FRAGMENTARY EVIDENCE

GIT JAKE

RONALD K MARSHALL

A JAKE HARPER & TJ ALVAREZ NOVEL

THE WAR AFTER THE WAR SERIES

BOOK II

"Greater love hath no man than this, that a man lay down his life for his friends."

John 15

"The better I get to know man, the more I find myself loving dogs."

Charles de Gaulle

"If you love something, set it free. If it comes back, it is yours. If it doesn't, it never was."

Richard Bach   Jonathan Livingston Seagull

This book is dedicated to all wounded warriors and first responders. They work long and hard to serve, protect and save life while having placed, and continually placing, theirs at great risk. Often making the final sacrifice.

FRAGMENTARY EVIDENCE

3

PRELUDE

Jake Harper came from a family of warriors and farmers. Each had fought different battles against other men, the elements, and their inner demons. Jake had lived it and fought the battle every day. The hardest battle was trying to not let others see his struggles, and not let the battle take away his nights. He had learned the best way to do this was to force pleasant thoughts into his pre-sleep consciousness. It helped when things went well the night before with those he shared his bed with. Lately, his efforts had been unrewarded. Rare was the morning he awoke feeling refreshed.

Jake sat on the porch in a wicker rocker watching the sunset. Faint clouds were moving in, caught up in the fading sun, looking like fiery tendrils pointing his direction--a surrealistic effect both soothing and intimidating. He walked inside and shut the door, stopping the chilly breeze which had been puffing in through the outer screen door. Elena was in the kitchen opening a bottle of wine. As he walked over to the eating side of the grey-tinted cultured-marble countertop, he commented on the evening's fading scene. Without turning around, she replied in an emotionless tone, "the weatherman said it might rain tonight." Jake started to ask what was bothering her, then decided to let it be. It troubled him that she seemed to be in a funk and seemed to take no joy in anything. A shame—those you love, and lovers should have to tread lightly as often as he and Elena did of late.

He stayed up long after Elena went to bed. He returned to the caned rocker on the side porch, listening to the night, enjoying the soft flash of the all too less frequent sightings of lightning bugs, and the moon's and star's shadowy light play through the ancient oaks. These, like the patterns of campfire embers and star constellations, always mystified him, just as it had for mankind from the earliest of times. They, like him, sought to make sense of their life on this tiny speck in the universe amidst the many wonders here provided.

Jake rocked slowly and quietly, his sixteen-gauge shotgun, loaded with bird shot rested on his thighs. He was waiting for the cackles from his frightened chickens. Some varmint or varmints had been breaking into his chicken coop and he was determined to put a stop to the nighttime foraging. He left the two dogs, Dusty and Maisy, inside with his wife Elena so they wouldn't raise an alarm or chase the intruder off before he could hopefully get a shot at it, trying, so far unsuccessfully, to ensure they or it would never return.

Off in the distance he heard a whippoorwill and a lone coyote's yelping bark. There came another sound. A truck turning off the McConnells Highway; the deep throated noise carrying up through the woods as it picked up speed. Rocks pinged off the metal, slung there when the driver gassed it coming up the hill from Turkey Creek.

Jake thought he recognized the sound of the truck. Whoever it was had been making a nightly pass-by for several nights, taking the foot off the gas pedal, drifting by in front of the house without lights, then flooring the truck once they were past. Jake wondered if this was possibly the vehicle which had frightened his neighbor Patrick's daughter when he was off working in the Bahamas.

He could hear the sound echo off the tunnel of trees just before it reached their house. True to the pattern as it topped the hill, Jake saw its lights disappear from within the tops of the trees and the motor quieted to a low rumble. Shortly afterwards, the brake lights winked on and off, then the brazen driver killed the engine as the truck coasted to a stop. Maisy, then Dusty, were raising their warning alarms, their cries coming from Jake's and Elena's bedroom door, open facing the road, their angry, insistent sounds carrying out into the night, ceased as the truck came to a stop. Jake eased inside the house and hurried to the bedroom.

Elena had turned off her lamp. When Jake entered their bedroom, he could barely make out Elena and the two dogs huddled on the other side of the bed. He moved quickly toward the door and looked out, focusing on the road to get a fix on the truck's location. Elena whispered loud enough for him to hear over Maisy's and Dusty's now muffled alarming warnings, "I heard voices from outside. They could have seen me before I closed the door." She heard the almost imperceptible ratcheting sound of Jake's twelve-gauge shotgun he kept behind the bedpost on his side of the bed.

"What are you going to do?"

Jake didn't reply. He reopened the door, eased the screen door open and softly stepped out onto the treated-wood porch, his right hand gripping the shotgun with a laser beam light attached underneath the barrel, clutched in his left hand, ready to be switched on whenever he got into a forward position.

Across the road, somewhat nearer than the lone coyote, came a louder, more discordant chorus from a pack of coyotes moving across Tindal's land. Were these goofballs coyote hunters?

He saw the flicker of fire, then smelled the strong acrid odor of cigarette smoke from the bold jerk who had stepped out on the passenger side of the truck, releasing the sound of heavy-metal music, which became muffled when he closed the door, then ceased altogether. The splashing sound of the smoker taking a piss was followed by a female giggle that came from the driver's side window as it was opened. Another flicker of fire and the sweeter smell of marijuana followed the whir of the window motor, then came the click of the passenger door latch reengaging. Before Jake could get into position, the truck motor turned over and the truck roared off past the gate where Jake stood. The passenger flicked his lit cigarette out the passenger window over the top of the truck. It landed on the other side of the gate across from where he stood. They must have seen him.

Within seconds, a loud pop sound, a firecracker or a weapon's retort, echoed through the woods from the direction their vehicle had taken.

He opened the gate, used a piece of gravel to extinguish the smoldering ember and picked up the extinguished fag. This was evidence that might prove useful at some point.

Jake listened to the rumbling sound fade away. He saw the lights come on before the truck disappeared over the next hill.

When he came back inside, he noticed Elena had donned a robe and was standing by the door holding Maisy. Maisy, then Dusty, freed from Elena's muzzling hold, began barking again. Jake reached down, patted Dusty's head shushing him.

"Who was it?" Elena asked holding onto Maisy, futilely trying to quiet her—her barking almost drowning out Elena's worried question.

"Probably some coyote hunters or kids out getting their kicks." Jake said offhandedly even though he wasn't sure that was all there was to it.

"I was coming out of my bathroom and heard their truck out front. I was naked Jake. I think they stopped because they saw me before I could close the door and turn off the lamp. It was the same truck that's been coming by day and night, wasn't it?"

"Possibly. I doubt they saw you. The moonlight is bright, they may have seen me. Maybe that'll make them think twice about stopping out front again. For their sake, I hope so. Go on back to bed. I'll join you shortly." Jake reached to hug her. She was having none of it.

"That's not the first time they've stopped out front. I've heard that same sounding vehicle a couple times when you're gone. I don't like it."

"Dusty will protect you. Have to be a fool to set foot past the gate with him on the other side. If not, shoot them--anyone that crazy deserves to be shot."

"You just don't get it do you Jake." She pushed past him and climbed back into bed.

To Jake's dismay, the truck hadn't been back, as far as Jake knew, since that night.

FRAGMENTARY EVIDENCE

CHAPTER

1

The sun made its slow ascent; its light piercing through the trees that stood tall at the edge of the front lines of the property. Jake felt the cool, rain-moistened air coming in through the screen door. He thought maybe he should get up and close the inside door but decided against it. He lay still listening, trying not to think of the restless night before and the day ahead. The mournful coo of a morning dove and the distant whippoorwill's naming call created soothing sounds, an uncommon peaceful respite from the noise of blasts from hunter's weapons, or, logger trucks rushing by—always followed by the incessant buzz and whine of mechanical monster machines and saws and the resulting crashing trees which had been the usual reveille ever since the end of turkey season. Deer season was about to begin--the ceasefire was almost over.

His wife Elena was lying with her back to him. She was sleeping, or pretending to be. They had met on-line while he had been finishing up his management duties constructing the Emerald Bay Resort on the southern island of Exuma in the Bahamas. He had been instructed to use a dating site as a means of communicating with other members of a joint task force for Operation Pink Flamingo. He had been enticed to be Homeland Security's eyes and ears for the op. Money was the inducement. He was on the verge of bankruptcy about to lose his ancestral farm--his refuge after a bitter divorce. Elena had caught his attention; she looked and sounded like someone worth getting to know.

He lay there thinking about his time in the Caribbean before returning stateside and hooking up with Elena. It had proven to be a once in a lifetime of adventures he would never forget. His housemate's girlfriend, the lovely enigmatic vixen Blakely Carmichael, and the boss' son's girlfriend Amy, had reawakened his libido—ultimately, almost costing him his freedom and life.

Jake knew he should be getting out of bed. But his little head demanded attention. It tented the sheets, having been stirred by the memories of Blakely and Amy and, for some strange reason, his teenage first love Ariel and his wife Elena--their bodies mentally commingled, an orgy of dream-induced thoughts. The awakening thoughts, carried over from last night, were invigorating pushing work plans momentarily aside.

For Jake two things epitomized life: a near death experience and discovering the blessed creation of the art of the act of making love. Jake had experienced both, and greatly preferred the second.

He and Elena had not made love in over three weeks. Not since the last night before the intruders showed up outside on the road.

Jake knew that was not the reason.

Early on in their relationship, Elena had thought of his constant libido as welcomingly enticing and humorous. Lately, she had begun to say he had a problem with being over-sexed, even venturing to say maybe the PTSD, she claimed he had, was the reason. As a daughter of a retired Marine, Jake had wrongly believed Elena would understand. For soldiers like him, sex was therapeutic, an embrace of the good things in life, a gift of the gods.

Jake's thoughts drifted back to a previous night and the following morning. The one before the asswipes had stopped out front. Seemed a lifetime ago.

He and Elena had watched a romantic movie, a chic flick his teasing way of referring to it. Then they had retired to bed, each with their own book. Movie, book, their usual routine, broken that night by Elena's stopping reading at the same time he did. And, to his pleasant surprise, kissing him lightly on the cheek and whispering an uncharacteristic, "good night" before she turned over to switch off her bedside lamp. Jake had lain there wondering and hoping this meant something.

The sound of rain on the tin roof had prompted him to turn off his lamp. He had lain there listening until his wondering ceased. He had, as was usual, drifted off wishing and imploring the night to keep his dreams on the up and up.

And, as usual he had awoken before her, hoping the night-be fore's promise was to be fulfilled. He rolled over and pressed his morning arousal into her sleep-relaxed, well-toned, enticingly shapely backside.

"Morning", she had replied, rolling over to caress his prodding member.

He slid his left arm under her head and pulled her face out of the pillow. He flicked the tip of his tongue out to brush her lips. She then moved in closer and kissed him back--her kisses amazingly eager, uncharacteristically intense. He then ran his right hand up under her nightie and down her back, lightly kneading and massaging her well-toned but supple muscles, giving her nice firm butt and shapely thighs added attention.

The growing eagerness had only briefly been interrupted when Elena had arched her body away from him, slid her flimsy nightgown up and over her head, tossed it aside and slid one of her legs over his, pressing her nakedness so he could feel her against him. Jake loved the sensation of her body on his, but Elena hadn't been, and wasn't much for foreplay.

They had for the last time, so it seemed now, made love, not the wham bam think you ma'am, what Jake called a sympathetic have-to fuck, that had been, up until that night, their norm. This had been a memorable feast with all the dishes served hot and heavy, every portion mutually relished. For Jake, he remembered it as the reckless abandon of Blakely, the youthful enthusiasm of Amy, and the unforgettable passion of Ariel--all the ingredients amazingly mixed in a pleasing way, a dream come true. Elena had become once more the ardent lover, reminding him of the times early on in their relationship that Jake had come to miss.

Her eyes, at the last moment, had sprung open, a distant fondness had flashed as if she too had been caught up in the not-too-distant feelings. A tremble had passed through from her to him as she had allowed herself, an all too rare, orgasm. Beyond both their expectations, they had each found themselves at that place where Elena had once stated only lovers could go.

Elena had remained on top of him only for a moment, gave him a brief kiss, then quickly raised herself over and off, and made a dash to her bath.

Jake remembered watching her, enjoying the quick glimpse of the beauty of her nakedness which she rarely displayed nowadays. Though they both usually slept naked when the weather was warm, she had stopped undressing so he could enjoy the view, depriving him of everything but her lovely backside before she would, with all haste, jump into bed and cover herself, leaving him frustrated and, until that morning, wondering why the sudden change.

He remembered listening as the water stopped running in the sink, followed by the soft sound of her footsteps approaching his side of the bed. He had turned his head to get a look, another brief glimpse before she had reached the bed and used the warm washcloth to remove the remains of their lovemaking, first from herself, then from him. He had tried to get her attention, she hadn't even bothered to look, her face had become set like a mask, devoid of any of the emotion that had burst forth only moments before. He had reached over and tried to pull her to him. She pushed away, left the cloth on his stomach, walked to her armoire, and hastily put on her running outfit.

"To what do I owe this unexpected pleasure?" he had asked watching as she dressed.

She hadn't answered. The dogs followed as she left the room.

The memorable feast, desert and all, the smell and taste a lasting, slowly fading, reminder. An old fear had crept back in despite what had happened and what remained to be relished. The anxiety, that had lain pushed aside, had attempted to raise its head again. A nagging mistrustful feeling had been created by secrets revealed when he surreptitiously read her emails. To voice what he had found would be seen for what it was, a violation of trust, and an invasion of her privacy. He had learned from previous marital experience, that when communication in and out of bed was not happening and you didn't know why, you better do whatever you can to get an answer. That was his excuse. What he had found was correspondence from her daughter's biological father, Tim, the slimy limey. She had not mentioned any of this to him.

Made him think about whom she had made love to that morning? Enough. Little man was demanding much needed relief.

He returned his attention to Elena. Her slender silhouette was caught up in the early morning light—her soft puffs of exhalated air barely discernible, her strawberry blond hair fanned out across her finely chiseled face, folded into her feather-down pillow, her body lying there under the soft cotton sheet--arousing, inviting. He turned toward her, raised himself up, nosed his way through her fresh-smelling hair and kissed her neck. No response. No movement, no opening eyes, no change in her breathing. But there had been no resistance.

He reached down, slid his hand down across one of her many treasured gifts, those nicely rounded buttocks. No reaction. Emboldened, as had been his habit, he ventured down, up and under her gown bringing his hand under and onto her silky mound. Tenderly, he used his middle finger to set the stage for what he so hoped would follow. Again, no reaction. Boldly he inserted his thumb into the place that engendered so many tasteful, sexually-fulfilling memories. This would have been a well-received opening act at the beginning of their getting to know each other and she would have pushed back into him, anticipating the lovemaking play to ensue.

It was not to be. This time she pulled away from him causing his ministrations to cease. She brusquely pushed his hand away and sat up. He brought the fingers up to inhale the aroma. If only. Once more his ardor was not to be reciprocated. He reached out to her. She quickly stood up. He was at a loss. Later today he would mention the slimy limey's name. It was past time to put it to rest. Or? Or what?

Elena grabbed her robe off the bottom bed post on her side of the bed. She went past the dogs and continued around the bed without saying anything. She went to her bathroom and not long after she came out dressed in her running outfit. She didn't look his way or acknowledge his presence. This shit needed to end.

"Hey. When you going to talk about whatever it is that's eating at you? She continued out of the bedroom. The dogs followed.

Jake wasn't sure his refusal to sell the farm and move to Louisiana was all there was to their distancing. Did she know he had read her emails? Had she left them on her screen on purpose? Damn. He didn't want to go through another divorce.

He took a deep breath and decided to do what he always tried to do, not let their differences ruin another beautiful morning.

He rose from bed, slipped into cargo work pants laid out on an old rocking chair next to his chest of drawers, then slid his feet into flip flops, grabbed a t-shirt and headed to the kitchen to make his strong coffee, which he drank straight. Sometimes on weekends, mainly on cold winter mornings, he would add a shot of brandy. Never on a workday.

Morning was Jake's favorite time of day, although evening sunsets over the ancient oaks were the more noteworthy.

Coffee mug in hand, Jake stepped out onto the drive-side porch, he considered the front porch. The quiet of daybreak always helped pick up his spirits. It was that brief interlude between when the nighttime sounds cease, and the daytime creatures hadn't yet found their voice. Pleasingly quiet.

Today he missed seeing Elena do her normal frustratingly arousing stretching routine. The smell of her, the only thing he had for his efforts, still lingered. It was pleasant, almost blocking out the rain-dampened freshness, laced with the smell of freshly mown hay, other familiar scents, and a hint of the steaming coffee. He almost hated taking his first swallow of the acrid taste of the coffee, knowing the piquant scent of Elena would be diminished. He tried not to be his usual analytical self. TJ often accused him of overthinking the situation. Couldn't be helped. The problems between him and Elena needed to be fixed.

He laid his cup on the rail and watched Elena and the dogs as they headed out the drive for their morning jog. He stared after them and his eyes took in the always satisfactory view of the olden red oaks, ancestral sentinels overshadowing the driveway's circular turnaround--their gnarly limbs, Spanish moss drooping down, bearing spiny leaves that had started to turn shades of red--the chilled morning's moisture looking like prisms twinkling on their surface. Some of the leaves had already changed to a tawnier, rust-like color, turned loose from the limbs, and had drifted down onto the drive and the indigenous evergreen shrubs and fern bed that lay below near the base of the tree, where large rough, grey-brown roots jutted up through the fertile soil--like arms and legs pushing up or holding on as they had done for longer than Jake could ever know.

Jake's never-ending, wandering thoughts drifted off once more, as they often did at moments like this, to the bygone days. Days trailing his grandfather which started out or ended at the barn, either having let the cows out, or bringing them in to do the milking. Try as he might, back then Jake had had a difficult time keeping up with his long-legged, big-boned, gnarly-knuckled, callused-handed grandfather—often finding himself left behind before blossoming daybreak or at the fading dusk and promised dark; when his childish imagination unbridled, watched wide-eyed the shapes of trees--grotesque shapes blotting out the star-spangled night sky and carrying the echoing sounds of night crawler creatures adding ominous tones—childlike cries of a bobcat, mournful calls of whippoorwills, deep-throated croaks of bull frogs and chirping tree frogs--all the things Jake now loved. All part of the life chosen for him--much preferred and thankful for having been given the gift--a life of natural wonder punctuated by hard work required to maintain his ancestral, self-sustaining farm. If only Elena could be as happy here as he was.

The "farm" as he called it was in the upper Piedmont, just south of Charlotte in the far western section of York County, South Carolina. The gravel road bordering two sides of his property had been an Indian and colonial trade path, that became a road which played a major role in the Revolutionary War. A graveyard situated at the highest point on the property bore foot and grave markers for the white folks of what was believed to be the site of the rebellious colonialists' Fort Lacey. Next to them and all over the hilltop, indentions, under the thick covering of leaves, the long-gone remains of what were thought to be slaves who had worked the surrounding property. Their reward, a hole in the ground. For years nothing but a depression. An unremarkable life and death, no marker, no name, as if that was all that need be said for hundreds of years of hard labor which made the nation possible.

Jake could only imagine how difficult it was for those caught up in a war that pitted neighbor, Whig, and Tory, against each other. With blacks and native Americans caught up in the action--many losing everything, some, their lives. Other generations, their ancestors still struggling, never knowing of this site or how to give them their just rewards or their heretofore recognition.

Jake would sometimes listen to the wind while sitting on that hillside, wondering if it possibly was unrecognized souls' mournful voices sending out their warning of the futility of dying for other men's uncompromising differences.

As if history's lessons were meant for deaf ears, a repeat of a divided country was still happening over a hundred years later. Wounds never seemed to heal. Today there was the fear that the festering scars of open dissension, created by the recent election, would continue. The Capitol Assault before the new administration could take office demonstrated it could and would. This on top of the worst pandemic since 1918, fostering attacks on Asian Americans, blamed for *The Chinademic,* so labelled by a bitter loser president and right-wing extremists.

The adjoining property now owned by his unfriendly, openly racist neighbor Thurmond Pinckney Tindal, had originally been an English King's land grant deeded to the Hill family. Jake had wanted to purchase a portion of the parcel when an attorney and the timber company, who had acquired it from the family, auctioned it off. At the time, he did not have enough borrowing power.

Once beautiful forests and farmland were now pine and sprouting hardwoods which would never be allowed to mature. The pine Tindal harvested in pieces continuously, except for breaks during deer and turkey hunting season. The noises sending Maisy and Dusty yapping and woofing at a feverish pitch, upsetting Elena, especially when she was in her office where she worked as a practical nurse dealing with homebound patients.

Jake kept some of his hundred acres as his grandfather had when Jake was a child. The difference was that he had allowed much of the hard-to-work, rocky ground to become hardwood forested, only thinned once since he took over as the caretaker.

He grew hay in the remaining field to feed the few cows he used for milk and other dairy products. His grandparents had lived off the land, Jake had witnessed the futility and confinement of trying to do that. Other than a small garden and the cows, the only other animals were a few chickens and a couple of pigs. Elena wanted horses, but Jake, who had been raised on another farm with horses, came to the same conclusion as his father, horses were a liability needing constant care and riding, which Jake's injuries forbade, and work left little time for.

Today Jake decided to go ahead and take care of all the feeding and watering. Elena had, until lately, taken care of the chickens and the garden, which was now past bearing, allowing the chickens to search, scratch and forage what was left.

He let the cows out into the upper pasture, away from where he had already mowed and rolled the tall fescue grass into round bales. This was the hay he would need for the winter. They would graze on the remains in the separate field until then. The bales needed to be wrapped before the next rain and there were some areas of fencing that needed repair which would have to wait. He didn't have time to do that today. He mixed the feed in a little water and slopped the pigs, topped off their water trough from the spigot he had installed last fall. He then filled the old cast iron tub at the edge of the pasture, which was used to provide water for the cows until he could afford to build a much-needed pond.

Despite the chilled air of a cold front moving through, the sun's heated fingers reached through the trees, pulled out rain-dampened moisture, causing his shirt to cling to his skin. Jake walked back up the slight incline past the chickens, humming their contentment, pecking and scratching at the corn he had thrown down outside their old wood-sided, metal-roofed house.

He went up the steps onto the wraparound porch of his grandparents' former home, now his and Elena's, redesigned and remodeled by him into his vision of what a farmhouse should be. He dried the sweat off his neck and forehead, then turned on the tv to hear the morning news. Nothing new about the news. Attractive faces, smooth voiced readers, their droning hum reciting the same old, same ole: more divisive election political crap, partisan tribal dribble, rumors, slanted half-truths and lies, Russian meddling, Middle East bullshit once more about to boil over, Iranian, Chinese, and North Korean threats, terrorists' threats and attacks, celebrity misdeeds and gossip brought on by the Me Too and Black Lives Matter Movements, fueled by Antifa and other deluded, bigoted misogynists and racists, so on and so on, day in and day out, week after week, seemingly never-ending. He preferred PBS's recitations.

One new news story briefly caught his attention--a report by the CDC that those who were vaccinated no longer need wear masks. What happened to the unvaccinated and the herd immunity? Seemed they changed their guidelines almost daily. No wonder the public stayed confused.

Jake grabbed another cup of coffee and a couple of blueberry muffins, set them on the eating counter and pulled on his work boots, packed his day pack with electronic and steel measuring tapes, his minicomputer notebook and another shirt and sandals for when it got hot or he got dirty. He packed his face shield and mask just in case he needed to go inside a crowded supply store, even though most people no longer believed they needed to take precautions. Too many never had.

He sat down and ate anticipating Elena's return and the arrival of TJ who was going with him to look at a job. This was TJ's day off. He would occasionally help Jake when he was not working his main two jobs--one as an undercover Metro Charlotte SWAT Vice Squad member, the other doing skip trace work for a bail bondsman. He was the best of what Jake called friends. Jake counted friends as someone you would lay your life down for and knew that person would do the same. To that end Jake owed TJ way more than TJ owed him. As a sniper overseas, TJ had put his life on the line to save, not only Jake's, but many more of their fellow soldiers' lives. He knew he could always count on TJ. TJ would say, "having one's back is not just being there when the load is heavy, sometimes a light one has to be helped before it gets heavy."

Thomas Jefferson Alvarez reminded many people of a young Dwayne Johnson, "the Rock", with his Afro-Cuban dark complexion, big boned muscular build, ever-present, full-of-meaning smile. Jake could not understand how he stayed in shape. Unlike Jake, he rarely exercised, unless you called playing with your dogs or lending Jake an occasional hand, exercise. In their military service days, TJ as a sniper could lug his weapon and pack loaded down with ammo and other essential survival gear without breaking much of a sweat. Even in the Philippine jungles, he seemed never to show a hint of fatigue while others, like Jake, would have their tongues hanging out.

He and TJ were called bookends by their wives. Both had us vs. them mindsets. For Jake it was mostly authority figures, for TJ it was the bad guys, particularly the gangbangers.

Jake often reflected on his and TJ's years surviving the challenges. The latest had been more personal for TJ; Jake's seemed to have been, and continued to be, more and more personal.

He had been receiving death threats. The reason he kept his weapons at hand. He dared not tell Elena and she hadn't asked why when he bought her an S&W .32. She was used to having guns around, her father collected and sold firearms. The only person he told was TJ. TJ and his wife Deane knew what living with threats was like.

TJ's recruitment by Homeland Security as part of Operation Pink Flamingo brought it home for him and Deane, forcing them to leave Miami's Little Havana, the Hood, their childhood home, where TJ's family still resided.

Jake had emotionally mixed memories regarding his part in the op. Some, like this morning's memories—the arousing sexual parts--were worth remembering. Always, there would be an unresolved nagging thought left over from the op--someone out there wanted him out of the way. His bet was on his avaricious neighbor, Colonel Thurmond Tindal.

No actionable evidence, as TJ so often reminded him.

At times like this, when his mind grew nostalgic, Jake often thought of the last words he would ever hear from his father, a highly decorated Vietnam Veteran—words said to him when he lay in a hospital bed, depressed because of the wound that had cut his career short; prompting his first wife Joanna into taking his children, running back home to Natchez, and leaving him unconsciously helpless to stop her. Alone with his demons.

His father had recited words he himself had probably heard said to him when the weight of that nation-dividing war had weighed heavily upon him: "We all fight a war each and every day. Not all enemies wear colors or uniforms, serve on the field of battle, or give warning. The human condition is a fight for survival son, from day one until you finally succumb. You have to never give up, survivors are the ones who fight on, no matter the cards they are dealt."

It had been hard for Jake to accept that advice then. The demons would always be there, he just hoped he would always want to be a survivor.

Enough self-pity, where were Elena and TJ? He needed to get going. Today he and TJ were scheduled to meet with a doctor's son about converting an old barn into a riding stable.

CHAPTER

2

Jake reached down onto the coffee table fetched the remote and turned off the television. He heard the roar of a speeding truck coming from the direction Elena and the dogs had gone. The speed limit was 25 on the gravel road and many people went much faster, which pissed Jake and Elena off. Several of Jake's dogs had been hit by speeding motorists. He looked out the window to see if he recognized the vehicle. It was TJ.

"What the fuck?" TJ never did that. Jake rushed out the door as TJ wheeled in and sped up the drive, skidding to a stop at the end of the walk. Elena was in the backseat. Maisy jumped up on the front passenger side window, yapping at Jake as he ran to the truck. TJ got out and opened Elena's door. Jake could see Elena's tear-streaked face her eyes wide open in horror. He ran around the truck and saw, over TJ's view-blocking-bent form, Elena cradling Dusty in her lap, his entrails hanging over his side onto a towel on the leather seat. Jake visually checked Elena over--her running attire was bloody but she appeared physically unharmed. TJ was trying to pick Dusty up and Elena was pushing his hands away.

"They shot him," she screamed.

"Who shot him?" Jake asked.

TJ spoke up in a stern voice, "Elena ain't no time for delay. Tell her Jake, got to get him stabilized."

Jake and TJ had seen enough damage to humans on the battlefield and each had had to treat fellow soldiers and had watched too many die for lack of immediate first aid. Jake had few memories of his ordeal. He had no idea how he had been treated until he had awoken weeks later at Walter Reed.

"Elena! Snap out of it! TJ's right. You should know that. We need to get him inside."

Jake could see her slowly struggling with the reality of the situation. She looked over TJ's shoulder at Jake, her eyes stretched wide, tears running, mingling with mucus dripping from her nose onto Dusty's prostate mangled body.

"We're not equipped to handle this. He needs to get to the animal hospital. Oh God," she whimpered.

"Not enough time." Jake hurried to the other side of the truck, reached in and commanded Elena to slide over as he began pulling the towel with Dusty toward him. TJ came around to give him a hand.

"We'll use the towel as a sling. Elena you need to go and get whatever you need to help stabilize him."

The only way Jake could tell Dusty was still alive was because of some trembling and the slight rise and fall of his diaphragm. His eyes had that distant stare that Jake recognized all too well. His body was trying to shut down due to the pain of the trauma. Who and what had done this?

Maisy had jumped over into the backseat, continuing her incessant yapping. Elena grabbed her, as TJ took the other end of the towel sling. Elena ran ahead of them with Maisy who thankfully stopped yapping.

When they got inside, Jake and TJ laid Dusty on the red mahogany-color, leatherette-covered pool table. Elena came in with her bag, pulled on surgical gloves then handed a pair to TJ and Jake. She pulled out antiseptic ointment and gauze then a syringe which she loaded with a pain killer she had retrieved from her metal combination-locked drug safe. After administering the pain shot, she instructed TJ to lightly lift Dusty and instructed Jake to hold his entrails inside and help as she wrapped the antiseptic ointment-coated gauze around and around the wounded area.

"Got saran wrap?" TJ asked.

"Good idea." Jake took off his gloves and went to the kitchen pulled open a drawer to get a box of plastic wrap. Slipping another pair of gloves back on, he and Elena wrapped the thin clear plastic around and around the gauze that covered Dusty's abdomen.

Jake pulled out his cell phone. "I'll call 911."

"Done that bro. Did it soon as got out of the truck after seeing Elena and Dusty."

"They could be a good 45 minutes depending on where the first responders' location is. We'd best take Dusty to Doc Hunter's. We should be able to get there in ten or fifteen minutes if we hurry. I'm ready, let's go," Jake replied.

He turned to Elena, "stay here and wait for the first responders, the police will want to talk to you." Turning back to TJ, he said, "I'll grab a lawn chair. We can put a clean towel underneath this one and use that as the liter to carry him on."

Elena started closing the house up. "I'm not staying here. You can call and tell them where we are going." The dogs were their family. She wasn't about to not be there. She was worried Dusty might not make it and she wanted Jake to be with her if that was the outcome. Not only that, she wouldn't say it, but she was scared, not knowing who may have done this. The thought that this could just as easily have been her made her tremble. They could still be out there. She had not heard the shot-- there had been no abnormal sound--how could that be possible? Was she the target? Oh God. She didn't want any part of this. Jake would have to listen. If not?

There could be no if not.

In TJ's truck, Dusty, once more with his head in Elena's lap and Jake holding Maisy riding shotgun, turned so he could watch Elena and Dusty. "What happened?"

Elena was nervously stroking Dusty's head. "We were jogging along; Maisy and I had just turned around at our normal spot and I had gotten just a few yards ahead. You know how Dusty will go bounding off jumping like a deer always looking for rabbits or squirrels to chase. I heard a sound, a yelp and glanced back. It was horrible. Dusty had to have just jumped across the ditch and had evidently taken one more stride before he dropped…His insides were all over the road where he lay." She trembled, wiped her running nose on her sleeve. "There was no warning sound before Dusty's yelp. All I saw was blood and guts hanging out, I froze. Maisy started yapping." Elena stopped, the tears once more running down onto her blood-streaked sweatshirt. She sobbed, "I almost ran away. I heard a truck coming and I ran back toward Dusty. It was TJ."

She sat there trembling with the memory and silently crying. "If he hadn't shown up, I don't know…"

Jake couldn't recall seeing her this upset. She had been an ICU nurse when she first moved to the farm. She had seen it all and never complained.

TJ kept glancing in the rear-view mirror. He drove as fast as he dared on the rough dirt road. The only sounds were Elena's sniffing and the gravel crunching under the weight of his tires. When they reached the paved portion of the road, he would be able to speed up, take care not to hit broken sections and potholes. The logging trucks and heavy dumps hauling gravel from the nearby quarry kept the roads in disrepair. He glanced over at Jake.

"Here's where it happened." TJ slowed his truck and maneuvered to avoid where Dusty had lain. "I came over this hill, saw Elena squatting in the road, knew something was wrong. There was Dusty. First, thought he'd been hit by some other vehicle. Stopped, dialed 911, asked for assistance, gave them my name and location, cut the call. Got out of my truck, asked Elena what happened. Got no reply. I ran back to the truck opened the back door, grabbed a towel. Told Elena help me get him up and in my truck. Maisy, was barking her fool head off, had to repeat myself. Elena was all froze up, not moving. When she look at me, could see she in shock. Had to pull her up, repeat myself, told her, "we have to hurry." Cop part of me wanted to stay, secure the scene, wasn't sure this not a live situation, a shooter still out there or not. Decided need to get Elena 'way, know Dusty he maybe die, need immediate attention. Elena and I we got him in the truck, grabbed Maisy and got to your house as fast as I dared."

He kept looking in the rearview mirror at Elena. She stayed quiet.

Jake saw Elena's continued trembling. The real shock had yet to set in. This was not good.

"I hope Doc Hunter is at his clinic." Jake looked at his phone. Almost seven.

"Someone be there by now," TJ replied. "They board animals. Either Doc Hunter or his wife, Doc Susan, they be there."

Jake kept watching Elena and Dusty. "He'll make it. You did a fine job with that field dressing." Jake hoped he was right. Losing Dusty would make their personal problems even worse.

Elena kept on stroking Dusty's head, the tears continued to fall.

They made it to the clinic in near record time. The golden-yellow sun had risen above the tree line of the hills in the direction of Brattonsville, a Revolutionary Period visitor site, home of the lead actor in the film "The Patriot". There were three vehicles at the back of the parking lot. One was a red Ford 350 diesel dually, that Jake recognized as the Doc's, parked next to the fenced holding and exercise pens. Jake saw one of the assistants inside the center section of the livestock barn at the back of the lot. Leading a horse to one of the stalls, he supposed.

"Doc's truck's here." TJ said. He began blowing the horn as he came to a screeching halt at the side entry with the side of the truck, where Elena sat hugging Dusty so he wouldn't slide off the seat. They were ten feet away from the emergency and personnel entry metal door.

The door was flung open and the young orange- and-blue-streaked hair assistant, hands on hips shouted, "What the…."

Before she could finish Jake and TJ had flung their doors open. TJ was opening the rear door when she started her question. Judith, the name on the name tag said, cut herself off, eyes enlarged, she quickly yelled over her shoulder," Doc," and moved to assist TJ. Before Jake could get Maisy in his arms and open Elena's door, they had disappeared inside.

"This doesn't make any sense," she sniffed, "how could this have happened? Who did this to Dusty? Who? It just doesn't make any sense."

"You sure you didn't hear anything?" Jake thought Elena must have blanked the sound out. People in combat and in traumatic situations were prone to blocking things out.

"I'm telling you there was no sound. You've got to believe me. Do you?" She looked at Jake her eyes were red and bloodshot." I don't want to talk anymore about it." Jake reached out to hug her, she pushed his hand away and went in the side door.

Jake went in behind her. Entering the operating area, he saw Dusty on a stainless-steel table. Doc Hunter was on one side and his wife, Doctor Susan Hunter, on the other with face shields on. Doctor Susan was staring through a magnified light, tweezers in her hand pulling fragments of what must have been the bullet, gravel, and other debris from the ragged wound. The bullet fragments she placed on a tray separate from the other debris.TJ stood off to the side with Judith, the receptionist and sometimes assistant. Elena went and stood next to the tall lanky Doc Hunter whose back was to Jake. He was pushing their makeshift bandage into a plastic bag which he set aside.

"Did you administer any drugs?" Doc asked looking over at Elena, who was staring at his wife with not so friendly intensity. His wife glanced up at Elena and their eyes met anticipating Elena's response.

"I gave him 10ccs of Xylocaine," Elena answered never looking away from Doctor Susan.

Jake watched the two women and wondered what was going through their minds. Was this professional rivalry or was this plain feminine territorial response?

Both women were attractive, about the same height, Doctor Susan, a few years older, was slightly heavier and filled out her scrubs in a genuinely nice way. Maybe that was this was?

Doctor Susan was the first to break eye contact and resumed her meticulous removal of the foreign objects. "We need to clear the operating room," she said looking over at her husband.

Doctor Hunter nodded his approval.

Jake saw Elena twitch and knew she was about to argue so he spoke up, "I hate to ask Doc, do y'all think you can save him?" Jake kept watching Elena hoping not to upset her any more than she already was. Her pupils were dilated, and he thought she was once more on the verge of tears. Watching her more closely, he could see a slight tremor. He handed Maisy to TJ asking if he minded holding onto her. He moved toward Elena in case her emotions overcame her. Not sure what to do if they did.

"This is as bad as I've seen. We'll do our best, but to be honest there is no way I can promise anything. A lot of what is needed is the will of him to want to live, and that seems to be working, or he would not have made it this far. We need to get the wound cleaned out and we'll do our best to stabilize him. We will isolate him, as you may know," he looked over at Elena who was looking from him back to what his wife was doing, "the risk of infection is a grave concern. Any ideas what did this? From the looks of it this appears to be fragments, metallic and plastic, I've never seen anything like this," he said holding up one of the pieces under a magnifying lamp a puzzled look on his rough-hewn face. Jake figured he was what many would consider ruggedly handsome.

Doctor Susan looked up at her husband, clearly irritated. He nodded again and said, "Why don't we go into one of the examining rooms and give my wife some space."

Jake laid a hand gently on Elena's back and tried moving her out of Doc's way. She wanted to resist.

Doc said, "Mrs. Harper as you know it is not customary to allow people in the operating room, and as much as I hate to ask, all of you need to accompany me and let my wife do her job. My wife is very competent, but she hates having anyone staring over her shoulder, including me. I'm sure you understand."

Elena let Jake guide her out of the Doc's way. TJ had already left with the assistant Judith, who had returned to take Doc's place in case Doctor Susan needed her while the Doc was with them. They went into the middle of three examination rooms and Doc closed the door, asking them to take a seat. Elena declined, so Jake remained standing.

"What happened? Were y'all there?" he asked shifting his weight from one side to the other, standing slightly askew.

"Elena was out jogging with the dogs when it happened. From my experience overseas this looks like a military fragmentary ordinance projectile wound," Jake said. "Elena says she didn't hear any shot fired and it's not gun season yet, as you probably know, so I can't figure out how this could have happened. Doesn't make sense."

"There was no shot noise. I know that for a fact. I was there. I don't care what anyone says or thinks. Maisy and I had just turned around to head back. I glanced back because I heard Dusty yelp. He had been coming through the woods, had jumped the ditch, and had dropped. He was only a few yards behind me and Maisy." Elena dropped her head, looking down at her hands which were again starting to shake.

"It was like a nightmare. My first reaction was to run. Maisy was yapping. I heard a vehicle, TJ's truck, and that made me turn back around. I ran back to Dusty," she said as she tried in vain to choke back the tears, which once more ran down her cheeks. "he was lying there, his insides all torn out. He was twitching. I heard a truck coming, so I knelt, thinking I had to move him, not knowing if I could or should. I looked up and saw it was TJ's truck." She stopped to catch her breath. "There was no shot. If there had been Maisy would have heard it and started barking."

"She's right," Jake said, "I hadn't thought of that. Maisy goes crazy yapping whenever she hears anything. This doesn't make sense."

"You think you might have blanked part of this out? Something like this can cause you to forget things, get them in the wrong order. Maybe the shot was too far away to have made much noise." Doc looked at Elena.

"No. I remember hearing some birds and squirrels, other than my breathing, that was all there was."

"Okay. I need to get back in there and help my wife." He looked at Elena, her fear and anger were playing across her face. Jake looked unsettled. From experience he sensed this trauma was not the only problem here. He wasn't about to go there. Not his problem. Saving the dog was.

"I will send Judith back out to the front and you can leave her your contact information. Soon as I know anything, I will let you know. The police will want a full report so I will have a copy for you later. Try not to worry, if Dusty doesn't give up, neither will we." He turned and left.

They joined TJ who was standing at the counter holding Maisy. Judith came out of the back and went behind the counter and took their contact information.

"Better head back 'fore the scene get messed up. The sheriff's deputies they could be there lookin' for us. Called dispatch, she said they on their way. That was ten minutes ago. Didn't say where they coming from; so, doubt they there yet."

CHAPTER

3

They arrived back on the road and as they topped the hill where Dusty's guts had spilled out, TJ slowed his truck. The sun, lighting up the bluer than normal blue sky, broke upon the pitted rocky road, granite fragments sparkled amidst the rust-colored dirt packed tight where only TJ's truck had driven over coming and going. They stopped well short/ of the fly-covered blood stain that surrounded a small crater where Dusty had lain. This time TJ stopped so no other vehicle would be able to drive through the spot. Jake was thankful no other vehicles had been through and disturbed the scene.

TJ told Jake and Elena not to get too close to the blood spot. "Need to preserve the area for the investigators, treat like an active crime scene until have some answers. Elena it okay you stay in the truck." He looked in the mirror and saw the flash of anger on her face. He opened his door. Elena and Jake followed. Maisy was left in the truck with the windows down enough for air, but not too much so she would be tempted to try to jump out.

"Don't leave your keys, Maisy has hit our automatic locks and locked us out several times." Jake told TJ before he closed his door.

TJ looked around. On the side of the gravel road, he saw a few taller hardwoods here and there among the small hardwoods and ten-year-old twenty- to thirty-foot tall pine trees. A dust-covered patchwork of leaves and weeds, whose flowers were dead or fading and bare blackberry brambles lined each side of the ditch. Ambient noise, his truck motor's pings, a now and then rustling of leaves drifting in a breeze that had begun to blow, otherwise, quiet.

Elena felt compelled to talk, convince herself and Jake and TJ that it was not something that had become scrambled by its horrifying remembrance. Being here, where it had happened, brought the whole frightening incident back again.

"Dusty must of come out from over there. He had to have jumped over the weeds and blackberries landing on the road about there," Elena wiped her nose and pointed about 15 yards up the road from where she and TJ stood. There were big paw prints on the rain-softened shoulder where she indicated.

"You can see where he took one or two strides before he went down. I was about ten yards up the road. About where Jake is now. I had looked back to see why he yelped. I took a couple more strides, stopped, looked back and saw him. The blood and gore…" She hesitated, doing her best to not start crying again. "I almost ran away." Elena trembled. She couldn't stop the tears. She wiped her eyes and nose on her sleeve. She gathered herself, then continued, "Maisy had stopped, she heard Dusty's yip, and had run back to Dusty, yapping like she wanted to prod him into getting up. I was scared, and I guess shock made me panic. I didn't think. I started running away. Maisy's yapping and the sound of TJ's truck coming made me stop and run back. I looked down at Dusty; Maisy was yapping at him, so I bent down and held her. The next thing I knew, TJ was talking to me." She stopped the retelling. Just stood there looking frightened. TJ and Jake were watching her.

Jake walked back and hugged her. He felt her stiffen when TJ asked the thought-provoking question. "You're sure you didn't hear a gun shot?"

Elena pushed Jake away.

"No. As I keep telling y'all, the only sounds were a few rustling animals scared out of hiding by Dusty, some bird sounds and my breathing."

"You said Maisy was barking? You sure that wasn't before Dusty went down." Elena's face hardened, her eyes were like daggers when she looked at him as he said, "I know from experience when something like this happens your thoughts get all scrambled."

"No. It was just like I said." She walked a couple steps away shaking her head in disbelief that everyone was doubting her story.

Elena felt the chilly breeze pick its way through the trees and fallen leaves into her worried thoughts, made her shiver.

TJ took a couple more steps toward the stain. Looking down he tried to make sense out of the deep indention in the gravel at a less than ninety-degree angle. "Major impact indicates the shot came from this angle." He had picked up a stick and was holding it so one end pointed down parallel to the deepest part of the indention and the upper end pointed almost straight up. "Shot come from direction of my truck, away from your farm and Tindal's home."

He studied the spot some more. There were the smoother areas where he and Elena had placed Dusty on the towel. In the area covering the bloodstain, he saw insects, stirred by the breeze, fly up, then land to feast once more on the bloodstains, ignoring the fragments, the same as Doctor Susan had taken out of Jake's and Elena's dog's wound.

"These fragments, the extent of the injury, says flechette round fired from a high-powered weapon--even if supersonic, should have been a sound." He looked over at Jake then Elena, they both had joined him. "Not doubting you Elena--this much damage, no sound--bit puzzling--deputies goina be scratchin' their heads, goina assume you the target. Finger is goina be pointed at you bro. You thought about that?"

Jake simply nodded. His eyes on Elena who glanced his way then looked off toward TJ. This was problematic. The police will be tearing into their personal lives. He hated the inevitable coming invasion; he knew Elena will also. He needed answers. The who and how were questions which would make their story seem unbelievable. As he was pondering the implications, he heard a vehicle coming from the direction of the farm. They all looked and saw a white truck with orange and blue flashers on the roof slowing down as it came up the slight incline. Jake and TJ moved in that direction to flag the truck down.

"Aw hell. It's Tindal's robo Barney Fife looking lapdog, Red, the game warden," Jake snorted, "That's the last person we need to see."

Red stopped his truck about twenty feet from where they stood. A simple vortex of dust and leaves followed in his truck's wake. They all watched him get out, hitch up his uniform pants and saunter over, eyeing each one of them as he came. His eyes settled on Elena, looking her up and down with a lascivious grin that dissolved when he saw the blood stain, then he gave TJ a hard stare before turning his obviously disdainful glare on Jake." Might have known it would be you Harper."

"Why is that Red?" Jake spoke up with his own obvious disgust.

He stepped a step closer, no longer keeping a safe distance, locking eyes with him, Jake felt he should step back, but wasn't about to give ground.

"That's Officer Crandall to you bud. Only my friends call me Red." He rose, rocking forward like he was daring Jake to make a move.

"Why is it every time there is trouble around here, it seems to always involve you Harper?"

"Maybe it is because whenever there is trouble for me you are involved Red." Jake, a few inches taller than Red, flexed his shoulders as he twisted his neck. Tension always seemed to inflict pain into the vertebrae which had been broken and fused. Arthritis was what he had been told at his latest physical.

TJ knowing Jake's body language stepped closer, ready to get between them.

"Got your 'killerboy' with you I see. Kind of light-skinned one ain't he?" Red hooked his fingers in his gun belt, his pants sagged, pulling downward on his skinny hips. He shifted his feet, stealing a glance at the Harper bitch. Not bad, even with all that blood on her.

Jake watched him as he leered at Elena—made him want to knock that snide look off the asshole's face. "Tell me something Red, did your daddy's sister have your daddy's baby willingly?" Jake asked.

Red couldn't let the Harper man's taunting insult stand, he had to do something. He briefly fixed his attention on the Harper man, turned his head and tried to lock eyes with the big darkie, straightened up, and reflexively, reached down to his holster. Jenkins had instructed him to provoke them, arrest them, and avoid any gun play—said, "that might draw unwanted attention."

He attempted a smile. "Good thing there ain't none of your kind as game wardens."

This time TJ started to make a move and Jake stuck out an arm to stop him.

"Always trying to start something aren't you Red? We don't need you sticking your nose in here, this is not your jurisdiction, so why don't you make like a fly and buzz on out of here."

"This is my jurisdiction," he said taking a step back, "if I say it is my jurisdiction. Look around you. My territory covers three counties. For your information, my jurisdiction is the state of South Carolina. So, I am well within my rights to arrest you three and take you in for questioning."

TJ pushed forward, stopping within striking distance of Red. Jake moved with him. Jake could see that Red was trying to get them to do something as an excuse to arrest them. Red flinched, moving his right hand as if he were going to pull his revolver from the holster.

"Big man with a gun, aren't you?" Jake spat on the ground at his feet. "Nothing would give me more pleasure, anytime, anywhere, you name it, no weapons, just you and me. Not here and not now. So why don't you go on back to your master Mr. Tindal, and leave this to someone who knows a thing or two before we both do something we might regret?"

Red unsnapped his holster.

"Before you pull that gun, you best think about it," TJ sneered, "may get one of us. Though I doubt it. My bet, Jake or I drop you like the sack of chickenshit you are before your weapon clears the holster. Never draw that weapon again. Guaranteed. Go on little man. Go for it."

TJ took a step away from Jake, put space between them just in case. TJ watched Red's eyes twitch from Jake back and forth to him. "Why don't you take my partner's good advice and get the hell out of here."

The tension was reaching the point of no return. There came the sound of another vehicle approaching from the direction of TJ's truck. No one reacted.

"It's the deputies," Elena said suddenly feeling some relief.

"Lucky thing for you two they got here just in time to assist me. I am arresting you two for threatening an officer of the law. I will let them read you your rights. You done stepped in it now...."

Before he could finish, TJ cut him off. "Can it asswipe, we know our rights and will be filing a formal complaint with your department and the governor's office. You'll be lucky if anyone let's you be a garbage collector."

Deputies Coulter and James got out of their car and strode over to where they all stood. Deputy Dan Coulter tipped his hat to Elena, "ma'am," he said politely his eyes staring through his shield at the dried blood on her warmup shirt. She looked angry and on the brink of crying. "Heard somebody's dog got shot out this way? Warden Crandall, you know anything about this?"

Red moved away from TJ and Jake over toward where the officers stood. Deputy Coulter put up his hand signaling Red to keep his distance.

"I want you to arrest these men. They refuse to answer my questions and threatened me with bodily harm when I attempted to question them."

"Is that right?" Deputy Coulter asked. "TJ, good see you man. Something here that I should know about, besides a dog gittin' shot?"

"Dog getting shot! Sir, that dog was Dusty, not just some ole dog!" Elena bristled, hands on hips. Her nose ran, she wiped it on her sleeve. "Our dog Dusty was shot right over there," she pointed at the blood spot, "I was here. But who gives a damn, he was just some ole dog. I guess you would prefer it had been me, not some ole dog?"

"Sorry ma'am. Mean no disrespect." He looked at TJ and Jake, pleading for intervention.

"Chief Dan, Deputy Coulter, we were here waiting for you to arrive. Red, so he would like it to seem, just happened to appear..."

Red cut him off. "Are you going to arrest these two or do I have to cuff them and take them in myself?" Red fumbled with his cuffs, seeming to have a hard time unhooking them from his belt.

"Sir, if you would kindly allow me to, I will listen to your request. Procedures must be followed. I hate unnecessary paperwork. I will take everyone's statement regarding the shooting incident, then hear your complaint."

Deputy Coulter was half Cherokee and half Caucasian and had suffered the indignities prejudiced rednecks, like Red, had bestowed upon the Native American peoples all his life, except when he had been a star running back for the Clemson Tigers. He looked like he could still do it and probably could if he hadn't blown out a knee in their National Championship game against LSU. Jake saw him eyeing his LSU cap and hoped he wasn't going to hold that against him.

"I have jurisdiction here and I want these two men arrested. Do you understand Deputy Coulter?" Red's angry face contrasted with his green uniform matching the red hair which had earned him the nickname. He had had his hand behind his back and was finally able to retrieve his handcuffs. He started swinging them to add emphasis to his intentions.

Deputy Coulter pushed his cap back, fixed Red with his ready-to-scalp-you-stare and replied, "I like that. Hear that Deputy James, jurisdictional issue, might want to write that down." He turned back to Red. "Soon as I hear what I came here to find out, you can fill me in on this jurisdictional issue. If that is not good enough for you, I suggest you take a hike, and we will handle this without you."

Red stormed back to his truck. Jake and the others watched him get in his truck slam the door and close the windows, then they saw him lean forward with his mic in his hand, his lips moving rapidly.

"Thanks Chief," TJ said with a grin.

"TJ, you have probably drug me into a whole pile of shit. Beg your pardon ma'am." Deputy Coulter looked over at Elena then back to TJ while keeping an eye on Red.

He resettled his cap.

"I hate when someone talks down to me. Can someone please fill Deputy James and me in on what happened to your dog Dusty." He looked around and settled on Deputy James, whose black face was frowning. He was staring back hard at his partner. "Don't worry, I take full responsibility for what I said. Keep out your pen and pad. Okay folks, let's get this over with."

Deputy James was about five feet eleven, a few inches taller than Deputy Coulter. He was slightly overweight with his gut beginning to hang over his belt. He had been on the force less than two years and had learned all he knew from his partner who was a good officer that treated everybody with an even hand but didn't always go by the book. The white officers and a few blacks called him Chief, some because they didn't like him, most out of respect. Deputy Clarence James had come to like and respect him but often worried when he strayed from the book.

"Alright. Just so we can move this along, who wants to go first? TJ?"

TJ turned to Elena. She was looking none too happy.

She had been standing there through it all, arms folded in a defensive gesture, wondering what turned this beautiful early autumn day into crap. All these men, their testosterone-infused machoism. None of them really cared how she felt. She just wanted to get out of here away from where Dusty had been shot. Maisy's yapping from TJ's truck lent a surreal quality to what was happening. Jake should've been more supportive instead of acting out some macho bullshit.

"Take me home dammit, let me get cleaned up and just leave me be," she felt like yelling. She felt the weight of her isolation on this island of fading greenery. She couldn't live like this anymore she needed to be where she had normal people to comfort her. The pandemic isolation, dealing remotely with patients, had made it especially hard on her. Jake had said he understood, he didn't. Like these people, he couldn't. Now this.

Jake was struggling to calm himself. He walked over to Elena, lightly put an arm across her shoulder to lead her aside. "I'm sorry. I know this is upsetting, but we must do this. Okay? Do it for Dusty." She shrugged him off and walked back a few steps, faced Deputy Coulter.

"Can we just get this over with please?"

They told what they knew about Dusty having been shot. When they got to the part about the trajectory and the lack of sound, Deputy Coulter stopped TJ and said, "You know a high-speed, high power load can travel a long way something like a mile I believe. In fact, I read recently that the new record for a sniper is two miles. My guess is you would know more about that than I would."

Jake spoke up. "There is more to it than that. Out here it is so quiet that you can hear anything, especially in the morning. And any time Maisy hears the least noise she starts yapping like she is doing now." The chatter of their police radio and Red's and the Sheriff Deputy's vehicles motors running, helped muffle Maisy's yaps—the noise too loud for anyone to appreciate the solitude.

"There was no hunting or logging going on--like today, you can hear for miles out here, especially at first light."

Elena showing frustration interjected. "Even if I didn't hear it, which I didn't, the dogs would have heard the shot, and they would have started barking. They fear any noise, in particular thunder and gunshots. Again, and again, I repeat, there was no gunshot sound!" She didn't know what she could say that would convince anyone of what she knew she had heard and seen. She wanted to just get away from here. Go back home. Her preferred home in Texas.

Deputy James had been scribbling notes. Deputy Coulter had been walking around the area taking pictures while trying to make sense out of what he was hearing. He stood over the blood stain, pulled out a pointer he kept in his belt and did a trajectory analysis same as TJ had done earlier. Then he pulled on some gloves and used his pointer to dig around in the blood-stained deep indention made in the hard-packed gravel.

"TJ, did any of you do anything to disturb the site?" He looked up briefly at TJ who said "no". Motioning him over, pulling out a plastic baggy, he used the pointer to dig out some of the fragments. "Any idea what kind of fragments these are? To make an indention like this in hard gravel would indicate an explosion or a shot at close range don't you think?" He pulled off his ball cap, scratched his head and looked at TJ.

"Not the legal MagSafe Amo, resin tipped with shotgun pellets that explode upon impact, they don't exit the victim, wounds showed no shotgun pellets. Had to be military." He looked back at Jake who was looking in over his shoulder as he crouched a short distance from Deputy Coulter. "That what you think bro?"

Jake straightened up. "Only thing that I know of could have done that is military flechette ordinance. Like you said before. And those are restricted. Analysis I would bet will prove that to be the case."

"Maybe ATF or the FBI should have a look. I'll send this off to them." He bagged the fragments. He and TJ stood up. He looked from TJ to Jake and finally Elena, who stood rigid at a distance from everyone. He glanced over at Deputy James, placed his cap back on his big head, asked him if he got all the information they might need. Deputy James offered to let him read his notes. Deputy Coulter took the pad read out loud what was written, then asked if there was anything else anyone wanted to add. Jake looked to TJ who said if they thought of anything, they would notify him.

He walked closer to where Jake and TJ stood. "Mr. Harper has it entered your mind your dog was not the intended target. Any reason someone may have wanted to scare or shoot at your wife?"

"No sir. And before you ask, I was at home. TJ can verify that and no I have no reason to, have never thought to, or had tendencies to do my wife harm. I believe my dog getting shot was no accident and someone out there was sending me a message. I believe that someone was Thurmond Tindal. If truth was known, Red was sent here by him to provoke a situation to deflect the blame."

Deputy Coulter smiled. Then his face grew stern. "Maybe a possible accidental shooting, don't know. The sheriff may not see it that way. Fair warning Mr. Harper don't give him any reason to think otherwise. The shooting was illegal, and the type of ordinance itself creates serious questions. I will be looking into this. I suggest you let me handle it. I think that about covers it. Exactly what it all means I'm not sure. We will ask the few people within the area if they heard anything. From what I know most of them are too far away. More than likely, were not awake, so they possibly heard nothing. Thurmond Tindal owns most of this land, does he not?"

"That's right and the firing range is up near our house. I was outside taking care of the animals and there was no gunfire to be heard."

"Deputy James and I will talk to the vet and the folks in the area but, I hate to tell you, at this point there is not a whole heck of a lot to go on. Maybe these fragments will get someone's attention" He looked around at all of them once more and shook his head. He rolled his eyes after fixing his stare on Red's truck.

"Now TJ, Mr. Harper, what happened to get Red's feathers ruffled?"

Jake quickly spoke up. "Like I said Red is nothing more than Tindal's lapdog. He showed up here out of the blue and started insulting us. He was not interested in what we had to say; he had his own personal agenda. We told him we were waiting for you and we didn't need him. He started all this jurisdictional bullshit." Jake looked hard in Red's direction. "It's personal. He and I have had numerous run-ins over things that happened between Tindal and me. Seems to me this is, but shouldn't be, another one of those. Should make you wonder what Tindal has to do with this. Are you going to arrest us?"

"Let me see what I can work out." Deputy Coulter looked from one to the other of them, nodded to Deputy James and they walked over to Red's truck.

Several minutes went by and the deputies came back to join them.

"He has agreed to have you appear before a magistrate." Deputy James handed Jake and TJ the arrest warrants. "I'm afraid that is the best I could do. If you'd like, I'll talk to the magistrate. You will need to go talk to him, I mean her, before end of day tomorrow. Y'all might want to call ahead I think they only serve warrants certain times of the day and they get kind of touchy about their schedules. You don't have to have an attorney with you. That's up to you two. Let me know if you hear anything about the gunshot and I'll do the same. I should have my report ready in a day or two. If you need a copy, you can come by the office to pick one up. As for the feebs, I wouldn't bet on a fast turnaround. Who knows, this may shake their tree. Good luck. Good to see you again TJ." They bumped fists. He nodded at Jake.

Jake had his hands in the pocket of the cargo pants. He felt the baggie with the cigarette butt in it. He had meant to give it to TJ. He caught up with Deputy Coulter before he reached the patrol car and held the bagged butt out to him..

"What's this?" Deputy Coulter asked.

"We've been having some truck come by. Same truck day and night He told how he had come to have the butt and what he had intended to ask TJ to do with it. "If it's too much to ask, give it to TJ. I think this ties in with Tindal. Just like Red's being here does. I'd like to know. It's spooking the hell out of Elena."

Deputy Coulter put the baggy in his shirt pocket.

"I advise you to stay away from Tindal and Red. You might want to think what motive, along with the means, Tindal would have to be involved with this."

He looked over at Elena standing next to TJ's truck and nodded. She stood with arms crossed and didn't acknowledge the gesture. He walked closer, stopping several feet away and told her he was sorry that this had happened and hoped their dog survived. Deputy James, standing with his hand on the passenger side of their vehicle, a troubled look on his face, was watching. The deputies got in their car, sat there until Red turned around and left before they did the same.

They got back in TJ's truck and rode back up the road in silence. Jake looked at his cell phone. No messages. Soon as they pulled in the drive, went half-way around the circle next to where Jake's and Elena's vehicles were parked and stopped, Elena bolted out the door with Maisy and hurried into the house.

Jake and TJ stood next to his truck. Pulling out his cell again, he called his customer, Mr. Donegal. No answer. He left a message telling him his dog had been shot and apologizing for not having called sooner and asking him to return the call if he was interested in rescheduling.

"Don't think be going there today bro."

"Probably not. I'll call you, if, and when I hear from him. What time you want to go see the magistrate tomorrow?"

"Midmorning most likely, on call tonight and tomorrow. Anything happens it's after the drunk perps and junkies get into the sauce or other preferred mind-altering substances, decide they want to share their misery with the world. Sometime tomorrow afternoon need to make a show at one of my Cis--supposed to have something for me having to do with a case I've been working." TJ wanted to but was forbidden telling Jake what he hoped to glean from his informant. If his hunch was correct, it could help their situation.

"Call you if anything comes up. Need to get home and get cleaned up. Deane may come home for lunch, don't need her, especially her, or anyone else for that matter, seeing me with blood on my clothes" He got back in his truck and left.

Jake went back into the house. Elena had taken a shower and came out of the bathroom, not even looking his way, and went into her office and closed the door. Jake noticed the blinking lights of the digital clocks on the appliance faces in the kitchen. 'Another damn power surge.' He went around resetting all the clocks and listened at Elena's office door. He heard her talking to someone, probably her daughter. He could not hear what she was saying but if it was her daughter, he was certain it would not be what a great guy he was. It would be well received. He walked quietly away and went to the kitchen to make a sandwich for lunch. Afterwards he went out to do some farm chores, hoping Mr. Donegal would call.

CHAPTER

4

Bud Jenkins, Thurmond Tindal's COO and Head of Security, had received the call from Game Warden Crandall telling him things weren't going exactly as planned. The sheriff deputies had arrived sooner than expected. He told Crandall not to rush the scene, to keep Harper and company there if possible. Hopefully, this would give those two bozos Butch and Billy time to take care of their simple task.

The big man's local lieutenant, Arturo Gonzalez had recommended he hire Mexicano members of his crew that spoke Spanglish. He had placed three of the beefier, less tattooed members that spoke more than a little English, on his security detail station down at the hangar and wharf. The other two Mexicanos worked as yard men helping Butch and Billy take care of the grounds and orchards. Those two chain-gang reject rednecks seemed not to mind the Mexicanos, in fact they seemed uncharacteristically friendly with them, which gave him pause. It wasn't like he didn't know what Arturo and his guys did. As part of his job, he had run background checks on everyone that he associated with. Most of these guys flew under the radar but if they didn't create any problems on the job or draw attention to themselves where Tindal took notice, he didn't care what they did on their own time. He hoped that Butch and Billy didn't fuck this up.

Butch Ferguson and his bud, Billy Donahue, had been instructed by Jenkins to park at the hunting cabin down the road from the Harper home. They cruised by the farmhouse in Butch's '97 Chevy primer grey 4x4 truck with mud covering most of the out-of-date license plate. There were several vehicles parked in an area off the circular drive, but they didn't see any sign of anyone or their big dog.

"There ain't supposed to be anyone here,"

"I wonder why all those vehicles are here and the gate is open?" Butch drawled in his deep smoker-tainted tone. "Every time I've been by here the gate is closed."

"Mr. Jenkins said they would be down the other end of the road. Sometin' doing wid the game warden. Said we'd have twenty minutes or so. Why 'on't we pull in and see if anybody comes out." Billy looked over at Butch. They were both sun darkened from working outside all the time. Butch was big boned and hard angled, whereas Billy was more rounded and heavier. Butch wore old faded and raggedy cuffed Carharts that barely covered his leather work boots. He had on a flannel shirt with the sleeves cut off, a pack of Marlboro cigarettes rolled up in his right sleeve, the fabric stretched tight by his oversized bicep. Billy preferred loose jeans, tennis shoes and corduroy shirts.

"We s'posed to park down at the hunt camp in case someone comes home whilest we here."

"Mr. Jenkins ain't here. How's he goina know? Let's see anybody home. Git in dere and git the **shit** done and over with."

"Yeah, you right. How he goin' ta know? Fuck doing all that walkin' bullshit. We do enough of that shit all the time. What you say Butch? Let's git 'er done." Billy slapped his right hand down on the open window area of the passenger side door. "Sure wish that Harper woman twer here. I'd like to git sum of dat thing."

Butch pulled in the drive and eased his truck up toward the house. He had left the radio off and hung his head out the window listening for any sound that would tell him if anyone was at home, especially that big dog. He heard a couple of roosters crowing and the mooing of a cow off in the distance.

"Soon as I stop the truck hop out and grab the ladder off the rack. Get the big 'un." Butch looked for a place to hide his truck from anyone passing by on the road. He pulled around the circular drive and stopped behind the big red oak that had shrubbery planted around its base lining the drive and would help hide his truck.

Billy jumped out and was sliding the ladder off the rack as Butch got out to catch the other end. He told Billy take the ladder around back of the house and he reached in the bed of the truck to pull out a box that contained three miniature Wi-Fi remote cameras. He joined Billy at the back of the house and helped him extend the ladder up into the gable on the screen porch. "Put one uv 'em up there next to that security light."

"What we going to do if someone comes home?" Billy asked as he climbed the ladder.

"You take the ladder and head down that way." Butch said pointing down across the field. "Go around the barn cut through the woods and head over to the hunting camp. I'll get back in the truck, and, if they stop me, I'll make up some bullshit reason about why I was here. Now hurry up."

They installed another camera in the oak tree near the truck, loaded the ladder, and then went back to the house.

"Think they have an alarm?" Billy asked as I stood on the front porch eyeing the lock.

There was an alarm company sign at the end of the walk near where they were parked. "Let's walk around the house and see if there is a box." They found the alarm box next to the electrical panel box which was not locked. Butch opened the panel lid, shut off the breaker main and they went around the corner to the screened porch.

They looked at the back door inside the screen porch and Billy said, "This one be uh piece uh cake." He pulled out his hawksbill knife from its sheath, took his wallet from his back pocket that had a chain attached and extracted a worn bank cancelled credit card. Using the knife he pried the door away from the jamb and used the credit card to push the latch bolt out of the keep. Fortunately, the dead bolt was not locked. Billy opened the door and Butch followed him inside, listening for any sound of any animal, dog, cat or otherwise. The first thing they saw was the pool table with the blood-stained cover.

"Can you believe this? They've got a damn pool table. Sure wish I had this mother." Billy was running his hand over the edge admiring the fine polished walnut wood. "What you think about that blood?" He was staring at the stained green felt where Dusty had lain. "Reckon we goina find somebody or somethin' dead in here? Kinda gives me the creeps. Know what I mean?"

"Does kinda make you wonder. We need to hurry up and find a place to put this other camera and git the hell out of here." He started walking slowly through the house and Billy followed. Butch went into the master bedroom and

Billy went into the master bath. Seeing a pair of lacy panties on a chair next to the garden tub, he reached down to pick them up, lifted them to his nose and inhaled deeply. "Hey Butch," he yelled, "come here."

Butch had been eyeing the shotgun in the corner next to the nightstand on the far side of the four-poster queen size bed. He turned and went into the bathroom to see what Billy wanted.

"Take uh smell of these. Man, she sure has a sweet twat. Sweeter than yer cuz." Billy had a big grin on his face. He tossed the panties to Butch who took a whiff, then he too inhaled deeply.

"Damn. You right." He stuck the underwear into his pants pocket. "And I done tol' you don't be sayin' nothing 'bout my cuz and that shit that happened. Neva happened. Got it?"

Billy reached out, "Hey! I found 'em."

Butch grinned. "You gave "em to me. And you had better not mention that shit again about my cuz. You wanna do big time. That is, my unc' don't kill us first. Let's install that other camera and git the fuck outa here."

"Why don't we put it in that recessed light over the tub? That way we could get a better look at that Harper woman's goodies. What yuh say?"

Butch looked at him sideways." You mean Jenkins would get a better look, not us fuckhead. She might even look up and see it. That be too risky. Come on, we need to put it somewhere up front. That way Jenkins can see what's happenin' in the main part of the house. 'Sides I hear Jenkins got some nudies of her anyways. Least ways that what them spics say."

"Shur wish she hadn't turn that light off udder night. Bet ole Harper ain't doing her like she'd like. Yer cuz shur got all hot thinkin' 'bout it. Okay. I git it."

They were unable to reach the area over the door from the upper room which served as Harper's office and had an opening that looked out over the dining room. Butch placed it in a corner of a window. This would allow Jenkins to see out toward the front, and, would allow him to see and hear anything going on in Harper's office and the dining area below.

Butch and Billy hurried out of the house. Butch went around to the panel box to turn the power back on. He knew they would know the power had been off. He figured they would think it had been one of the power surges that happened now and then. He heard a vehicle coming from the direction where the Harpers would be coming. He ran back to the truck. Dumbass Billy was leaning against the front of the truck taking a piss. "Cut it off man and cover up that wet spot. A vehicle is coming up the road. Hurry up and git in." Butch jumped in and heard Billy scraping his tennis shoe in the drive's gravel. Quickly he ran around and jumped in the passenger's side. "Don't slam that door, it's almost out front." They watched as the game warden's white truck went speeding by and down the hill. Butch cranked up and headed down the drive.

CHAPTER

5

Warden Red Crandall hated the Harper man and his dark-skinned buck sidekick. He had started his hate from the first time he met him. The Harper man's all-American good looks and cocky attitude, like he had a chip on his shoulder and dared anyone to knock it off. And the darky, he needed to be roped and drug, threatening him like that.

The Harper man jes like his grandfather, the clodbuster. When he got up in age, he carried his shotgun and walked his fields and surrounding woods, threatening anyone he caught. After he died and before the Harper man showed up, it became open season hunting ground. The hunting club that Thurmond Tindal joined wanted to keep hunters from straying across onto their club land and asked him to help them by keeping other hunters off the untended, unposted land, that would become the Harper land.

He didn't know Jake Harper and his first hoity toity wife had taken possession of the property until one day he was checking the land and the Harper man confronted him, catching him off guard and threatening him with his shotgun. He had not been in uniform, but even after identifying himself, the Harper man told him to leave and not come back.

Over the years there had been many problems between the Harper man and Thurmond Tindal which he had had to investigate. Mr. Tindal wanted the

Harper man's land, had made generous offers to buy it, but the Harper man refused to listen.

Colonel Tindal paid him good money to make the Harper man want to sell and leave. You couldn't very well tell Mr. Tindal "no".

Thurmond Pinckney Tindal's land surrounded Jake Harper's family land. His latest acquisition across the river, once called Pinckneyville, would bring his total holdings to three thousand acres, stretching from Turkey Creek to the Broad River and beyond once completed.

His palatial home sat on a hill above the Broad River and off Bonner Horton Road. An Italian Cypress tree-lined drive wound from a gated entry, over another hill through the pastures, around a pond, ending at a circular courtyard with a fountain in the center. To the right was a six-bay garage which housed his daily personal vehicles on the lower level and his collectible vintage vehicles on the upper level. Behind the garage were the guest suites and below were Bud Jenkin's office with surveillance monitors and the lab where R&D was performed to develop the projects and house the technicians and staff.

A marble columned portico, wide enough for two vehicles, extended from the fountain to the flagstone entry steps. The two-story high entry had a chandelier whose prismatic light sparkled off the marble floor and wall tiles that surrounded a small fountain with its kneeling nymph statues' cupped hands allowing water to flow through splayed fingers creating a soothing ambiance. On the first floor was a library, off which was his office, a receiving room, an entertainment room with antique billiard table, and of course in the foyer the wrought-iron-railed marble staircase that wound up to the second floor living quarters, though he and his wife used the elevator that was accessed through a door behind the staircase just before the powder room. Below was his assistant's office. Out of sight and snooping ability, a chef's envy gourmet kitchen with all the latest accoutrements, his wife's fantasy, though the meals were prepared by a cook not a chef and served in a dining area that could serve a family of twenty. There was only one ungrateful, busybody, know-it-all, stepdaughter, and she, with her brood of three, lived, thankfully, in California. The dining room had two sliding glass walls leading out to a terrace with its winding wrought-iron staircase which led up to the veranda outside Tindal's pride and joy trophy room.

The trophy room had a bar in the center that was surrounded by hand-carved wood bar stools and a sitting area with a glass humidor for Cuban cigars. The wall outside the main house and the two side walls contained stuffed animals behind glass—a buffalo, an antelope, a black bear, a fox, mountain lion, bobcat, snakes, and iguana--all in a natural museum like setting. The main attraction in Tindal's eyes was the elephant and an early hominoid holding a spear in a savannah setting, next to which was a moonrock with a framed picture of the first moon landing. Tindal saw these images as symbolic of his life.

He had been raised in Charleston by a single mother who served as a nanny for a widowed professor of the Citadel whose children treated Tindal as their inferior playmate. He never knew his father and he was never sure his mother did either. He later learned his mother, so prim, proper and a woman of great strength had been a madam for the Charleston elite and politicians.

Through hard work and the goodness of the professor, whom Tindal suspected, knew more about his absentee father and his mother than was ever acknowledged, Tindal was admitted to the Citadel and went on to serve as an Intelligence Officer in the Army, followed by several years in the CIA, then the NSA, parlaying his insider information and contacts into becoming an extremely successful weapons supplier and now a manufacturer for the military and the Petrochemical Industry. It also helped he married into a politically connected family. His wife, an only child with parents who doted upon her fortuitously, had received a tidy trust after their marriage.

Using his connections and her wealth, he had built his business into an enviable position. He was privy to national secrets, his company had top national security clearance. Daily he conversed with generals and politicians, as well as masters of industry and finance. His position, like his home, was a place fit for royalty and that was how he saw himself.

Tindal had business to attend to, but like today, he often spent mornings and evenings before going to his office to reflect upon his life and to look out from his trophy room to take in the view from above.

The terrace flagstone steps wound down the hill past an Olympic size swimming pool to another courtyard. On the other side of this courtyard was a hanger that housed a small Lear jet, a turbo prop Cessna and several drones that were used to surveil his property, along with the latest version, an unmanned aircraft which was about to be demonstrated in hopes of landing lucrative contracts, both military and industrial.

This morning's fiasco could complicate the situation. Meant to be a test run, some fool programmer had missed a glitch in the data. Now the major, Bud Jenkin's was charged with containing the situation and preventing any adverse blowback.

He stood behind his ornate mahogany desk. On it was a small device which could open a holographic screen. Or if he so desired by putting on specially designed eyewear, he could navigate the e-verse virtually with nothing but his thoughts. His former NSA technical aide, now Security Chief, Jenkins had set this up. Once the thrill of having the ease of access wore off, he began to wonder where his thoughts and e ventures went, who could access them? He found it hard to trust anyone. The more you rise on the ladder of success, the more people there are on the lower rungs who would pull you down and the more people above who are doing what they will to keep you below them. One must be vigilant, wary, and willing to do whatever it takes to maintain and climb higher. Trust no one and never let anyone below you know too much.

The former president he had helped put in the oval office knew this. That was why he had been there instead of some self-righteous, feminist bitch, that the Chicago Daley political machine chose not to succeed their other minion. It had been back to business as usual without the brakes of tree hugger regulations slowing things down. Tindal knew he needed to move fast. His man had been robbed, the election stolen, pointing the pendulum back the other way. Nevertheless, his people were in control at the local and state levels.

That Harper man, he had discovered, was one of those tree huggers. Why, having been a military vet, was beyond understanding? He himself had disagreed with the president and those competitors who insisted on a border wall. He hoped to convince the choosers technology would defeat its purpose and technology was the best solution. Like Israel, use drones and robots, preferably his drone, to guard the border and the energy companies' pipelines. Southeast Petroleum's Atlantic Coast Gas Pipeline was coming. He wanted his piece of it to come through here, guarded by his drone, to do that he needed the Harper man out of the way. Bad timing for this incident to happen. Just a damn dog but the liberal weenies would be all over it. Didn't need that bad press, not now, not ever. The choosers love secrecy.

He heard the truck come around to the side. Looking out, he saw the less useful, dumbass Game Warden get out and come up the side steps to his outer side door. He opened the door and the man stopped on the landing and seemed to puff himself up like a toad. Tindal stepped back, "No need in putting your damn mask on, come in and close the door behind you." Tindal walked back behind his desk and remained standing. "Hope you have something worth coming here for."

He started to say something. Tindal held up his hand, walked out of the office into his office anteroom, closed the door, pressed the instant messenger post, and instructed Bud Jenkins to join him in his office. As he reentered the office, he was pleased to note that Crandall had not moved, hat in hand he was looking around and quickly turned back to face him with a look of a kid with his hand caught in the cookie jar.

"I've asked Major Jenkins to join us. He should be here momentarily." They stood in silence. Tindal watched Crandall who stood staring at his feet.

Jenkins chose to take the tunnel that led from his office to the below-garage elevator that brought him up to Tindal's office anteroom. He had been busy pushing the techs to find any more errors in their program that had caused the incident this morning and make sure all fail-safes were installed so nothing like that happened again. Especially since the demonstrations Tindal was counting on for their old military comrade and the pipeline geek were set to take place soon. Personally, he didn't care about the demo, but he did care if the drone was all it was supposed to be. He had his own agenda to worry about and the drone was essential to that end. He despised interruptions but for now Tindal was in charge.

"Now that Mr. Jenkins has seen fit to join us, Warden Crandall would you tell me why you chose to interrupt our day with your presence. I hope you have good news."

"I went to the scene as you requested Mr. Jenkins. I think I may have taken care of the Harper man and his boy, who happened to be there." He looked over to Jenkins. "As I told you, the Sheriff Deputies showed up and I had them issue arrest warrants to the two. This will cost them and…"

"Hold on," Tindal said holding up his hand. He looked from Crandall to Jenkins and said, "Is this what you meant by handling this? You were supposed to handle this. I expected you to use your influence with the sheriff to make this go away."

Jenkins did not flinch. He stared back at Tindal. "I am doing what needs to be done to make sure this never happens again. We are under a tight schedule, as you know—your instructions. The Sheriff was out of town and the deputies had been dispatched by the time I talked to my other source in his office. I sent Red here to run interference. Hopefully, he did as I told him. There was nothing else to be done."

Tindal hated being talked to by subordinates as if they were his equal and he especially hated that to happen in the presence of anyone, especially another subordinate. The major had a smug expression and the warden seemed to be enjoying the moment.

"This is not some trivial bullshit. An incident like this could snowball into a major media feeding frenzy and while I would suffer a financial loss. I would be forced to cut my losses if you two can understand what I mean."

Warden Crandall began to fidget. Jenkins continued to stare at Tindal. "And what would you have me do, other than what I did? I fired one tech who was to have checked the program. If I had gone to the scene myself, my name would have been linked to the investigation. Red was never there which assures your deniability. What else should I have done, sir?"

Tindal looked from one to the other. "You say you issued arrest warrants, what for?"

"Threatening an officer, assault and battery and obstructing the investigation," Crandall hurriedly replied with a muffled edge of excitement.

"I take it they will have to appear before a magistrate. Do either of you know the man? I would like to speak to him."

"Her sir. It will be the newly elected woman, Judge Gerard, sir."

"I don't give a good goddamn who it is. I want to talk to whomever it is ASAP; you understand? I hope she is a good Republican not some feminist liberal Democrat or Green Party do-gooder. She'll most likely know who I am and know what I can do for or against her."

Tindal moved from behind his desk. A tall man of above average weight, he had grown used to physically intimidating people, harbinger of his military days. He towered over the warden but was not much taller and only a little heavier than Major Jenkins. The warden stepped back toward the door. Jenkins stood his ground and waited to hear what Tindal had decided. He hoped he wasn't to be fired. Not now. The goal was too close, and the plan was taking shape.

Tindal looked past Jenkins and told the warden to go see the magistrate in person and have her call him. When the door closed behind Crandall, he looked hard at his former aide, "Do not ever test me again, are we clear?"

"Sir? I was not testing you. I did what I thought was in your best interests. If you wish I will resign."

Tindal walked back behind his desk. "Are you willing to walk out on a mission? The man I thought I knew would never even consider such a cowardly deed."

"Nor would I unless asked to do so."

"This Harper problem should have ended when he was out of the country. I want it to go away. The political winds seem to be shifting and we needed this to be laid to rest yesterday. Am I clear?"

"Yes sir."

"Then why are you still standing here. We both have work to do. In two days we have some important visitors coming here. Make sure we are more than ready. Carry on!"

The last spoken as a military command from a superior officer rankled Jenkins but he spun like a dutiful soldier and went out the door without another word. Let the bastard think what he does, his day was coming.

Tindal watched as his man Jenkins disappeared out the door. He would call the DA and sheriff himself. They owed him, like every politician in this county and the state. Hellfire, in the entire nation, every damn one of them that he felt served his best interests. And once these new contracts were approved and his plans put in motion, he would be the most powerful man in the county, potentially the whole state. Mother would be proud. One problem, Harper…He had to go. DoD was concerned about securing the area and the pipeline needed to run through Harper's land.

Attempts during Operation Pink Flamingo had failed. Jenkins and that damned Russian Pietr Okneyev had failed to handle the situation. Thankfully, he had suffered no blowback. Maybe Sam was the answer? His daughter Elena's future financial security, her mother, Sam's wife's care ensured. Should be incentive enough. Besides, Tindal thought, what Jenkins and I know--the unauthorized, clandestine Laos mission during our days in the CIA, his lies under oath, should doubly ensure his cooperation. Sam was in too deep to back out now.

CHAPTER

6

They parked in the back of a row of newly renovated buildings. There were no open parking spaces on the main street of York. The only indication of the magistrate's office was the small placard under an antique looking wall light over a heavy wooden door in a recessed alcove. There was a sign on the door of a head wearing a mask, so they donned their masks. TJ held the door for Jake.

The office would have been dark were it not for a series of lamps on end tables between wood with fabric-cushioned high-back chairs, squeezed in on each side of the room. Heart pine board floors had been worn smooth by over a hundred years of foot traffic from various merchants, customers, and wares. Jake, behind TJ, had been taking it all in. His observation was interrupted by a "may I help you?" inquiry to TJ. Jake looked past TJ, who had stopped a couple steps back from a dark-stained wooden desk behind which sat an attractive olive-skinned, dark auburn-haired, dark-eyed woman with a no-nonsense expression who had briskly put forth the question as though it were a challenge.

"Yes ma'am. Hoping might have a word with Judge Gerard?" TJ made his statement sound like a question.

"Regarding?" she asked looking from TJ to Jake.

TJ handed over his warrant. Jake had left his in his truck.

"Thomas J. Alvarez. If you would please show me some identification. TJ pulled out his wallet, extracted his license and police ID. She looked at the IDs and with a slight shake of her head handed them back. I believe the officer who issued this summons was just here. Did you see him?"

"No ma'am. I mean yes ma'am. But did not speak to him."

"And you must be Jackson B. Harper?"

"Yes ma'am, I go by Jake."

Judge Gerard arched her brow. She eyed them both trying to keep the bitterness out of her tone and off her face put there by Warden Crandall's insistence, no, demand she talk to Thurmond Tindal. Her refusal was met with a thinly veiled threat which prompted her to tell the warden she did not work for Mr. Tindal and was under no obligation to speak with him, nor would she, and that he had brought her the warrants which she would investigate and she *would* follow procedure. Then she ordered the warden out of her office.

Now here were the parties that precipitated that incident. Still shaken and inwardly seething, she eyed them both. "I don't recall speaking to either of you two, did you attempt to call? I don't believe so. The warden shows up here unannounced and here you two are. Do you think your time is so vital, or do you think that my time is not?"

Jake turned to leave. TJ started an apology but was cut off.

"Mr. Harper! Where do you think you are going?"

Jake hesitated, hand on the knob. He turned around. "I apologize for this untimely intrusion and I do not wish to take up any more of your valuable time. TJ, you coming?" he started opening the door.

Judge Gerard quickly stood. Her chair pushed back and banged into a wood commode behind her. "Mr. Harper, one minute. Did you call?"

"I called, got no answer, I guess you were too busy. Then I got too busy and forgot. Sorry. Guess I made another mistake."

"Since you are here. If you would, please have a seat. My day is already off schedule, may as well continue. I don't know if you knew, but it is normally explained that you should call to schedule a time for coming in. I take it that this was not explained, and I am sorry if that was the case. Perhaps we both owe each other an apology and if you and Mr. Alvarez will have a seat, we can get this out of the way. Please," she said waving her hand toward the chair next to TJ.

"Sorry for this inconvenience. Jake and I appreciate your time ma'am." TJ said as Jake came back to take a seat.

She waited until Jake was seated.

"Mr. Alvarez, or should I say, Officer Alvarez?"

TJ did not reply. "Either's fine your honor, although in this situation I guess Mr. would be appropriate."

Sitting back down in her chair, she reached into a drawer removed a recorder and asked each of them if they minded her recording the session. When they each said they did not mind, she read them their Miranda Rights including the right to not write or say anything that might incriminate them, the right to an attorney, and, if they desired an attorney, they must not say or write anything without the attorney's presence. Do you understand this Mr. Harper? Jake replied in the affirmative. She repeated the process to TJ and he also replied in the affirmative. One question before you say anything. Did Officer Crandall or either of the deputies at the scene read you your rights as I just explained to you?

"No Ma'am?" they each replied.

"Duly noted. I have read you your rights and I hereby issue you the warrants for your arrest on charges of Assault and Battery against Warden Arthur Crandall. He agreed to drop the redundant charge of threatening an officer and reluctantly, obstructing justice. A hearing will be set for each of you to appear before this court in two weeks on October 28th to determine the validity of these charges. If you are found guilty you may face a fine of $500.00 and or 30 days in jail. I have no reason to believe either of you is a flight risk, so bail is waived upon personal recognizance. If you fail to appear, the hearing will be held, and a ruling will be made based upon any evidence presented at the hearing." She turned to each of them and asked if they understood what she said. When they both said yes, she asked if they wished to waive their right to remain silent and proceed with a plea or seek counsel and await the hearing.

"Ma'am, pardon us, we need to step outside for a moment." TJ said standing and nodding to Jake who had gotten out of his chair.

They went out of the alcove to the parking lot. Soon as they were outside, they removed their masks.

"What do you think man?" Jake asked, leaning against a rail of a handicap ramp out back of what had been a feed store. "We could pay the fine. I don't think she would give us jail time. But I hate giving in and admitting guilt for something when I feel we did nothing wrong. Especially where Tindal and that suckass warden are concerned. How about you?"

TJ stood looking out at the nearly empty parking lot. "Turning out to be more than a simple mess bro. Pleading guilty goina jeopardize my job both with Metro and as a bondsman. I have no choice." He shook his head. "Man o' man, I may be fucked either way." He shuffled off turned and came back. "Guess only good choice wait for hearing, get some legal advice. Think you can afford the fine? What you think Elena goina think?"

"Elena. She's way more than a little upset with the whole situation. Things haven't been so good at home. Her dad has been diagnosed with cancer and she wants to go home for that and to be with her family, especially her daughter who keeps pushing for her to move to Louisiana or back to Texas. Now this." Jake looked down, cleared his throat and spat.

"Been in far worse jams bro. Damn sure you know what I mean. I guess it's one of those times to boogie down, see how the chips fall. Let's go tell her we'll see what happens at the hearing." TJ led the way.

They slipped on their masks and went back in. The judge was on her cell phone. She waived for them to take a seat.

"Thanks Dan I'll let them know. We never had this conversation, ok?" She set her cell on her desk. "That was Deputy Dan Coulter. He and I could get in trouble possibly be brought before the county commissioner." She looked down, then back up, a frown had formed It was obvious she had been considering what to say or not to say. "Okay. I need your word that what I say goes no further than these walls and your ears. Absolutely. No if ands or buts. Dan and I both ask this of you."

She stood from her desk. Jake admired all female forms that were shapely and fit-looking, no matter the size. Judge Gerard, Jake figured in her early to mid thirties, was a well-toned, above-average-size woman whose business attire did nothing to hide her femininity. No doubt she could turn heads. He felt a slight flush and found himself embarrassed for where his eyes and thoughts had gone. She was studying Jake and asked if they would keep what she said to themselves. He cleared his throat, half croaking, "yes ma'am."

TJ looked over at Jake and almost laughed then replied in the affirmative.

Judge Gerard heard the humor and saw TJ's crinkled smiling eyes, she realized her dark complexion had darkened. "I have some water in that small refrigerator, or, if you prefer coffee, there is a carafe back in the kitchenette? She reached over to retrieve bottles of water and offered them each one. Jake took one of the proffered bottles almost dropping the handoff in his attempt at not touching her fingers. TJ watched with humor Jake's fumblings and declined with a polite "no ma'am."

Once they all settled back in their seats and the awkward exchange passed and Judge Gerard had a couple swallows while Jake raised his mask and gulped half his bottle, she said "Let me start by saying, Warden Crandall brought serious charges against you two. Had his behavior not been what it was, we would not be sitting here. What I told you before about the scheduled hearing and what a guilty verdict will mean, that may or may not be the case."

They both sat forward. "What does "may or may not be the case" exactly mean? TJ asked first.

"A hearing is the normal procedure. In my time as a Judge, that has always been the case. However, the District Attorney will decide whether to have this presented to the grand jury to be tried in General Sessions Court. This rarely happens and not before the magisterial or municipal court has presented the warrant or made a recommendation. Someone spoke to the higher ups, including the sheriff who questioned Deputy Coulter and Deputy James. I am expecting a call from the DA and that means there will probably be a change of venue and everything that was ruled here today will be overruled." She stood as if to dismiss them. "My advice to you two would be to hire legal representation as soon as possible before a new summons can be issued."

"Why did you warn us?" Jake asked.

"Let's just say, as a minority woman who has busted her butt to get to this point in my career, I resent seeing justice abused by people of privilege and power. I wish I could say more but…I hope you two receive the justice the system is supposed to provide. Good luck. And remember, Deputy Coulter and I said nothing." She walked them to the door.

They walked over to Jake's truck which was the closest. Resting their arms on the back bedrail, they stared at the other buildings on the other side of the lot. These had once been warehouses and behind them, out of sight down a hill, once stood one of the first auto dealerships in the country.

"This sucks. Elena wouldn't talk to me last night and was still in bed when I left this morning. I called Doc Hunter, Dusty is not out of the woods. Still a big if on recovery or what kind of life he will have if he survives. I left Elena a note and told her what Doc said and that I was meeting you here. I took care of the animals. I wasn't sure when or if she will get out of bed. As I told you, she wants to go to her daughter's. This may delay her leaving but I'm not so certain that will be the case. She will need to testify at the hearing. Damn."

"Hearing. Sounds more like indictment--a trial. We're being railroaded. Better call Deputy Coulter, see what he can tell me." TJ pulled out his cell phone and told his phone assist to call Deputy Coulter. He put it on speaker and after a few seconds a voicemail clicked on and TJ asked the deputy to call him if he would. "Hopefully, he will call back soon."

"How did Deane react when you told her?" Jake turned around to face TJ who had stood back from the truck, paced a few steps, and came back.

"She upset 'bout Dusty, asked how Elena and you taking it. Told her about Warden Crandall and what happened. She said he's a dick--thinks there no way these charges stick. Not goina be happy to hear we being indicted. Money's tight. New mortgage, new car and truck payments, education loans, on top of everything else. With her salary as a counselor and my puny officer salary, we live month to month. This a major problem bro."

Jake opened his door and sat down behind the steering wheel. "We may need to see a lawyer. One that doesn't cost an arm and a leg."

"Does such a thing exist? I'll call Tony Peyton, the bail bondsman. Maybe he recommend someone. Anyway, need to give him heads up about possible bonds for us. Let's eat; put together a game plan. Always think better with a full stomach. What say?"

"How about Turkey Creek Saloon? It's not too far out of your way and it's on my way home. I need to check on Elena."

"Lead the way." TJ closed Jake's door and walked around the front of his truck, raising a fist, the black heritage sign of strength and hope.

Jake pulled out onto the side road to avoid the downtown area which had begun a revival with an auction hall, arts and craft shops and antique stores next to cafes that served home cooking and various specialty cuisine. The back alley came out next to the newly renovated historic Robert Mill's designed Court House. Soon they were on Highway 49 headed toward Sharon where they would turn on Highway 211 to Hickory Grove. Turkey Creek Saloon was just beyond there, hopefully far enough from Tindal's place to keep from running into him or his men.

CHAPTER

7

TJ followed Jake. Hadn't been too worried before they went to the magistrate. Now he could not help but worry. Losing his place on the vice squad would happen if he were sent to jail. Otherwise, the charge would result in disciplinary measures, suspension more likely, reduced rank possibly. He could lose his PI license. Most likely, a temporary suspension with probation. Either way, he and Deane would be in trouble financially. They had been in worse shape while he was in the military, the reason he took his twenty and got out.

The bonus pay he received as a member of the joint task force called Operation Pink Flamingo helped. All the money was used on the move from Miami, a down payment on the new house and to offset bills for their former, now rental home, in Lil' Havana and to help out with his mama. His work for Special Agent Hardy and the continuing op made it possible to set money aside. Not enough to last long if unemployed.

He missed the military more than he dared admit to Deane. Not just the steady pay, more than that was the adrenaline rush of combat, knowing it was you or them, no ambiguity about who the bad guys were and what to do about it. Feelings, the risk of imminent death made life more meaningful.

Had hoped joining the Miami Dade Swat Team make leaving the military less painful. Too much red tape, political bullshit in and out of the department. Backstabbing and lack of comradery. Race and ethnicity issues during his father's Vietnam days, the Affirmative Action era, were why many white noncoms left the military--many of the racist bastards became police, rose through the ranks—no surprise to people of color why the racial injustice never ceased. Back then a small amount of military, not including his father, were promoted as a result. Even today, there might be increased numbers of black commanders, but they feared being labelled not tough enough on the under-classes, turned their backs on their police brothers like him. Realization a motherfucker.

Jake's father also served in Vietnam. Jake's father had survived. His had not. In the end it did not mean a damn thing. In combat, TJ had learned, there was no time for any such bullshit. Everybody bled red was the way he saw it.

Politics. Racial prejudice. In the Miami barrio where he and Deana grew up and their mothers still lived, he was not Cuban enough. Outside the barrio, he was too Cuban and of mixed race,

One thing he had learned all too well, in combat zones, your political affiliation would not save you or your buddy's ass, which applied to police personnel on the streets also. Only seemed to work for those who kissed ass to gain rank.

Guess that was what helped him bond with Jake. They were nonaffiliated. Both kept their us against them thoughts and feelings separate from duty.

They crossed paths in Ranger training and later some missions in 'Stan. Wasn't until they both were sent as trainee trainers to the Philippines, attached to the world elite Philippine First Scout Ranger Regiment, they really got to know each other. Those Rangers were eager, fearless, and willing to die for their country in their struggle against the Jihadist, Islamic extremist groups, the Huckbalahap Guerillas and Moro Islamic Liberation Front (MILF). In that regard their war was the same fundamentalist struggle as the Middle Easterners.

Before that, neither he nor Jake ever served in a training unit, never trained or served in jungle warfare. Desert dry heat of the day, extreme temperature drop at night and the ever-present dust of 'Stan, became replaced by tangled mass of vines, trees, snakes, insects, crocodiles, high humidity, and the relentless torrential rains of the Philippines. Urban warfare, door to door, village to village with demoed concrete, dunes and rock became more complex in the Philippines. Most instructors already deployed were former Vietnam vets working alongside the Scout Ranger instructors--local customs were taught, adhered to, strictly--same for any overseas deployment. The language not so hard for him, but Jake, Tagalog near impossible. The Scouts spoke better English than most instructors did Tagalog. Jake's smooth southern accent, a hint of cracker, hillbilly thrown in, slaughtered their tongue and brought laughter for Jake's efforts.

The soldiers, like younger generation soldiers and youth everywhere were tech savvy--second nature for them. Not so much for older veterans like him and Jake. Not only were the Scouts further into technological things than older trainers they were far more dogmatic about their Christian Religion.

Most of the Scouts, like him were raised Catholic. He had stopped attending Mass and going to confession once he finished his military training. Talking to a priest about killing not something you do in military or as SWAT team member. Praying was difficult, another thing he rarely felt the need to do. If God was all powerful, knowing all thoughts, what was the point? To ask His protection and help for taking another life seemed sacrilegious, asking forgiveness, hypocritical. Religious fanatics who did this, no matter their beliefs, were fucked as far as he was concerned.

He and Jake rarely talked about their beliefs. Any remarks, usually derogatory--cursing people and conditions in their operational theater. Jake said he never cursed until he got in the f…in' military.

He hadn't been able to contain himself. Here Jake was cursing like a sailor telling this. Jake said he rarely prayed when overseas. He too felt it sacrilegious to pray for killing, but felt it was okay to ask, what he called guardian angels, for protection for himself and his fellow combatants.

He and Jake had slowly shared stories about their backgrounds.

Country boy Jake rebelled against his authoritarian father, tried to earn his respect—said joining gang was rebellion; joining Army was to earn father's respect.

He barely knew his father. His rebellion the barrio, the Hood--gang warfare a constant part of day-to-day existence. His experience, unlike Jake's, was not by choice. He joined the Army to get out of the Hood, also because Deane, pregnant at the time they started Junior College, wanted family with marriage. Working minimum wage jobs, living with his mamacita in her small home, the military looked like his best choice.

Deane lost the baby while he was in Basic Training at Fort Benning, Georgia—made him think to go AWOL--Deane saying absolutely not--his mother telling him she take care of her. Deane had been then, as she was now, the one who always put their welfare first. One of the best human beings he would ever know. She stood by him through training, Ranger School and three deployments, Iraq, Afghanistan, and the Philippines. They tried to have children twice more, she miscarried. Those were some of their saddest days.

Another emotional day was when Jake had been hit by the Satchel IED.

They had been in a convoy, on what was supposed to be a training exercise outside Marawi City in the Southern Philippines. The memory still fresh like it just happened—the entering into a small enclave, Jake in a troop carrier just ahead of his, some kid on a motorized bicycle lobbing a satchel on the street in front of Jake's transport, explosion back of the engine compartment, vehicle flung into the air like a matchstick toy, driver and front seat Scout officer killed instantly along with four Scouts, who sat near the front of the rear troop compartment, Jake, near the rear of the truck, coming down on its top, landing head bent down cracking three vertebrae, rendering him unconscious, him and rest of the vehicles' troops immediately unloading, setting up a perimeter, watching as Jake was loaded onto a stretcher--not knowing his fate until much later.

Jake, in an induced coma for two weeks, was airlifted to a naval hospital in Hawaii, then sent to Walter Reed, Fort Jackson and finally Charlotte for rehab. Over the course of the next year, he learned Jake's condition from Jake's parents, finally Jake himself. Never, first wife Joanna. She took their children back to Louisiana while he was recovering, divorced Jake while in the coma-- before he could even get back on his feet. He knew little about her, except Jake's claim of her family's mob connections; couldn't help but feel she was not worthy of the benefits she took from Jake. The last he heard she died from an apparent overdose. Her family took custody of the children.

That was a turning point for both of them. Still in the Philipines, he had helped in the Battle for Marawi, returned stateside and served as a Ranger Special Trainer for two years, took his twenty and joined Miami Dade SWAT team as a sniper, then as an undercover officer, then recruited for a task force run by Homeland Security. Meanwhile Jake, medically discharged, became a farmer and contractor, met Elena on an internet dating site while working on a resort project in the Bahamas. Then he too got recruited by Homeland's Hardy for Operation Pink Flamingo—Jake told he would be eyes and ears only--turned into much more for both Jake and him. When the job ended, Jake returned stateside.

He and Jake kept in touch. Next time he saw Jake was the wedding. Shortly afterwards, he and Deane made their move to Charlotte—the main reason, threats to Deane due to the ongoing op--rejoining Jake, a bonus.

He had not owned up to Jake about his continued UC work with Homeland.

Now this. He wondered if Jake's enemies were behind the shooting. Had Elena been the target? He knew Jake well enough to know he wondered the same thing. Jake was fixated on Tindal. He may be right. Not Jake's only enemies, nor his.

52

CHAPTER
8

Turkey Creek Restaurant Saloon and Purgatory Dance Hall was on Purgatory Branch of Bullock Creek. Not on Turkey Creek. There were two parts to the facility, the dance hall, and the restaurant saloon, separated by a deck that had a view of Purgatory Branch which had a spring fed pond that was surrounded by Cypress and Judas trees, Cattails, Canna Lilies, Spider Lilies and Horsetails giving it a swampy feel. Adding to that feeling was the Cypress wood siding, weathered grey, and said to be from a Santee River plantation built in the days when Cypress Trees proliferated along the southeast coastal plain.

In Jake's opinion, the foresters were ruining the environment by replacing native species to plant polluting pine "crops" that could be harvested in fifteen to twenty years. He lived with Tindal's crap surrounding him and his own efforts to keep a more diverse, balanced environment.

Jake loved the feel of Turkey Creek Saloon. He tried to come here every Friday afternoon. Fish Friday, he called it. His family always had seafood on Friday. A Jewish or Catholic tradition. His family was neither. His grandfather had been raised by Greeks after he ran away from home at fourteen. Maybe that was how their tradition started. No one left of his family that would know, so he could use the story of his grandfather without any rebuttals.

They sat on wood chairs in a corner along the rail, each with his back to the rail and with nothing but woods and the pond behind them. Normally, out of trained habit they would prefer to sit with a wall behind them, keeping an eye out for any threat approaching.

Mabel was their waitress. She was one of the owners, the other owners were her husband and a silent investor. A bosomy woman dressed as though she were in an Irish Pub of the late Nineteenth Century. She had rosy cheeks, always a welcoming smile and a cheery voice with a coastal twang. "And what for ya and ya friend to drink Mr. Harper?" She asked as she put menus and silverware from an apron on the shiny urethane-coated wood table.

Jake looked up into her smile, "Mabel. I'll have a Turkey Creek Dark. And my friend TJ, what will ya have TJ?" Jake asked trying to imitate Mabel that drew a chuckle from both.

"Bottle or draft?"

Jake preferred bottle beer normally. But at a microbrew, the beer from a tap was usually fresher. "Draft will be fine."

TJ ordered a Turkey Creek Amber. "Either bottle or draft will be good thanks. Long as it's cold I don't care."

"Honey. That would be up to you. Bottle and draft are always cold. Everything here is either hot or cold." She replied with a laugh, her ample breasts bouncing.

"Draft then."

"Brew their own I take it?" TJ asked when Mabel left with their order. TJ tried to see inside but there was just enough sun peeking through the trees to create glare on the windows keeping him from seeing what lay within.

"I thought you might have been here before?" TJ shook his head. "They brew beer, wine and whiskey. They have a pretty good rating locally and nationally, so it seems. I've seen a pop-up ad on my phone and computer. Also, the meat comes from Hickory Grove Meat Processing and the produce is grown locally. I hear their hamburgers are exceptionally good. I know their seafood is as good as you'll get anywhere around the area and the chicken is very tender and fresh tasting. My favorite vegs are fried okra, squash, and home fries. You can't tell they've been fried. None of that oily taste."

TJ seemed to be distracted. "Sounds good bro. Whatever you're having, I'll have the same."

"On the way over, got to thinking about how it is with us. Known each other what ten, twelve years, little longer? Like we were plopped down next to each other on this planet and happened to come to like each other. Ever think about that? Lotsa fellow servicemen and policemen got a bond. Don't have many of those. You one of the very few. Guess it had to do with my MOS, I don't know.

All the time I've known you, I can't recall you talking about socializing, going out with other people or having them over. Am I wrong? Ever think about that?"

"What brought this on? Is it this shit we're in? Let's eat first then we can talk about crap, if that's what you want."

"Nah bro. You said you and Elena having problems. Got me thinking, Deane and I haven't seen much of Elena in the last year. You don't talk about you and Elena going and doing anything lately. And we came to realize that we don't know much about Elena. Ever get out, do things, see other people?"

"Not much lately. We used to get out, try different restaurants, catch a movie. Don't meet many people in my job I want to socialize with, not a joiner, never have been except the Army, no church, no clubs, or other group things. Elena is a military brat, grew up constantly on the move, her family was her world, still is, especially her daughter. Being away from them has started becoming a problem. She doesn't want to get out much of late. I come here by myself, mainly on Fridays. Deane and you are the only friends we ever did much with, and, because of all our schedules, the pandemic, like you said, socializing has become rare. So yeah, you are nearly my only friend, but I don't think it strange we became friends and remain friends, even though y'all don't ever come around."

Mabel came with their beers and Jake ordered the Barnbird Special with sides of fried okra, squash, and smashed tatters. TJ had the same.

"And Mabel I'll need one more order to go." Mabel pulled her pad back out of her apron and wrote it down.

TJ studied Jake. Man done got too serious. Could see the change. When he first met Jake, he'd been loose, always joking, couldn't remember last time he heard one of Jake's corny jokes.

Jake knew there was more to the conversation. "Okay, what?

"The Bahamas? Cuba? Haven't heard you talk much about what happened. Amy? Blakely? Come on bro. Deane says Elena act like she been told nothing. Like y'all hardly know each other's past life. She says you all bottled up. Scared you goina explode. Asked if you talked with me 'bout it. Told Deane haven't felt like we needed to—reminded her we sworn to secrecy about the op, her included. Ain't no rule 'bout personal stuff though." Jake was staring hard at him. "Okay. Don't have to talk if you don't want to. Just thinking, might help your marriage if you got out more, you know did things, opened up more to Elena. Over three years. 'Bout time bro. Couldn't hurt."

Jake grimaced. He didn't have an answer. He had to compartmentalize his life. There was before his near-death experience in the Philippines and after. Everything else was like it was happening to someone else. He dared not say that. Not to Elena, not to anyone, especially not that head-shrink the feds sent him to. Not even to TJ. He never felt comfortable talking about his personal life. This thing with Elena and her renewed interest in her old boyfriend he now felt had been at the root of their problems. As for his past life, Elena never seemed to be interested in knowing about his past life. In fact, she never asked about the Bahamas or Cuba, strangely nothing about Joanna or his children, except to use them as an excuse for moving to Louisiana. That was the extent of their discussion. He wasn't going to go there with TJ in this public place.

Jake raised his mug toward TJ, "Here's to friends and possible fellow jail mates. May Bubba be your cellmate and not mine."

TJ chuckled while he eyed Jake as they clinked their beers together. "Okay bro. When you ready to talk, I'll listen."

They sat there drinking their beers. A cool breeze began to blow, bringing the scent of gardenia and a hint of moistness. Jake looked back over TJ's shoulder at the water-garden plants. He didn't see any gardenia, but he noticed some billowy clouds off to the west over top of the cypress trees.

TJ broke the spell. "Speaking of friends and places, ever go back to that place we had your bachelor party?"

"You talking about Dilworth Billiards? Rarely. Elena never cared much for going there. Why?"

"What about your friends from there? Eric, the owner, your old op friend, Special Agent Bob Hardy, ever hear from them?"

"Saw Eric last time I was in there about a month ago. Didn't see Bob or any of the other members I used to drink and shoot billiards with. Probably a good thing I didn't see Hardy. He has a lot of explaining to do. He fucked me over more than I'm comfortable talking about."

Jake took a long drink from his beer. He wondered where TJ was going with this questioning. Like TJ just said they had been sworn to secrecy; he had been not so subtly threatened, told not to talk to anyone about his involvement, especially TJ, which he thought strange.

"Guess everybody has gotten older. Families demanding more of their time. And Charlotte has changed. A lot of the members worked in downtown and stopped by there to avoid rush hour. Now the metro area has exploded, more outsiders and the younger generation isn't into places like Dilworth. Why you ask about Special Agent Hardy, you still in contact?"

"Occasionally, task force shit, periphery of an overlap on an op. He asks 'bout you. Don't believe you ever told me how you got involved with him in that op, why you dropped out?"

Was Jake somehow currently involved? Like him, not able to say? He watched Jake to see his reaction, hoping he might answer. Hardy wouldn't like him bringing up the op with Jake, warned him not to. Too bad. He couldn't see any reason not to. Hadn't. Wouldn't. Could be Jake might know things to aid the investigation. Who knows, might have to.

Their food came.

Jake didn't answer. TJ let it slide. They ate in silence. Both were letting their eyes drift around trying not to be too obvious about observing the other patrons sitting outside. There was another couple in the opposite corner, a man and a female companion who seemed to be enjoying each other's company oblivious to everyone else. Jake wondered if this was a romantic rendezvous. Probably not. Too small a community with too many loose lips. Unless they were not from around here. He didn't recognize them. 'Can't help your suspicious mind,' Jake thought, 'and again, the trigger Elena's email from her daughter's bastard father?'

TJ noticed the couple and let his attention move on to two rough looking rednecks sitting on the dance hall side of the door. They were dressed like farm hands with faded flannel shirts, worn denim pants with the leg bottoms hanging in and out of mud-streaked boots. Their ragged billed baseball caps were pointed in the direction of the couple. Smirks, and from what he could tell, raunchy remarks, drowned out by the music coming in from the overhead speakers. The biggest one looked over at him and their eyes locked. He nodded toward them and the other one started staring also. Their contempt was obvious. They were mumbling to each other. One of them appeared to mouth something that included Jake's name and they laughed. "Know those guys?" He asked Jake as he turned his head away from them. Started watching them out of the corner of his eye. Jake had noticed.

The voice inside Jake's head said he knew one of them.

"The beefier of the two seems familiar and I believe I've seen both of them around town together. Probably redneck rump rangers."

TJ joined him in a chuckle." Typical good ole boy drunks. Good bet, opioid or meth heads, seems to be a lot of that around these days." He noticed they had two empties in front of each of them. They had been slouched over, beer bellies pushing their shirts out, now they were sitting straighter, swinging their heads, looking at them then breaking their stare to peer toward the restaurant entrance.

Mabel came through the door, ignored the upraised bottles from the two 'necks and went to the other couple's table. The man handed her a credit card, and she came over to their table. "Y'all all done?" She asked gathering and stacking their plates, her ample breasts swaying half exposed, she seemed to pretend Jake was not noticing. "Can I get ya anything else? Another beer? Desert? Got fresh blueberry pie and chocolate cream also," she asked straightening back up with a teasing smile Jake knew was not a come on. Just Mabel being Mabel. She was happily married; her husband was not one to be trifled with.

"TJ?"

"Not for me."

"Me neither Mabel. Mabel, do you know those two over by the door? They seem familiar and they keep giving us some hard looks. Seems they got something going on that's troubling them."

She looked over at them. They were waving their bottles.

"Those two? They come in here almost every day. How they can afford to, makes you wonder? Use to play the poker machines back when they were popular and poor ole folks was throwing their whole paychecks away. We got rid of them before they was declared illegal, on account of trash like them hanging around here. Wasn't good for business. If I could keep them out of here I would. Keep looking for a reason. Butch, the bigger of 'em and his cousin Billy are sod busters for that Tindal man. You know the man who owns most of the timber 'round here. He come here once. Acted all high and mighty like his stuff don't smell. Had some of the local politicians with him. I don't care 'bout none of that stuff. Treated them like everyone else. Tindal seemed to be none too happy. Hasn't been back. Not that my husband or I care. He was a lousy tipper. Most times people like him are."

She reached down to take their empties. "Sure you don't want desert?"

"No thanks. We have to get going," Jake said.

Mabel took their empties, turned, and walked back ignoring Butch and Billy.

"Figures," Jake said, "Tindal's boys."

Mabel came back with the other couple's receipt. They signed it and were walking out when Billy made a crude remark causing the man to turn his head. They walked on out, down the steps and out of sight. Butch and Billy were laughing. Mabel stopped and stared at them then came to their table with their receipt. They stared up at her as she banged two more Bud Lights down on their table along with their check. She spoke loud enough for Jake and TJ to hear, "Last two. Drink up. Pay your tab and git out!"

Butch made some remark as she turned her back to come to Jake's and TJ's table. She flushed but did not turn back around.

Jake started to stand. Mabel motioned him back down.

"Don't pay them no never mind. "Ol' buster, he like some dog in heat. Thinks all us women just can't wait to crawl in the back seat with him. Hard to believe they's some do. Not this ole gal. My man Avery more'n enough. If'n I was to go sneakin' around, it'd be with somebody special not with no stinkin' white trash like them two. Know what I mean?" she said with a throaty laugh, slapping her pad against her skirted thigh. She took Jake's credit card as TJ protested, extending his card also which Jake told her to ignore.

"Now I remember what it was about Buster." Jake said after Mabel went back in the restaurant. "Been a long time ago. Right after I moved onto the farm and sent word by way of Red, after catching him on my land, that I better not catch anyone else coming onto my land. I put up no trespassing and hunting signs all the way around to make sure there could be no doubt. Some kept getting ripped down and several times I heard gunshots over from the direction of the graveyard. So, I started making routine rounds at dawn and sunset. And low and behold guess who I caught up a tree sitting in a stand smoking a doobie? Caught my attention as I'm sure it did for any deer anywhere down wind."

"When I walked up, my Remington pump pointed up at him and cleared my throat, he almost fell out of the stand. I told him to leave his rifle and bring his ass down before I shot him down. His hand twitched on the rifle. I could tell he was about to be even stupider than he already was, so I pumped the shotgun, ejecting a shell, all the while with the shotgun pointing at him. "That was the birdshot shell," I told him letting him know I meant business. "The one in the chamber is a slug with your name on it. If I were you, I'd get my ass down." He took his hand away from the trigger, taking hold of the rifle by the barrel, slung it over his shoulder and climbed down, begging me not to shoot him."

"I asked him who he was and why he had ignored the postings? He never answered. I told him to unsling his rifle and put it against the tree and get the hell off my land before I had him arrested or decided to go ahead and shoot him, then call the authorities. When he stood there staring at me with that eat shit look and didn't put his rifle down, the thought entered my head that shooting him possibly might be the only, if not the better option. He tried to laugh it off. Then the smug bastard turned and started walking away. I came close to bashing him in the head and calling DNR. But then I remembered who the newly appointed game warden was. I had caught Red's sorry ass back on my land a little over a week before, figured I'd be wasting my time."

"I went back to the house, got in my truck and tried to find where ole Butch there left his vehicle. No luck. Now I know why. He came from Tindal's hunt club. I believe I've seen those two shits around town. Funny how things happen. Over there sit those two pieces of shit. And me with more trouble from Tindal. Don't you find that strange?" Jake took a swallow of beer. "Maybe we should rattle the cage. You know shake the tree. See what falls out."

"Not the time. Or place. Need to go see an attorney like your girlfriend Judge Gerard said." TJ replied.

"Girlfriend? First time I ever laid eyes on her. What are you talking about?"

"Looked at her like a kid with a schoolboy crush. Almost laughed out loud. She noticed. Can't deny it bro."

Jake said," you're crazy, she looked good and I admire good looking women, that's all. Hope you don't go telling Deane. She might let it slip to Elena. Speaking of which we need to get going. Wonder what's taking Mabel so long. Why don't we go see? Since you've never been here, you can see what the inside is like."

They got up and walked across the deck.

Billy with his back in the corner looked up and waved his beer bottle at them. "Hey buddy why 'on't you bring us two more Buds. Git yourself one and yer darkie friend one too and I'll pay you for 'em."

Jake and TJ ignored him and as they opened the door, he yelled "hey…."

Inside the place was nearly empty. No Mabel. Two good ole boys that looked past their prime sat at the long wooden bar. Behind the bar was a mirrored wall with glass shelves upon which sat an assortment of partially filled booze bottles. Above the bar were various sizes and shapes of glass and stem ware. TJ looked around. The place looked like an old western saloon with round wood tables and round back wooden chairs. A piano and speakers sat on a raised stage area in the far corner. Up high were exposed yellow-tinted beams of heartwood, cypress, or pine, he guessed. They extended out the gable end toward the parking lot. The floor was the same kind of wood, unfinished, worn smooth by the soles of boots and other shoes that had walked and danced across their surface. On the walls were posters, collectibles so they appeared, of musicians from musical events that occurred from the 1950s Hank Williams to the present-day Bob Dylan.

Mabel came out from the back of the bar kitchen. She was preceded by a man pushing a hand cart loaded with cases of beer and wine. When she saw Jake, she apologized, "I'm sorry. This vendor showed up and I got distracted. Guess I'm getting old." She went to the end of the bar, entered something into the electronic register, inserted Jake's card and handed it to him with his receipt to sign. "Don't ya worry about any tip. Lousy service don't deserve no tip." She laughed.

Jake gave her twenty percent. She offered them free beers which they refused. She gave Jake his to go order.

They came back out the door onto the deck.

"Hey Harper. 'on't see no beers." Butch said looking over his shoulder, turned so his chair was against the wall facing where they had been sitting. Ain't too neighborly. Though I hear you might be puttin' yer place up fer sale. Guess I'll be back huntin' there 'fore long."

Jake and TJ walked on away from them toward the steps.

"Seen'd that pretty lil' filly woman of yer's udder day," Billy said. "Know you ain't doin' her no good. Heared they's sum nudies of her. If'n you want sum, might be able to hep you out." He and Butch laughed.

Jake stopped abruptly and turned back. TJ stuck his hand out and grabbed his arm.

"Dat's right Harper you and your colored buddy need to git. Tell yer ole lady I's sorry 'bout dat mutt gittin' shot."

TJ let go of Jake's arm. Jake set the to go order on a nearby table. They walked side by side back to the other guys' table. Butch tried to stand. Jake pushed him back down. TJ moved over to Billy and held him with a claw-like grip on his shoulder. He was squirming and trying to get TJ's hand off and squeaking, "Hey let go. Dat hurts."

Butch did not struggle. He looked up at Jake with a sneer on his face. Jake wanted to knock that look off. He bent down, his face inches from Butch's head. Any fear of possible coronavirus contamination pushed back by his anger. He could smell the yeast of the beers from the bastard's breath and a pungent sulfurous odor mixed with diesel coming from his clothes. Overriding all that was a feral musk like an animal in the wild. "You want to run that by me again?"

"What you talkin' 'bout? Billy jes runnin' his mouth. Guess he can't handle the alckyhol."

Jake moved so he was facing Butch. Butch tried to lurch forward. Jake used the momentum to slam him face down onto the deck. There was a whoomff as the air was pushed out of his lungs. Butch pulled himself up onto his knees, tried to grab Jake as if to tackle him. Jake kneed him just below his chin, picked him up and slammed him back into his chair, his head banged into the glass of the wall. Lucky for him, it did not break. Pushing his left forearm into his neck,

Jake quickly replaced his forearm with his right hand, pinning Butch's oily head against the glass. He could feel him trying to swallow and his eyes bulged. "If I were you, I would speak when asked to. Otherwise, you might find your balls in your mouth and your tongue up your ass a distinct possibility. Am I getting through to you?" He felt Butch trying to swallow as he gave a slight nod.

"Good boy. Now, let's start with your buddy's comment about my wife. When and where did you two see her?" He relaxed the pressure. Butch tried to turn his head. Jake could feel his attempts to swallow. "I asked you a question." Jake squeezed again.

"Okay. Okay." Butch croaked, as Jake released the pressure and he reached up to message his neck. Jake knocked his hand away. "Come on man. We ain't done nothin' to you. We jes seed yer ole lady the other day, maybe a week ago. Some old Marine buddy of Mr. Tindal flew in. Yer ole lady, she come by. We heared he was maybe her old man. That's all."

"What did the man look like?"

"Bout yer height. Little heavier. Grey hair cut like military. From Texas so I was told. That's all I know. Mr. Tindal took him and yer wife in the big house. She left after a couple hours. He stayed till the next day. Seems he knew Mr. Jenkins also. Saw them together up on his terrace. They was sitting close and talking. Heared they all were in some war together."

Sounded like it was his father-in-law Sam. Jake couldn't help but wonder why Sam didn't come by. And why had Elena not mentioned this? Her old man and Tindal, Jesus, he never would have thought that. Not in a million years. Elena was probably told not to say anything to him. Made Jake wonder if Sam really did have cancer.

Billy had stopped squirming and TJ relaxed his grip but kept his hand on his shoulder. Jake looked down onto the deck at the cigarette butts from the spilled ashtray. The one butt he could see bore the same brand as the one that had been tossed out of the truck that fateful night not long ago. He fixed Butch with a cold piercing stare. "What was that about nude pictures of my wife, asshole?"

He tried to shift but TJ retightened his grip, a pained expression flashed onto his face. "Jes what we heared. The Mexicoons we work wid in the yard. They tell us stuff. Seem to hear and know ever't'ing. Said they'd heared sum uv 'em tech geeks had 'em. All I know. Swear."

"And my dog? What do you two know about that?" Jake asked Butch.

"Nuttin'. Heared he got shot is all. Like Billy said the Mexs seem to know everything. They talk to us when we wid 'em. That be all we know."

Jake put more pressure on Butch's neck. He could feel the bones and knew just a squeeze more and he could crush them. "Where can I find these Mexicans?" Butch's eyes showed his distress. He pulled and pushed at Jake's arm, but Jake only tightened his grip.

Mabel had heard or been told about what was happening. She came out and was moving in their direction. TJ locked eyes with her, held up his free hand and shook his head. This was not the first trouble Mabel had witnessed, she had stepped in on numerous occasions. As much as she disliked Butch and Billy, she could not witness any violence on the premises without intervening. "Do I need to call the sheriff's deputies?" she asked in a not so cheery tone.

TJ looked at Jake. Jake's eyes were locked on his target. "We were just leaving. No need in calling the police. Isn't that right boys?" TJ asked looking at Billy who didn't move or say anything. TJ went over to Jake, "Come on bro. Not here. Not now," he said almost in a whisper as he laid a hand on Jake's shoulder and felt Jake's tension slowly ease off. "Jake, we need to git going. Butch and Billy, ya'll need to mind your manners, but don't bother to get up, just apologize to Jake and to this fine lady for your rude behavior and we'll be on our way. How about it?"

"Uh huh. We ain't…" Butch started to say, and Jake cut him off with the near crushing squeeze. His legs started jerking and Mabel yelled "stop before you kill him." She grabbed Jake's arm.

Jake almost didn't hear her. Blood seemed to be rushing inside his ears. Since his injury, bouts of anger rose inside him, threatened to take away his hard-won self-control, making him a tortured stranger, running on adrenalin-fueled rage. He shook his head, forced himself to let go. Only then did he realize TJ's and Mabel's hands were on his arms. He looked around, regained his focus, saw the fear and anger on Mabel's normally pleasant face. He hoarsely said, "I'm sorry Mabel but this joker owes you and me an apology and he's going to give it if it's the last words he speaks. Now apologize." Jake turned back to Butch and leaned in closing the gap, once more squeezing his grisly throat.

Eyes bulging Butch croaked, "Aw'ight."

"What was that? Didn't sound like an apology to me?"

"Pologize. Mabel git him off me. We ain't done nuthin'…" He wheezed through gritted teeth."

"OK. He said it. Now let them be or I will be forced to press charges."

"How about it Billy? Need to hear you say it also."

Everyone looked over at him and TJ moved in closer, he cringed.

"Like Butch say, sorry."

Jake and TJ looked hard at the two of them. Jake said, "Don't move until we're gone, and, if I see either of you come by my house or anywhere else again…" He let it hang. He glanced at Mabel and said, "I'm sorry. I meant no disrespect to you."

Jake went over to their table and grabbed the packs of alcohol wipes, handed two to TJ, wiped his hands off, then his face. TJ did the same. Jake walked over and retrieved his to go order. On their way down the steps, Jake heard Mabel telling Butch and Billy, "I ain't going to tell you again. Pay up and git out. Don't come here again."

TJ was saying something that sounded like "grasshoppers in a frying pan." Jake glanced over at him.

"What was that? Sounded like you said something about grasshoppers."

"Grasshoppers in a frying pan, an old Cuban expression meaning you were losing it back there bro. Good thing me and Mabel were there." TJ chuckled. "You know bro you make me feel better about myself, make me feel almost human."

"What the fuck you mean?"

"Nothing bro. Just need to lighten up, clear your head. Don't want the shit piling up, isn't that what you used to say?"

"Lighten up? You heard them. If they had said something about Deane, we would be waiting on an ambulance and the deputies about now. Those are Tindal's boys. The threats started when I was in the Bahamas, now the shit with Dusty, the game warden, something tells me it's all tied to Tindal. It's time to have a closer look at him, his employees, his operation. He's got that place secured like he's expecting an invasion, even has a private airfield. And that stuff about Sam paying a visit, Elena not saying anything about it. This pisses me off."

"Sure hope those assholes not covid carriers. Don't want or need that shit."

"Be alright by me if Tindal and the rest of them dropped dead. I damn sure wouldn't shed a tear."

They stopped by Jake's truck. Jake put the takeout order in and retrieved a bottle of hand sanitizer. He squirted a generous portion on TJ's hands, then his own.

"Thanks. Come on bro calm down. Don't jump no conclusions. Talk to Elena, straighten things out. Get it off your chest. Goina do some digging, talk with people owe me favors, might be able to find out something that we can take to a lawyer. Judge Gerard is right, we need legal representation. There's a lawyer I know, maybe he'll see us tomorrow. I'll call let you know. Oh, meant to tell you, talked to Deputy Coulter, said he took those bagged fragments to his forensics guy and he was sending them to the FBI for analysis. Problem is, could take a week or more. May not do us much good."

Jake opened his truck door then stopped before getting in. He heard Butch and Billy at the other end of the lot. Butch was rambling around in the bed of the truck, threw a couple of bottles into the brush near the pond, tossed another one to Billy, took his bottle in one hand, opened the door, and got in the truck. He lowered his window and yelled out to them, "you and yer spick-coon ain' heared the last of this." His tires slung gravel as they sped out of the parking lot.

Jake recognized the sound of the truck. He told TJ what he now knew.

"I hope they do come by my house again."

"Let it go bro. They nothing but mouth. Don't need no more trouble. Just go home, talk to Elena, don't go accusing her, not with what she just went through, okay?"

Jake climbed into his truck answering, "something I remember someone once said, he looked hard at TJ who looked right back, *vengeance is best served cold*; around here we say, *what goes around comes around*. Don't worry I have people to see and things to do before I check out of this life. It'll be what it'll be, that's the way I see it. Right?"

"Right redneck motherfucker."

"Family fucker, remember? And yours could be next."

TJ 's face lit up. His eyes didn't change. "Call if you hear anything. And check your phone, see if you miss my call. Got it?" TJ closed Jake's door.

Before TJ turned loose of the door, Jake asked, "Don't go pretending like you're going to let this shit go."

"We take it to them bro. First we get this legal crap behind us." He leaned back off the door. Looked off to the west. The wind had picked up and clouds were forming. "Better get going, looks like a storm brewing." He smacked his hand on the bedrail of Jake's truck and walked off.

CHAPTER
9

Mary Elena McElroy Harper stared at her monitor. She had two post-coronavirus, active patients which she had to keep a close watch on. She went through the motions of reading and recording what she saw and the answers to the routine questions she asked each of them. Her mind was not there. Sarah, the one recovering from breast cancer surgery, asked if she was okay. Elena told her about Dusty and had to fight to keep the tears at bay and not sound as devastated as she felt. Sarah said, "Deary keep your head up. I'll pray for you and your dog. God will help you get through this. You'll see." Elena hoped she was right. She didn't dare tell the woman she was not the praying kind. She thanked her and begged off saying she had to check on another patient.

She wanted to call the veterinarian again but knew she would be told the same thing, "They would call if there was any change." Where was Jake? Why didn't he call? She kept checking her phone for any missed calls. Nothing. Was he ignoring her? Usually when they said hurtful things to each other she was the first to break the ice. Apologies were neither of their strong suits. His way of apologizing was to hug or make a joking remark about something unrelated to what had happened. Lately she noticed he had been quieter and was having more outbursts over what seemed to her to be minor stuff, not at her directly, but she felt she was the reason. The "I love you" was being said less often. Had he stopped loving her? She was not sure that was not the case, or, for that matter, if she still was in love with him. Had they really been in love?

They had met on an online dating site while he was working in the Bahamas. Four months of talking online and by phone before they met in person. He flew to New Orleans to see his children, she told him he could stay at her condo with her and her daughter. She felt she knew him, he seemed to be someone she could trust. Their conversations, while getting to know each other, went beyond intimate. She was anxious, not sure how it would go, turned out way better than expected.

A stroll through the French Quarter, followed by Mojitos and a good meal at an outdoor café. Finishing up in her bed enjoying some of the best sex she had had in a long time.

At first coming to the farm was an adventure, a reawakening of a wild sex life. Then came the coronavirus pandemic and the isolation became like being in prison. She missed her daughter, seeing her family. She had no real friends here. The feeling of isolation had not gone away, and her sexual appetite ceased to match Jake's. Things important to her seemed to be changing between Jake and her. She was less and less certain this was where and how she wanted to spend the rest of her life.

And Jake yesterday, the incident with Dusty. Not once did he think about her. Had she been the intended target? He didn't seem to consider the possibility. Said nothing even after TJ brought it up. Then he seemed to overreact when the warden showed up. She had seen in his manner and in his eyes the fierceness, the animal desire to strike with possible deadly consequences. He never threatened violence toward her. She knew he never would, but his anger scared her, made her angry because she felt helpless. Was this PTSD? What had triggered it? She felt it was more than the pandemic. Would it get worse? Made her afraid of what he was capable of, might do.

Her patient duties finished Elena thought about what she should prepare for dinner. She used to enjoy cooking. Jake was a home cooking aficionado. Said he learned how from his grandmother. He gave her a hard time for being more of a recipe type cook. But her interests in cooking like many other tasks had begun to wane. She knew this was a sign of depression and she needed to do something before it completely overwhelmed her. And she knew what that something was.

Fuck dinner. Jake would have to make do with leftovers.

She took her revolver off her desk, went to the kitchen, hesitated briefly thinking about Jake's comments about her drinking more lately, decided fuck that. Fuck you Jake. She poured herself a glass of wine and walked outside. Maisy was sunning herself on the front porch as though nothing had happened.

There were dark clouds to the west and the wind had picked up sending leaves sailing across the drive and onto the walk. A storm was brewing over the Broad River in the direction of Sharon. Would it move to the northwest or come across the farm? With a storm in the area there would be less cell phone reception and no internet or satellite tv. That meant if there was any news from the vet or Jake trying to call, they would probably not get through. Another thing she hated about being here.

Elena had grown up on military bases with her siblings, her friends, and their friends always around. Then she had left home at sixteen, having finished high school early. Nursing School had been easy plus there was a lot of social activity and partying. She began bartending at an upscale restaurant, the owner was into some shady dealings. She did some things she would never admit to anyone.

After college, she went to work as a nurse and went out with her fellow nurses. On one of their ladies' nights out, a band from England was playing and a band member asked her and her friends to join them backstage for the after-performance party. That was where she met Teddy, a big burly handsome keyboard player who was also a surgeon at a hospital outside London. One thing led to another and the result was Jennifer. Elena had been just shy of twenty when she was born. She found out he was married with other children back home. He sent her support money and would visit whenever the band was in the states.

Elena had not talked to him since hooking up with Jake, but they stayed in touch via email. The band was on tour again. He wanted to see her and Jennifer. Jennifer was excited but scared to go without her mother. Jake knew of him as Jennifer's father. She had never discussed Teddy's and her relationship and had not told Jake about Teddy's recent invitation. The thought of seeing Teddy again was exciting. It was the thought of him that engendered an orgasm the last time she had sex with Jake. She felt no guilt and wondered what that meant.

She also felt no guilt about her father's visit. Her father Sam had forgiven her her indiscretions, what he called *indulgences,* her way of paying her tuition and other bills—experiences she had pushed into the back of her mind--no longer spoken of. It was her father's connections which somehow solved the problem with the club owner who had demanded she get an abortion, continue her employment; and he and her mother had forgiven her pregnancy--embraced their granddaughter. He became the father she had always wished for, barely known-- a retired marine, veteran of two wars; and, until Jake had gotten him to admit the thing few people knew, including her and her siblings, a CIA operative. Elena wished Jake and her father could have put their differences aside, been hospitable.

It did not surprise her that her father had come into the area without wanting to stay with them. He and her mother had done so a couple times each year, choosing to stay in a hotel. What surprised her was that he knew Thurmond Tindal and his man Jenkins. She knew he was coming and honored his request not to tell Jake. How could she not?

While Jake was at work, she met her father at Tindal's palatial home. Mr. Tindal, Colonel Tindal, was how her father had introduced him, was a gracious host and Bud Jenkins, the Major, acted as if she were a person of interest. She did not know what the nature of her father's visit there was. Elena knew her father had an import export business since his retirement she was never certain what he imported or exported. She kept her suspicions to herself. On the few occasions, she voiced her suspicions, her mother told her, in a tone she rarely used, she would never discuss her father's business with anyone, not her or anyone else. Elena heard the same when people asked questions about her father when he was away on active duty.

Lost in her thoughts, she had not noticed the storm had come. Maisy, scared of loud noises, startled her when she felt her pawing at her pant leg. She heard the closeness of the rumble, saw the flash, the crack of lightening. By the time she and Maisy went inside, the rain pounded the metal roof with sudden fury. "Damn it Jake, where are you?"

CHAPTER
10

Jake could not shake the anger or the feelings of despair. He felt as though everything was crashing in on him. Adding to the turmoil was the storm brewing to the west headed his way and there was no avoiding it.

Huge billowy clouds like giant cotton balls caught in a wind tunnel moved in and out of view obscuring the last fiery rays of the setting sun until there was nothing but a dark void into which leaves, limbs and other debris flew onto his windshield. His truck was being pushed toward the shoulder and he had to slow down, having to fight to keep from sliding into the ditch, and being slammed into one of the trees. Many were bent over the edge of the road, close to the point of breaking. Then as if the gods of nature had changed their mind, his truck was yanked back toward the other lane.

Fortunately, Highway 49 was devoid of oncoming traffic and all Jake had to worry about were the larger limbs of trees, sheared off, thrown into the road. The sky, now crimson and lavender, opened and rain, as if poured from a bucket, made visibility nearly impossible. With the rain came the ping of hail bouncing off his windshield and hood. One loud rifle shot sound caught his attention. He slowed, pulled over on the shoulder under the protection of an oak tree, hoping none of its limbs would come crashing down. 'God, he needed to piss. He had hoped to make it home first. Damn, the rain gods were making their presence known and he dared not.'

When the worst of the storm subsided, he pulled back out onto his lane and slowly continued toward home, hoping no damage had occurred and Elena would not avoid him as she had last night and this morning. Perhaps she tried to call; the storm made reception sporadic. More likely, she had not tried. It would be better to let things slowly return to normal. Come on Jake, that's no longer possible. The situation TJ and he were in demanded answers. Many of those had to come from Elena. And he needed to piss.

He made it to the turn off at the intersection of Highway 322 then crossed over Turkey Creek, which had gone from a slow lazy meandering stream to a swirling rush of muddy water reaching the top of its bank. The thermometer indicator on his rear-view mirror showed the temperature to be in the low seventies, a fifteen degree drop from when he left TJ.

He lowered his window to let in the cooled, refreshing air as he turned onto the unpaved road that ran alongside this end of Turkey Creek. The gravel road had washed in places and was littered with limbs, leaves and other debris. He slowly wound his way, dodging larger limbs that had been sheared off and fell across the road. He had to stop and move some of the ones that were impassable.

As he climbed the hill up from the creek, he was travelling between two different worlds. His land on the left consisted of tall stately hickory, red oak, and other hardwoods, broken here and there by cedar and cypress. The trees and their biome niche had their own near perfect world. Jake believed the trees and their surroundings communicated through electrical and chemical actions and reactions, maintaining a balance. A balance which man disrupted, especially people like Tindal who only appreciated plants' commercial value.

A memory, that shaped who he was and his aversion to senseless killing, happened here in these woods.

His grandfather had taken him out after the first frost, he was told this made it safe to handle and eat wild game. He used his grandfather's 410 shotgun to shoot a squirrel out of a tall oak before the furry tree rat, as he had heard it called, could duck behind a limb. He still remembered running over to pick up the still warm, limp creature, its eyes fixed in death as if staring into his own. The joy of his first kill had been tempered by a sadness he dared not speak, and had stayed with him.

Jake carried that memory into his first bitter taste of combat. When the first onslaught of shots that were meant for him and his fellow soldiers rained down on their patrol, wounding and killing, the victim's desperate eyes fixed on what had been and would never be again, deepened his sorrow and became fixed forever in his mind, haunting his dreams.

The right-hand side of the road was owned by Tindal. The stately hardwoods had all but vanished replaced by pine trees as a crop, harvested once they reached commercial-use height. This had been hunt club land ever since his grandfather died. Tindal had been part of that club and now was the owner.

The land's woods and fields had been tended to and farmed by his grandfather in a sharecropping venture with the Hill family. At the top of the hill had once stood a three-story farmhouse that had been there when rice in the lowlands and cotton in the upper regions were aristocrat-makers in South Carolina and all across the south.

Jake had offered to pay Tindal to allow him to dismantle the house and salvage the materials. Tindal bulldozed and burned the pile of materials and constructed an unattractive metal building as a hunt camp in its place with a shooting range behind it. This was the backside of Tindal's land holdings, the least attractive part. The entry was used by the hunters, loggers and heavy equipment operators, the noise makers, and blue collar workers--to Tindal, commoners--in and out, dawn to dusk. A piss-on-you to Jake.

Water in the ditch was backed up at the culvert that diverted the rainwater under the road from Tindal's side to Jake's land, deepening a gully, tree roots exposed holding on to the sides for dear life. Jake saw the debris had clogged the culvert. Beer cans, styrofoam cups, paper napkins and food wrappers, stained from the red clay-colored water, hanging in and out of plastic bags, along with leaves and other natural washings creating a dam. Jake knew this would little by little end up littering his land, until he came to pick it up. Sometimes he dumped the residue in a pile by Tindal's hunt club back entrance gate. Too often it would remain there until he went back to retrieve it.

"I will never give in to that bastard,' Jake thought. 'He's behind all the shit that has happened, the threats, attempts on my life, everything. Doesn't matter if I can't prove it. With what has happened to me and now Dusty, I will fight him till the end. So help me God I'm coming for you Tindal. I'll get you if it's the last thing I ever do.'

CHAPTER
11

TJ could have taken shortcuts to outrun the storm. Instead, he decided to stay on the main roads. Cell service had been intermittent due to the area and the storm. He had missed several calls, two from Bob Hardy and two from Deane that he needed to return. He punched in redial for Deane. It buzzed and buzzed. He was about to end the attempt when she answered.

"I've been trying to reach you."

"Sorry, service hasn't been the best, everything okay?"

"People have been trying to reach you. Your office has called several times and I didn't know what to tell them, so I let the call go to voicemail. What is going on?"

Deane rarely got excited. She sounded alarmed and he wondered if someone said something they shouldn't have.

"I'll call them. Anything else?"

"TJ, you ran out of here this morning without telling me anything except you were meeting up with Jake. Said you thought you would be back before lunch. It's almost dinner time and not a word from you. That's not like you. Then when I couldn't reach you, I got scared something else had happened. All of this trouble with Jake and their dog… had me worried."

While he listened to Deane, he checked for missed calls using his truck's dash display. Saw several from Deane. Then a surprise--Elena called a couple times. Made him wonder what that was all about? No voicemail from her. Homeland Undersecretary Hardy left a voicemail.

"Sorry babe, need to call into the office. Be there shortly."

Hardy's message was the code for call back pronto.

An agent named Marcia answered, "Tasco. Where may I direct your call? The service would have automatically checked his call and alerted Hardy to an incoming call from him. This was supposed to be secure, but like all systems it was vulnerable to hacking.

He disconnected. Almost immediately his truck monitor said *Incoming. Caller Unknown*. He called out *Answer*.

Undersecretary Bob Hardy's smooth tenor voice said, "You've been out of pocket. We need to meet. How soon can you be at our usual?"

"Almost home. Need to stop by there. Should be there within the hour depending on the traffic."

"An hour. Eighteen Hundred. See you there." The unlisted, secure call was terminated.

TJ pulled off the road and drove back the hundred yards to their triple gabled brick ranch with the wrap around porch. The fenced in back yard that was the play area for his two rottweilers, Buster and Bonzo, was empty.

The dogs rushed past Deane when she opened the door and he knelt to receive their liquid greeting that nearly knocked him over. "Sit," he commanded, they hesitated only briefly before doing so. "Stay" was the next command as he rose to embrace Deane.

"I wish they listened to me that well," she said hugging him before he could caution her about the contact with Butch and Billy. He told her after her hasty peck on the cheek. She stepped back and wiped her mouth. "Great. Dog sugar and possible virus contamination. Just what every woman hopes for. Dinner is on the table." TJ didn't immediately head to the kitchen, she looked over at him, knew the expression. "Can't you at least eat your dinner?"

"Had a late lunch with Jake. I wish I didn't have to leave, but I have a meeting in Charlotte in an hour. You know how the traffic can be." Deane was not pleased. She hated when she had to eat alone. Too many times she had to save food which he often took for lunch the next day.

"I'm sorry love. Maybe we can do something this weekend. Go out to eat. Catch a movie. Think of what you'd like."

"What I'd like is to have enough money so I could have my husband with me like a normal family."

"When have we been normal?"

"Exactly," she replied and began putting away the food.

TJ took a quick shower and changed clothes then he went to the master closet, changed his shirt, stuffed his service revolver in his pants and put on a weatherproof lightweight jacket. He didn't have to check; he knew it was hidden from Deane and anyone else. She was used to the weapons and had become proficient with her own .38. But if she saw him carrying, she would worry. He changed his shoes from black sneakers to his lace up service shoes. As he came out of the closet, passed through the master bedroom to the den, she was standing there with an insulated cup that he knew would be strong unsweetened coffee. They had a longer, deeper kiss, said their usual "love you" and her, "be careful", his, "be back as soon as I can, and I'll call".

The meeting was to be at Dilworth Billiards near the center of Charlotte. Getting there was no simple task at rush hour. TJ could have stayed on Highway 49, gotten off onto Interstate 77 at Carowinds Boulevard or parked and taken the light rail. He chose to drive using the Interstate route because he didn't know what Hardy might have in mind, or if the Vice Squad would call, plus he needed to see one of his Hispanic gang CIs who was a computer hack.

Dilworth Billiards had not changed much since TJ met Hardy at Jake's bachelor party. Antique billiard tables took up most of the space. At the back was a long wooden bar with mirrored and glass shelves on the wall. Eric, the owner was seated in his usual spot on a wooden barstool to the left, reading the paper. Often, he would be engaged in conversation with one of the other members, greeting everyone by name with a friendly smile when they came near.

"Haven't seen you in a while. How have you been?" he asked when TJ walked up to him, keeping a practiced safe distance. TJ told him he had been too busy, regretted not having time to stop by since the shutdown ended. He asked had Bob Hardy been by. Eric said he had not seen him in a while. He asked TJ about Jake, what he had been up to? TJ told him Jake was busy also without going into too much detail or about recent events. They made small talk until another member came in. He turned to Susan, the manager/ bartender, exchanged greetings, ordered a Shiner Bock, and went out to the well-landscaped patio. He stood and watched the goldfish in the center fountain pool while he waited.

The area was enclosed by a vine-covered wood fence with Crepe Myrtles on the street side. Four story condos towered in the backdrop of the far wall behind a Tiki Hut bar area. Blooming vines enclosed the trellised sides and soft Jazz played through small speakers mounted in the rafters of the structure.

Bob Hardy came from inside with a cloudy liquid in a crystal drink glass. He walked over to TJ and they shook hands. They moved over to the bar. Hardy set his drink down, waited, watched to see if anyone might be in earshot.

"Why the face to face?" TJ asked.

"Heard some unsettling news concerning our friend Jake and yourself. Care to elaborate?"

TJ was not sure how to respond. He turned to face Hardy. "Elaborate? About what?"

"It was brought to my attention some source is searching for information about you two. That set off an alarm. I checked all protocols, did a security breach check, ran your names. Imagine my surprise when I found out you and Jake had been issued warrants, arrested. Assault and battery charges, a game warden, care to explain?"

TJ told him about the incident. Hardy listened without interruption. "Any idea 'bout the nature of the search? Who doing it? TJ asked.

"All I can say is the search came through well connected, top security channels and that is what set off the alarm. This puts your undercover SWAT relationship, ties to Homeland Security and me in a precarious position, our file is supposed to be unavailable. If some senior DOJ member wants to, he can start an investigation which could be problematic in ways you cannot even begin to imagine."

"Jake believes, got me beginning to believe, Thurmond Tindal the problem. Could have something to do with him?"

Hardy ignored the question. Instead, he said, "this could jeopardize your work for us," reached down, picked up his drink and took a swallow. "Where do we stand with the op from your end?"

TJ previously worked undercover in Miami as part of Homeland's Operation Pink Flamingo, investigating possible cartel attempts to purchase black market weapons. This led him out of Miami to Charlotte because of ties to a local gang called the El Diablos, connected to a suspected CIA counterintelligence agent, Mark Poponovich, Jake's acquaintance while in Cuba, who was acting as a local investment executive. TJ, suspected, but had no proof, that this investment company was tied in with the Palmroy's foreign investment group. He had been told to back off.

Intelligence indicated Mark was involved in laundering cartel drug money used to make the weapon purchases. Illegal diamonds and gold were being smuggled into the country through the Mexican borders into Texas, California and Arizona on the west coast and Miami, Charlotte, and Chicago east of the Mississippi.

TJ had several informants, one of which he planned to see later. An IT operator for the local gang. TJ had little doubt he and his brother were tied in with the Mexican Cartel from Juarez. Hardy told him Homeland needed to know the connections. For security reasons, TJ and Hardy agreed to keep his involvement with HS from being disclosed to all but his SWAT Team Commander, standard for any undercover work.

"Sounds to me, you think my cover been blown?"

"I'm saying you need to be extra careful. I don't know what triggered this. You are not a name, just a coded number. For people like you, any attempts at access should be taken as a warning. All operations have data tracking, only accessed on a need-to-know basis, requiring access codes, which are firewall secured. I am not certain the operation and your involvement in it have not been compromised. The alarm went off, the computer notified me that your code number was being scrutinized. Does not mean they have connected your code number to your name, possibly not, and so far, no connection back to HS. If they had, someone would have been asking. For damn sure I would have been contacted by your SWAT Commander. Which hasn't happened."

Bob Hardy picked up his glass, swirled the almost melted ice and the semiclear mix around, it was almost empty. He set it back down and turned to stare hard into TJ's face.

"What I need to know is if you have mentioned anything to anyone, Deane? Jake? Your mother? Anyone? Anything about HS? Do you have any reason to believe you could be compromised? Do you have anyone asking questions or acting as though they suspect you?"

TJ walked over to the fountain and back. Could David Gonzalez, his CI informant, have hacked into HS? He would need to check on this. He turned back to face Hardy. "Haven't had anyone ask me anything and haven't mentioned anything to anyone, not Deane, Jake, my mother, no one. You didn't answer me 'bout Tindal?"

Hardy looked toward the inside. There was the crack of someone breaking a rack of billiard balls, smack of someone making a shot heard over the soft music playing overhead.

"I have no reason to believe Thurmond Tindal is behind any of this. What occurred between this Warden Crandall and you two has no direct link to Mr. Tindal, you two are assuming this."

Hardy's reply didn't sound convincing. "His name came up, didn't it?"

"That is not the reason. Thurmond Tindal has been vetted by HS because he does contract work for the military. That is in the public record. He is former Army, served in Kosovo and the first Gulf War. Has been a military supply contractor since his retirement from active duty. Personal friends with many military and government bureaucrats, high ranking officials, numerous representatives, senators, and former presidents. So, tell me why he would be involved? He has too much to lose."

"The man wants Jake's land. Been doing crappy things to make Jake's life miserable for years. Many which involve this warden. He owns the warden, just like he does local police and other government employees. You know this. Just 'cause he has political ties and contracts don't mean anything in my experience. Tells me he has security clearance, that's all. He better hope Jake's and my suspicions don't prove true. Jake's goin' after him. Can't blame him. Jake, rightfully so, in my opinion, believes Tindal behind everything, including what happened in the Bahamas and Cuba."

"You and Jake need to get your heads on straight. You especially. Don't add to your troubles. As for this current problem, it could have been an errant shot by a hunter and the game warden heard the report on his two way and decided to investigate."

"Numerous problems with that theory: Elena heard nothing, the shot fired from too far overhead, the wound and the ground impact indicate a high velocity fragmentary round, the game warden arrived too soon, was not interested in doing an investigation; plus, the magistrate said Tindal's putting pressure on her and pulling strings. The DA now pushing for unprecedented legal prosecution. It's Tindal. No one else has motive and means."

"You know Jake made a lot of enemies. Could be any number of them. Could be Elena was the intended victim. I'm sure you and Jake thought about that."

"Yeah. All the other enemies would have gone after Jake or his family, not his dog. Tindal one of those enemies. *The* enemy as far as Jake's concerned."

Hardy was puzzled. He had received a memo from DoD. The memo stated a new drone type weapon was being tested for possible procurement by the military. The tests were scheduled for tomorrow, would be attended by military and industrial inspectors. He was tasked with vetting all personnel and people of interests in the area and putting in place all land, water, and air security measures. The place for the test was on Thurmond Tindal's property. Ridiculous. No way would Tindal have allowed this incident with Jake's dog to have happened, even if it was technically possible. Homeland's team had been surveilling the area, setting up the security protocol. Nothing had been reported. They would have noticed a drone.

"And how do you and Jake know his wife Elena wasn't the target?"

"Like I said, silent shot, came from overhead, most likely from a UAV, and the wound and shell fragments indicate restricted military ordinance. I know from personal experience, if Elena had been the target, she would have been mortally wounded. Seems to me whoever did this wanted to scare Elena and or provoke Jake into doing something to cause legal troubles. In Jake's and my opinion, the warden was sent to ensure this happened."

Hardy shook his head. "I don't see any way Tindal would be involved. He is under too much scrutiny. I can't say why, but it has nothing to do with what happened yesterday. Of that I am certain. Maybe instead of blaming him, someone could talk to him, ask him if he wouldn't mind talking to someone to see if this whole thing between the warden and you and Jake could go away."

"Who might that be? You?"

"Perhaps. There are reasons this could be done on a need-to-know basis. It would be better if you didn't know, definitely, not Jake. I will see what I can do?"

"We would appreciate any help you can provide. But, if we right, and it's Tindal set off your security alarm, there's no way he be willing to help Jake." TJ studied Hardy. Something was up.

"Let me work on it. I need you to put this investigation onto a fast track, reports are something big is happening. The border wall and the illegals' surge is causing a lot of political backlash, Homeland is under a lot of pressure to produce. There is growing opposition in Washington and across the border, someone is trying to stop the op, may be where the alarm originated. How your code came up is the big question? I'll be working on that. Be careful. You of all people know what these people are capable of. Keep me informed."

TJ knew what these people were capable of, at home and abroad. He didn't know if Hardy really knew like he did firsthand, or if his knowledge was reports and news footage. At this point in time, he wasn't sure if his legal troubles or security issues needed the most attention.

"Yeah. Well, you do the same. We trying get us an attorney, would love not to have to worry 'bout it. Let me know what you can do. So you know, got several gang banger insiders need putting the heat to, see what they know. See if this one CI hacker know 'bout the breach. But, if this personal problem don't get handled, won't be no follow through."

"I'll see what I can do. Get me something. Turn the heat way up. Otherwise, I may not be able to do you any good. In the meantime, tell Jake to stay away from Tindal and make sure you do the same. Nothing better happen to Tindal. I hope we're clear about this. Make sure Jake understands."

TJ simply nodded. Hardy was holding out on him. Telling Jake stand down, waste of breath, not going to work. Jake see right through and figure out who gave the order. Hardy had to know this. He would do what had to be done. So would Jake.

"We better go back inside before someone thinks something hinky is going on. Come on. I'm buying." Hardy started for the door.

"Need to get going. Deane had dinner ready. Need to be there before it gets too late."

"I should know something by morning. You need to concentrate on the op. Do not get caught up in Jake's problems. Verifiable evidence, not fragmentary. You and I don't need the kind that blows up in our face. Keep that in mind. I'll let you know if I can convince Tindal to help make this warden thing go away." Hardy picked up his glass and walked back inside past TJ who held the door.

CHAPTER
12

Fighting Tindal, the killing of the squirrel, Dusty getting shot, his spell of bad luck memories seemed never ending. Beginning with his near fatal IED encounter and the flashbacks that came unexpectantly day and night.

Sargent de la Cruz's sanguine face staring out as to nothing, the last image Jake remembered before awakening in a hospital, a doctor shining a light into his eyes. A strange voice inside his head that he didn't recognize that he later attributed to having been a result of the drugs they used.

Jake couldn't explain his restlessness to Elena, the cold sweats, the need to get up and walk around until almost time to be up for the day. She had stopped asking. Was this what was causing the distance that seemed to be growing? Their relationship was hot and cold. Had it always been this way? He didn't think so. Her wine consumption had increased. Once a little at mealtime, had become a bottle, sometimes more per night. What had changed? Was it his fault? His business had increased keeping him away more, but he couldn't recall any prior complaints. Did she know he was checking her phone—reading her messages to her family and Jennifer's biological piece of shit father? Why was she hiding things from him? Teddy and Sam? He knew they needed to sit down and have a heart to heart but Elena had deflected all attempts he made to do so.

He couldn't wait any longer to take a piss. Afterwards, he opened the gate and drove up the drive. As he reached the roundabout in front of the house, his phone chirped, indicating he had missed calls or messages. Four were from

Elena, two from Deana and two from TJ. The last from TJ not ten minutes earlier, flagged with 911, emergency, call back immediately. He tried to hit return for TJ and the reception died. "Damnit." He would try again if he had reception inside the house.

The house was dark. The front door unlocked. He called out for Elena. No answer. He set the to go order on the island then walked through the house. No Elena. Her cell sat on her desk. He started to check it but decided to look for her. Maybe she was checking on the cows or chickens. He went in his bathroom and washed his exposed skin and changed into a clean shirt. Still no Elena or Maisy. Strange. Her car was here. He decided to look down at the barn.

The sun's last rays were behind the giant oak where he had stopped his truck. The shadows were dying, replaced by twinkling silhouettes, a small sliver of moon was visible. He heard the chickens settling in, a low squawk as he walked by, normal sounds, a flutter of wings. One of the heifers let out a lonesome deep-throated moo from the direction of the barn. No sign of Elena. No yap from Maisy.

The barn door was ajar, a dim light faintly glowed piercing the dark interior. He approached with caution. Not sure what lay beyond. His radar on high alert, feeling apprehensive, he thought of calling out, decided to look first. Jake slid past the opening, then pushed the door further open. The hinges made a whining sound and Maisy started yapping. Stepping inside, he saw the light of a small halogen penlight on the dirt floor its beam rocking off to a side like it had been dropped. By its light he first saw Elena's feet, then he quickly noticed her silhouette. She was sitting in a corner on a milking stool, a revolver on her lap, a shotgun pointed at him. He reacted by moving aside then quickly toward her to push aside the weapon. He saw her scared and tear-stained expression turn to anger; her stabbing eyes stared up at him.

"You know you should never point a gun at anyone unless you mean to use it. I hope you didn't intend for that someone to be me." She didn't reply.

Maisy continued yapping and Jake told her to hush. She came to him with her happy whine, and he reached down, picked her up, his eyes on Elena.

"I'm sorry I didn't know you had tried to reach me. I didn't have reception."

He set Maisy down, reached down, tugged her to her feet and hugged her. She was stiff, her arms stayed at her side, the revolver in one hand, the shotgun in the other. He reached down and took them into his own hands, propped the shotgun against a rail and stuck the revolver in his back waistband. He heard another sob escape and saw tears fall onto her chest.

"What is it? Is it about Dusty? Did someone from the vet call?" She shook her head in what felt like a no. He reached his arms around her and hugged her tight. Then he gently pushed her back, brushed the hair back from her eyes, tears continued to run streaks down her dust-covered cheeks.

"Something happen, what's wrong?" Her face was twisted not in remorse but in anger. Jake felt relief, this was not about Dusty. Was she this upset with him about something? He couldn't imagine what he could have done to provoke this uncharacteristic anguish.

Elena stopped shaking. She pushed past him and walked over to lean against a stall. Inside was a four-month-old baby calf and her mother. Elena turned to look at them then looked back at Jake who started toward her. She put her hand up. He stopped.

"You didn't think to check, didn't care, either way, what does it matter. You went storming out this morning without a word."

"Whoa. I looked and you appeared to be asleep. I didn't want to wake you. I left a note."

"No Jake. You could have called. TJ called Deana. She called me. All day Jake, not a word."

"You went to bed last night without saying anything to me. I figured you needed time for yourself. I knew how upset you were about Dusty."

"Dusty yeah. But not just Dusty. You Jake. You and TJ and the warden. It didn't seem to be about me, Dusty or what I witnessed. You never considered that maybe I was the target. Just macho bullshit. When we got back here afterwards, you acted as though nothing had happened. I heard you on the phone talking about work, then later with TJ."

"You went into your office and slammed the door. Later you came out and ate something, went back in your office without saying a word. What was I supposed to think?"

Jake shifted his weight. Watching Elena for a sign that she was less angry.

"Look. I'm sorry. You're right. I should have been more sympathetic yesterday. I did consider the possibility you were the target. I dismissed that because you insisted there was no weapon retort, and because of the type of injury to Dusty, and the type ordinance that caused it. Then that prick warden showed up. We have a history. He is Tindal's boy. He was there to cause trouble. TJ and I got suckered into it." Jake moved over to stand next to Elena. There was a moment of silence as they both watched the calf nurse its mother making slurping sounds that filled the silence.

She wiped her eyes and nose on her sleeve. Without looking at him, she said, "I guess you haven't talked to TJ?"

"We stopped by Turkey Creek and had a late lunch. I left there and came straight home. Why?"

"Moms called. Dad checked into the VA. The tests for the spots they biopsied were positive. He has melanoma. They suspect other related problems."

"That's not good," Jake replied thinking to question, deciding to wait.

"And Dusty, the vet hasn't called. And…" Elena started trembling again and the tears started dripping. "That truck came by again, going slow. Went past. Wasn't long it came back and stopped in front of the house. There were two men. They just sat there for what seemed a long time. I grabbed the shotgun."

Jake didn't say anything. He had a good idea who it was. He hoped they came back again while he was at home.

"Then shortly afterward, someone called," she said in a shaky tone. "All I heard was breathing. It went on and on. I kept saying hello and asking who is this? When no one answered I hung up. The phone indicated a caller, no ID and I didn't answer. Then a few minutes later a text came through with a picture."

"What kind of picture?"

"It's on my phone. I tried calling you twice. Then I called TJ. He and Deana got pictures also. I broke down. He said you should be here soon, said for you to call him back. I was scared. I had to get out of the house. All I could think to do was take the revolver and shotgun and come down here. I didn't hear anything but the cows and the chickens. I didn't hear you. I nearly shot you. What am I supposed to do? Who is doing this?"

Jake reached over and took her hand. It was cold and shaking. "Come on. I need to see what you are talking about."

He put the revolver in his belt, reached out took her hand and gently pulled her to the door. Maisy scooted ahead of them. The outside solar light at the eaves of the barn and the chicken coop cast a dim light, lighting their way to the wet brick paver, motion sensor lit walk and on up onto the porch.

Jake put the shotgun back on the rack. All the other guns were locked away in a gun safe. He came back to the spare bedroom that was used as Elena's office. Elena had retrieved her phone, brought up the text and picture, handed it to Jake. The picture showed Elena spread out on one of the wooden lounges Jake made which was in the back yard by their small nature pool and fountain. She was completely naked. They often sunbathed in the nude on summer days when no hunters were close by. Both enjoyed the air over their skin lying next to the pool with the soothing sound of the water. This often led to some spontaneous lovemaking, something Jake missed.

The picture had been taken from overhead. After what Tindal's boys had said at Turkey Creek Saloon, there was not much doubt who was responsible. The caption text said, "Keeping an eye on you."

"What did TJ say?"

"Just what I told you."

Jake looked, there was another missed call from TJ.

"Jake, I can't live like this. I don't feel safe here anymore. You are gone most of the time. We counted on Dusty. You said Maisy was our alarm and Dusty was our first layer of defense. Now with what happened to Dusty and this. I can't take living here anymore. We need to get away. I need to be there for moms." Elena plopped down in her office chair, wringing her hands, then wiping them on her dust covered jeans.

"I can't up and leave. Who would take care of the animals? What about Dusty and this problem with the warden? You will have to be here for that. No way I can leave, I wouldn't if I could. Tindal is behind this, all of it. He's determined to get his hands on my land. I will not let him intimidate me. I am not some damn coward who runs when assholes like him threaten me!"

"See. That's what I'm talking about. You get so worked up over everything. All I hear is Tindal this and Tindal that. Even if it is him, you can't prove it. We can't afford to fight him. You are going to end up losing this place trying to fight him. Then what. That's what worries me. We have nothing to fall back on. That scares the hell out of me. What about me? Do you ever stop to think what this is doing to me. To us?"

"What about us? And your father and you and Tindal? When were you going to tell me about Sam's visit?"

He saw the shocked look on her face. She looked out the window and said nothing.

"What was that all about? Is that why you've been acting distant? Tindal tell you to talk me into letting him buy my land? What was Sam's part in all this?"

"I went there to see my father. That was all there was to that. I didn't know he was coming until he was here. He told me that he and Colonel Tindal and Major Jenkins knew each other from their military days and occasionally they had some mutual business arrangements. Mr. Tindal and Mr. Jenkins were very nice to me. I find it hard to believe he would have anything to do with what you accuse him of. I think you want to believe this and refuse to think otherwise." She looked up at Jake and shook her head in dismay.

"I see. You think Mr. Tindal is some bogeyman of my own creation. I guess I don't need to ask what about us? I guess you're planning to go running off to Texas. Makes me wonder, does Sam really have cancer or is this an excuse you and your daughter cooked up so you can go meet up with her bastard father?"

"You're fucking crazy. Are you going to blame me for Dusty and everything else?" Elena said, her eyes flashing anger.

"I don't hear any denial."

"That's what I'm talking about. It's you that is pushing me away. Maybe we both need to get away from each other. Let you decide what is more important." Elena stood up and went out of her office.

Jake wandered out of the room and went into the kitchen. He put Elena's takeout into the refrigerator, was tempted to grab a bottle of bourbon, then thought this might not be a good idea, so he got a glass of water from the faucet and went by the billiard table and out to the screened porch.

The night had a chill to it and the rain had cleared the air. The smell of fresh-mown grass, moist and pungent, already baled, wafted up from the nearby field. Jake walked out onto the porch steps, looked up, so many stars, it was almost like a million pen lights pointed down. No. More like a million eyes staring down, eyes of far greater intelligence, wondering what we these primitive creatures were up to, shaking their heads, thinking what the fuck. Jake felt the same way. He checked his phone for reception, saw he had bars and hit redial to call TJ.

TJ answered by the third ring. "Hey bro. You home?"

"Yeah. Would have called sooner, Elena and I had to talk. She showed me the picture, said you had received some also?"

"Got pictures, plural. Deane's holed up at the house. Called the Sheriff's office, told them threats had been made, requested they send someone by to keep an eye on your house and mine. Deane says there's a patrol car out front, asked them to wait for me. Anyone showed up there?"

"Elena didn't mention it, haven't seen anyone since I got here. It usually takes them an hour or more to come here the few times I made a report. What did you receive?"

"Check your phone. Should've got them 'bout twenty minutes ago."

Jake looked in his message folder. There was a picture of Deane in the yard and one of an older woman inside a window. The text said, "You have been warned."

"Got them. I guess the older woman is your mother?"

"That's right. That is my mother at the kitchen window in Miami bro. Her house is only fifteen feet from the house next door and that window is about ten feet up off the drive that separates her from the older couple next door. Don't make sense, not sure how they got the picture? My brother Leonard, he's looking into it. Got his boys watching her house."

"The picture of Elena was from almost straight down. I believe our buddies from Turkey Creek had something to do with the ones of Elena. They mentioned Tindal's techs. This really pisses me off. Elena is threatening to leave."

"I hate it bro. Hang tight, don't make things worse. Got to check on a lead, see someone might be able to shed some light on what this about. Keep your eyes and ears open, watch what you say and do. Sent me a retired police officer, a fellow PI I know and trust to my place, he goina relieve the deputies already there. Watch your back. We need more info before we see an attorney."

Jake heard a car coming from the direction of McConnells. He told TJ to hold on that there was someone coming down the road. The car stopped out front on the road. Jake could hear the strong motor and the chatter of a two-way rising in volume, car doors being shut, the radio sound became less noticeable. Maisy started yapping her head off. "I believe the sheriff deputies are here. I need to go to the door."

Jake broke the connection.

Light from a flashlight shone through the glass of the front door as Jake came back in the house. He reached down, picked up the yapping Maisy telling her it was alright, be quiet. He flipped on the front porch light and opened the door startling one of the deputies who was about to knock. The other deputy chuckled.

"Mr. Harper? We are here because of the report of a threat. Is that correct?"

"Why don't you come in? Jake stepped back so they could enter. He closed the door and directed them to the eating counter which served as the separator for the kitchen and dining areas. They declined a seat and remained standing as Jake went around to the kitchen side.

"What was the nature of this threat? Why were we called?" The older, beefier officer who had chuckled at the younger slender officer's earlier fright asked. He pulled out a form from a metal file case and laid it on the eating counter, reached up to his shirt pocket for a pen and looked across to Jake preparing to write.

Jake looked at both officers who were staring at him. He wasn't sure of what to say. He assumed TJ had told them what happened. Guess not.

"The reason someone called is that my wife got a phone call from some jerk who wouldn't say anything, just heavy breathing. She received a text accompanying a picture, it said, 'keeping an eye on you'. Understandably, she was frightened. I wasn't home and she couldn't get me on the phone, she called a friend who had received photos also. He was the one who called to request you people come by. This is all I know. I haven't been home long, just found out about this."

"I take it your wife is home, I need to talk with her," said the heavier one, Catledge was on his name tag. The other was Baskins. "Would you get her Mr. Harper?"

"She is still upset. I'll see if she is up to talking to you." Jake walked back to the bedroom, gave a knock, and opened the door a crack. Maisy darted through. Elena was lying on top of the sheets staring up at the ceiling and did not look his way. She had put on a pair of plain white cotton pajamas. Her hair was wet and pinned up in a braid.

"The police are here and need to talk to you." Jake said flatly.

She didn't move or reply.

"You need to come talk to them Elena. Do you want them back here?"

That caused her to look at him. Her look was an angry squint. "Why don't you show them the picture that ought to satisfy their curiosity," she replied.

"Are you going to come talk to them or not?" Jake turned to leave the room. "I'll tell them you don't feel up to talking."

He went down the corridor past the spare bedroom and walked back through the dining area to where he left them. "She is too upset to talk right now."

"Mr. Harper, I need to get information from her for my report. Also, I need to see the photo and the text. If she doesn't want to talk tonight, she can come by tomorrow and give her statement then."

"I don't think she will be willing to show you the picture and I wouldn't want her to, because she is undressed in it."

Officer Catledge straightened, then smiled. "This picture, did you know about it or did you take it?"

Jake looked hard at him. "If I had, I certainly would not have told you about it. Starting to sound like you suspect I might have something to do with this. Is that what you think?"

"Did you?"

"Not just no, but, hell no! This is bullshit. You need to leave." They didn't move. Jake walked to the door and opened it. "If you don't leave now, I'll file a complaint with your IA."

That made Officer Catledge turn beet red. "You do that Mr. Harper. I guarantee that a full report will follow. This will make the DA happy, add to the problem you and your buddy Mr. Alvarez already have. Seems to me, this is part of bullshit play you two cooked up." He could see the anger flashing from Jake. "Oh yeah. You didn't think I would run a check on you? Seems you have a problem with authority, perhaps anger issues. Now you either let me see your wife to make sure she is okay, or I will search your house and she better be okay or you can file your complaint from behind bars. Have I made myself clear Mr. Harper? What's it going to be?"

"Yeah. I have problems with assholes who abuse authority. Follow me asshole. Keep your distance. Wouldn't want any possible contamination you two might be carrying." Jake closed the front door and went back toward the bedroom followed by the two deputies. He tapped and Maisy started yapping as he cracked the door. Elena had rolled over facing the bay window her back to them. "These officers demanded to come back here to make sure I hadn't done something to you," Jake said, "I told them you didn't want to talk, they insisted."

Elena didn't move for what seemed forever. Maisy came around the bed yapping, and Jake reached down to pick her up so she would stop.

"Mrs. Harper," Officer Catledge said stopping just inside the door, "sorry to barge in here like this, but I needed to make sure you were not harmed in any way. If you say everything is okay, we will leave you be."

Elena sat up. "What do you mean am I alright? No. I am not alright. Please leave. Get out of my bedroom. Now!"

"Satisfied asshole? Get the fuck out of our house." Jake followed them back down the hallway, stepped out onto the porch and held the door open. Officer Catledge walked over to retrieve his metal clip pad and the deputies left without saying anything else.

Jake went to the refrigerator, thought about getting another beer, then changed his mind. His stomach was knotted up. He got a glass of water and a sniffer of cognac, changed his mind, and took the nearly full bottle and went to the upper porch to wait for TJ's call.

CHAPTER
13

TJ left Dilworth Billiards and walked a couple blocks to the South End Brewery area where his truck sat parked at the end. There was less light here and less foot traffic, making his change into his tactical clothing inside his truck safer--out of sight of prying eyes. When he arrived earlier, he had looked for any security cameras and picked this spot because he had not seen any. After checking to make sure he couldn't be seen, he slipped his Springfield polymer KD M Competition Model pistol into its holster. It had been modified with a ramp blade to prevent jamming and with the m 9x19mm ammo and his expert eye, he knew if he ran into any surprises, they would soon find out what that meant, though he hoped that would not be the case. He retrieved his Ka-Bar and strapped it onto his calf, then locked his other tactical weapons and gear into the special locker that was bolted down under the rear passenger seat. Satisfied, TJ drove his truck to the better lit area near the brewery, grabbed his face shield, engaged the alarm siren that could wake the dead, and walked another block to catch a trolley to the downtown terminal. At the downtown terminal he switched to another light rail car which would take him to the NoDa area of Charlotte. There were few passengers. He was the only one wearing a mask and gloves.

Whereas Dilworth had been a middle-class neighborhood with cottage style homes occupied by merchants and bankers from the city center, North Davidson started as the blue-collar section of Charlotte. The early residents of NoDa worked in the area textile mills and factories before and after WWII. In the middle of the Twentieth Century, textile mills began going out of business-- many moved overseas for cheaper labor. The support factories little by little began closing or moving outside the city limits to avoid higher tax rates. Toward the end of the century, yuppies and the art crowd began to move in. The run-down factories became galleries, restaurants, and music venues. They bought up and renovated the mill homes and several developers built high-rise condos. Twice a month they had an art / pub crawl that brought in outsiders to see and be seen. Easy marks for the ones preying on the unwary late at night.

On the edge of NoDa are the neighborhoods of smaller, less desirable homes owned by slum lords, occupied by the poorer displaced residents of the urban renewal projects. Many of these people were unemployed, temporary workers in service trades and immigrants trying to get a start at a new life in the states. And, as is often the case, this is where the illegals and gangs from west Charlotte and Pineville came to recruit and prey upon the less protected, less likely to seek or receive protection, residents.

When the NoDa and downtown area crime rates began to grow, the city was forced to do something. Gang warfare had begun to rise. Arrests of MS-13 and other highly dangerous gangs' members was on the rise. No longer could it be said this was just local gangs with no national affiliation. A commission was appointed, they put together a task force of local and national experts and the police escalated their presence in neighborhoods like NoDa and Plaza Midwood.

This was TJ's area of expertise. Having grown up in Little Havana with gangs like "Big Money Team" and "Latin Kings", understanding the culture and lingo, no problem. Working the streets undercover in Miami at first challenging and nerve racking had become second nature, but you could never let your guard down. The gangs had some of the best humint from those they exploited inside and outside the correction system. Too many of those whose profession it was to protect the public fell into or were coerced into cooperating with the criminal elements. They also had some of the best hackers and IT experts that could penetrate the most sophisticated, supposedly "secure" systems and they were connected internationally--organized crime at its worst.

TJ exited the light rail and walked the few blocks east into a poorly lit area. He turned into an alley that was used for access to short parking areas, or in some instances, carports and garages. One of these garages was the computer repair shop run by David Gonzalez, the *Cacique,* second in command to his brother Arturo, the *Inca,* enforcer of a branch of Latin Kings in Charlotte.

They had been here less than a year and were keeping a low profile as far as local law enforcement could tell. NoDa was a tinderbox, just a matter of time until gang warfare once more erupted with MS-13 and other unaffiliated local gangs. Drive-by shootings were happening way too often. Homeland was wanting to know possible ties of the gang to money laundering activities, hoping to take into custody those further up the food chain before ICE and the other task force member groups moved in, arrested, and deported them.

An ICE agent had put TJ onto David and Arturo less than a month ago.TJ had used the deportation leverage to convince David to cooperate. Putting together bits and pieces of what he had learned, he had fragmentary evidence of their connection to the Latin Kings. But he did not have much that could be used to tie them to the cartel's money laundering and weapon purchases. TJ was operating on other people's time schedule. Hardy made this clear. If something big was in the works as Hardy said, then he needed to put more pressure on David. Learn if there was a connection to Tindal.

The back-porch light was on. Other than that, the house was dark. The garage had no windows, but the walls were thin, so he dialed the number of the dedicated phone he had given Gonzalez. No sound. He had texted him to let him know he was on his way. The pingao had better not have skipped. A laser dot appeared on his leg. TJ jumped back into the shadows, anticipating a bullet would follow. He had quickly retrieved his sidearm and listened. The only sounds were the nearby street and city noises. Then he heard locks disengaging and the door swung open to reveal the short-statured, pudgy Gonzalez. His round face smiling. His smile faded when he saw TJ's pistol. TJ flipped his visor down and moved forward out of the light, shoving Gonzalez back then closing the door.

"You early. Not expect you." His face was lined with laugh lines so that even his frown looked comical.

TJ pointed to his face-shielded eyes then his ears and swirled his finger. David looked puzzled, then his face lit up. "No. my friend. No one see or hear us."

TJ pulled out a miniature scanner from the pocket of his cargo pants and walked around the space. There were computer parts everywhere, on shelves, on a rug that covered part of the concrete floor, and on the table, where a mirrored lamp, like a jeweler would use, was on. Beneath it sat a bar stool where David had been, TJ assumed. He had to move cautiously so as to not step on anything. Satisfied with the results of the sweep, he moved over to the laptop computer. The screen saver ocean-scape picture was lit-up indicating David had been using it.

"Busy?"

"Little this, little that. You know how it is. You need me do something?" He was looking from TJ to the laptop. The smile grew and shrunk as if on cue.

"You can find out pretty much anything online, so I hear. Same sources say you're better than most, you are the man that your brother, the local Aztec relies on as his Cacique, right?" TJ looked down on David watching his smile fade.

"This Aztec and Cacique that Latin Kings. We El Diablo. No Latin Kings. My brother, we from Mexico, We El Diablo, this protect us from Latin Kings, others who wish us harm." He tried to smile but it wasn't working.

"I told you before if I caught you lying to me what would happen. So cut the bullshit. I know other people that do things with computers and I know who and what you are. Comprende?"

David Gonzalez dropped his eyes and TJ followed their track. On a shelf beneath the computer, he saw the butt of what appeared to be a weapon. David moved but TJ was quicker. He reached in and pulled out a taser.

"You weren't thinking of using this on me, were you? I've never had to use one, except in training. Hurt like hell. Maybe I should let you find out for yourself." He swung its tip from David's chest to his crotch then to his face and watched his potential victim's eyes grow big. "I got shot in the chest. Felt like I had been hit by an electrified power pole. Wonder what it would do if I shot you in the nuts or the head?" He kept moving the tip up and down. "You want to change your story?"

"Why you want to scare me? I tell you I know nothing. You shoot me, still know nothing." David's eyes were on the taser. They were enlarged but showed defiance. His lips, pulled back into a snarl, had a slight tremble, his yellowed teeth showing. "You say I Latin King. I no Latin King. Latin King try recruit my brother, me, we play 'long. No say no to them. They no threaten, they kill. Comprende?"

TJ looked hard at him. What he said went against the intel he gathered from his sources. He had been doing this a long time and knew official channels relied upon their sources which were not always accurate, as was the case with outside sources which often were rumors or unreliable witness interpretations. Many operations, TJ knew firsthand, went horribly wrong based on corrupted

Intel--innocent people went to prison or were killed. You had to trust your gut, look at the facts.

Facts? Someone had threatened his family and Jake's as well. Jake and TJ believed Tindal was behind the threat. Tindal's boys said the Mexican yard hands told them they got information from techs that worked for Tindal. Who were these techs? How did the yard hands know about these tech's info, the picture of Elena, the picture of Deane, the picture of his mother in Miami? They called him 'killerboy' implying they knew something about him. Makes no sense. He never had anything to do with Tindal, or any of his employees. Were they the ones doing the search, setting off Hardy's alarm? David Gonzalez, the Mexican computer whiz, was he the connection to Tindal's yard men?

"What do you know about a man named Thurmond Tindal?"

David looked down and away. Could be he was confused by the change of direction. No. He knew something.

"I not know this man Tindal."

"Thurmond Tindal has men who work for him who know you and your brother. They say your brother, you, are Latin Kings." A slight flinch.

"They lie. I know no Tindal. No one say we Latin Kings. No Latin King say they Latin King. Why you say this? You try get me tell lie."

He was good--to be expected from number two cartel frontman laundering drug money, among other things. The reason why Latin Kings and other cartel-related gangs so hard to bring down.

"Need you to get information for me 'bout a Thurmond Tindal and his companies--work they do, employees, including the Hispanic yard men you say you know nothing about. Connections, anything, everything. You the computer whiz, should be easy. No bullshit, better check out. By tomorrow, make it happen, otherwise," TJ stopped talking, waited on a reaction. The smile was no longer there.

He reached out, grabbed David by the shoulder with his gloved hand, sweat beaded the pindao's forehead even though it was chilly in the garage workshop.

"Don't fuck with me. Be shame ICE know 'bout this. Or FBI." TJ waved his hand around, picked up a thumb-drive, dropped it back beside the monitor with its grinning skull screen saver. "All these toys. Wonder what they might say? Get me the information. And, cover your tracks. You not only one know how to tap; know when their system being tapped." David had pulled inward, like a turtle when attacked. TJ squeezed his shoulder. David winced. "By tomorrow. Now let me out of here." David looked up at him. There was hate and fear in his stare. He turned and started toward the door. This gave TJ time to reach into his pants pocket and pull out a miniature surveillance devise. He set it up onto a low hanging beam. He wasn't sure about getting video, audio was what he was more interested in, certain calls would be made.

David unlocked the door and waited for TJ to go past. TJ motioned to him. "You first." He stayed back until Gonzalez went out without incident, then he went out keeping his eyes and ears tuned to what was happening around them. Nothing that set off his internal alarm. Once outside he turned back to David. "Tomorrow and it better be good."

TJ worked his way through the back alley, zig zagging, going one way, then he doubled back to make sure no one was following. He pulled out the surveillance devise miniature monitor and slipped it over his right ear and eye then put his cap back on. To the casual observer he looked like any other tech savvy person staying connected.

He had no doubt David would do the expected. Problem was, if he wasn't careful, Gonzalez would set off NSA alarms, initiating an investigation—resulting in questions he, and ostensibly Hardy, would rather not answer. A risk he decided to take. Things needed to happen, this had become personal, for him, for Jake, for their families. Standard operating procedure needed to be put on the back burner.

Gonzalez flinched when asked if he and his brother were connected to the Mexicans employed by Tindal. Their spies? On who? For what? Who hired them, and why? Getting close to the missing link to the cartel laundering operation, he could feel it. And Tindal, how much did he know? Hardy thought Tindal had too much to lose, hadn't stopped many people in same position. White collar and political crime were bigger problems than all petty, local hustler crime. BolsToy, the Palmroys, thinking of them continued to rankle him. Bolstoy dead. The Palmroys' political connections keeping them from further questioning. Was there a connection between them and Poponovich and the cartel? Tindal Industries, was it a front?

Too many questions, too little information, not enough time, always the case for law enforcement, the bad guys always one step ahead.

TJ went to the bath in the transit terminal, took a piss, checked himself in a mirror, smiled. He grooved out to a tune only he knew. 'Got to get the mojo working, get down, get down, do the get down boogie.' Time to rock 'n roll. Let these motherfuckers know they best not fuck with the J'bros.'

A foursome waited outside, two couples, drunk on alcohol, oblivious to him. He moved off, pulled out his cell. Time to check in. First with Hardy to see if maybe he had talked to Tindal. Would Tindal see this as an opportunity to make their lives hell, or would he see this as an opportunity to put them into his debt? TJ bet it was the former.

Hardy didn't have any news. No, he had not talked to Tindal. Deane was fine, watching one of her shows on tv. He told her he might be late and that he loved her. He got in touch with his PI buddy Paul who was standing guard. He said everything was kosher. He was streaming a movie on his laptop. That concerned TJ, but the man said he had one eye and ear tuned to another laptop monitoring surveillance units. There was one on all sides of the property.

The call to Jake had been difficult because of the intermittent signal. Jake, sounding somewhat thick-tongued which TJ wasn't certain was due to the signal, until Jake told him briefly about what had occurred with Elena and the episode with the deputies. TJ didn't blame Jake for hittin' the bottle. If he had been a problem drinking man, he would likely done the same. He and Jake wondered where the info about them originated. TJ told him it was probably all part of the nature of the small-town police department. Jake was still pissed, felt it was more than that. TJ did not tell Jake about meeting with Hardy or his CI.

Jake had changed since his near-death encounter. Not in ways which mattered--still the best of friends. Others didn't know Jake the way TJ did. In the Philippines they got to know each other. Jake with his smooth southern accent--not the rough peckerwood-one TJ had expected. TJ found Jake had depth. You name it, he could talk about it--could convince most people he was an expert. A prolific reader. TJ had learned Jake came from a long line of well-versed story tellers. Many thought he was full of shit, TJ included, until he got to know him. Couldn't believe how open-minded he was. Took the tension out of being out in the jungle. Funny too. That's what changed. The IED, Joanna leaving, taking his children, took that part of him, left a bitter shell. He seemed to have some of his old swagger back after the Bahama and Cuba gig. He and Deane thought Elena was the reason, that she was good for him. He hoped things between them got better. All in all, TJ considered himself lucky to have Jake as a friend. The J'bros will ride again. No way the lowlifes goina get away with doing this to Jake's dog, us, and our families. Fuck them.

"Get some rest bro. Tomorrow we going to teach them they shouldn't have fucked with us."

CHAPTER
14

Colonel William Randolph Baker, DoD, arrived aboard a Kiowa OH-S8F UAV capable helicopter. He came from Bethesda to review the new drone specifications and observe the test run to give his report to his superiors at DARPA-- required before approval and authorization would be granted.

He landed on the dedicated pad out front of Tindal's hangar early in the morning. The day after Jenkins had allowed the photos to be released.

Jenkins couldn't get his mind off Elena. He stared at the Harper woman's photo days on end. What a shame such a good-looking piece of tail was the daughter of Tindal's and his former service member friend and intelligence colleague. Sam would be hard to handle if he knew of the photo. Tindal knew about the photo but had not wanted to see it which surprised Jenkins. Tindal preferred deniability concerning many things: photos, the Harper man's dog, anything which might turn up in an investigation. Just like the days in the military and CIA, Bud was to provide cover. Suited him fine, his files left no doubt as to who knew what. Tindal had asked him to make the Harper man's life miserable and do what he thought necessary to keep his attention away from them and their plans.

Photos were taken using miniature drones. He directed the two moron field workers, Butch and Billy, to place additional surveillance devises in the Harper home. He had enjoyed the photos and their reactions.

The Harper woman was at the breaking point. The earlier meeting when her father Sam was present started the ball rolling. She had said her husband, the Harper man, would never consider leaving, he refused to talk about selling, moving to Texas or Louisiana. Tindal told her the amount he was willing to pay if Harper would sell. She was interested, promised to try again. Didn't happen. The photos might do the trick.

The Alvarez man had proven more difficult. He tried. Not a hell of a lot there: military service, SWAT team career after discharge, rumored to be part of Operation Pink Flamingo Task Force. Had to be something else, the man's record was too neat, the same as Tindal's, Sam's, his files. Had the Alvarez man been in intelligence? Was he now? He had asked Tindal's techs to search deeper to no avail. The task had been passed on to Arturo Gonzalez, he was waiting to hear what he found. Rather, what his brother David could come up with. If there was any blowback, let it fall on their shoulders. If no one could connect him to any of this within the next couple weeks he would be safe, and on his way. If it led to Tindal so be it. Perhaps there was a way to make that a part of the plan. Meanwhile he had to appear to be on Tindal's team, ensure these tests ran smoothly.

Jenkins sent a man with a golf cart to bring Colonel Baker's personnel and their bags up to the guest quarters. He personally went in a separate cart to bring the Colonel. Tindal was waiting with the IT guy from Southeast Petroleum, Thomas Ridley. Ridley had arrived earlier in a Cessna 182 which he piloted himself. Jenkins had shown him around while Tindal was taking care of other business. He seemed a no-nonsense engineer, no humor, and a limp handshake. Was he gay?

Colonel Baker was another animal altogether. Always eager for entertainment, life of the party, joking and laughing, relying upon his military escort to remind him when he was getting carried away, which was every time that Jenkins could recall. In the past, he noticed the colonel's hands tended to wander when in the company of the opposite sex. Tindal told him to be certain there was plenty of Woodford Reserve for cocktails, Remy Martin Cognac and a Behike cigar at the completion of business, and female companionship waiting in his quarters for the colonel's bedtime pleasure.

Bud Jenkins knew the colonel, had most of his life. He had served in the same unit as a junior officer toward the end of his Warrant Officer father's career. The colonel had been instrumental in getting Jenkins into OCS.

The colonel asked Bud why no one was wearing masks.

"Like you and your staff, all guest's temperature is checked, and they are questioned about any health issues and vaccinations. Colonel Tindal has instructed me to have the place sanitized twice a day. Any staff that work in the lab or in the house are not allowed to leave or return without following strict protocols. I trust you are monitored and tested similarly?"

"Certainly."

As they rode along the winding road up to join Tindal, he gave the Colonel his opinion of the other guest.

"I had the staff make certain his quarters were on the other end away from you and your personnel. If Colonel Tindal and I had known what he was like, we would have tried to schedule him for another time."

"No problem. Washington is full of that kind. I'll try my best to steer clear of him and try to remember not to say anything that might cause an embarrassment. By the way, I was sorry to hear about your father. I would have been there if I could."

Jenkins knew that was not true. There had been a Reserve detachment to do a gun salute and present the flag to his mother. Other than that, no one. They didn't want to be seen attending his father Devin's funeral. "None of you bothered to attend. In fact, I don't remember a card or flowers that bore your name."

"Bud you of all people know my not attending had nothing to do with what happened to your father. I do as I am told. I called and spoke to Christy. Didn't she tell you?"

"No. She was too upset. His death and funeral opened old wounds."

"Devin was a fine officer and a good friend. I was proud of what he did for our country in Vietnam and afterward. It was a great honor to have served with him."

"You mean the Iran Contra Affair and Oliver North, were you proud of that? As I recall your name was never mentioned, yours or Tindal's. My father took the heat, kept his mouth shut. Is that why you and Tindal recommended me for OCS?"

"We recommended you because we knew you would make your mother and us proud. You've done that, have never disappointed us."

Jenkins wanted to say, "And Tindal kept me close at hand to make sure nothing was ever said." Instead, he said, "My father drank himself to death. He felt disgraced. Where were you during that time?"

"Why are you bringing this up? Okay, if this is what you wish, might as well clear the air. It was not just the Iran Contra Affair. There was evidence that your father had been involved in the cover up of American knowledge of Abdul Kahn, the Pakistani Nuclear Scientist who sold nuclear bomb making plans to Libya, Iran, and North Korea. Where we are today is a direct result of Mr. Kahn. I never believed your father had anything to do with allowing Kahn's theft and selling of the plans, but he refused to cooperate with the investigation. That poisoned the well. Any direct contact with him would have been a death sentence for a career. Your father understood that. We talked about it. The Marine Corps exonerated Oliver North, the Army, your father. Which is why he was given an honorable discharge and allowed to collect his pension. I was part of that investigation and spoke nothing but praise for your father. Later when your application was submitted for OCS, Tindal and I were more than happy to support your candidacy. Your father thanked us. He never blamed us for what happened. Do you? Is that what this is about?"

"That's right. Tindal and you were left untouched. My father took all the heat. And I wasn't given any chance to prove myself, I was always watched, labelled as the son of a father forced to resign. It wasn't until he was dying that I knew anything about Tindal's and your connection to my father. Tindal and you were never there for my father when he took the heat, nor when he turned to the bottle to drown his humiliation. Tindal is on his way to becoming a richer man and you are a top dog at DoD's DARPA. My father is in the ground."

"I didn't exactly escape unscathed. My rise throughout my career has been slow. If I don't get my star the next go round, my career is over. Maybe I can get a job with one of the defense contractors. Maybe Tindal if this project works out. I could end up on the same team as you, that is, if you are still planning on sticking around?"

"It always pays to keep options open. I believe this project will be a big moneymaker and if Tindal is willing to share the wealth, I'll stick. We haven't talked about my future here, I figured there will be plenty of time to discuss that when this project is given the green light as I'm sure it will be."

"That is what I wanted to hear from you. Come on, no more of this bitter talk. You are going to be part of something big if what I have read proves true. Who knows, maybe we all will get what we want. Speaking of which, how is Miss Francine?"

"She sends her regards. She said she has made sure she will have someone available tonight."

"Splendid. I guess we better go on up. Business before pleasure." He laughed and clapped Jenkins on the back like all had been put right and to rest.

"Yes sir." And fuck you too. You and Tindal will soon know what it's like to be on the other end.

Tindal was waiting for them at the top of the step landing to the veranda. He had a frown upon his face. Standing next to him was the Ridley man. Bud wondered what the problem was. By the time they reached the top, Tindal's frown became a smile.

"Colonel Baker. So good to see you. Hope you had a pleasant flight? I love the views over the Blue Ridge, especially this time of year, don't you?" He reached out and shook the Colonel's hand, then they embraced, patting each other on the shoulder like best friends.

"The scenery was spectacular and the flight uneventful. Gave me time to rest up after I reviewed your proposal again. I am looking forward to seeing the demonstration."

"I am sure that you won't be disappointed." He turned to his right. "This is Thomas Ridley from Southeast Petroleum. Mr. Ridley this gentleman and officer is Colonel William Baker from the Department of Defense."

Ridley stepped forward and shook Colonel Baker's hand. "My pleasure sir. You may call me Tom."

"Tom, my friends out of uniform call me Will. I saw a Cessna aircraft sitting off the edge of the runway, is that how you arrived?"

"Yes. I flew in earlier from Georgia. Didn't have the views you were able to enjoy."

Tindal turned to Jenkins who stood off to his left. "Mr. Ridley says he will be leaving out earlier than expected tomorrow. Seems there is a weather front supposed to move through, thinks this will be a problem for his flight. Were you aware of this?"

Bud now knew what the frown was about. "No sir. I checked the weather for this area and was told there was a slight chance of evening showers. Nothing that would interfere with our plans." Bud pulled out his phone and checked the weather app. Nothing had changed. "The weather forecast is the same as reported earlier sir."

The Ridley man had pulled out his phone and checked to make sure he had not been mistaken. "You are correct for this area. However, I will be flying south and there is a better than fifty percent chance of thunderstorms directly in line with my flight path, could continue into the next day as well. I am scheduled to meet with the board on Friday and I cannot miss that meeting. You wouldn't want me to miss that meeting, Is there a problem? I was told everything was ready."

Tindal looked at him then back to Jenkins. "We'll do what is necessary to accommodate you. Bud, see to it that we move tomorrow's schedule up."

Bud struggled to keep his composure. "Should not be a problem. If you excuse me, I will tell the technicians of the change of plans. I will get back to you after I see how soon we can make this happen." He turned to go, Tindal placed his hand on his arm and led him a few steps away from the others.

"This is important," Tindal said, "make sure this happens. You tell them there better not be any foul ups. Get back to me ASAP. We will be in the dining room."

The techs were not happy. They said they were preparing a run through to make sure everything was running smoothly. Dr. Lisa Guthridge told him this had been Dr. Perkins' and her project. Dismissing Dr. Perkins was a mistake, his input was essential. He told her he didn't want excuses, just results. After another heated discussion, Jenkins told her he expected them to have the miniature prototype set up in the auditorium in four hours.

"Work through lunch. Just make sure this happens."

After a lengthy lunch and a tour of Tindal's home, Jenkin's escorted them to the theater-like auditorium. At the foot of the stage on a table was the scaled down version of the drone. It looked just like a beehive. Jenkins pulled Lisa aside. "Tindal wants a demonstration inside the auditorium."

"We've never done that before," she said, "could be dangerous."

"This thing is supposed to be able to maneuver itself in tight spaces, 'to search and seek', is what the specifications we presented say. Tell your people to make it happen. While they do what they need to do, I need you to run through the specifications with our guests. Remember, no foul ups. Make sure your people understand." Jenkins walked back to where Tindal, Colonel Baker and the Ridley man were. Tindal looked up and arched his brow. Jenkins nodded.

"Gentlemen if you will, take a seat," Tindal said, "we are ready to present Tindal Industries Nano UAV system which we call The Bumblebee Hive, or, simply, The Hive."

The lights went dim and the screen lit up with a picture of The Hive. Lisa spoke with the speakers turned down low. "The Hive is an autonomous capable platform with an operating speed of one hundred miles per hour at an altitude of five hundred feet and a maximum speed of one hundred fifty miles per hour with a maximum vertical limit of one mile. The Hive is less than three feet in diameter. It is propelled by twin jet propulsion engines and with solar capabilities can stay aloft for up to twenty-four hours. The guidance system is equipped with infrared and sonar radar linked via satellite and Wi-Fi to a central remote control anywhere in the world, at a command control center and/ or with personnel on the ground. The system has been made virtually unhackable and will block the signal if communication comes from an unknown source."

"The Hive has twelve nanobots, which resemble, as you can see, bumblebees on steroids. The Hive serves as the base, the launch platform, the arming, and the recharging station for the Bumblebees. As in nature, the Bumblebees have different functions. Of course, there is no queen, unless you consider The Hive as such, or perhaps one of the techs." Jenkins glanced over at Ridley when Lisa said this. He gave a quirky smile Tindal and Baker chuckled. "Some Bumblebees fly out and look for threats. If threats are detected, The Hive will have an instant response. Depending upon the nature of the threat as perceived by The Hive and confirmed by a controller, other Bumblebees will be launched and monitor and communicate while the recon bees return to the Hive for recharging and reprogramming and arming. If the controller verifies the threat and chooses to, The Hive will be given a fire command and it will send a mini missile with a fragmentary charge, and/or it will launch the armed bees. The bees can be armed with disabling darts containing drugs or chemicals, smart tech flechete rounds or other debilitating projectiles. At the Hive's disposal are also mini smoke bombs and/or explosives to create camouflage or inflict disabling injury. The Hive is also equipped with a wi-fi and satellite signal disrupter for escaping detection and avoiding destruction.

"The Bumblebees are capable of maneuvering in tight spaces and have sniffer radar and infrared guidance systems allowing them to be used in search and rescue operations. They are equipped with high resolution micro cameras with night vision capabilities. They are solar battery powered and can be recharged in the Hive as stated. Using a built-in low power mode, they can operate autonomously up to twelve hours in a darkened space.

"Gentlemen this is the most advanced battlefield UAV design in the world. The Bumblebee Hive will surveil and protect domestic borders, pipelines, or natural and manmade disaster sites, as well as battlefields in war zones. We will now give you a demonstration so you can see for yourselves The Hive's potential."

Lisa pointed a laser beam in the direction of The Hive on the table. Instantly it began to hum, followed by a tiny light like a firefly would emit, then it rose about ten feet where it hovered. Within seconds a tiny infrared speck streaked out of its lower ring and began maneuvering around the auditorium.

Jenkins stood and said, "Lisa, have your controller maneuver the Bumblebee so that it hovers over each one of us and takes our picture in this low lighting then I will turn the lights on, and I want the bee to autonomously take our pictures in bright light so we can show our guests its photographic capabilities."

The bee completed the task within seconds. Jenkins walked over to the desk where the controller sat, reached underneath, and pulled out an Elmer Fudd looking dummy with a small replica rifle in his right hand and placed it on a stool. He set the dummy in front of the stage. He nodded to Lisa who in turn nodded to the controller. All eyes were on the dummy as a sound like a firecracker was followed by a puff of smoke emitted from the dummy's right shoulder, a ragged tear appeared, the dummy tilted, shot leeward off the stool, and the rifle holding arm dangled. Jenkins watched as everyone flinched. Ridley jerked. Jenkins thought he was trembling. While doing a background check on Ridley, he seemed to recall something about a sister who had been at the Columbine Massacre. Perhaps he should have warned him. The Bumblebee returned to The Hive and The Hive landed back on the table.

"Gentlemen, if Elmer had been a real threat, he would now not be," Jenkins stated.

Tindal stood and clapped, followed by Colonel Baker. Ridley remained seated, a shocked expression on his pale face.

"I had not expected this type of demonstration to have happened in here. Well done guys!" Tindal said nodding his head to Lisa and the controller. "Well done indeed."

Colonel Baker turned to Jenkins who had rejoined them. "No dog and pony. That was impressive." He leaned in close to Jenkins, "Mr. Ridley seems to be at a loss for words. You might have to resuscitate him."

Jenkins looked over at Ridley, "I hope this wasn't too real for you Mr. Ridley. Perhaps Lisa can show you the pictures and you can see what The Hive could do for your purposes?" Ridley didn't acknowledge Jenkins presence. Jenkins walked over to Lisa, told her to get Ridley, see what she could do to smooth out the situation. "Show him the photo images. Just do something, anything. Tindal will be pissed if we don't get him over the shock."

Lisa walked over with Jenkins to where the others stood. Jenkins turned to Tindal and said, "Perhaps Colonel Baker and Mr. Ridley would like to see the photo images so they can see the quality of their resolution?"

"Mr. Ridley? Colonel Baker? Would you like to see the images or is there something else either of you prefer to see?" Lisa asked giving each a smile. She walked over and handed Ridley some of the photos. She noticed his liver-spotted hands were shaking. She sat down beside him and gave him her best motherly expression as she whispered, "Are you okay? Perhaps some water or fresh air might help."

"I'm okay. Just wasn't prepared for the explosive response demonstration. Those weren't included in the material I received. Not something our people would be interested in. Guess that's why they weren't included," he replied in a near-whisper response.

"I'm sorry. The Hive's offensive capabilities, for your company, could be reprogrammed. I should have made that clear."

Colonel Baker and Tindal watched Lisa talking to the gas man. The man was clearly shaken. Too bad. He cleared his throat to get Tindal's attention. "I would like a further run through of all The Hives capabilities, the ones you spoke of-- the specs that DARPA reviewed. Preferably in an outdoor situation."

"Certainly. Jenkins would you and Lisa have the outdoor demonstration set up." Turning back to Colonel Baker, he said, "Bill the outdoor demo was scheduled for tomorrow, but if you wish, we could have an abbreviated demo this afternoon? Tindal knew from prior visits, the Colonel loved live action, but knew he would be contemplating tonight's live entertainment as well and how that would affect how he would feel tomorrow.

"How long will the demo take? I enjoyed what I saw and am anxious to see more, my report can't be complete without a full demonstration. If that is not possible for today," he paused looked at Ridley," perhaps you should ask Mr. Ridley since he is on a tighter schedule?

All eyes turned on Ridley.

"And you Mr. Ridley?" Lisa asked, her hand resting on his arm.

Ridley looked around then focused on Lisa as if he was only now aware of the others. He seemed to gather himself, straightened his shoulders, a forceful expression took hold of his face. He gave Lisa a brief smile, then stood, cleared his throat, and locked eyes with Tindal. He spoke louder than what had seemed his normal response thus far, "the photos are good. I will need a copy of the file that I can present to our chairman and the board. However, Southeastern is more concerned with the durability of The Hive, the battery life under adverse conditions such as clouds and operational ability in extreme wind conditions. Much of our projected use will be over varied terrain, including mountains where weather conditions can change suddenly, without warning. Do you have a wind tunnel?"

"We used the hangar as our wind tunnel. Because of its aerodynamic shape, it outperformed all conventional UAVs' stated specs. It can fly above most storm fronts when greater winds are anticipated. As for the battery life, The Hive can stay aloft for twenty-four hours before recharging is needed. That includes the Bumblebees. The battery company says the batteries are warranted without regard to conditions for ten years. Before then, who knows, a new battery with infinite life is said to be close to fruition."

"If it would be possible, I would like a demonstration of the wind effect."

"Colonel, would you like to see the wind test?" Jenkins asked. "We have a recording of previous tests. You were sent a copy. But, as the saying goes," ain't nothing like the real thing". I'm sure you agree. We can have it ready in about an hour. You interested?"

"That would be fine by me."

"Good. Lisa, please have the men prepare for the test and one more thing," he turned back to Ridley, "afterwards we will leave The Hive and Bumblebees operational in the hangar area overnight to demonstrate their battery durability."

He looked back to Lisa, who did not like two more unexpected demands, barely disguised as requests.

"Thank you, Lisa. We will be at the hangar," he looked at his watch, "at 1500 hour. That's a little more than an hour from now."

Tindal said, "Mr. Jenkins, why don't you give these gentlemen a tour of the lab while I check with the staff about tonight's dinner and tend to some other pressing business. I will join you at the hangar for the test."

Ridley moved toward Tindal. "Mr. Tindal, may I have a moment? I have a private matter to discuss to which our chairman wishes an answer."

"This way. Colonel, if you and Mr. Jenkins will pardon us?"

"Of course."

Tindal led Ridley to the corridor where the elevator that went up to his office was. "Mr. Tindal, our chairman has asked about the land section adjacent to yours which you said you were acquiring. He would like to tell the Board that our plans can be submitted for public approval. Have you acquired that land?"

This caught Tindal off guard. "Tell Mr. Dennison I am still in negotiations and hope to have an answer before the end of next week. I wish I could have an answer before then, seems the other party had a personal tragedy. I am giving them requested time to deal with this. I feel confidant everything will be in place by next week."

"I will let him know. Thank you."

Ridley left to join the others and Tindal took the elevator to his office. Business indeed, something had to be done about this Harper situation.

CHAPTER
15

David Gonzalez did what TJ expected. By the time the streetcar reached his drop-off at the Southend Terminal where he left his truck, David had made the call. Walking toward his truck, he heard him telling someone about his visit. Hearing only one side was frustrating, he hoped it would soon be rewarding. His bet, the party on the other end, was Arturo. Sounded like Hardy was correct, something big was going down. Arturo, or whoever, kept interrupting. TJ's, Jake's, Tindal's, and his man Jenkin's name were mentioned several times. David, as he suspected, apparently knew a lot more about Tindal than he had admitted earlier. David bragged he did not disclose any connections to the Latin Kings, this drew an interruption, TJ heard nothing for a minute or two. Confirmed, he was talking to Arturo.

"No. Arturo, we no talk 'bout Kings, no Paponovich. Alvarez man he know nothing."

Shocking hearing his name mentioned numerous times, the Harper man and woman, David sounded excited. TJ listened very carefully, heard David say something about hacking into surveillance cameras and devises, said he could do this. David assured Arturo he make sure plans not change. The call ended. TJ heard David's fast tapping on his keyboard.

The ride back to his truck took longer than the earlier ride due to the increased traffic and passengers getting on and off at the last two stops. The NFL Carolina Panthers' game had ended, and the last partying fans were on their way home. Many, too many, wore no masks. The new CDC guidelines didn't require them for outdoor events. Problem was not all were vaccinated.

Once back seated in his truck, TJ called Jake, told him to check his home for hidden cameras and listening devises. Jake wanted to know what the fuck TJ was talking about. TJ said he had intercepted a call from a CI, had heard their names in connection with said items. Jake said he had no way to do that. TJ told him to just look at lights, lamps, corners, anywhere that was easily accessed and would give a good view for cameras or give access for listening devises.

"Hey, look bro just look…if you don't find anything, then keep your conversation to a minimum and turn out the lights. Unplug your tv, most people don't realize their smart tv and phones can be used to listen and give a hacker video access. This hombre is a very good hacker, can do all this and more, so be careful. Hell, it is very likely they are listening to our conversation at this very moment." Jake wanted to say more, he decided it would be better to do some checking first. Further conversation could wait until they were face to face in the morning.

TJ's next call was to Undersecretary Hardy's office number, he answered just as TJ began leaving a message.

"Did you talk to Tindal?"

"No. I've been busy. I'll try tomorrow."

TJ then told him everything he heard. "You were right, there is something big going down. From what I heard, it involves Tindal or his man Jenkins, the Latin Kings, Paponovich and money laundering."

"This requires careful action, no jumping to conclusions based upon a one-sided conversation. You don't know what this has to do with anything or anyone. I can't do a thing. This is not actionable information. You had no warrant. I can't get one based simply upon what you heard."

"Answer me this, how is it my CI knows about Tindal and his man Jenkins? Why would he know their names unless there is some connection?"

"Do you have a recording of this conversation? No…. I didn't think so. No physical proof. Nothing. You can't prove any of this. Neither can I. I repeat, we have no actionable evidence. And need I remind you, you are deep undercover. I am not about to use you or anything you say without physical and verifiable evidence."

"In other words, you don't intend to do anything. Jake and I, and our families, are in danger, and you tell me you need physical evidence. I hope that doesn't come at our expense."

"I didn't say I was not going to do anything. I am gathering information and evidence to build a case which I can take legal action on. I expect you to proceed very carefully. Get me evidence I can use, let the chips fall where they may, but don't expect me to go after someone like Tindal with what you have heard. If I expose you and your sources using this, we both would be out of a job with major lawsuits to fight. You and Jake need to wait, I'll talk to Tindal. Go see a lawyer. Get me something I can use for a wiretap. We'll talk tomorrow." Hardy disconnected the call.

A sheriff deputy patrol car waited at the end of their drive. TJ was a somewhat apprehensive because of the incident Jake had earlier. He drew up alongside and introduced himself. They were polite. He showed them identification, told them he was a member of Charlotte SWAT, that he appreciated their presence, but they need no longer stick around. They left.

TJ and Deane's house was not noticeable from the street. The porch light winking through the limbs of the live oaks was the only thing indicating its presence. He let Paul know he was approaching. Paul said he had heard the deputies' radio and had seen TJ's lights and figured it was his truck he heard entering the drive. TJ pulled under the carport, got out and walked back to Paul's new Chevrolet SUV.

"Nice ride. You must be doing alright?" TJ remarked.

"Other one was getting over the hill, like me. Wanted something more technologically smart and less conspicuous. My old one kinda stuck out and made a lot of noise. See you got new wheels also."

"Pretty much same as you. Gotta keep up with technology, especially in our line of work. Anyway, I guess it's been kind of quiet?"

"Nothing to report. Deane came out and offered me coffee about twenty minutes ago. Fine woman you got partner."

"Don't I know it. We've known each other most of our lives. Anyway, I know you'd like to get going. Been a long day. I need to go inside. I'll be pretty busy over the next several days, going to try to get Deane to go stay somewhere else. If you not too busy with the weekend coming up and all, I'd sure appreciate it you could swing by and check on things."

"No problem pardner. Well, I better get on home. Maybe I'll catch my ole lady doing something she shouldn't." He laughed. "See you pardner. I'll send you my bill."

"You do that. Thanks Paul. Let me know you ever need anything."

Deane and the dogs met him at the door. He bent down and petted the dogs, this time avoiding their attempts to lick him. He straightened up expecting a hug and kiss instead Deane looked up at him and said, "I've been receiving weird calls, says caller unknown."

"Does that mean I don't get my hug and kiss?" She didn't move in closer. TJ saw Deane's twelve-gauge Remington semiautomatic shotgun leaning in the corner. Her revolver was on the lampstand next to the sofa.

"You seem to be prepared?"

"Those calls spooked me. The caller was breathing heavily and said nothing. I hit redial--"*Caller unknown.*" No answer. Soon as I hang up, they call back. I could hear Latin music in the background and voices. They're trying to scare me--I know. I wasn't sure if Paul would be able to do much. You always said not to call unless it was an emergency and…"

TJ reached out to pull her into his embrace. He hugged her and they kissed. "I'm here now." He said out loud then whispered, "Continue talking, better still I'll cut on the tv, I need to do a sweep inside and outside" He walked over and cut on the tv. "Put it on the local sports report. Turn it up." The announcers were talking about the Panther's. "I've got to take a shower, change clothes," he said out loud. Deane looked at him puzzled, then her lovely Cuban-American face showed concern.

"I know they won, let me know if the highlights come on before I get in the shower." He went in the bath, turned on the shower then pulled out the sweep from his cargo pants, went quietly outside after mouthing to Deane to hold the dogs inside.

The detector picked up nothing active outside. He checked carefully around the windows and doors. No sign of any devises or any attempt at jimmying the windows or doors. TJ was certain he would find nothing inside. The dogs would take care of ninety nine percent of intruders, but there was always that off chance someone could slip some mild knockout drug or gas and then later an antidote to revive them. Or distract them at one end, while someone else slipped in the other end using a lock pick tool or program that could disable the locks and the alarm. TJ knew Gonzalez was capable of this and much more. After he and Jake met with an attorney tomorrow, they would need to pay David Gonzalez another visit. It was time to get proactive, get the physical evidence Hardy demanded.

Back inside, he did the sweep. Moving as quietly as he could. Deane held onto the dogs, hugging them, and having to endure their licks and tugs as they followed with their eyes his every move. He found nothing. He then took their cells and removed the batteries, turned off the tv and unplugged it.

Deane waited until he came back to her and the dogs.

"What's going on? Why all that? You're starting to worry me."

"Sorry. Just learned tonight this thing with Jake's and Elena's dog is much more than just his being shot. And those pictures...plus the calls. Jake said Elena had received similar calls. Someone putting this into a whole different league...a dangerous situation involving Jake, Elena, you, me and our families."

"What about the police, the FBI? Can't they do something?"

"Not without proof...evidence that will get the DA to issue warrants, make arrests. As of now we don't have anything verifiable. Jake and I the ones on the local law's radar. It's up to me and Jake. We plan to go see an attorney tomorrow. Buy us some time while we figure out who's behind all this and why. Meanwhile you and Elena need to go somewhere safe until we sort this all out."

"Go somewhere? I don't have anywhere to go. I don't know anyone well enough, other than Jake and Elena, and that's out. Besides, I have a job. I can't take off without scheduling something. You promised me when we left Miami to come here that we could live normal lives. I'm not going to let someone take that away."

"Deane. This shit's serious." She made a face, didn't like him using slang, swearing or cursing. Always the counselor.

"Sorry. Anyway, I need to know you safe. Can't you take sick days? The flu has hit and with the coronavirus and all. Tell them you think you have the flu. That should satisfy them. Buy me a coupla weeks. That's all I'm asking."

Deane started pacing. The dogs looked from her to TJ and back. "

What about your family? Your mother?"

"My mother refuses to leave. You know her, she can be stubborn. I talked to my old SWAT commander, he said they would step up patrols as time allows. I also talked to brother Leo, his crew owe me. They don't like anyone coming into the Hood. Mama's not happy, she said she would allow some of his men to watch her house, escort her when she goes out, said maybe they go to church with her, see the priest. We laughed about that."

He walked over and sat down on their twin recliner sofa. Deane remained standing. Other than their bed, this was the only new furniture they had bought since moving to the Carolinas. The other furniture had been purchased from antique and second-hand dealers. Deane had used her creative touch to make this home both comfortable and cheerful with a Cuban flair of colors. He didn't have the heart to tell her it could all be lost if he failed to stop this assault on Jake and him.

"What are you going to do? We can't afford a lengthy legal trial. What happens if you lose?"

"We'll cross that bridge when we come to it and I don't plan to come to it. Jake and I will have to prove the warden acted to provoke us. I have evidence, right now that I can't use, that points to Jake's neighbor Tindal being behind this. We need verifiable evidence--a week or two--need to know you and Elena safe. Goina go by their place tomorrow, sweep it for any electronic bugs. Got to have evidence can be traced to whoever bought it. My CI, confidential informant, knows more than he has admitted. There's connections there—the cartel gangbangers, Tindal, this warden trouble—they connected. Those photos we received, they're proof we're being spied upon and threatened. Tomorrow when Jake and I go see an attorney, we'll tell him to talk to the magistrate and Deputy Coulter. They can help tie the warden to Tindal. With their help, the attorney can build a case, put pressure on Tindal, perhaps get charges dropped."

"Gotta get Elena to go with you. Buy Jake and me time. Get her to give her statement to the magistrate. You gotta tell the magistrate what you know also. Then you two need to take the dogs and go somewhere, Asheville or someplace away from here in a secure hotel that allows dogs."

TJ reached in a cargo pocket and brought out a couple throwaway phones. "Use these, not your regular phones, leave your regular phones off with the batteries removed, and don't talk to anyone but Jake and me. I'll keep you up on what's going on. Oh, and before I forget..." TJ got up went into the master closet, pulled out several pairs of shoes from the back corner of the closet, tugged the carpet loose to get access to a floor safe, removed some documents, turned to find Deane standing behind him.

"Take these." He handed her a driver's license, credit card, Social Security Card and Passport, all in a fake name with her picture. "Register using these for a rental car, your hotel and whatever you have to purchase."

"What…how…why do you have these?"

"My undercover work. It's my job to gather evidence, testify against some very dangerous individuals. Some of them have ways to find me, us, like now. This will help ensure your safety."

He closed and relocked the safe, reset the carpet and placed the shoes back, stood up and faced Deane who seemed speechless.

"You okay?"

She shook her head no. "How come you never discussed this with me? Don't you think you should have? I can't do this. It has to be illegal."

He took Deane's arms in his hands. "Deane, you have to. These people have ways to track you. They will find you, use you to get to me, then they will do things you wish no one did to another human being, leave you dead or wishing you were. I can't let this happen. Other than the source, no one knows of these documents. These identities are people who never did or no longer exist. Now is not the time to argue the legality or morality of using them. Please."

She pulled loose, stood there shaking her head, turned went to their bedroom, closed the door after ordering the dogs out, sat and put her head in her hands.

"You should have discussed this with me before now. TJ you promised to tell me everything unless it was confidential information. Don't you see, you violated that trust?"

TJ walked over to sit beside her. She shifted away. "If I had? I knew you would react just the way you reacting. Deane you sometimes too good for your own good. I did this in case what has happened, happened. If you think I was wrong, I understand. But our wedding vows were for me to love, hold, keep you safe, that is what I have attempted to do, will do as long as I draw breath. What love requires of me Deane."

He slid over and hugged her to him. She stiffened and resisted, then relaxed and turned to stare at him, her eyes moist.

"I love you. Just promise me you won't ever do anything behind my back again; that you won't do anything that gets you killed. You are all I have left."

They kissed. He felt her begin to relax.

The kissing became more passionate. TJ unbuttoned her blouse, gently pushed up her light-support bra. He gently kneaded her breast. She took his hand in hers, pulled back, her eyes meeting his, slowly she used her other hand, unbuttoned her blouse completely, her eyes never leaving his.

He reached behind undid her bra, sliding it down her arms, it fell to the floor. He stroked her swollen nipple, their kissing resumed, more intense, an intensity borne of hunger and desperation created from what lay behind and lay ahead.

Deane knew TJ and their lovemaking It was passion born out of fear, for both; the thought not spoken--they might never see each other again. It always pained her. It began with losing her virginity to TJ when they were teenagers. Living with the dangers in the Hood--each day a threat.

Then his military days, the last night before deployment, he was like a sex-starved man she hardly knew. After she lost their last attempt at being parents, he seemed more patient, his needs more emotional. She came to understand. And the sex was good therapy for them. She no longer minded. She learned from working with other veterans, sex was their release. And she needed it also.

She pulled his hand away, stood and removed her clothes, kneeled, pushed him back, unzipped his pants, pulled them down, removed his boots, pants, and underwear. She removed her skirt and panties, eased down onto her knees, flicked her tongue over his penis, took him into her mouth, a few strokes while she reached up to lightly tease his nipples.

She released him, moved up, helped him off with his jacket and shirt, licked his nipples. A few seconds of licks and kisses, their hands caressing and kneading the intensity away, finding the other's sex ready, his firm, hers wet. She raised up to guide him inside her. He stopped her. Said he didn't want to finish too quickly. He eased her off him. TJ then licked his way to her breasts, down across her stomach, then pulled her to the edge of the bed. He slid off to kneel where she had on the bedside rug. He spread her love lips and drove his tongue in and out.

Soon she couldn't take his oral thrusts with his thumb on her clitoris any longer. She pushed his head away, pulled him up, leaned down to remoisten him, laid back, guided him into her. Their Latin passion didn't last long but long enough for them both to be satisfied. They lay there, him on top until his organ slid out. Satisfied, spent, he rolled off, a final kiss, each enjoying the aftermath, the unspoken fear pushed briefly aside once more.

After a short time of holding each other and soft kisses, TJ eased off the bed, went through the house to check and secure the locks, turning out lights, making sure the dogs had food and water and came back to bed. They lay there, went back over the plans for the next day, kissed, covered themselves and lay back with their own thoughts. Deane drifted off to sleep, TJ lay awake going over and over what had to be done.

CHAPTER
16

Jenkins checked with the tech who stayed up all night monitoring the steady hovering of The Hive. Everything was operating normal as had been the case with all the tests run during the developmental stages. He asked the tech to text him when Lisa was up and ready for the days demonstration which he had scheduled for 0900 hour.

He sent a text to Contessa, Colonel Baker's overnight companion, instructing her to get moving and to check on Ridley's companion, a transvestite calling herself Kimi. He told her to text him back to acknowledge receipt of his text, plus, another reminder, the car would be waiting in the garage in twenty minutes, meet him there. Five minutes later he got her acknowledgement. Everyone showed up on time. He asked how it went and Contessa said the Colonel was certainly kinky and had tipped well. Kimi said Ridley was embarrassed, angry at first. She assured him nothing went beyond their room. Using her talent, he soon became completely compliant, his groans and moans assured her he had enjoyed her ministrations.

"I believe I got his cherry. He slept with a smile on his face."

Bud thanked them, gave her the tip, Ridley had failed to provide.

He told them to keep themselves down in the rear of the limo, out of sight, until they were out the gate, warning them they were not to speak of this to anyone, reminding them of the nondisclosure. He told the chauffeur to get going. He wanted them out of here before Colonel Tindal, and more importantly his wife Lou Anne, were up and about. He figured Tindal knew and, as was his custom, preferred to pretend not to.

Bud hurried to his office, checked to make sure his recorders had captured everything. He saw Ridley was preparing to leave, so he shut the system down and secured it with a few keystrokes. He liked the fact the system's security was promised to be unbreakable. Bud was skeptical. Soon, it would not matter.

The sun had just risen over the tree-lined hillside. Dappled sunlight played over the orchard which extended from the Broad River up to the road.

The daytime security detail arrived as Bud Jenkins went down the hall and looked in the lab. No Dr. Lisa Guthridge. Two other techs were at their stations, preparing for today's demonstration. He took the garage elevator up and went out the side entrance as the first rays of sunlight lit up the far side of the river. A security man was taking Ridley down the hill to the hangar. Before Bud could reach the bottom of the hill in another ATV, Ridley had run his preflight check of the plane and was prepared for takeoff. Without acknowledging Bud's presence, he swung the plane around, taxied to the end of the runway, swung the nose back around and was airborne within a matter of minutes. No "good morning", "kiss my ass", no sign of having seen Bud or wishing a *fair the well*, not a good sign. Oh well. He could remedy the situation, if he so desired, the video should make him compliant. From what he heard from Arturo Gonzalez last night, he doubted that would be necessary.

Arturo's brother David's encounter with the Alvarez man, who was an undercover policeman, had made the Gonzalez crew anxious to accelerate their timetable. Bud had told Arturo this would not be a good idea. He told him that once DoD approval was given, Tindal would be announcing his plans to build a manufacturing facility for The Hive, tentatively scheduled for the York County Fall Festival this upcoming weekend when local politicians would be on hand.

"This is the original schedule. Stick to it," he told Arturo.

Arturo replied, "you not one to decide. We do as I decide."

"I'm the one that can make this happen and will do so when I am certain of success. Mr. Tindal is taking measures to get the Alvarez and Harper men out of the way, so hang tight and let things play out. I suggest you get your brother somewhere he can't be found until we are ready to put everything in motion. One more week and everything should be ready. Your brother and you should be making sure the money is there, where promised, transportation issues ready to go. You do your part. I'll do mine."

Bud was worried that he might be dealing with amateurs. They might be good at what they do, this was another level. Uncle Sam would waste no time. The agencies would go all out to recover The Hive, punish all involved. Talking supermax. The Gonzalez Crew thought in terms of the physical Hive with plans to duplicate it for use in their operations against other cartels and their border drug war. He knew the real value were the key components, the specs and software, plus the military satellite system software.

He made other plans, real professionals, people he knew could make things happen, not fuck things up. He had a bidding war going with Tindal's approval. Tindal wanted to use the bids as backups, put pressure on DoD and Southeast Petroleum to meet his price, promise him future contracts, let him be part of space mining ventures. Tindal was all about Tindal. Bud decided he would play along, do whatever he had to, fuck over the Harper man, get him out of the way, whatever. Play stupid, pretend he didn't know Tindal planned for him to be the fall guy in case things went awry.

Bud had other plans. The way he looked at it, he had given Uncle Sam more than twenty years, they had given him nothing but a title, a piece of crap retirement. Tindal offered crumbs. He didn't plan to end up the patsy, bitter and broke like his ole man had been. Tindal and others were getting rich off the system and off him. It was time to cash in.

Meanwhile, he had to make sure today's demo went without a hitch. Colonel Baker needed to be impressed. Bud knew he would be. Baker had told Tindal after dinner, when they were enjoying the cognac and cigars that if everything went off without a hitch, he was certain he would be able to get the go ahead this next week. He had asked if Tindal had lined up a manufacturer. Bud heard Tindal say he would be making the announcement the next week if given approval. Bud had been reading Tindal's correspondence, pretended excitement, played up to Tindal to keep suspicion at bay. The pompous ass wouldn't see it coming.

CHAPTER

17

Whippoorwill, whippoorwill, whipporwill, then another sound, like an ancient pipe organ, asthmatic-like rasping breath noise, followed by a louder repetition of whippoorwill.

Jake lay there listening. His head throbbed. He shouldn't have drunk so much before crashing.

How could a sound, romantic and charming when heard from a distance when you were outside, be so disturbing when heard up close in early morning hours? This was their mating call—the way they marked their territory--warning other males to stay clear. Unfortunately, one of those birds' boundaries was the old pear tree outside the guest bedroom where Jake had retreated to the night before.

Last night when he had been ready to crash, he found Elena in the center of their bed. She had staked out her territory. He decided to not lay claim to the too small leftover. He had stumbled into the guest bedroom and hadn't bothered to pull back the covers. Sometime during the night, he had managed to pull the bedspread over himself. He was still dressed in the clothes from the day before.

Might as well get up. He swung his legs over the edge of the bed then remembered TJ's text saying he would be by early to run a sweep of their house before they headed out for breakfast. He wondered if Elena would bother to get up. Probably not until she heard his vehicle leave.

Jake put on a pot of coffee and went out with Maisy for her morning potty call. He doubted Elena planned to resume her morning routine.

The day had a biting chill, the moisture on the vehicles looked close to freezing. An early frost was not unusual. Normally cold weather would not set in until after Thanksgiving, accompanied by frequent rain with an occasional ice or snow event.

Jake welcomed the refreshing chill, but Maisy wanted no part of it. He let her back inside, went down to the outbuildings to tend to the farm animals. When he got back to the house, Elena had been up, gotten a cup of coffee, retreated to the bedroom. Not planning on running today. He went back to the bedroom, heard the television, and peaked inside. She was sitting in the corner chair, Maisy on her lap. She did not acknowledge his presence even when he told her TJ was coming by and they would be going to see an attorney after TJ checked on something for them.

Thirty minutes later Jake heard TJ's truck coming up the road at a normal pace. He got up from his recliner, turned off the sitting room television and went outside to meet him.

After the shooting incident, Jake had started closing the gate whenever they came and went. TJ knew the combination to the gate and let himself in. He left it open, figuring they would be leaving soon.

Deane had been unhappy about having to leave the house, not knowing when she would be returning and under what conditions. He waited to leave until after she contacted her administrator and lied about having come down with what she thought was the flu which had stricken many others in the school and across the nation. She hated lying and told TJ she would have to present proof from a clinic when she was ready to return to work. She was concerned about how she would be able to do that.

While he packed a duffel bag with clothes as if he were being deployed, she packed two suitcases and a carryall for herself. They loaded these and the dogs' beds and toys in her SUV and he put his things in his truck. He had her promise to have Elena go to the magistrate, then go with her to a rental car company at the airport, leave her car in the long-term parking and head west toward Asheville.

"Make sure Elena doesn't use any credit card and have her disable her cell phone or leave it in the car at the airport. Pay only with cash or using the card I gave you. They shared a long kiss. He gave the dogs a farewell petting, climbed in his truck then followed her out the drive. She was going to a diner on Lake Wylie to wait for him to let her know when to call Elena.

Jake met TJ at the same spot where he had when TJ had brought Dusty after he was shot.

"Morning bro. You look as bad as I feel."

"Didn't get much sleep. Hasn't been one of my better weeks."

"Know what you mean. Elena up?'

"She's not talking to me. This shit has traumatized her. For some reason she blames us, says we're the flip side of the same coin, whatever that means. Don't expect much hospitality from her."

"Well…guess better start the sweep outside."

TJ pulled the small detector out. Immediately it picked up the camera in the tree near where he was parked. "Damn Bro." Jake went to one of the sheds, got an extension ladder, grabbed a plastic shopping bag out of his truck, put on gloves and brought the game camera down after switching it off. They checked the chicken house and barn, then the trees and the outside of the house, where they found another in the back gable of the screen porch. Jake figured this was the one used to take the picture of Elena. Inside, they went through the house locating two more. They saved the master bedroom for last and Elena watched but said nothing. Jake noticed she had put on jeans and a sweatshirt since he last saw her.

"Elena, sorry all this happened. Guess you blame me also," TJ said. "Hate to ask, but you need to run a diagnostic on your computer. We've found surveillance cameras outside and in your house. Anyone do that, probably has tapped into your computer, other things, possibly your tv, phone…"

"What the fuck are you saying? You mean someone has been spying on me? Well, that is no big shocker. Did you not see the picture I was sent? I wouldn't be surprised if the whole damn world has seen it. I guess next I will be considered a reality porn star. What does it matter about my computer? Once my patients and family hear about this, I'm done for." She sat there her face twisted in anger, tears dripping off her chin. Jake moved toward her, and she held up her hands to ward him off. "Just go away. I'm tired of this whole fucking mess. Do what you got to do and go."

Once they were in the kitchen, TJ turned to Jake. "Told Deane to call her and go with her, see the magistrate, give her statement. Afterwards they need to leave the car at the airport, get a rental, head to Asheville or somewhere up there. It's not safe for them at home bro, take my word for it. We and our families are in danger, big time. You got to get Elena out of here. You and I need see a lawyer, then make ourselves scarce. It's time to go on the offensive.

You need to pack up like we're being deployed. You got anybody who can check on your animals? If so, set it up. We need to get going."

Jake had not moved. He stood there looking at TJ as if he was listening and not listening. His mind elsewhere.

"You listening? They know we found their surveillance shit. They'll be making a move. Say what you got to say, do what you got to do, you got to get Elena out of here, we've got to get out of here, now!"

"I hear you. Short of dragging her out of here, I don't think she'll do anything I tell her to do. You saw her. You think she would listen to me, or you? If they come here, they'll have hell to pay. I guess you better go, do what you got to. I won't leave her here."

"Damn bro. Only thing happens they come here you both become statistics. They'll burn you out or they'll come in here and then you'll be forced to watch as they rape Elena until she has no place left to fuck. Shouldn't have to tell you this. You were there, you've seen it. This is war. They won't be taking any prisoners. Man up bro. Do whatever you have to. Won't be pretty but, if I have to, I'll drag you both out of here? I'm not leaving here without you two."

Jake smiled. "You damn right it wouldn't be easy. Especially with Elena. I guess I need to give it a try."

TJ heard Elena screaming obscenities at Jake. Maisy began yapping, Elena yelled shut up. He walked back down the hall outside a spare bedroom near their master bedroom, listening, staring out the front window toward his truck and the direction of Tindal's camp, figuring that would be the direction someone would come from. Jake came by him without saying anything, went to an armoire, then back to the bedroom with an armful of Elena's clothes. That set her off once more, some of the fire seemed to be missing. He heard Jake say, "either you pack your shit, or I will. You are going voluntarily, or I'll pick you up and carry your ass out of here. Now what's it going to be?"

TJ smiled, thinking, "Atta boy."

"You really need to see someone Jake. You're fucked up, PTSD or some shit."

Jake didn't reply.

Elena packed everything she could in her Prius, including her computer and current patient paperwork. She was angry with Jake, didn't see how their marriage would survive this. She half listened as TJ told her what he and Deane had planned. She did not say what was on her mind. She didn't tell Jake bye, no hug, no kiss. Jake didn't say or bother either. They stood there, two no-it-all men, idiots, thinking they were being chivalrous, preparing to fight a fight they couldn't win.

It was ludicrous. She and Maisy headed out the drive in the opposite direction for meeting Deane. This was it. She had thought about it all day the day before, last night as well. Just go, she told herself, her daughter had agreed, felt this was for the best.

"I miss you. Come to Louisiana. You deserve to be happy. Poppy's right, Jake is never going to leave there, except in a box. If he really loved you, he would leave. The jerk has children that live here. Never made sense why he stays there. Come on mama, maybe he'll come to his senses."

She would call her daughter to tell her she was on her way as soon as she had cell reception.

CHAPTER
18

Jake grabbed his duffel, packed all his weapons and ammo in a strong box in the bed of his truck. He called Patrick--didn't know of anyone else. Patrick begged off the last time when Jake had been in the Bahamas. Strange vehicles stopped in front of the house, frightened his daughter, Jake felt certain he knew who that was now, Butch and Billy. Since returning, he and Patrick had repaired their relationship, Patrick's son Ben was grown, took no shit off anybody, Butch and Billy wouldn't mess with him. Patrick said he and his son Ben would take care of it. He hated telling Patrick a half-truth. Jake told him they had a family emergency, would be gone possibly two weeks. Patrick was friendlier with Tindal and the warden which made any harm coming to them less likely. Jake hoped so. No justification would he feel if anything happened to them.

Jake followed TJ. They stopped off at the McConnells' Diner to grab a bite to eat. It was too early for the lawyer TJ arranged to see. They would eat, stop by the vets' to check on Dusty. TJ called Deputy Coulter. He said he would meet them, get the cameras, and personally take them to the FBI lab. The feeb techs could check for fingerprints, determine point of purchase and to whom they had been sold.

Jake was concerned Deputy Coulter would be found out, so he decided to take pictures of the cameras' serial numbers. This way they would have a backup. TJ agreed. He took pictures also. His would be downloaded, sent to Homeland Undersecretary Hardy. Jake was not told this.

Jake, followed by TJ, turned off Highway 322 onto 321. Where once there had been two nice brick hardware and feed stores, there was one of the two run-of-the-mill service stations, the other sat on the opposite corner. Next to it was the Town Hall with the Post Office adjoining and the volunteer fire department in the back. McConnells Diner was not far down 321.

They went in the diner. The place was half empty, the locals had come and gone onto work, just a few older retirees Jake did not recognize who had pulled two tables together. From the sound of it, they were busy gossiping, still hashing out the coronavirus, the election, and Black Lives Matter doubts. They looked at him and saw TJ accompanying him. That created a pause--old prejudices die slowly.

The diner was owned and operated by Barbara Davis, a tall statuesque Scotch Irish woman with larger than normal nose and ears, pushed forward by her greying hair, a pencil normally tucked behind the right one. She was brusque, had a no-nonsense demeanor. She stayed back in the kitchen and her two daughters tended the tables. Both were also tall, more pleasing to the eye, with homespun manners, typically smiling, full of good humor. Must have come from their father, Jake thought, no doubt it was their presence brought the male customers back. That and Barbara's cooking, pricey for the area, way better than average. It was a favorite with truckers and travelling salespeople during the week and the weekend buffet brought the locals on Saturday night and after church goers on Sunday. Never stopped, despite the coronavirus state and county mandates.

This was Jake's first time coming here since the restrictions were lifted. He liked it here. They appreciated veterans and didn't mindlessly say 'thank you for your service', without really giving a crap like most people did. Jake thought it was better to say it to his dick after a good romp. He chuckled at the thought. TJ wanted to know what was so funny. He told him and they both laughed.

Deputy Coulter arrived by the time they had been given their silverware, glasses of water and cups of coffee. They told Jenny, their waitress, they were expecting someone else. She had Deputy Coulter's on the table, waiting for him.

Another nonwhite joining them prompted the older diners to pay and leave, the ambient noise dropped. They ordered, ate, and went out to TJ's truck to do their talking.

TJ told Jake and Deputy Coulter what he had learned from sources unidentified. He did not want to disclose to Deputy Coulter anything more than what the deputy already knew--that TJ was a Charlotte Metro SWAT team member and a private investigator. He saw no reason to tell him he also worked undercover for SWAT and Homeland.

Jake knew about the SWAT undercover work, he often thought odds were TJ continued his involvement with Homeland's task force. He wondered why TJ failed to disclose to Deputy Coulter the source was his SWAT CI. He did not say anything, figuring TJ had his reasons.

Deputy Coulter listened and didn't say anything until TJ asked why the sheriff and DA were so keen to prosecute Jake and him.

"I'm not sure."

Jake spoke up. "Do you think it's because an election is coming, and Tindal may be giving money to the assholes' reelection committees?"

"I wouldn't know about that. What I do know is Red, Warden Crandall, was in the Sheriff's office with the DA for a long time. After he left, Deputy James and I were called in and we told what we had witnessed. I told them that Red and you had a history and from what I saw this was a case of bad blood between you two. They wanted to know why I had not considered your wife as the target and you as a possible. I told them from everything I saw, it was a shooting accident like I put in my report and that I had not witnessed anything worth prosecuting. I also said your dog had been shot and you were justifiably upset. And that Red had not seemed interested in gathering evidence. They asked if I thought your dog being shot was any excuse for Assault and Battery of an Officer of the Law. Officer James was scared to say much. I told them we had not seen or heard any threats of physical violence. The Sheriff told me I should keep in mind who was believable you two or an officer of the law. I told them TJ was an officer of the law also. Clearly, this was not what they wanted to hear. We were dismissed. I called the magistrate so she could warn you."

"I wish I could be more helpful. If this thing goes to trial, I'll testify to what I saw. I can't guarantee what Deputy James may say. He told me yesterday he had a family to worry about. He and his wife just had their first baby. I told him to tell the truth. I wouldn't count on him." Deputy Coulter's radio squawked. "I need to get going. You said you had some evidence needing to get to the FBI. I took the other to them. Including your cigarette butt Jake. Normally, I would let our forensics look at it first. After listening to the sheriff, I decided to give the feds some of the evidence along with my report. I hope something comes back that helps."

TJ handed him the plastic bag that contained the cameras. "We appreciate what you've done for us. Feebs should be able to get prints off these, find out who bought them by sales records. If it points to Tindal's men, an attorney should be able to get a search warrant. Tindal and his pals' names keep coming up. We gotta connect the dots, get these charges dropped. Maybe cause the warden, sheriff, and or, the DA to be charged with corruption, along with Tindal."

"This big risk. Have to be careful. If gangbangers come 'round, let me know. That one thing the sheriff and DA cannot ignore. Stay in touch TJ. Good luck." Deputy Coulter shook hands and walked around to his cruiser. Jake and TJ watched him get in, speak into his mike, pull to the end of the parking lot, wait on two gravel trucks and a semi to pass, then he pulled out heading north on 321 towards York.

Jake turned to TJ. "Why didn't you tell him about being undercover with SWAT? I thought you trusted him?"

"Compartmentalization and deniability. Saw no reason to tell him. The less he know, the better for him."

"Does that apply to me also?"

"You know all you need to know. For now--may change--may have to for both our sakes. Don't give me that look bro, we goina meet my CI soon as we leave the attorney. We better get a move on. On the way here, I heard that gangbang puke talking to his brother, big chief, frontman, gang boss, saying he was packing up, would be ready to leave this afternoon. He also said he was tracking the targets, that's most likely us, and he have men intercept targets. My CI is an electronic and computer whiz, capable of hacking any system. All of us're potential targets. Called Deane. Said Elena not answering. She was headed to your place, told her no need, Elena not there. Got no answer when tried her phone. May be out of cell tower range or she may have her phone off. Any idea where she may be headed?"

This alarmed Jake. "I can't be sure. I told her to go to York and call Deane as soon as she had cell service. She went the opposite way out of the drive. Not her normal way to York. Possible, but not likely, she could have decided to go by way of Sharon. If I had to bet, I would say she didn't turn her phone off. I would not be surprised if she's headed west, probably on her way to her daughter's house in Louisiana." Jake tried her cell repeatedly as he talked. No answer. "She's not answering. Damn!"

TJ asked Jake if he had contacted his stepdaughter and his other children.

"No. I overheard Elena talking to someone last night. I checked her phone while she was packing, she called her daughter. Doubt Jennifer would tell me anything. We seldom talk. Elena doesn't know my other children. They wouldn't have heard from her. No need in calling them."

"You might better let them know what's going on. The cartels have nationwide affiliations. Remember they targeted my mother. You need to see if Jennifer heard from Elena, warn her of the danger she and Elena in, and better give your kids a heads-up. Need to make those calls on a different phone before we leave here, then turn that phone off, take the battery out. Here, use burners, takes longer to trace 'em." He handed Jake two phones. "Don't use them unless you have to. Sooner or later, my CI or the authorities may try tracking us. They'll be looking for recent burner phone purchases from you and me."

Jake made some calls. Surprisingly, Jennifer answered, said she had not heard from her mother.

"I know better. Don't give me your bullshit lies. Elena is putting herself and you in a bad position, a dangerous position. You need to call your grandfather and tell him I said you need protection. If you hear from Elena, text me?"

She said it was his fault. He cut her off. "Do like I told you. Now." He disconnected.

He called his son and daughters. They didn't sound very happy to hear from him and were angry when they heard what he had to say. Knowing how little they listened to him, he decided to call his ex-father-in-law, their grandfather, who was said to be an associate of the Dixie Mafia, though, as was the case with his kind, he vehemently denied the accusations. Jake hated calling him. They had never seen eye to eye, much of that was because he felt Jake had done the family wrong when he got his daughter pregnant before marriage and refused to join the Catholic Church. Jake was surprised when the man who called himself Hank Michaels answered. Jake would not have been surprised if that wasn't his real name, he should be in prison and as far as Jake or his family knew or admitted, hadn't been.

He listened to what Jake had to say and then cursed him for bringing more trouble for his family.

"Mr. Michaels, Hank do we have to keep going through this? Stop. No. You listen. Joanna took our children, left me when I was laid up and couldn't do anything about it. I couldn't always be there. For that perhaps I bear some of the burden. She knew, you knew, when we were married what being in the service meant. Her addictions killed her, other people provided the weapon, not me. I know you blame me, told this bullshit to my children, and have continued to do everything you can to turn them against me. Seems to have worked. I'm tired of talking about this. Can't you just shut up and listen. I know. No, it's not the same ole problem and this isn't some more bullshit. I wouldn't have called if I didn't know how dangerous this is. That's right curse me. I can't be there to protect my children. It pains me to have to rely upon you." Hank continued cursing. "Same to you." Jake cut the call.

TJ waited, listening. "Damn bro. Glad don't have to deal with that shit.".

Jake tried Elena again. No answer. No voicemail.

They pulled out and drove to the vets. Doc Hunter said Dusty was stable but was not out of the woods yet. Jake insisted on seeing him and one of Doc's assistants had him don a surgical gown and mask and led him into the isolation ward. Jake saw Dusty bandaged lying with his eyes closed, his chest barely showing signs he was breathing. He called his name. He thought he saw a slight twitch. The assistant said he doubted Dusty heard him because of the sedative. Jake wanted to believe otherwise. Come on Dusty, I'm here. You have to survive.

TJ was waiting at the reception area. Doc told him Officer Coulter had picked up the bag containing the fragments taken out of Dusty. He took statements. Doc said he and his wife stated this wound, this type fragments, were a first for them. What he didn't want Jake to hear was, even if by some miracle Dusty survived, the amount of trauma and lead poisoning would certainly limit the quality and length of his life.

In the vet parking lot TJ told Jake he planned to take David Gonzalez hostage.

"We need place for questioning him. Remote, defensible, push come to shove."

Jake was surprised that TJ was willing to do something as illegal as kidnapping. Personally, Jake had no problem with the idea. Seeing Dusty hardened his resolve. That and threats to him and his family. Enough was enough.

There's a place little more than an hour from Charlotte on Lake Wateree belongs to my family. Most are second, vacation, weekend homes. Not many people come there this time of year. A few fishermen are about all."

"We should leave one of the trucks someplace remote, safe from whoever comes looking."

"I know someone who has a vacant warehouse in Rock Hill. I can leave my truck there. Padlock the door, should be safe for a week or so."

"Have to assume they'll be tracing our vehicles." TJ walked over to his truck and came back with a small devise, raised Jake's hood, and attached it to the GPS antennae. "This'll disable your GPS System."

TJ looked down inside the engine compartment after he installed the blocking devise. He walked around to the passenger side, crouched to make sure.

"Damn bro, take a look at this."

Jake came around and knelt to see what TJ was talking about. There was a hole through the rear of the front fenderwell.

"What the fuck?"

TJ walked around to the driver side. Just behind the fresh air vent at the back of the hood was another hole.

Jake joined him.

"Looks like a bullet entered here and went out the other side," TJ said looking at Jake. "Any idea when this could have happened?"

Jake shook his head. A thought suddenly occurred to him. "When I was headed home in that storm yesterday it started hailing. I heard one loud ping. I thought it was the hail. Damn." He paused, scratched his head. "I didn't see any other vehicles. I can't imagine anyone being out in that storm." Jake was puzzled. "I serviced my truck less than a week ago. I would have noticed. That loud ping. Had to be when. Who?"

"You thinking what I'm thinking?" TJ asked.

"Those fuckheads. Had to be them."

"No way to prove it."

"If it was them, they'll brag about it. They come by my house again they'll get theirs. Payback is a motherfucker."

 TJ hoped Jake didn't get the chance. Wouldn't if things didn't work out.

"We better get going to see the lawyer." TJ closed Jake's hood. Jake kept staring at the hole.

"Let it be for now bro. Are you listening?" Jake looked up. TJ saw the look. "Come on bro. We have to get moving. Okay?"

Jake nodded. "You're right."

"Good. Now listen up. Once we get to where we're leaving your truck, we'll take your battery. That way, even if some of these fuckers somehow find your truck, they'll have a hard time stealing it. Be on the lookout for an older van, abandoned one preferably, we'll hotwire it."

This statement really threw Jake a curveball. TJ really had his attention now. He couldn't believe TJ would think this, much less say it.

"What the fuck for?"

"Got to have it to put the CI in when we pick him up. Old ones don't have chips."

"Seriously?" TJ grinned. "Unfucking believable."

Jake thought about who might have such a vehicle. He hated the idea of stealing one. Getting caught would mean losing everything. TJ had to know this. Unbelievable.

"I know a used car salesman in Charlotte who probably would have one. And he knows how to keep his mouth shut." He didn't tell TJ the guy was an old high school gang buddy who, so Jake had heard, ran a chop shop.

Another of Jake's heavy drinking years' friends, Jimmy George, met them at a warehouse. It had been a cotton warehouse. Jimmy used one section for his delivery business, another for storage, with more than enough space for Jake's truck, protected by a state-of-the-art alarm system. They stashed Jake's truck and went to see the attorney.

The 3H Law Firm was located a few blocks away on Main Street in a newly renovated building as part of the York County Historical Society and Downtown Economic Redevelopment Associations attempts to bring life back to center city.

Jake knew the building. It had been the site of the Civil Rights Sit-In by a group of African Americans given the name The Friendship Nine. Theirs was one of the first demonstrations at the beginning of the Civil Rights Movement in 1961. They had come from nearby Friendship College and attempted to be served at the food counter of the Whites only diner. Duly arrested and jailed, their names recently cleared in 2015 by Judge John C. Hayes III, a judge Jake knew. He had done remodeling work on the judge's personal home. TJ read the plaque inside the door, "hmph." was all he said.

The attorney's office was on the third floor. They took the elevator. It was as slow as molasses on a cold winter morning. Gave Jake time to admire the polished brass, thick hand-carved mahogany woodwork inside the elevator which also formed the wainscoting, chair rail, crown molding and door casings of the corridor. The 3H Law Firm Door was at the end, the name etched into the frosted glass top panel of a heavy mahogany door. Inside was a small waiting area furnished in a Victorian motif.

They donned their masks and entered. Seated behind what once must have been an old bank teller setup was a receptionist, dressed as though she was in a fifty's theater Old South production.

"May I help you?" A poor attempt at southern coquette, a tilt of her head, a put-on smile. Didn't work for Jake.

TJ couldn't resist. Using a southern black tone, he said, "You's new, ain't you? Sure do like yo' getup. I'm TJ Alvarez and my whitey sidekick here he be

Jackson Harper, but you can call him Jake. Weuns have an appointment to see Mastuh Henderson. If you would, please lets him know we's here. We would be ever so grateful."

She blushed and her mouth dropped open. Without another word, she swiveled around in her chair, got up and went down a short hallway. Jake and TJ heard her say, in a more flat-toned southern accent, "Daddy, there are two gentlemen here to see you, a Mr. Alvarez and a Mr. Harper."

A distinguished, lawyerly-type man, tall, thin, dark-turning-grey-haired, wearing a shirt, vest, and tie, noticeably not your everyday off-the-rack clothing, followed the young lady back to the desk. She sat down. He, who turned out to be her father, pushed back the saloon style half-door came out, reached out with both hands like he intended to give a low five then high five to TJ.

"Damn TJ. Good to see you. Come on back to my office. Jolene this is my friend TJ. You must be Jake?" Jake replied in the affirmative. "Jolene is a drama student at Winthrop, as you probably can tell. My receptionist is out with that dreadful flu going around, at least we hope that's all it is, so Jolene is helping out between classes.

They sat in two high back leather chairs. The lawyer rocked back in an expensive leather swivel chair behind his desk.

"Mr. Harper, Judge Hayes mentioned your name to me when I was looking for someone to do some up-fitting at the house. My wife had already engaged someone else. Perhaps another time, she's always doing some changes. We bought one of the homes in Judge Hayes' Winthrop neighborhood."

"Appreciate the thought. If I can ever be of service, please let me know," Jake replied.

"Certainly. TJ, how have you been? Been about what three years since you helped me out? He looked from TJ to Jake and saw the puzzled look on Jake's face. "I'm sorry Mr. Harper, I guess you are wondering how TJ and I came to be on personal terms. Your friend and mine, TJ, saved my life. You may have heard or read about the Bank of America attempted robbery in Charlotte a few years back. I was one of the hostages. The hostage as a matter of fact. Had a sawed-off shotgun put to the side of my face. Negotiations had failed and I was certain I was a goner. One minute the gun was pressed to my head, the next it was gone, and the would-be shooter was on the floor in a pool of blood. The rest of what happened was a blur. Within seconds all of us, the hostages, and the would-be robbers, were stunned by flash grenades and smoke bombs. Other than the one robber, we all escaped with minor injuries. I later found out TJ was the sniper who saved my life. I will forever be grateful." He looked at me again then turned to TJ, "I can't believe you never told your friend about saving my life."

"Oh, he's way too modest," I said. "I could tell you a lot more about this man's heroism."

"Enough. Ok? Appreciate the sentiment and all, but telling campfire tales not why we here. Don't mean to sound rude Alex, but Jake and I have a major problem." TJ told him about the incident with Jake's dog and the warden, about seeing the magistrate, learning the DA was going to the Grand Jury for an indictment for Assault and Battery on an officer of the law. He told him about the evidence that had been collected at the scene, by the vet and the cameras that had been planted at Jake's and Elena's home. He then told him about the pictures that had been sent with threatening messages and about his undercover work and planting of a camera and what he had heard because of that devise.

Jake kept his eyes on the attorney while TJ talked. The attorney kept a poker face. Jake had the feeling this wasn't news to him.

"There is an ongoing investigation by Charlotte Metro and the feds into the Mexican gangs and I worked undercover in Miami for several years and this area for over six months, gathering evidence for indictment. The incident involving Jake's dog, the warden's accusation, other previous problems, points to Thurmond Tindal and associates, employees, whatever. Mr. Tindal or his employees are, without a doubt, in bed with a Mexican cartel. At this time, we not sure what's going on—do know there's money laundering, drug smuggling, and human trafficking in play. I believe the investigation is the cause of our troubles. If we are locked up, that will be the end of it. We could lose everything including our lives if we get sent to prison. Therefore, we came to you."

"Wow! That is quite a story TJ. Anything you might want to add Mr. Harper?"

Jake waited to gather his thoughts. He felt this man's daughter wasn't the only drama student. TJ cleared his throat. Jake decided he might as well try to trust TJ about this man.

"Mr. Tindal, the game warden and I, we have a history. Most of it not cordial. You probably are wondering about a motive for Mr. Tindal's actions. For me, it seems there will always be before Thurmond Tindal and after Tindal. I'm sure the Hill family, like all many wealthy plantation owners back then, weren't saints and had plenty of slaves. Not that this means anything concerning our problem, but I think it's past time we put that in the past. I doubt Tindal would agree."

Jake saw the discomfort in Henderson's face as he looked from Jake to TJ. TJ simply nodded. He and Jake had had this conversation way back in their getting acquainted days in the Philippines. The recent Black Lives Matter clash meant little to TJ. His family had suffered many indignities in another part of the world and in America as well. TJ looked beyond that. He saw himself as a soldier and lawman first and foremost. Jake wasn't sure about the attorney's thoughts and didn't care.

"Tindal is a throwback. He sees himself as some aristocratic plantation owner and he wishes to increase his holdings. Anyway, to put it simply, he wants my land and has wanted my land ever since he purchased the adjacent tracts. Over the years he has used the warden to harass me. I recently found Mr. Tindal had surreptitiously met with my father-in-law and my wife to pressure me to sell. I have refused. Now my dog has been shot. This is not the first dog that has been shot or disappeared since Mr. Tindal took over the hunt club on what is now his land. He has thousands of acres, three roads he could have used for his firing range and hunter staging building. Instead, he sited them less than a quarter mile from my house. No sir. People don't know Mr. Tindal like I do. He will stoop to anything to get what he wants. Having me locked up on these charges is his latest effort to take my land. This was my grandfather's land and has been in my family over one hundred years. I'll not have the likes of Tindal getting his hands on it."

Jake noticed the attorney had looked uncomfortable whenever TJ and he said Tindal's name. "You know Mr. Tindal, don't you?"

"Most people in York County know Colonel Tindal, Mr. Harper. Sounds like you are implying a personal connection. Let me just say upfront, I have been asked to run for state senate the next go round. Mr. Tindal is a major contributor to both parties; moreso to the Republican Party, which is my party affiliation. He has been present at campaign parties and I have been introduced to him as a potential candidate. That is as far as my personal involvement with Mr. Tindal goes. Would it pose a problem for me in handling your case? Possibly. If he is as underhanded as you accuse him of being, he could cause me not to be nominated. I haven't decided to run and would not consider it, if not for my wife."

"But I wouldn't be sitting here if it wasn't for TJ. I owe him my life and believe me or not that is why I would do everything possible to get the charges dropped, or, if need be, acquitted, and the same would go for you. If you doubt my integrity, ask our friend Judge Hayes. There is a good chance he would be the presiding judge. He too knows Thurmond Tindal. Do you think that would change the way he would handle the case?"

"I appreciate your honesty. If you want to run for the Senate and need Tindal's support, you better not take this case. If you decide not to take our case and you feel like you owe Tindal, then I would appreciate you not letting him know you even spoke to us. TJ may feel differently but that is the way I feel. Just being honest with you."

TJ sat quiet, not moving. He knew Alex felt ingratiated to him, but he didn't know him well enough to bet Jake's and his life on his integrity. In his experience, most people put their ambitions ahead of everything else. That especially applied to politicians.

"Jake's right Alex. If you want to run for office, you better not get involved."

"TJ. I would never sell you out. My wife might get upset. It won't be the first time and damn sure won't be the last. I'm not getting any younger and I have a good practice here. This is my home and I hate moving. Sleeping in my own bed means more to me than anything at this point in my life. All that glad handing, baby kissing and travelling around giving speeches has been causing me to doubt my desire to be a politician. I guess kissing Mr. Tindal's ass wouldn't be worth the cost to my pride. So, if you still want me, I'll take your case. Pro bono. No argument on that, ok."

"Now. As of this moment, neither of you has been summoned by the Grand Jury. My first action will be to try to head that off. I'll speak to the DA. Maybe I can convince him you have evidence that could be embarrassing for Mr. Tindal. Could give him pause. Buy time. I will talk to Deputy Coulter to get an indication to how soon this evidence will be available. TJ how soon do you anticipate this case you are working on will lead to indictments?"

"I have every reason to believe this will be happening within the next couple of weeks. My superiors are pushing me. I have reason to believe the feds are ready to make their move. If you can buy us a couple of weeks, that should give me time enough to do what I have to do."

"Even if they call you to appear, unless they call a special Grand Jury and even then, nothing will happen before a couple of weeks." He stroked his chin and sat back. Attorney Henderson looked out his window. Jake and TJ did the same, thinking something outside caused him to look. A tree-lined parking area and tops of other buildings was all there was to see. The room was silent except for Alex drumming his fingers on his desk.

"This will not be an easy one for either side." He said as if to himself while continuing to look out the window. "Today's political climate, with you being an officer of the law and both of you being veterans, works in our favor. The other side will be using the officer of the law card when seeking an indictment. Jake your dog being shot will draw a lot of sympathy. And TJ, the African American ACLU will be all over this if the DA goes ahead and pushes for a trial. Jake your history with Tindal and the warden is a two-edged sword, have to be careful about using it."

"This is how I will play my hand and maybe I can get the DA to decide this will not play well for his reelection. I like the odds. Yes sir, I think the DA will not like this."

He turned back to face them. "I'll get back to you as soon as I know something. As for Thurmond Tindal, his influence only goes so far. If he is involved in some criminal activity, that influence will disappear, would make him radioactive for the sheriff and DA."

"Mr. Harper steer clear of the warden and Mr. Tindal until TJ's work is finished." He stood and they did the same. He extended his hand then withdrew it when he realized his mistake. "Sorry. Hard to break the habit. Damn shame. Hopefully, the new vaccine is as effective as predicted. Anyway, good luck TJ. You'll be hearing from me. Let me know if you find anything I can use. Mr. Harper, good to see you. When Susie decides on her next project, I'll have her call you."

"Thanks. That would give me a chance to repay you. If you see Judge Hayes, tell him I said hello."

"Will do. In fact, I may be having lunch with him real soon. Always helps to give him a heads up on possible cases. Who knows, he may discourage the DA. Y'all take care."

On the way down in the slow elevator, TJ asked, "What you think?"

"Sorry, but I don't really feel better about our chances with the DA. Tindal's influence worries me. It seems we can't get away from that son of a bitch."

"We'll see about that." TJ said pulling back the elevator's metal scissor door. "Let's get the van and pick up that piece of shit gangbanger. Speaking of which, better check my spycam, see what's happening."

"Good morning. Thought you might like to hear I had an interesting conversation with the new clients that we talked about earlier. Yeah, I'm now their attorney. Thought you might like to know," Attorney Henderson said to the man on the other end of the call. "Mr. Alvarez informed me the feds are close to an indictment." Henderson listened, then replied, "if I hear anything more, I'll let you know. My name need never come up. Would not be good for any of us. That's not a threat. Just keep my name out of it."

Attorney Henderson leaned back in his chair and looked out the window. What were the connections of Tindal to the DA? Had to be more than money. The DA said Tindal was launching an enterprise which would put the county on the map. Said we could get in on the initial stock offering. However, the feds involvement was troubling. And how did this Poponovich get his name? What was his connection to Tindal? He would have to be careful. Politics was a dirty business. Something strange was going down and he couldn't afford to get caught in the middle of a federal investigation. But he needed the money he was being offered. The coronavirus pandemic hit hard.

He would have to think about this. After all he did owe the Alvarez man his life. It was the Harper man that Tindal was after. Perhaps there was a way to cut a deal for the Alvarez man.

CHAPTER
19

Thurmond Tindal was upset the Ridley man left without saying anything. Bullshit excuse, the weather, a front moving in west of the mountains. The damn front wasn't due in until tonight. There were showers possible off the coasts of South Carolina and Georgia, but nothing that should affect flying.

He had seen the videos Jenkins had installed in the guest suites. Two more of Jenkin's slip-ups: the Harper man's dog, not telling him about the transvestite. The videos did give him leverage if need be on the Ridley man, Colonel Baker, and if anyone found them, he would pin it on Jenkins.

Colonel Baker was on the veranda, a coffee cup in hand, facing the direction of the hanger, didn't hear Tindal's approach.

"Good morning."

He turned to face Tindal.

"I take it you slept well?"

"Very well indeed. Nice to be away from Washington, enjoying a quiet morning with a great view like this."

"I never tire of it. Though with all my businesses scattered across the Southeast, I haven't allowed myself the luxury as much as I would like. With this new project, if I get the go ahead, I hope to change that."

"If everything goes as your people have led me to expect, I see no reason why approval will be anything less than a formality. Couldn't help noticing, you have a rather small, mostly Hispanic security detail. Highly unusual."

"Bud ran security checks on all personnel. Those Hispanics all served in the military, honorably discharged. One or two may have been DACA, Dreamers, some call them. Bud assured me all are citizens. There are other non-Hispanic members of the detail also. What you don't see is a virtual detection system that has multiple layers that start on the river and extend around the property covering the visual range, with several other circuits that tighten in on the house and lab and twenty-four- hour monitoring, backed by drone coverage, including The Hive which is tied in with military and civilian satellite systems-- state of the art. If everything goes as planned, the pipeline contract, with DoD acceptance, The Hive will become one of the best weapons in our War on Terrorism."

"And make you an even richer man. Let's say you get the go ahead, how soon could you start production?"

"I have arranged with Boeing at their Charleston facility to begin right away. Meaning within this calendar year. But, as I indicated last night, my goal is to set up a manufacturing facility, with Boeing and other investors, over there." Tindal pointed across the river. "I purchased a thousand-acre tract that was once Pinckneyville, my middle name as you know, with the intention of setting up a manufacturing facility that will be a major economic boost to this area. It also helps with securing the area. I have received the go ahead from my investors and have had the plans approved locally and by the state. Federal approval is pending, our senator and representative are on board, waiting on DoD approval. I'm counting on you to help with that, could get you that star. If that doesn't happen, you could come to work with me. Your knowledge of DoD's DARPA's procedures and personnel would be a major asset. I'm certain I could make it worth your time."

"I appreciate your consideration. I will keep your offer in mind. This could be a serious problem if it got out while DoD is looking for my approval of the project. I'm sure you are aware of this. This conversation never happened. How soon can we get today's demonstration under way?"

"Whenever you are ready, I will tell Bud to get moving. Should take no more than an hour. The Hive has been operational all night."

"Gives me time for a quick breakfast, take my constitutional and freshen up. Oh, speaking of personnel, where did your techs come from?"

"The ones you saw are former military IT engineers. One Air Force, one Army, and one Navy. The team leader, Dr. Guthridge, Air Force Reserve. She has worked with DoD and NASA. Others, not here, are from top think tanks of universities. Came over with the acquisition of Marberry Manufacturing. Dr.

Perkins was the original developer of The Hive concept. Dr. Guthridge and her team developed the prototype."

"Where do I need to go for the demonstration?"

"Use the remote in your suite, buzz Major Jenkins when you're ready."

The demonstrations went off without a hitch. Including The Hive and Bumblebees autonomous system demo. The Hive was also demonstrated using the latest on-ground personnel connectivity in a virtual battlefield situation using mental commands that had been developed for flying combat jets in the military. The Hive, unlike the Bumblebees, had in its arsenal not only exploding aerosol gas pellets and drug darts, but also R.I.Ps, smart bullets and mini missiles. They demonstrated their capabilities without any problems. Colonel Baker witnessed everything, gave enthusiastic applause to every action. He was given a brief turn with the virtual system and couldn't restrain himself. He was like a kid finding his most coveted toy under the Christmas tree. What he didn't know was a tech was his copilot and kept him from making a costly mistake.

Bud Jenkins mentioned the chip implant that would allow the operator to control the Hive without the virtual setup.

"One thing at a time. You know Congress is slow to give approval for these new tech ideas. Too many voters scared of Big Brother, invasion of their privacy."

Later sitting on the veranda as his aides prepared for his departure, Tindal pushed to know if the Colonel was on board and when he could expect to know something. "Next week York County is having their annual Fall Fest. The Governor will be there along with all local politicians running for office in the next year's elections. I would love to announce my plans then. Do you think that will be possible?"

"That is not up to me. I will report what I have seen, do what I can. This has been difficult politically with the upcoming election and all. That can be good and bad. The new president has his own agenda and no one, but him, knows what he is going to do. He keeps everyone guessing. The parties are using this to strengthen their positions. My guess is like everyone else's as to what that will mean for the military or any budget going forward. Right now, it is a wait to see game for everyone. I will do what I can. I know you were a big contributor to the former president and other local and state politicians. But at this point, who knows."

Tindal was not encouraged by what he heard. "There is a lot riding on this project. My investors may not be as patient as some expect. Some have hinted that they have foreign interests willing to purchase our product, willing to give favorable tax incentives for setting up production in their country. Personally, I would prefer that not to happen. Financially for me that would not be the best scenario and as a patriot, I would rather have our government and good ole American companies reap the benefits. But there has been a lot of money invested for R&D, material, and labor. These top minds don't come cheap. I can only wait so long, then these investors will vote to go to the highest bidder. You might want to let the decision makers know this."

The Colonel stood up and looked sharply at Thurmond Tindal.

"Thurmond, you and I go way back. I have never questioned your patriotism. I would hate to do so now. What you just told me would not be received very well in Washington. There would be some who would see this as a threat, blackmail. You know what our national policy is on those counts. The repercussions could be enormous for you and these other investors. Tax breaks could be withdrawn, as could military contracts. I don't think you or your friends want to go down that road."

Tindal didn't like the Colonel's tone. No one need threaten this project. He stood and locked eyes with the Colonel.

"Colonel Baker, Will, as you say you and I go way back. I consider us friends and have entertained you here numerous times. It has been brought to my attention, that on those occasions, you have enjoyed the company of female companions of questionable character. I'm sure your wife would not be very forgiving, and I am absolutely certain a man of your standing with your National Security Clearance would most likely be treated with less than an honorable discharge, possibly military imprisonment. Public humiliation would be a certainty. I wouldn't want that to happen to someone I call friend. Let's be clear, my investors and I aren't the only ones with a lot to lose. I would suggest, you do everything in your power to not disappoint us."

Colonel Baker turned beet red from his neck into his face. "This is something I would have thought beneath you Tindal. Friends don't threaten friends. I will have to consider your threat and I will have to decide if I can live with myself if I acquiesce. Either way, you can be certain this is the last time I will set foot on this property." He turned to leave.

"Colonel Baker," Tindal said as the Colonel headed to the veranda steps, "I will expect a favorable answer. If everything goes well, I expect you to attend the ceremony next week. If you show, none of this happened. I will destroy the tapes. The offer for a job will still be there. Think about this when you write your report."

The Colonel continued marching; didn't reply.

CHAPTER
20

Elena's thoughts were on the long drive ahead. She and Jake had made this trip numerous times together. This was her first time alone. Noticing the fuel gauge was below a quarter tank, she decided to stop at the Amoco in Jonesboro to fill up. When she got out to pump, she saw the sign to pay first before pumping. Normally she would have gotten back in the car and driven on to where she didn't have to go inside, but she wanted a coffee. Remembering Maisy was in the car, she reached in and grabbed her key fob. Maisy had locked them out of Jake's truck one time when they got out to fuel up and use the rest room. She was notorious for jumping up on the door arm rest to look out whenever they exited the vehicles and left her inside. More than once she had hit the lock button on the door panel. That one time had cost them an hour's delay, as they waited on AAA to send a locksmith to get them in Jake's truck. Jake had put some rubber door stops and a stiff wire in the bed of his truck whenever they came back from their trip, in case he forgot his keys were in the ignition and the door got locked.

Walking toward the station building, she had to hesitate as a van came into the lot and cut across blocking her entrance to the store. This irritated her and she was tempted to say something to the driver, but he didn't get out. She saw the Hispanic driver was on his phone. He was wearing a mask. She forgot to bring hers. Oh well. She had received the vaccinations.

Inside she got a coffee and went to the register. The older woman asked her how much she wanted to pay for the gas. Elena had no idea. She remembered Jake said the car held 15 gallons so she told the woman she would need 10 gallons. The attendant looked irritated and entered twenty-five dollars plus the cost of the coffee. Elena swiped her card, signed the receipt, grabbed her coffee, and headed back to her car to pump the gas.

She noticed the van had backed up to the opposite side of the pump where she was stopped blocking her view of her car. She noticed the prick driver was still on his cell phone as she went around the front of his van. She opened the door to put her coffee inside and hit the release on the gas door. Straightening up, after she reached to return the hose for the pump, she was startled by the feel of a damp rag pressed over her nose and mouth. She was lifted off her feet and shoved inside the side door of the van. The last sounds she remembered were the hysterical yaps of Maisy and the slamming of the van doors.

CHAPTER
21

Jake and TJ took Interstate 77 to Charlotte. It took a little more than fifteen minutes. Good thing it wasn't rush hour, you could double or triple the time. Rock Hill and the surrounding area had become part of the Charlotte Economic District. They exited onto Tyvola Road and went to South Boulevard. Two blocks back off Tyvola was Homeland Security's office. TJ need not guess what Hardy would say if he knew what he planned to do.

The car dealership sat back off South Boulevard in what had once been a restaurant. Jake's friend had added a metal building behind his office that was supposed to be a repair and maintenance shop. Jake suspected this was used as the first step in the chop shop business. His friend's cousin had run a similar operation near Heath Springs, South Carolina when Jake and Bitch, his buddy's gang name, were street racing and swapping parts to keep their cars in top condition. Bitch had been running moonshine and pot for his cousin which led to their being popped by the SBI. A young punk who was a gang wannabe had ratted them out. They received probation and got that thrown out when Bitch joined the Marines and Jake joined the Army. Jake had run into him a few times over the years and had heard from people who knew their background that he was back to his old ways, but now had the protection of the Dixie Mafia. His cousin had hooked up with the gang in prison and brought Bitch onboard when he was discharged.

"Jakie boy, long time no see. What's happening?" Bitch remarked, as he came out to meet them when they stepped out of TJ's truck. He reached out to bump Jake's fist. They held their distance. They eyed each other, each taking the other's measure. Bitch looked taller and more muscular than Jake remembered. Jake noticed the Confederate flag and Born to Die tats along with the Marine Emblem tats on his well-toned arms. Bitch looked hard at TJ when he got out to join them. "This a friend of yours?" he asked with contempt.

"That's right Bitch. This is TJ and you best not piss him off."

"Semper Fi. Ya look like ya were in the Corps?"

"Army Rangers," was all TJ said.

"That how ya know my ole pal Jakie. Bet ya two served together, am I right?" TJ nodded and they held eye contact until Bitch said, "Well I guess if Jakie says you're ok, then ya must be. Ya ain't no cop, are ya?"

Jake broke in. "Enough of this pissing contest. Bitch, I need an old van. You got one that runs and has good tires?"

Bitch broke eye contact and looked at Jake. "Look around, I don't carry anything that doesn't run or have good tires Jakie. What ya need it for?"

"I do home repairs and I need something my employees can haul tools and materials in without someone being able to steal them and keep them dry from the rain. Nothing fancy, an old work van that, if they beat it up, I won't be too upset about."

"Got a '97 Dodge Van, one owner, bought at the Darlington Auction. Got a big six that will haul about anything and she looks like she has been in a garage all her life. Ready to roll. Since ya are an old pal, I can let ya have her for a thousand. How's that sound?"

"Come on Bitch. I didn't come prepared to spend more than five. You got anything else?"

"That's the only older van I have. Hell, I'm damn lucky to still be in business with all these self-driving cars. People just ain't buying the less technological ones anymore. Give me until tomorrow and I might be able to fix ya up."

Jake said, "Can't wait. Got a job to do starting tomorrow and I need the van today. Guess I'll have to try somewhere else." TJ started for his truck and Jake said, "Thanks anyway." He stuck out his hand and Bitch didn't move to shake.

"Fuck Jakie. Tell ya what I'm gonna do, I'll let ya have it for the five today and ya can bring me two fifty whenever ya back on this side of town. How's that?"

Jake thought about it. He knew they needed to move fast. Listening in as they came up the Interstate, TJ had heard Gonzalez cautioning others as they were packing up his garage for the move. "Okay. Deal. But we're in a hurry. Got to get the materials from a man on the other side of town in less than an hour. How about I give you the five and you give me a Bill of Sale right quick and we'll go over everything when I come back by."

"Come on in the office. I'll make out the Bill of Sale and get ya a temporary tag and the key."

Jake nodded to TJ, who he saw had his headphones back on. Inside the office, Bitch was writing the VIN and other info on a Bill of Sale. "Oh. By the way, have ya heard about ya old squeeze Ariel?"

That name caught Jake off guard. Ariel had been a girl from their little community. Her family had a farm not far from Jake's parents' farm. She was a distant cousin with the same last name. A kissing cousin was how people described the relationship. She had been Jake's first love and the first person that had been the other party in finding out what making love meant. When her father found out, he had her sent off to school in Europe. "What about Ariel? Last I heard she was in Europe."

"She's some big-time news gal now. Saw her on a Columbia News Station. She was a looker when ya two were messing around. Now she's a knockout. Musta got hitched, calls herself Ariel Gaspard now."

"No shit. That's good to hear. Maybe I'll get in touch." Jake said as Bitch handed him the paperwork to sign.

"I bet she'll remember ya. Didn't see no ring. Who knows maybe ya can hook back up? Ya married?" He asked as they went out the door.

"Yeah. Second go-round. Got three kids by my previous one. Hey, I appreciate this Bitch. Be cool man. I'll get back here as soon as I can. And I'd appreciate it if anyone asks that you don't tell them anything about who bought the vehicle."

Bitch put the tag on and started her up. "Listen to that motor. Ought to last at least a hundred thousand more miles. Keep it between the ditches Jakie, I mean Mr. Jones." He looked at Jake and winked. "Don't forget to get the permanent tag within ten days. Drop by and let's catch up on things. See ya."

CHAPTER
22

TJ pulled out onto South Boulevard, retraced their route back to the Interstate and Jake followed. TJ called him on his phone. "Hey man goina swing by downtown near the SWAT lot, leave my truck in the City Police private secured yard until we're done. We'll pull over before we get there and transfer some of our gear to the van. Follow me."

In an old, abandoned warehouse that had once been Tremont Music Hall, they made the transfer. TJ told Jake to bring his handgun, two magazines and the illegal suppressor only. The rest would remain secured in TJ's truck. They would pick up the other gear on the way back. Jake trusted TJ's planning. It had been a while since Jake had been involved in this type of activity, unlike TJ. TJ knew about the suppressor and pretended not to know. His saying to bring it was surprising. As was what they were about to do.

Jake once more followed TJ. They went up Tryon Street to Morehead and then came out onto College. TJ pulled in, entered a code and Jake went around the corner and pulled in an honor system pay lot as TJ had instructed. Sitting there he thought about Ariel, trying to remember what she looked like. It was said you never get over your first love. Jake could remember the feelings, her taste, her smell, how his every waking moment was about her. He wondered what she looked like now.

He remembered the hurt when he found out she had gone to live in England. Gone. Not a word. He had already decided to join the Army and wanted her to be there for him. How young and innocent they had been. He tried to get these thoughts out of his head. There was a feeling of guilt. He was married and these thoughts were like dreams that went nowhere. Elena. He needed to see if she was answering, find out where she was. He tried several times. No answer. She was ignoring him. He hoped that was all it was.

Fifteen minutes later TJ crossed the street and jumped in. He had brought a black holdall bag which he put in the area behind his seat.

"You know how to get to NoDa?"

Jake said, "Of course." He paid the box and went to Tryon Street, downtown Charlotte and headed north. As they travelled in silence through the manmade canyon, TJ with his headphones on was listening to their target site. Jake looked around thinking, Charlotte's skyline had changed drastically in his lifetime. Its history erased. Now, like all the urban development that had sprung up everywhere, you couldn't tell much difference between it and other cities of similar size.

They got on the John Belk Freeway and exited off onto North Davidson. It took fifteen more minutes to reach Gonzalez' neighborhood.

"His house is two blocks from here. You get to the garage from a back alley. We know he has company, so we've got to be locked and loaded. Don't shoot except in self-defense. We don't want to make too much noise and alarm the neighbors."

Jake pulled over and they pulled out their sidearms--TJ decided to take his Springfield pistol, and Jake retrieved an untraceable Sig Sauer P226 9mm that TJ had given him--a gift after he and Deane had moved to Charlotte. Jake had modified it for a silencer. He would have felt more comfortable with his Remington semi-auto 12 gauge with aught and double aught buckshot for close quarters, but TJ said that would not be necessary.

TJ pulled out two Kevlar bullet resistant vests, two pairs of skin-tight leather gloves, two ski masks, two respirators, two stun guns, and six grenades. He handed Jake a couple. "One with the yellow marking's loaded with knockout gas, orange one, a stun grenade."

"Had me wondering there for a moment. Where did you get these?"

"Better that you don't know."

"Go one block past the front of his house, pull in any unoccupied driveway. I'm going to head out on foot, come in from the alley. Keep the engine running, lock the doors, cover the tag with some tape. He handed Jake a small roll of duct tape. Expect they in a moving van, won't be expecting us. I'll be waitin' in the shrubbery up the alley. Cut in behind the house where you park and come over to the alley. Text 111 on your phone before you get there, that way know it's you. Put your vest on, bring your pistol, stun gun, and grenades only. Don't go shooting, unless no alternative. In and out, that's the plan."

"No shit."

TJ smiled. "Hear me out. Not to your liking, say so. Here take these." He handed Jake a handful of zip ties.

"I'm going to go up one side the alley. You come up the other. The shrubbery will give us good cover until we are on them. The alley is a one-way, narrow lane. We'll move and cover, I'll go first. Check the back of the truck first, work our way forward. Any there, we use gas grenades, stun them when they come out. Doubt they'll be many, assume they armed. Remember, we don't want noise, don't want to fire our handguns unless we have to. I'll secure any that are in the back of the truck. You get the ignition key and cover me."

"Next, the garage--come in on each side, again gas grenades, you know the drill. If they don't come out, or start shooting, we flashbang them. We just want to stun them, we need Gonzalez alive. He'll be the short pudgy one, the only pudgy one hopefully. Everything goes righteously, we should be able to get in, secure everyone, and be on our way fast. If they have their vehicle almost loaded, we'll load everything else we think we'll have some use for, including Gonzalez and the others. I'll take their truck, you get the van, and we'll get the hell out of here. I figure the police can respond in fifteen to twenty minutes max, that is, if anyone notices and calls, so that is our window of opportunity. Come on we'll drive by. I'll show you the house and we'll see what they have in the alley. Then we'll circle back around, and you can drop me off. What you think?"

"Hope don't end up a shootout. If so, I hope I live to tell you, you fucked up."

"Yeah. Right. You ready bro?"

"Ready as I'll ever be." Jake hopped into the driver's seat and followed TJ's directions.

Sure enough. There was a small moving van in the alley. A couple drives beyond, TJ pointed to another house. The house looked vacant as was the drive. Jake circled around and dropped TJ off when he told him to stop. He grabbed his bag and Jake watched him cut across the street and go up the alley. Pulling the van into the vacant drive, Jake got out taped the tag, grabbed his bag, and walked back behind the house. He cut left behind the fence of the house next to

Gonzalez, kneeled down, opened the bag, put on the ski mask, placed the gas mask on top of his head, slipped his handgun into his waistband at the back of his dark cargo pants, clipped the grenades onto the front waistband area, pulled on the gloves, grabbed the stun gun, stood up, crossed the back drive of the other house, keyed in 111 on his cell, and quietly slipped through the head high shrubbery.

He came out less than fifty feet from the garage. The door was open, he could hear voices, but no one was in sight. Crouching down, he retreated behind a shrub. Jake heard voices from inside the back of the van which was just beyond the side of the garage. Suddenly TJ appeared and tossed a gas grenade into the back of the van. There was a pop, then Jake saw one of the Hispanics appear at the back. He was holding his throat and coughing. TJ stepped out from the side of the van and shot him in the chest with the stun gun and depressed the trigger sending an electrical current into him and he fell to his knees. TJ caught him before he hit the loading ramp, pulled him down, zip tied his hands and feet together, and motioned Jake forward.

TJ picked him up and laid him out in the back of the truck. Jake stayed low and hurried up to the driver's side door, while keeping an eye on the garage opening. There was no one in the front of the truck. Jake grabbed the key and hurried back to the corner of the garage. TJ came out the back of the truck. He had his gas mask on. Jake pulled his down, cleared it to make sure it was working properly. He grabbed a gas grenade, his thumb on the pin. He signaled to TJ who quietly came down the loading ramp. He came over to Jake. Staying back out of sight, they waited to see if anyone would come out of the garage.

There was no movement and no sound. TJ motioned for Jake to pull out his stun gun by waving his, then he extracted another gas grenade, pulled the pin, and gave Jake the signal before tossing it in. Panicked voices started shouting in Hispanic, followed by shuffling sounds and crashes of boxes and some metal clanging.

TJ and Jake moved in; stun guns ready. One man lay on top of some boxes, a metal shelf rack across his legs. He was coughing and gasping for breath. Jake knelt zip tied his legs, removed the metal shelving, and flipped him over face down, pulled his limp arms behind and zip tied them. That done he looked over as TJ was pulling a pudgy short man up, hoisting him onto a shoulder and walking as quickly as possible, stepping over parts that had spilled out of some unloaded boxes, heading for the door. Jake reached down and picked up his captive and followed TJ into the back of the moving van.

TJ and Jake stopped at the end of the loading ramp and slid their masks up. Jake could feel sweat seeping down and dripping onto his neck. He gulped in some fresher air. TJ did the same, said, "Come on, we need to see what else needs taking and hurry the hell out of here." He slid his mask back on and Jake did the same then followed him into the garage.

TJ grabbed David Gonzalez' laptop and Jake picked up a tray of zip drives that had been pulled onto the floor next to where he had been sitting. TJ reached up on top of a beam and pulled down his spycam and motioned for Jake to follow him. Once more outside he pulled his mask up. Jake had hurriedly done the same. "Go get the van and meet me back at the old Tremont parking lot."

TJ laid the laptop on the back of the truck ramp. Jake looked inside at the bangers. They lay motionless. He closed the door and latched it, thinking, now that's a switch, locking drug and human traffickers in the back of a moving van. He heard TJ closing the garage door. He slid the loading ramp back under the bed of the moving van and grabbed the laptop.

Jake went back to where he left his bag and threw the sweat-dampened gas mask he had wiped off into the bag on top of the laptop and box of thumb drives. He pulled his sweat-wet ski mask back down to hide his face.

Without wasting time, he quickly retraced his steps to the van and was heading back through NoDa, when he saw three Hispanics on motorcycles heading in Gonzalez' home's direction. He called TJ. "Got three bikers headed your way. Looks like Hispanic gangbangers," he said when TJ answered.

"On my way. I'll cut over a few blocks, come back a longer way. I should miss them."

"Ten Four. I'm going to pull into this vacant parking lot on North Davidson. I forgot to take the tape off the tag. I'll wait here for you to come by. Stay on the phone and let me know if you run into any problem."

"Roger that."

Jake didn't have to wait long. After TJ went by, he pulled back out. He kept his eyes on the mirrors. "Go through town. I don't think they'll look for the van there."

They pulled into the parking lot and TJ came back to the van with his bag, stowed it behind the seat and they sat there for a moment. There was a good deal of traffic on South Tryon. The business day was coming to an end. The amount of traffic would only increase.

"What now?" Jake asked.

"Pull around on other side of the moving van, keep the rear sliding door beside it, leave just enough room for us to get in between. We'll load Gonzalez. You got his laptop right?"

"It's in my bag under your seat, along with the box of zip drives. I say leave the other stuff. What did you plan to do with those other fuckheads and the other shit? They can identify us. I know you thought of that."

"Don't matter. They won't talk to the police, bet on it. They know what will happen to them if they do. Whether it's jail, prison or back in their country. I'm not worried about them. We need to get Gonzalez, and get the fuck out of here, before some patrol car comes by and gets curious."

They loaded Gonzalez. Closed the moving van. Some of the bangers were coming around and started making noise.

"Go back downtown. Need to get my truck. All the stuff we might want is in it. Then we head to wherever your family's place is."

The quickest way is the Interstate," Jake said as he drove back up South Tryon. "Or we can go a longer way down Highway 521 through Lancaster."

"Should be alright if we take the Interstate. It will be cluttered with rush hour traffic going south."

David Gonzalez started moving around and making moaning and retching sounds.

"Hope that fucker doesn't vomit in here. He smells bad enough as it is. Smells like he pissed and shit himself. What if he starts yelling or banging on the sides or something?"

TJ unbuckled and climbed into the back. He pulled out some more zip ties and secured Gonzalez to the bed rails, his feet on one side and his hands to the other. He tied a rolled-up handkerchief as loosely as he dared around his neck and in his mouth. "David, I would try not to vomit if I were you. You might choke on it and I wouldn't like that. Comprende?"

David stared at TJ wide eyed, trying hard to swallow.

Jake dropped TJ off, pulled back into the building traffic, and went around the corner to the same parking lot. As they waited, he tried Elena's phone again. Still no answer. He left her a voicemail, asking her to call him. He heard David Gonzalez trying to speak. He had turned his head to stare at Jake. It looked like he was grinning as he was making what Jake perceived as trying to tell him something. Jake recalled TJ telling him David had said something about his brother tracking them and their families. He climbed into the back and pulled the handkerchief gag out of David's mouth.

David belched and Jake moved back some thinking he might vomit. David with a smirk on his mouth said, "Harper man, you and your friend make big mistake. You and your families no longer safe. Have your wife, maybe your friend wife. Big mistake you have me. My friends find me no matter where you go. You can no hide anywhere. They find you. You let me talk maybe they let wives go. You let me go, I tell them no harm your family. No let me go and you and friend have problem. You friend ask comprende. I say comprende to you."

He broke into a big grin.

Jake looked at him and said, "If your brother has our wives and anything happens to them or our families, you will die many times and beg someone to put your ass out of misery. You will call your friends and tell them we will let you go if they harm no one and let our wives go. Before I believe you or them, we will need to hear them tell us they are ok. Understood?"

"Need my phone. I tell them what you say. Maybe let wives go I tell them you set me free."

There was the sound of a horn, three longs and a short repeated twice. Jake looked out the window and saw TJ had pulled out of traffic and was stopped blocking the entrance and exit to the parking lot. He put the gag back into David's mouth. "I'll have to talk to my friend, and we'll decide what to do. You better think about what I said about what will happen to you."

Jake pulled out onto Fourth Street when he could. He was several vehicles back from TJ. He called TJ and told him what David had said.

"Talked to Deane, said the dogs and her somewhere safe. But she has not heard from Elena, not been able to reach her. Have you tried her daughter?"

Jake said he had talked to Jennifer earlier and she claimed to have not heard anything from Elena either. "I'll try her and get back to you before we get too far down the Interstate, I need to know something. We may need to pull over in Rock Hill, I'll let you know."

"Ten Four. With the traffic, be better if we pull over south of Rock Hill."

"Ok. Exit at Highway 21. Pull in one of the truck stops. I don't need to be saying too much with this asshole listening. I'll wait to make any calls."

Jake was getting worried about Elena and these threats. Where was she? If these fuckwad bangers did have her, what would they do? He knew from experience that negotiating with terrorists was not something you did, and rarely, had a satisfactory outcome. But that was other people, this was Elena. If they had not had this incident with Dusty and the game warden, none of this would be happening. Everything led back to the incident; everything led back to Thurmond Tindal and or his employees. He and TJ had no proof. A lot of circumstantial evidence and this fucker's threats; not anything law enforcement would listen to, or act upon. TJ was certain the piece of shit in the back was a key part of whatever had happened. Didn't matter, if he wasn't before, him and his crew were now, damn sure a threat to their families. Even if they turned him over to law enforcement, there was not much chance he would cooperate. TJ was right about that. Without proof, he would probably be held, then deported. If so, if not. Fuck them. Elena may be in trouble. Could it be the cartel?

There was something else, the deputies last night wanted to accuse him of doing something to Elena. Why? Seemed like somebody put them up to it. Was this part of Tindal's frame up? Would he stoop that low? He wanted Jake's land, was said to have taken a contract out on him.

Was he involved in Elena's possible disappearance? Jake couldn't picture him chancing harm to Elena. Sam, his friend, Elena's father loved his daughter, no question. Would Tindal do something to Elena and risk Sam's response? Jake knew Sam well enough to guarantee the outcome would be dire. Could Sam be a party to Tindal's actions? Only if Elena was involved. Jake couldn't believe that to be likely. Sure, Elena wanted him to sell the farm and move closer to her family, but Jake refused to believe she would go this far. No way. She knew what would happen if the truth came out.

Where did that leave him? Up shit creek without a paddle in a canoe with holes in it.

He played the possibilities in his head over and over, only one likely conclusion, Thurmond Tindal was somehow involved, directly or indirectly.

They reached the exit with Jake wondering what they could do to prove Tindal's culpability.

TJ pulled into the Circle K Fuel Depot and pulled around to the side where one other vehicle sat toward the back. An employee or someone sharing a ride were the two likely possibilities. When Jake pulled to the stop beside him, he came over and sat down in the passenger seat.

"Whew bro, how you stand it in here? Need to roll down the windows. Let's stretch our legs." TJ got out and Jake grabbed his phones and did the same.

He called Jennifer. She said she had not heard from her mother. She was worried. Said she had been trying to call him and it kept going to voicemail, why wasn't he returning her calls? He told her he had his iPhone turned off. She said she had been frantic and had called her grandparents. They had not heard anything either. "Granddad says if he had not heard from her soon, he was going to be heading that way." He shouldn't be going anywhere. Moms had said he was going in the VA next week for the cancer treatment and didn't need to be going anywhere. He won't listen. You know him. That's a long drive and at his age, he shouldn't be doing these long trips anymore. He says he will do what he damn well pleases. Jake where do you think she could be? Why isn't she answering her phone?" Jake asked her if her mother had told her what had happened with Dusty and all. She said she had.

"I told your mother to call your grandfather and have him get you to come there. Why aren't you at their house?"

"I can't miss my classes. I'm trying to catch back up after missing most of the last two quarters. Moms said you were blowing this thing out of proportion. And…"

"Listen to me Jennifer. I don't have much time to explain. Get yourself in your car and go to your grandparents. Tell Sam to call me and tell him I said not to leave Susy and you alone."

"You're scaring me Jake. Are you saying momma could be in danger?"

"Jennifer, I've got to go. You do to. Tell Sam to call me. Just go to his house now!" Jake disconnected the call. He hoped she did as he told her. What should he say to Sam? Hey asshole why don't you ask your friend where my wife and your daughter are. The call was not going to go well. But having Sam here could only make things worse.

TJ had been on the phone talking to Deane. She had gotten a suite with a kitchenette He told her that she probably would not hear from him for a while. "If anything doesn't seem right, do not hesitate to call the number I'm going to give you and ask for Sergeant Sanchez. He's my SWAT partner. I trust him." He gave her the number and had her repeat it back to him. "You should be fine. Do as I tell you. Don't go out unless you have to. Don't worry about us. I love you."

The next call was to the police desk. He covered the phone with a cloth and disguised his voice by sounding shrill and excited. "I live over here near Tremont and I was walking my dog. There is a big truck. You know them moving truck kinds. It be over at that old music place. You know where those bands they played. I hears banging and shouting coming from that there truck. It weren't no English."

"Ma'am this crank call? How'd you get this number? Why didn't you call 911? What's your name?"

TJ disconnected the throwaway phone call. "That will get those bangers off the street." He said as Jake came walking over.

Jake told him what he had been thinking on the drive down the Interstate. "If they have Elena, which was a distinct possibility, where would they take her? You think she's ok?"

"We have their number two man. Number one's his brother. That piece of shit," he flipped a thumb toward the van, "knows everything about their whole operation, maybe he knows about the Latin Kings' money laundering, human trafficking and drug running in this area and beyond. Elena's their bargaining chip. Tindal or no Tindal, the man has no say so when it comes to their operations. If he's involved, they won't be asking him what they should or shouldn't do, for damn sure he won't be calling the shots. No, we're the threat, having him, they're scared, puts us close to blowing their operations open. Elena will be fine as long as we have their man. Our best bet's to keep him where they can't get their hands on him."

"As for Tindal, time will tell if he has anything to do with any of this. Since the bangers know his name, there's a connection and fat boy over there's goin' to tell us what it is. And once we learn what's what, we can use it to help clear ourselves from this legal shit Tindal's man the warden put on us."

"Tindal's involvement has more to do with him wanting my land than anything else. We both know Dusty's shooting was no accident. I can't think of any reason for his coming after you though. Unless like you say, you've stumbled onto some connection which threatens him or his business or something he's trying to cover up. Having us locked up and kidnapping Elena doesn't seem like something he would do otherwise--too risky, and he wouldn't want to risk fed involvement. Plus, Elena's father Sam is a friend of his. Only way her father would involve himself with Tindal on this is if Elena herself is involved. And I don't want to think that."

TJ was walking a few steps away, then back as Jake talked, he stopped, looked at Jake while rubbing his chin to help cover his face. It was not a good idea lingering out here. He hadn't spotted one but they would be smart to believe the store's security camera probably has its eye on them.

"We ain't getting' any closer to knowing standing out here bro. Not very smart exposing ourselves like this. Let's get out of here and get to wherever we're going. That's the best thing we can do for Elena and our situation."

CHAPTER
23

Undersecretary Robert D. Hardy was sent word from the FBI and ICE about the moving van. A team was dispatched to the Tremont Street scene. The police and paramedics were the first on the scene and were not happy when the feds showed. Hardy learned they had received an untraceable anonymous tip which prompted their response. Tattoos on the three Hispanics identified them as members of the El Diablo Motorcycle Gang, which the SWAT Team Commander and Hardy knew was the gang TJ Alvarez was working with as an undercover agent in their ongoing investigation. Reluctantly the SWAT Team Commander Kelly Jones informed the feds of his operation and his intent to take control of the gang members and the boxes of evidence found in the van. They refused of course and Hardy and HS took charge of the investigation.

Within an hour, they had found an address label which led them to the garage in NoDa. There they found evidence of what had been a well-conceived operation resulting in what they believed was the computer repairman and the other gang members' abduction. No one in the neighborhood had heard or seen anything, other than one older lady had noticed a van parked in a drive of a vacant home two doors down where a masked man carrying a bag got out, went toward the back of the house, and returned fifteen or twenty minutes later. She had a hard time giving any other description of the man or the van.

Undersecretary Hardy and the SWAT Commander Jones tried calling TJ with no luck. The same with Deane's cell. Hardy then tried to reach Jake and had no luck. He knew cell phone reception where Jake lived was not particularly good.

Concerned with the lack of response, he dispatched a team to TJ's home. A half hour later, he received word that no one was home. With darkness less than two hours away, he sent the team to Jake's farm.

An hour passed before the team reported via satellite phone that they had surprised a man and his wife, Ben, and Carrie McDonald, who were there to tend to the animals. They told the agents Jake had said he and Elena would be gone for two weeks due to sickness in the family and had asked them to take care of the animals and check on the farm. They had checked the man's id and he did live at the other end of the road. The couple thought it strange that they would both be leaving since they had heard that one of their dogs had been shot and was at Doc Hunter's Veterinarian Hospital in McConnells in serious condition.

Something told Hardy, TJ's and Jake's families being gone at the same time was no coincidence. TJ had not mentioned anything to him about any trip when he saw him yesterday. With their pending legal troubles, it was highly unlikely they would have gone anywhere. TJ had said he would be meeting with his CI and expected to have something that could prove vital to their investigation. A van with some members of the gang and possible evidence, the disappearance of TJ, Jake and their families with no communication happening…Damn.

He told the agents to stay put at Jake's farm, give the neighbors a card and tell them if they hear from Jake or Elena to notify him. "After they leave, I want you to go in the house and check for signs of foul play, hasty departure, anything that doesn't seem right. Before you go in check for an alarm system, if there is one, disable it. Get back to me with what you find."

Hardy dispatched another team to TJ's home with the same instructions. He then had other personnel find all they could about Deane and Elena. Check with their friends, families, their places of employment. Try not to alarm anyone, pretend to be a creditor or something, you know the drill. I need this information ASAP. Before he contacted the FBI and raised an alarm, he needed to gather as much information as possible. If he had to issue missing persons' alerts, he needed to come up with a damn good reason without raising a red flag. He had no idea how he could do that. Dammit TJ, where are you; what are Jake and you up to? He hoped and prayed TJ's cover wasn't blown.

Those pings. Had someone found a way past their security protocols? If so, who? And what would they have done with these people?

As darkness descended, Hardy sat at his desk waiting for his people to give him the information he requested. The first response was from a female agent who had been contacting Elena's family members. The first person had been her daughter. She immediately went hysterical and had passed the phone to her grandfather. The grandfather demanded to know who she was and what the hell had his son-in-law done to his daughter. She tried to calm him down to no avail. After assuring him that she had no reason to believe anything had happened to his daughter, that she was with the alarm company, the alarm had gone off and she had not been able to get the primary residents to answer, so she was notifying the other parties that the police had been dispatched and his granddaughter was on the emergency call list. He wasn't buying it. She assured him that she was who she said she was, and she gave him the alarm company's number which would ring into another agent's number. She had alerted the other agent of the possible call. "Sir I felt I should come to you with this. I couldn't get much information, but it seemed obvious that something is wrong, and it was like they had been waiting for a call."

"Thank you, Agent Pierce. Good work. Any luck on Mrs. Harper's employer?"

"Yes sir. She works as a Nurse Practitioner with PNAmerica which employs Nurse Practitioners that work from home. I got her email address and sent a message. No reply yet."

"I also checked on Mrs. Alvarez' information. She is a school guidance counsellor and works with the VA as a counsellor also. She called in sick saying she was coming down with the flu. I told the school administrator I was with the VA and I told the VA coordinator I was from her school. Anything else sir?"

"Do a search on emergency clinics, hospitals, accident reports, the usual. See if anyone with their name or fitting their description has shown up."

Hardy pulled up the preliminary police report. Nothing there just like the other agencies' and HS' reports. The gang members weren't talking. He had a decision to make. If TJ, Jake, and wives turned up dead, he would feel responsible if he didn't seek help. The FBI and local police would be reluctant to issue a missing person's alert in less than 24 hours unless he was willing to disclose his relationship with TJ. That would end TJ's use in the investigation and possibly with Charlotte Metro SWAT. It would create more distrust with other federal agencies and local law enforcement. There was enough of that already. The next 12 hours would be critical. He had no choice but to use Homeland's resources until then.

CHAPTER
24

Elena woke in a darkened room; a wet tongue was licking her. She reached out and pushed Maisy away. There was some light coming from a hole in the ceiling. She sat up and looked down at her clothing. They were wrinkled. She didn't feel anything physically had happened to her other than she was a little woozy and her stomach felt funny. Maisy jumped down and started her twirling around and around chasing her tail, her show of aggravation or her attempt at getting attention. She tried to stand and felt weak, so she sat back down. The memory of what had happened immediately caused her to panic. What drug had they used? Who had done this? Where was she? Why had someone done this to her? All kinds of thoughts and questions flooded her mind.

The room looked like a luxury hotel room. There was the queen size bed with an expensive bedspread which was wrinkled from her having tossed and turned. Next to the bed was a thick Persian rug. The rest of the floor was dark stained wood. On each side of the bed were two bedside antique tables with ornate lamps and shades that were off. She reached over and turned one on. Across the room was a mirrored dresser. On one side was a wingback chair, on the other was a wheeled clothing stand like you find in luxury hotels used by bell people to bring client's clothes from the entrance to their rooms. She saw her largest suitcase on bottom and hanging clothes on its brass rail. Above the dresser mirror was a television. The far corner had a door which led to a bathroom. She could see a footed cabinet with a polished brass and nickel faucet below a cut-glass mirror. Along the wall, paralleling the bed, was a pair of windows set high up with glass panes that allowed a modicum of light but appeared too small to allow any possibility of entry or escape. Under the area of the windows was a desk with a reading lamp and pen and pads sitting in front of a comfortable looking chair. Nearest her, next to the wing-backed chair was a door she figured to be a closet. To the right was a heavy paneled metal door leading to place unknown in the corner where the light shaft's dim light shone. Maisy was sniffing at its bottom. Other than the sound of air coming from HVAC registers set in the two-tiered ceiling and Maisy's sniffing, there was complete silence.

She rose on shaky legs and went to the bathroom. After using the toilet which sat in the corner next to a footed tub with shower, she washed her hands and splashed water on her face. She dried her hands and ran her fingers through her hair. Her toilet kit sat on a bath stand next to the sink. Everything was inside like she had placed it before leaving the farm. She took out her brush and brushed her hair. Feeling better but thirsty and hungry--she had not eaten anything since lunch the day before.

Elena walked out into the large bedroom, went to the door, and tried the handle. As she figured, it was locked. On the wall next to the door was a light switch and what looked like a speaker box with a button on one side. She pushed the button and yelled, "Hello, can anyone hear me? Please answer me if there is anyone listening." No answer. She depressed the button and held it repeating her plea. Still nothing. Had they locked her in this fancy prison and forgotten about her? Not likely. She scanned the ceiling. In the upper tier she saw what appeared to be a small camera. She waved at it.

There was a click and the door suddenly swung inward and startled her. Maisy started yapping. Elena reached down and picked her up, clutching her to her breast as if this would offer some protection. A tough looking Hispanic woman stood there holding a tray with two covered dishes and a pitcher of what appeared to be tea, a glass with orange juice, another empty glass and silverware rolled up in a white cloth napkin. She quickly stepped inside, closed the door, and took the food over to the desk, set it down and walked back towards the door.

Elena stepped in front of her and asked who she was? She stared at Elena as if she did not understand. Elena repeated the question in Spanish? The woman tilted her head, looked her up and down but did not reply. She asked where she was in English and Spanish. The woman tried to step around her, and Elena moved to block her, holding onto Maisy with one arm and reaching out with the other arm to grab the woman's arm. Her hand was immediately grabbed,

Elena was twisted and shoved onto the bed. Fortunately for Maisy she landed on her back. The Hispanic woman produced a knife from under her skirt and pointed it in Elena's face. Maisy got behind Elena and continued yapping. Without uttering a word, the woman backed over to the door and depressing a button on a remote held in her other hand, the door swung open and she backed out into what Elena saw was a narrow corridor.

Elena felt like screaming. Tears of anger, hurt and frustration ran down her cheeks. She had cried more in the last several days than she could ever recall doing. Normally a stoic who endured other people's suffering without allowing herself to get caught up in emotion, sympathetic not empathetic, she now was lapsing into self-pity. Why was this happening to her? When would this be over? She hated to admit she should have listened to Jake.

Bud Jenkins' monitor view of Elena gave him pause. Even in the rumpled state she was in, he couldn't resist the urge. He wanted to go in her room and have his way with her. Maybe before he left here, he would show her what he was capable of. Who knows maybe she would like it so much she would be willing to go with him? Not likely. And that would cause an issue with her father Sam. But with all the money he was going to have, he could have ten more, younger and less needy than a spoiled American woman like her. All in all, why not have her and the others too? Something to think about.

That Mexican whore-dyke was another matter. If Bud didn't watch, she would probably rape the Harper woman, then cut her throat. Good thing Arturo had warned him.

But for now, he needed the fucked-up bitch to help with the Harper woman. Arturo needed the Harper woman to get his brother back. Hopefully, that would ensure her safety.

Bud saw David Gonzalez as a threat. He was too good at the hacking crap. Bud wondered how much he knew about him and his plans. He could not help but ponder who had him? Not likely the feds or this place would be crawling with them. A competitor? Arturo will be looking to insure that is not the case. How much did Arturo know that he was not sharing?

Bud Jenkins didn't really need the Hispanics any longer. He had them convinced that taking the prototype was the way to go. With his knowledge and the prototype, they could duplicate The Hive to use for their purposes. He had told them The Hive had a self-destruct program that only he could deactivate. The self-destruct was true, but he was not the key. That was built into the program. Bud knew how to override that command, but he was not about to let anyone know that was possible. Had David Gonzalez found this secret? He was certainly capable, but Bud wasn't sure David had found any reason to look. With David out of the way, Bud could bargain with the other bidders and obtain a better price without worrying about David exposing his plans.

Mark Poponovich had hinted he was willing to deal directly with him. Risky. But then risk was more profitable, as long as you knew how far to go. That was the problem with Mark, he didn't know him. Could Poponovich be testing to gain leverage? The cartel, like Uncle Sam, will stop at nothing once they find they've been had. Having Mark as a partner was a big risk. As the saying goes, 'Two people can keep a secret, as long as one of them is dead.' Bud didn't want to have to add murder to his list of crimes. He wasn't sure Mark Poponovich had the same scruples. Could he be behind David Gonzalez' disappearance?

David Gonzalez needed to stay gone. His disappearance would keep Arturo and his gang members busy looking for David while he laid false trails and implicated others, ensuring his safe get away to live the life Tindal had, and his family had been denied.

CHAPTER
25

Jake again led the way. He decided to take Highway 21 instead of getting back on the Interstate. Once they got by the Highway 5 exit, there was little traffic. The four-lane narrowed to two lanes and they continued on to the other end where there was a bridge over the Catawba River, a damn for power generation stretched across the river on the left side and rock outcroppings lay to the right.

On beyond the bridge, Highway 21 continued to Lancaster, passing by what had once been Springs' Park. His father had often talked about going to this waterfront recreational park, created as a local place for employees of Springs Industries, a cotton manufacturing company that was the largest employer in the area at the time, started by Colonel Springs. The Park had included a miniature train kids could ride around the park on, a wood floored roller rink with calliope for music, swings, slides and other playground equipment, an Olympic-size swimming pool with diving platforms extending in tiers of ten feet, up to thirty feet and a cleared landing area for boats. The park had closed with the closing of the mills, the foundries, and warehouses when the heirs decided to move production overseas where cotton was being grown and labor was cheap.

Jake had been too young to remember the park. His only memory was the boat landing.

They took the turnoff before where the park had been onto Highway 97, a curvy, two lane that wound along parallel to the river. At the highest point on the road was a community called Liberty Hill where numerous antebellum plantation homes reposed on the higher bluffs. Some were visible, others sat back down tree lined lanes, with rusting wrought iron fencing and gates. Down one road was a former governor's palatial home that had had a view out over what had been fields tended by slaves that stretched for miles to the river, which now was not possible due to the pine trees that had been planted.

When cotton was king this had been a very wealthy community, home of South Carolina's first millionaire. The old heirs had died out or their families had sold and moved on, hoping to have left the costly upkeep to a younger group of wealthy patrons. The stores and other buildings had all but vanished also. The only remnants were a small post office and the Liberty Hill Presbyterian Church which held Sunday Services where an older organist played the antique organ accompanied by the voices of the remaining parishioners.

The highway wound down from Liberty Hill to a smaller community that was situated on each side of the bridge over Beaver Creek, which was also the name of the community. The community consisted of several restaurants, a service station with a dock that held fuel pumps for boaters, a post office, a volunteer fire department, and a marina where boaters could dry dock their boats, have them repaired and serviced or get refueled.

Jake went to the marina, parking back from the open service bay. He went back to ask TJ, who had stopped behind him, if his truck had a trailer hitch with a two-inch ball. TJ said he had one under his rear seat and wanted to know why. Jake told him, his family had a small pontoon boat stored here and figured it might come in handy as another escape method if push came to shove.

TJ got out to see if he had one. He did. Jake went in the back, service area and spoke to the older mechanic named Charlie Quin, who listened to Jake's request, telling Jake to see Paul upfront while he took the lift back to bring his boat around to the parking lot. Jake went upfront and signed the paperwork and got the key. Charlie and TJ were hitching the boat to TJ's truck when Jake came back out to the lot. He tipped Charlie a twenty and thanked him.

After Charlie left, Jake told TJ they would continue 97 toward Camden for a couple miles where they would take a road that made a big loop along the river out to where Beaver Creek branched into the main channel of the Catawba.

"This will give us two ways in or out by road or we can use the boat if we get boxed in. That is if his buddies try to find us and get lucky, which I don't see how that will be possible. You'll see why when we get there. Unless it has improved, cell coverage is as bad there as it is at the farm. We better grab whatever provisions we might want and need from one of these stores before we head there. How long were you planning on us being here?"

TJ looked around. "Damn bro, this damn sure in the middle of nowhere. As to your question, it shouldn't take more than a day, two at the most to find out what we can from him and those thumb drives. I always keep some bottled water, snacks, and energy bars in my truck for when I'm on a stakeout. Does your family's place have a refrigerator, stove and microwave?"

"It's not that primitive. Yeah, it has those things. I guess we could get some sandwich makings and chips, maybe a twelve pack of beer. That sound okay to you?"

"Doesn't matter to me. Get whatever you want and I'm sure I can make do."

"Why don't we grab dinner at the restaurant across the bridge after we stop at the store for the other stuff? TJ didn't look too enthusiastic. "You look like you don't want to. Is there a problem with that?"

"Several. Not a good idea showing ourselves to too many people. We need to get that fucker out of that van, always a chance someone may get nosy and see or hear him. And there will be people other than those bangers looking for us. Not to mention, we need to git some answers. Elena's missing in case you forgot."

"Fuck no man I haven't forgotten. But I figure we've got him, and like "you" said they're not likely to do anything to her while we have him. Isn't that what you said? Don't tell me you've changed your mind?" Had TJ been saying this to keep him from worrying?

"No bro, Haven't changed my mind. But rather than standing here, we better get on with it. Why don't we split up? You get the shit from the store and I'll grab the takeouts. You know what they have that you want?" TJ looked up at the sky. Dusk was settling in. "Looks like the sun will be down in a little over an hour, almost behind the trees now. How long will it take to get to this cabin? Like to have a look around before dark."

Jake knew TJ was right, they should split up. Problem was, he had no idea what the restaurant people would think of a big, dark-brown-skin stranger coming into their place by himself dressed in SWAT fatigues. "You're right. We could save time and we maybe would be less noticeable if we weren't together, but…"

"But what?"

"You ain't from around here and these people don't know you. They're suspicious of strangers, and much as I hate to say it, they'd be really suspicious of a big brown-ass dude like you, especially dressed like a commando. Now don't get upset with me. I'm simply telling it the way it is. It won't take that much longer for me to do both. I can place our takeout order, go across the street to the store and be back by the time our food is ready. You can stay with our friend in the van and be giving him some friendly advice while I take care of the rest. How's that sound?"

"Typical honky bullshit's what I'm hearing. Okay white man dressed like us, huh? Don't like it, but had to take it most my adult life, especially up here. You right, we don't need the attention. What kind of food do those redneck crackers have?"

"All kinds, mostly seafood, mostly fried. I guess I'll get a seafood platter, with bass, shrimp, oysters, fries and slaw."

"Hate fried but guess I'll have the same. That way you can't fuck it up."

"Fuck you. When have I ever fucked up an order for you?"

"Too many times to count. Anyway, time's awastin'. We need to hit the road."

By the time they got to Jake's family's place, the sun, looking larger than normal, was casting its orangey glow on the thin, violet-streaked, cirrus clouds, almost past setting behind the trees on the far shore, its reflection sparkling on the river's ripples created by the dying breeze. Jake felt the temperature dropping once he stepped out of the van. He went around to the meter and flipped the master breaker turning the power on. A light came on in the kitchen. The last person here must have left when it was dark or, as some were prone to, it stayed on the whole time they were here, and they never gave it another thought. While Jake went inside to check on things, before unloading, TJ walked around reconnoitering the surrounds.

Jake nearly lost it when he opened the refrig and caught the smell of rotten food someone left behind. He opened the windows the back door, then pulled the garbage can over, unloaded the funky crap into its bag and carried the contents outside. Once having loaded their provisions in the cleaned refrig, he went in search of TJ.

TJ was standing at the end of the deck, taking in the sights and sounds of the few boats passing further out in the channel. Fishermen coming in or going out to catch and release fish from their favorite spots, afraid to eat their catch, due to upstream industrial contaminants which polluted the waters of the area river basins. Jake had seen the warning signs posted at the loading ramp.

TJ turned, he heard and felt Jake, the structure slightly trembling as he approached, a passing boat added a rhythmic sway.

"Nice place. Pretty quiet. Compared to Lake Wylie and Lake Norman, damn quiet. Does this water have a name?"

"Beaver Creek, part of Lake Wateree, another damned up portion of the Catawba River. We should back the boat trailer down the ramp, have it ready to unload, just in case. Our guest may feel left out by now, hopefully, ready to engage in a little conversation. I put our food in the oven to keep warm. I don't know about you, but I'm getting damn hungry. I get ornery and mean when I'm hungry. Might not be a good thing for our guest considering how I feel about everything else that has happened. It's been a lousy day."

"Direct me back. Have a backup camera and four-wheel drive but can always use another set of eyes. Been a busy day, probably'll be a long night as well."

"We need to take the van up-stream in case we need to make a quick exit."

"Be better we take the truck. That way we can leave most the gear in it, take out what we can carry in a hurry. Besides, don't want to leave my truck so those fuckers can get their hands on it.

"There's a place not too far from here we can take it, which means, we have to unhook the trailer. We can put a lock on the hitch and chain it to the dock."

Jake went back the way they came past Liberty Hill. Several miles later they took a left and wound down a narrow road to a boat landing. There was an unoccupied truck with a trailer hitched to it off to one side. Jake walked back to TJ's truck and pointed off toward the vehicle.

"On the other side of that truck is a dirt road that goes up to a lookout, place where people camp. I'll guide you. Back your truck up there out of sight. Out yonder," Jake pointed to the river, "is a small island, where kids go when it's warmer to party. If we have to, we can come back here by boat, stop on the island. From there we can see the area where your truck is."

TJ followed Jake's guidance, retrieved his tactical SWAT helmet with night vision and heat sensory capabilities.

Jake pulled the van around under the deck on the water side away from the road. They carried the smelly Gonzalez up the steps onto the deck and through the back door. TJ had his feet and Jake his arms. They placed him in the tub. TJ pulled his Ka-Bar knife from its sheath on his belt, cut the zip ties on his hands and feet so he could get his circulation back. They gave him a bottle of water which he first declined then hastily accepted when TJ started to put the gag back in. After ten minutes or so, they trussed him back up and regagged him. He had asked to be allowed to use the toilet and get cleaned up. TJ refused, told him if he cooperated, he would be given that privilege. He started cussing and that was that.

"Ever noticed reheated fried food never tastes the same as when it is served immediately after preparation?" Jake asked finishing off his beer to get the last bite's taste out of his mouth.

"Not much on fried food. Prefer my seafood fresh and grilled." TJ replied. He stood up, pushing his stool back from the eating counter. Guess it's time to see what's on those zip drives. He walked over to Jake's open bag lying on a cushion of the wicker sofa and pulled out the laptop and the box of drives. Once more seated at the counter, he opened the computer and inserted a drive. A prompt appeared asking for a password.

Jake stood looking over TJ's shoulder. "I was wondering if you could get a drive to run without unlocking the computer. Seems not. Looks like we will need to ask our guest. Think he'll tell us if we ask politely?"

"He will, we polite enough. You want to do the askin'?"

"Might need assistance, why don't we both ask," Jake replied.

David Gonzalez lay on his back in the tub. His eyes were closed. He didn't open them when Jake cleared his throat, so TJ reached over and cut the water on. Gonzalez jerked and his eyes flew open, water ran down from the top of his head into his eyes and he sputtered, eyes blinking rapidly, twisting his head back and forth. Finally, he stopped, lay still looking up at them. His stare showed open hostility.

"Sorry to disturb your beauty rest," TJ said solemnly with a hint of sarcasm, "we're having a hard time doing our homework on your computer. My friend and I were hoping you might want to give us your password."

David made no effort to answer. His eyes had a hint of humor and the corners of his mouth curled up slightly around the gag.

"I take that as a no," Jake said looking from Gonzalez to TJ, "What do you think?"

"Guess our friend here ain't going to act polite. Maybe he'ld be more willing we take his clothes off, give him a nice cold bath. The stink may be bothering him. Damn sure offends me." TJ pulled his razor-sharp Ka-Bar knife off his belt once more and cut Gonzalez hands loose, reached down, yanked his flannel shirt up over his head. Jake bunched the tail around his forearms pulling Gonzalez child-size hands together and held them tightly while TJ cut the ties on his ankles. David started thrashing and moaning, twisting trying to get free as Jake held on and TJ unbuckled David's pants and yanked the soiled jeans down to his ankles.

"What the fuck? TJ exclaimed.

Jake was busy trying to contain the whimpering wild man. He glanced over at TJ who held David's stumpy legs. Following TJ's stare, he looked down past David's pubescent female-like sagging breasts and pudgy flab of a waist and saw what TJ was looking at. There was a small penis projecting out of what looked like a vagina. "Jesus is that for real?" Jake had heard about transsexuals, hermaphrodites and, out of curiosity, had seen pictures online, the reality was shocking. Jake let go, TJ relaxed his grip, David slid down drew himself into a ball, and lay there, curled up in the tub. Jake looked over at TJ who seemed paralyzed.

TJ reached past Jake and David with his left hand, trapping David's knees against the side of the tub with his right and turned on the shower, spraying all of them. "It pissed on me," he explained. "What is the right call, him, her, an it? What do think of yourself as David?" TJ reached under the shirt and pulled the gag loose.

David shook and croaked. "I kill you. Your families, they dead. All of them," he squawked between sobs. "You think my brother no find you. You see. He knows where to find me always. We kill you." He remained curled up and stopped talking.

TJ turned off the shower and he and Jake went over by the sink. They both kept looking back. TJ scrubbed his hands and his right shirt sleeve.

Jake said, "Wow. Never would have thought to see someone made that way. Must have been hard growing up like that. What do we do now?"

"We get him, her, it, whatever you call that asshole. Don't go pitying that piece of shit. Whatever childhood problems he had, has nothing to do with us. He chose to be a cartel fucker, probably like most, when he was a kid. I had to choose, so did he. Has nothing to do with his sexuality. Didn't matter in 'Stan did it? Male, female, old people, kids, they can all be killers. He's a banger, a terrorist on American soil, plain and simple. You heard him. Given the opportunity, he and his fellow homies will do just what he threatened."

Jake knew TJ was right. But memories of being bullied as a skinny kid in a place where his war-hero father had done better than most--resentment, jealousy, part of it--seemed he was always singled out, not knowing why--had no choice, learned the hard way--had to fight--joined the gang for protection-- to belong, fit in. The Army had made him a warrior, a true fighter. TJ was right.

"Sorry you got pissed on," Jake tried not to laugh, and failed. TJ failed to see the humor.

"Aw, come on now. You'd be laughing your ass off if it had been me. Okay. You're right. Fuck'em. They have Elena, I'll do whatever we have to do get her back. Problem is how do we get *It* to talk? I'm thinking tires."

"Tires? What the fuck bro? Burn him. That's Klan shit bro."

"Nah man. You see, we have some old tires out, off the pier. Fish swim in and can't get out because there is netting around them with a one-way flap over an opening, catch lots of catfish in them. Those fuckers sting the hell out of you if you aren't careful getting them out. Have to be careful, snakes, lots of those get caught in there. Bet we put a couple of those around his waist and he starts feeling the movement, a few whisker stings, maybe fang bites, bet he'll want to talk then. What you think?"

TJ gave the idea some thought. Ole cracker Jake. He grinned. "Would scare the fuck out of me. If not, I've got jumper cables. Just one problem--sound carries over water."

"Yeah." Jake looked in at Gonzalez. Still curled up, his head toward the back shower wall.

"Wait a minute. There's some old diving masks down in storage. Should be able to use one as a muffler. I'll go get one and we can try it out."

Jake left and TJ went back over to the tub. He pulled Gonzalez head around. The anger flashed out of the banger's eyes. TJ grinned.

"Your threats don't worry me. Known worse than you. Grew up around some bad homs. In the Hood, you and your brother be scared to leave home. Spent most of my life fighting motherfuckers that would think nothing of cutting my head off. Your brother may find you, then again, no one may ever find you. First you going to tell us what you know, starting with your password. If you don't tell us while we in a nice frame of mind, we will be forced to do things to you that won't be so nice. Either way you will talk. That I guarantee."

Gonzalez tried unsuccessfully to divert his eyes. He spat at TJ. Wasn't much. Didn't go far and TJ dodged the attempt.

"Try that again, stuff soap in your mouth. Now, going to ask you nicely just one more time, what's your password?"

"Fuck you. Never tell you."

"Would tell you to go fuck yourself. You probably already do that, be wasting my time. Don't mind doing this the not so nice way. Your kind don't deserve niceties. My friend Jake's idea make you wish you had talked. You ever been baptized?"

David flashed a puzzled look, went back to his hate-filled glare.

"Didn't think so. Your mama probably Catholic like mine. Did you even know your mother? That's right your father beat you, probably called you a freak. Your brother killed him, let's see, he was ten wasn't he? You were only eight, right? You both had to run and hide. Your mother's brother helped you escape the law. Is that when you became a banger? Your uncle and brother were already ganged up, you joined for protection." TJ nodded toward Gonzalez' crotch. "Must've been difficult. See, you should know, warned you, everything out there 'bout you and your family. You somehow passed your initiation. Bet you killed a poor helpless kid from a rival gang. Uncle loaned you out--gained leverage within the Juarez Cartel, used your hacking ability, like an idiot savant, came natural for you so my intel says. Then you and your brother were sent to Chicago, used the cartel connection with the Latin Kings. You say you not with Latin Kings, we both know that's a lie. You and your brother got sent to Charlotte. Hooked up with a motorcycle gang called El Diablo. Strange, neither you nor Arturo have motorcycles, yet connect with a motorcycle gang, do little this, little that, think it's time to make the big score, huh?"

TJ watched Gonzalez expressions change when he said, "know what, my intel speaks of a connection to a banker named Mark Paponovich. What's confusing about this guy, no background information. Like he didn't exist until he shows up working in management for an investment bank known for laundering funds. We know there's a connection because we've been monitoring you guys for over two years that all three of you have been in Charlotte. There are rumors going around that something big's 'bout to happen. You've been really busy lately. Trying to play me off, giving me shit information, keeping me looking, not finding anything worth a damn in the direction you point."

"We discovered communication with Thurmond Tindal, his Hispanic employees. Been trying to figure that one out also. Which brings us to Jake, me, and our families. Jake's dog gets shot. One of Tindal's boys, the game warden shows up, we get arrested. Shortly afterward our family members receive photos with threats and subsequently Jake's wife gets taken hostage."

"Got personal. You're going to connect all the dots. We know you can. Better believe when we're done, we'll know why you fuckers chose to fuck with us. When it got personal, didn't have to guess, already knew who could help change the odds, my ole CI David Gonzalez. Whether that's the last thing you do, well, that's up to you."

Jake was standing in the bathroom doorway holding the face mask, listening to TJ, also watching David Gonzalez, seeing his facial expressions as TJ wove his tale. Jake walked up and TJ held David's head in place while Jake placed the mask over his head. TJ took his knife and cut a shallow line down David's stomach toward his crotch. David squirmed and screamed into the mask. It took both of them to hold him. TJ was careful not to cut too deep.

"Don't believe anyone anywhere close by heard a thing. Gonzalez you ready to start telling us what we need to hear? TJ asked you politely what the password was. How about it?"

Gonzalez eyes were bulging in his head, his face and neck flushed red as he strained to look down where TJ had cut.

"I can't hear you." Jake sounded the words in a sing-song jingle manner. Nod yes when you ready to talk."

TJ waved the blood-streaked knife in front of the mask. "Maybe he needs persuading, a deeper cut perhaps, give those fish in the river a bigger opening."

"Yeah, make that cut a hole, take him out in the lake, pull one of those tires filled with catfish and snakes up from the bottom, push it down over that fat stomach, let them nibble away. Maybe a nice big water moccasin will work his way inside. What do think about that David?"

David jerked and pulled against the restraints.

"We're waiting. Nod your head if you ready to talk."

Gonzalez nodded his head vigorously almost shaking the mask down from his forehead.

"I'm going to pull the mask up," Jake said. "If you attempt to scream, we will put the mask back in place and you will be taken out to the river. Understand?" He nodded. "You prepared to tell us your password?"

 Once more he nodded.

Jake reached up and pulled the mask out so they could hear his reply. He yelled out in Spanish something Jake didn't understand. He placed the mask back and looked at TJ, "did you get that? Didn't make sense to me."

TJ pulled a pen and pad out of his vest pocket and put his face in front of David's mask, so their eyes met. "Going to cut your hands free. Write down what you said. Try anything you have my guarantee it won't end well for you. And better be the correct password not some command that locks the computer. If that happens, we will no longer need you. There are experts good enough to get into that computer without your help. Waste our time, your last hours goina be awfully slow and painful. Comprende?"

David bobbed his head. TJ cut him loose and Jake used a washcloth to dry his hands, then handed him pen and paper. With shaky hands he placed the pad on his left knee and wrote a sentence in Spanish using numbers and symbols.

TJ scratched his chin. "Maybe? For your sake it better be."

TJ and Jake zip-tied Gonzalez' hands together and went back to the computer.

CHAPTER
26

Jake sat down beside TJ and entered, what they hoped was the password. TJ read it out to him. The screen pinged and opened showing a page of icons. Jake handed him one of the thumb drives. He inserted it into one of the ports. TJ exclaimed, "Bingo!" when a series of photos appeared--picture after picture of Hispanic gang members in various shots. Some were posed, many taken from a distance showing gangbangers partying and committing various carnal and criminal acts. Among these were the photos which had been sent to TJ's and Jake's families. TJ and Jake cursed.

What came next threw them a curve. Here was a set of blurry pictures of what vaguely appeared to be a gigantic bee-nest-looking flying disk and more fuzzy pictures of what could have been over-sized bumblebee-like objects darting in and out.

"That alien looking object must be a UAV. I recognize that place, that's Thurmond Tindal's property." He scrolled down slowly, pausing every few frames, transfixed by what he saw. "That's Tindal's place alright. Out of curiosity, when I got back from the Bahamas, I had to take a look at that big fucking house while it was under construction. I was on the other side of the Broad River. That's where these pictures were taken. Wonder what that thing does? Why would Tindal have that weird-ass UAV?" He scrolled down some more. Look at that," Jake said leaning in closer, partially blocking TJ's view.

"Check this out." The photos were close-up shots which more-clearly showed the bumblebee-looking objects moving in and out of the hive-looking UAV.

"Damn. What the fuck's that thing?" TJ said after he nudged Jake so he could see.

"A weaponized UAV, Look." He scrolled further. A group of shots showed lifelike dummies being shredded, as if they were being shot or hit with an exploding shell. "I believe we've found how Dusty was shot. Motherfuck!" Jake stood up and began pacing. "Son of a bitch. I knew Tindal was responsible. This proves it. That bastard. Wait till I get my hands on him. This proves his involvement."

TJ saw the pissed-off look on Jake's face. "This proves nothing bro."

Jake nodded, came back, and stared at the images while TJ took over scrolling-- no pictures included Tindal.

"We need to check the other thumb drives. So far, no picture of Tindal. In fact, no people's pictures are in these photos.' TJ's phone started trilling and vibrating. "I need to take this. Deane is the only person besides you that knows this number. He got up answered with hello, went out on the deck.

Jake scrolled back through the drone photos and saw TJ was correct. He took out the thumb drive and inserted the next one. A lot of Spanish with charts and figures, spread sheets. The amounts were mind boggling. He inserted another thumb-drive, more spread sheets, more photos of Gonzalez brothers' associates.

Boats, mountain areas, resorts, far more expensive places than normal people like himself could afford. He recognized a few places in the Bahamas, was surprised to see Cuban places he had been to on his last great misadventure. He was about to stop looking when a face caught his attention. He zoomed in, it was Mark, or at least that was the name he had given when Jake and this dude had shared the rent for the house in Cuba. Zooming back out and slowly scrolling he found several more photos of Mark, many with the Gonzalez brothers. He looked up when TJ came back in the door. He seemed to be troubled.

"Everything okay? You got that we-fucked look." Jake thought, oh no, something happened to Elena or Deane.

"Yeah, problems. Deane been trying to reach me, Fucking phone doesn't show missed calls, has no voicemail. Not good. Bad shit bro. We made the news--pictures, you, me, Deane and Elena. The DA issued warrants, not only for the Assault and Battery, he added other charges. Named you a person of interests in the disappearance of Elena. They found her car abandoned outside Lowry, blood stains on the driver's side. They tried to find you, Deane, and me.

When they couldn't locate us, they issued a bulletin requesting information from anyone who might have seen any of us."

"The story's been picked up by the networks. Been on national news broadcasts. Your stepdaughter and her father called in. Report said you contacted them about Elena and about threats being made against Elena and our families, including them. Your father-in-law said you made the threat story up to cover up what you were doing or what you had done to Elena. Your stepdaughter said Elena had told her she thought you were suffering from PTSD, that she was worried what you might do, especially after Dusty was shot."

"The DA, subsequently, issued fugitive warrants, stated you should be considered armed and dangerous. Speculated I might be involved. They reported the van and the bangers we left in Charlotte. My name leaked out somehow. Deane is frantic. She wanted to call into the hotline, waited to talk to me. I gave her our attorney's name and number, told her to talk to him, he would handle it. It's better she call, possible his line is tapped, authorities hoping we might call. Told her not to use her name or tell where she was and to disable that phone afterwards. She's not too happy, can't blame her."

"Fuck bro, the shit has hit the fan. I doubt that damn attorney has or will do diddly squat. He probably *will* notify the authorities."

Jake sat there listening to TJ, not wanting to believe this was really happening. "Jesus, Joseph and Mary, this is worse than I could ever have imagined. Armed and dangerous fugitive. How could this be?"

"Don't know bro. Anyone who has seen us today and sees this, will be calling in expecting a reward. Why would your father-in-law want to fuck you and by association me?"

"I'll bet you a dollar to a dime, Tindal is behind this. I told you my father-in-law is a friend of his."

"Not good. Shit's piling up bro. People can shoot us and claim self-defense. Goina lose my job and my soon-to-be-former SWAT team will be on the lookout, like the rest of the country. The honky's will love it—shoot the colored boy and his nigger-loving friend. We fucked. Sure hope Deane gets Henderson and he says something besides turn ourselves in. We got to get our shit together, fast. With me bro?"

"Guess we need to do what we gotta do and get somewhere more isolated. And that means even less electronic connection. Better learn all we can while we have access. Come over here. Look at what I found. See this guy here," Jake zoomed in on the picture of the person called himself Mark Castle. This guy and I shared a house outside Havana. That's him, with the Gonzalez fuckers. Have any idea who he is?"

TJ looked at the picture then at Jake. "You sure this is the guy you met?"

"Absolutely. Why?"

"That my friend is Mark Poponovich, the investment banker, suspected of laundering the cartel's money. Homeland's Special Agent Swanson's team came across him when we were doing our investigation. Been trying to connect him to the Gonzalez brothers, here is proof they know each other. Holy shit bro. The task force needs to see this."

TJ stood back up. "Doubt anyone will be interested in listening to anything from me." He walked to the kitchen side of the island. "Got to find some way to get our story out there, create doubt. What we need is an unbiased investigation going." TJ started pacing.

Jake was puzzled by what TJ said about Mark. He wondered why Swanson didn't tell TJ about him and Hardy, their encounter with Mark and Mark's crew in Cuba. Hardy felt certain Mark and crew were CIA, Swanson knew this. Jake's thoughts kept straying back and forth from one problem to the next. He ran his hand through his short wavy hair. Felt clammy. He needed a bath.

Out of the jumble, a thought. Maybe? Ariel.

"Hey." TJ stopped pacing and looked at him. "There might be a way-- something Bitch said. Ariel. When we bought the van from my old buddy Bitch, he mentioned Ariel, my first and only real love. I told you about her."

"Yeah bro. So?"

" She's a news person. Works at a television station in Columbia. If I can get word to her--me, us, this story--no doubt she would jump right on it."

"What news person wouldn't? Think she'll be straight-up, or twist it to make it sound sensational?"

"Sensational? Damn man the only way this could be more sensational is if we killed someone. The DA is probably working up to charging me with that. As for Ariel, unless I'm wrong, she'll be on our side? I'll know, soon as I talk to her."

"Sounds like you're excited at the prospect of getting back in touch, see if the fire's still hot?"

"I'm married, my wife's missing, makes that scenario highly unlikely." "Besides, that was a long time ago. You got any better ideas?"

TJ had been searching for options, had thought of Hardy. He needed to get in touch with him. No doubt Hardy would be leading an investigation into his disappearance. Good chance he had already connected the dots to what had happened earlier: gangbangers locked in back of moving van; a mysterious phone call; his, Deane's, Jake's and Elena's disappearances; his CI missing; an unoccupied gangbanger house in the NoDa area with computer parts, other records matching ones in moving van; signs of an assault; by now, the house linked to missing gangbanger, his CI; and now, a leak linking him to it all.

Jake wouldn't like the Hardy idea.

"Go with it bro. Can't hurt. Deane hasn't called back." He checked the phone. No service. "Fucking spotty phone service. Big problem. Going outside, see if can get anything there."

Jake watched TJ leave to go out to the deck.

His mind wouldn't stop churning. Why did he feel guilty? Elena, where are you? He wished there was a television, the last one was stolen, no one bothered to replace it. He wanted to see the news, maybe see Ariel, find out more about what was being said about them and Elena's disappearance. Why was her car found abandoned? What about the blood? Was it hers? She would have fought. Was she badly injured? Damnit. He needed to know.

Elena and Ariel, his dream. Wasn't the only time he dreamed about her. He wondered if she had changed much. Bitch said she was even better looking. He looked out through the glass storm-door, saw TJ checking his phone. He checked his cell, one bar. He walked over to the laptop, no connection. Must come and go, like it does at the farm when a storm's in the area. He wondered what Ariel thought when she heard his name, when she reported the story on her broadcast--did she tell anyone she knew this person? Did she believe the accusations?

The internet hadn't come back. Neither had his phone service. Had the marina shut their Wi-Fi down for tonight? Without internet or phone service, he had no way get in touch with Ariel.

Concentrate on Elena. If, which seemed more than likely, the Gonzalez brother has her, where would he be holding her. And Maisy, he almost forgot about her. I wonder what they did to her. That damn dog sure would bite someone if they try picking her up. I hope they didn't harm her. Could that have been what happened, she bit someone? Would explain the blood."

TJ came back in. "The phone service sucks even outside. There's a coupla boats just sitting out there, no lights on either one, no sound. Could be fishermen, seems they'd be making sound. Could be police boat patrol units."

Jake eased off the stool, walked to the den's window and peeked out through the shutters. Too dark, he couldn't see the boats. The marina lights across the way were all he saw.

"Used to ski with some buddies of mine out there at night, no lifevest, no running lights. You fell, you hoped you were seen when we came back around to pick you up. Also knew a young woman got her head cut off when a speedboat rammed into the party boat she was on. Didn't have any lights on. The speedboat operator didn't see them. When you're young, you do foolish things. Might be just water boat hookups. Did that also."

TJ wondered what the fuck. Damn that story, TJ thought, Jake fucking with my head. Hate water, that's the kind of shit scares the fuck out of me. Combat, not a problem. He went over and strapped on his pistol. Jake might not be worried, didn't mean he shouldn't be. No way they goina take him out in the water. Good thing, Jake didn't know he wasn't about to go with him to take Gonzalez out and drag up no tire either. No fucking way. He'd played along, seemed to have worked. Damn that Jake could come up with some fucked up shit.

"What's with the pistol? If that's the police, they come ashore the security lights'll come on. I activated them before I looked out the window. Should've done that when we got here. Relax TJ. You like, I can turn the spotlight at end of the dock on, light their ass up."

"Forget it bro."

Jake came back and sat down. "Look, no internet, keeps going in and out. What I was going to tell you was, while you were out there, I got to thinking about Elena, who has her and where? Seems fairly likely the cartel bangers have her, and like you said our trump card is that fucker in there. We could try to trade him for Elena, but I can't come up with any way to do that and come out of it alive. You got any ideas?"

TJ had to put his phobia aside. The main thing, Deane was safe. That was all that mattered. Jake needed his help, they needed to find Elena--make a trade, get the info out there. Not likely to happen here and he wanted to get away from here, the sooner the better. The best thing would be if they turned themselves in and used Gonzalez and the files as bargaining chips. Except, he knew, there was no way Jake would agree.

Okay, he told himself, get your mind back in the game. He took a mental deep breath.

"Any trade has to take place in a public place. There's several problems with that. One, these bangers never goina agree; two, let's say they did, no way any of us goina walk out of any exchange alive. And three, think about it, we're wanted, they ain't the only ones lookin' for us, getting in or out of a public place becomes way too problematic. Be best we work a deal with the authorities, turn our ass in at the same time the bangers show for the exchange."

"We've been in worse situations."

"Convincing Arturo, getting' law enforcement to cooperate, requires time, time we don't have. Need a better place than here, one with reliable communication, quiet, private, goina take some persuading to convince our guest and his brother it's in his brother's best interests to make the trade. Be better to let a professional negotiator do this…my commander, Hardy, our attorney, someone like that." TJ walked to the refrigerator, got the rest of the beers out, walked back and set them on the counter.

"No thanks. Only make me more depressed."

"These ain't for us. We need to get done with It in there, go where we can get reception. And, unless you've got some drugs that will make our guest compliant without killing him, this all we got. Don't have time for the tire thing, too risky, some boater might see us.'

"You think he'll drink those?"

"One way or another. Yeah, he will."

Jake walked over to the laptop. "The Wi-Fi is back. Let me do a quick search for Ariel first." He began a search for a Columbia news person named Ariel Harper, the last name he knew her by.

TJ looked over his shoulder, watching. "Don't send her an email, call her."

TJ straightened up, turned and walked around through the den to the bath to check on Gonzalez. He looked asleep, or was he pretending? He went back to the kitchen.

Jake waited on TJ to return. "Signal's liable to drop again. If I can get through, my hope is she'll recognize my voice. Not sure which number to call, the numbers listed are for departments at the station." He was staring at the web site. The connection signal broke. You are no longer connected prompt appeared. Damn. Good thing the info remained.

"You reckon anyone would answer any of these lines? After all it is after ten."

"There has to be a hotline. The news crew will be there getting ready for the late newscast. They wouldn't want to miss out on a big late breaking story." TJ looked over his shoulder. No hotline. "Try the news team number."

CHAPTER
27

The laptop Wi-Fi power indicator showed between one and two bars. Jake punched in the number. It rang and rang, went to a recording. He was in luck, there was a menu for personnel. He punched in 12 for Ariel Gaspard.

"Ariel, in case you don't recognize the voice. Been a long time, this is Jake. Hopefully, you haven't forgotten…"

He was cut off by a voice, sounded not exactly southern, a foreign-to-his memory-sounding edge, somewhat familiar, answered--"Hello Jake." She paused. "How could I forget you? Forgiving you, well…. Anyway. I can't talk now. I'm getting ready to record my spot for tonight's broadcast. Unless you're wanting me to do a quick announcement concerning your contacting me. You're one of the big stories as I'm sure you're aware."

Not what he wished to hear. What exactly did he expect?

"Thanks, but no. No announcement. Not tonight. The phone service sucks so I may lose you. I'm willing to meet, give you an exclusive. We can discuss the details, the when and where later. Here's the number. He gave her the number for a burner phone. "Don't tell anyone you talked to me, okay? I've got to go."

"Wait Jake. You got something to write with? Here is my personal number. Call me." she recited the number and he repeated it back. The signal began to drop. "… me…a couple hours…set…up."

"Losing you." Gone. No signal.

He turned to TJ. "She sure didn't sound like the girl I once knew. Different, more mature, very feminine, with an accent. Reminds me of Cajun, kinda South Carolina low country, something like that, but more sophisticated." He went to the den and found a pen. He wrote her number on his wrist. He entered the number in the burner TJ had given him.

"Don't get carried away. You're married, remember?"

"Of course. It's confirmed she's in the news business. Got to figure out how we can meet with her, not here, I have a place in mind, but first, back to business at hand, we need to know what our friend in there knows about Elena and Maisy, hate to leave here without knowing everything he knows that might help. I say we do what you suggested, see if getting him drunk will loosen his tongue?"

Jake got up and walked over and reached up to the cabinet over top of the refrigerator and pulled out a nearly full liter bottle of tequila. "Forget the beer. Might want those for us later. This'll work faster. And he is Mexican."

"Some would call that racial profiling. Hold up a minute, I need to step outside, try Deane again. I should have heard something before now."

While TJ was outside, Jake stared at the computer screen, willing it to work. The signal returned. He rejoined his search, went to the station's broadcast news, hoping to see Ariel. He waited and watched, thinking should he trust her not to report his call, the way his relationships had gone lately, he felt the 'trust but verify' mantra was best.

The lead off story flashed Jake's, TJ's, Deane's and Elena's pictures with a brief damning interview with the York County Sheriff and DA. They were at his farm. The place was crawling with law enforcement officers, local, SLED, FBI, and Homeland Security, surrounding the Sheriff and DA. Standing nearby, his old buddy, Homeland's Bob Hardy. Why would Hardy and HS be there?

Ariel came on near the end of the news segment. Damn she did look and sound great. Wasn't reporting about them, she was doing a follow-up piece on the Charleston Confederate Monument removal and the on-going Black Lives Matter, the Floyd and Brown killings' protests in the city and across the state.

The filming took place at Middleton Plantation, one of the earliest settlements in America. Ancestors, black, white, and mixed race and religion, descendants of the original settlers, who met yearly were interviewed. They had put aside their differences, united, forming a cohesive bond. Politics be damned. They refused to let the monument, the police shootings or other racial and political issues divide them.

Jake agreed. This was the Twenty First Century. You would think, like these descendants, mankind could look beyond petty racial and tribal issues. Tackle the major ones which threatened all mankind--global warming, etc.

They went to commercials. The signal dropped once more.

Ariel. Damn, he couldn't believe it. Should he get back in touch? He doubted she would appreciate his sentiments about her chosen profession. He would have to try not to sound critical, abstain from negative remarks when he saw her. If he saw her.

He and TJ needed to find a place for the possibility of an interview. Had to be secure, had to be defensible if push came to shove. Where to go? Somewhere in the direction of Tindal's property, close, not too close Jake felt certain Elena was probably somewhere on Tindal's property. He hoped it was not voluntarily. He didn't see her being complicit in framing him and TJ. Deane said something about blood being found in her car. Was Elena hurt? Had they killed her accidently or deliberately? Would whoever was involved go that far? "God don't let this be," he prayed.

TJ came back inside. "She finally got in touch with Henderson. Just as we figured, he told her to tell us to turn ourselves in."

Jake told him about the news report.

"They were at my house out by the drive. Every local, state, and federal agency had people there. Homeland's Bob Hardy was there. Why would he be there? I thought Homeland dealt mainly with threats to national security? What threat do we pose? I don't get it."

"You sure Hardy was there?"

"Hell yes. I saw him. Why would he be there?"

"You were friends. We haven't done anything that should be considered a national security threat. Did he say anything or did the reporter indicate anything about national security?"

"No and no. I don't think Hardy was there because of me." Jake had been watching TJ as they spoke. His eyes flicked left when he said Hardy's name. "TJ, we've known each other a long time, well enough to tell when we aren't being totally up front with each other. You know something about why Hardy is there. I would bet on it. Whatever it is you better tell me. This shit we're in means we need to be on the up and up with each other. What is it that you aren't saying my man?"

TJ motioned Jake to follow him outside. He wasn't about to tell Jake he left a message on Hardy's office machine saying he and Jake had nothing to do with

Elena's disappearance, that he had uncovered information that would bust the investigation wide open.

Once they were out on the deck, he went to the rail, looked out toward the river. Peaceful, chilly wind gusts, not cold, a taste of rain in the air. Sounds of a couple boats, a car crossing the bridge, frogs croaking, wind-caused ripple-splashes against the trailer and dock, the lights from the marina and distant cabins strobing across the water surface. A lone dog bark came from a cabin on their side. TJ listened, no alarming cadence to the bark. He glanced at Jake who joined him.

"Well?"

"Hate being paranoid. There's people, both sides of the law, good as our friend in there when it comes to hacking. Reports about smart devices, your cell phone, tv, etc. being hackable. absolute, a fact. By now, law enforcement people working the case will have figured out there was a computer missing from all that stuff we left. More likely than not, something was left behind, identifies that laptop. Simple matter of time, they'll tap into the laptop. That laptop makes tracing our location possible."

"What's that got to do with Hardy?"

"Those were foreign nationals back there. Members of a Mexican Cartel I've been working undercover to investigate. The task force is Homeland, ICE, the FBI as well as Metro Charlotte and other local law enforcement in the Carolinas and elsewhere. A continued effort, Operation Pink Flamingo, the op you were involved with. The only thing that ended was your involvement."

"Hold on. I was laid off, then dismissed. Hardy reinstated me to help in Cuba, almost got me killed, never paid me what he promised, no contact when I went back to the Bahamas, not a word. Comes to my wedding—at Elena's behest--there and gone. Don't give me this bullshit about ending my involvement. Not true then. Not true now. They owe me, I don't owe them shit."

"Okay. If you say so bro. Doesn't really matter. Want to hear me out or not?"

"Just don't ever throw Hardy's bullshit at me."

"Hey. That's between you and Hardy."

"Got that right. Go ahead, tell me about you and Hardy. How is it you never told me you were still involved with Operation Pink Flamingo?"

"Op stalled--political bullshit. As for me, just one of the few SWAT undercover agents working with the task force. Okay? That's the Homeland involvement."

"Our worry, by now, Hardy'll have decided, we've committed a felony crime. The press'll be all over this, Hardy's there trying to control the situation, because of your former involvement, you, Elena, me and Deane missing, my ongoing involvement. Satisfied?

"For now. I have to think about it. Where does this leave us?"

"Need to find out if Gonzalez knows where Elena is. Then get the hell out of here. For all we know, law enforcement or his fellow bangers have tracked us, could be getting close. Need to go dark, as soon as possible."

"Do you know where his brother lives? Did David and Arturo live in the house in NoDa?"

"Sometimes. Both moved around, stay with various other members of their gang, sometimes hotels, flea bag joints in high crime areas. Usually, they stay in separate places, occasionally together. David spends more time in that garage workshop, often crashing there. Why?"

"While you were talking to Deane, I was thinking where would they have taken Elena? My conclusion was Tindal's place. It's in a remote area with heavy security and the authorities would never think to look there. If Arturo had her, someone would have to always guard her. That is risky for a lot of reasons. I believe he would want every member of his group looking for David. What do you think?"

"Can't see Tindal risking everything getting involved in a kidnapping. Too smart, too much to lose. If Elena's there, safe bet he knows nothing about it. That's a large place, be easy someone put her somewhere without his knowledge. But for lack of options, good place as any to start. Have to be careful, your place is close, be covered in law enforcement. Plus, Arturo's looking for David. For now, he's our only bargaining chip. Can't afford to lose him."

"Could be he has Elena at Tindal's place."

"Like I said, not likely. We talking Latin Kings, Juarez Cartel, networks, she could be anywhere by now. Maybe our guest can enlighten us? Need to finish and get the hell out of here."

CHAPTER
28

They closed the bathroom door, walked over and stood next to the tub looking down at David. He lay motionless, his hands covered his sexual parts. He refused to open his eyes, wouldn't look up.

TJ switched the shower on. The cold water made him jerk, one hand flew to cover his face, his eyes flew open, his curses echoed inside the small space.

"Beginning to think you were asleep," TJ said. "Have something to reward you for your cooperation." Jake waved the tequila bottle over his head, down in front of his eyes. "You do like tequila, don't you? Jake here thinks all Hispanics like tequila. Personally, I prefer beer. Jake help me sit him up so he can more easily enjoy his drink."

They reached down to lift him up. TJ grabbed the upper arm, Jake pulled the other arm away from David's crotch, handed it to TJ. They zip-locked them together. With his other hand, TJ grabbed a handful of hair and yanked his head back.

"I kill you," Gonzalez said with a grimace. "My brother, he be here soon. He kill you." He shook his head from side to side when Jake tried to put the bottle to his lips.

Jake poured some of the tequila on his cut abdomen. Gonzalez let out a shriek and thrust his body up, arching his pelvis pushing his sexual organs into view. The blood had begun to dry. The tequila made darker red streaks run across his stomach and down toward his crotch into the tub, mixing with the yellowish urine in the water.

"Take a big swallow and we'll put some ointment on that cut and let you get dressed," Jake said. "How does that sound?" Jake once more pushed the bottle toward his lips. "It will help with the pain while I doctor that cut. Wouldn't want it to get infected, got plans for you."

"You lie. You take password, say you let me go. You lie. You soon see I no lie 'bout brother. He be here soon. I treat wound while watch you die."

"No. You no understand. Drink or we make you drink. Understand?" TJ said mockingly. "We no afraid of your brother, long as we have you, he not do anything. Comprende? Now what's it to be, you drink, we treat that scratch, let you get dressed. Or we pour tequila down your throat, hope you don't drown in it. Does not matter to us."

Gonzalez shook his head no. TJ let go of his hands. Jake took them in one hand and clenched the bottle in the other. TJ pulled Gonzalez' head back, took his freed hand pinched David's jaw, forcing his mouth open. Jake started pouring the tequila. Gonzalez body bucked, twisted and the tequila splashed out of his mouth as he spluttered and choked. Jake waited until he stopped. TJ signaled with a nod. Jake then pushed the lip of the bottle over the top of his tongue and poured more slowly. Gonzalez gagged and wretched but was forced by TJ's clamping his lips onto the bottle to swallow more of the liquid. He continued bucking and tears ran out of his wide-open eyes.

When over half the bottle had been forced down Gonzalez throat, Jake stopped and they stepped back in case he got sick. Gonzalez closed his eyes rolled over onto his side and moaned. TJ motioned to Jake and they went back to the kitchen.

"Need to let the alcohol do its thing, Might throw it back up. Won't make a damn, still be in his system. If have to, use the threat of more. Eventually, he'll talk. Meantime, need to get loaded up, ready to go. Might want to think 'bout where we can go, somewhere more isolated."

"Already have, Sumter National Forest. Upper end is over half-way back toward my house and Tindal's property. There is a park—doubtful any people will be there--not this time of year and not with the covid shutdowns. There used to be a ranger station, Park Service closed it due to budget cuts. And they've been closing the park around this time of year. There are campsites with small corrals for horses, bathroom facilities and cook pits. Plus, and a bonus for us, there is a fire tower that is no longer used. We can use it to keep an eye out for anyone that comes into the area. It would give us a strategic highpoint with cell coverage also. A good place to have Ariel come and we could watch to make sure no one follows her. Sure would be nice to have the pontoon, but that would mean having a trailer hitch and it would take time to go back for your truck. I don't recall the van having one. Need to go check to see if it does."

Jake went out on the deck and down the steps. They were in partial luck. The van had the mounting hardware but no hitch. He went to the under-cabin storage and rummaged around inside. Voila! Jake found a sliding hitch with four balls attached and a locking pin. About time something went their way. He took it out and slid it into place and used the lock pin to secure it. Now if their good fortune continued and Gonzalez could tell them where Elena was held hostage. He went back up the steps to tell TJ about their good luck.

TJ was in the bathroom questioning the drunken Gonzalez who apparently was not being cooperative. TJ had the tequila bottle in his hand waving it in front of Gonzalez as an inducement.

"I know no Mark Pavbitch." Jake heard him slurring the answer as he came back into the bathroom.

"Guess you want more. Jake the tequila doesn't seem to be helping our friend here to remember answers to our questions. Very impolite. What say we take him out to the lake and put one of those tubes with the catfish and snakes around his waist?"

TJ reached down and pulled his Ka-Bar out of its sheath and waved it at Gonzalez. Time to play the Jake gambit.

"Guess we goina have to open you up further, give the snakes easier access to your guts?" TJ touched the tip to Gonzalez stomach and his prone body recoiled pulling his knees in tighter against TJ's hand with the knife. "Might need to help me with this Jake. Our guest not being very cooperative."

Gonzalez started screaming. Jake retrieved the mask off the tile floor and went over beside TJ. Gonzalez saw the mask and began screaming Spanish words and TJ held up his hand stopping Jake.

"Say again. This Mark man, works for bank, supposed to do what?"

Gonzalez started talking in slurred Spanish telling TJ answers that Jake translated in bits and pieces. TJ repeated in English which made Jake feel better.

"Said Mark have money ready, pay man called Jenkins for drone Arturo call Hive." TJ asked about Elena, he admitted having tracked her car along with Jake's truck, said had problems tracking TJ's truck. "He swears he does not know 'bout Elena."

TJ thought he was telling the truth.

"We need to get out of here. Any luck with a hitch?"

"Yeah. What are we going to do about him? You think we ought to let him get dressed? It is getting kind of cold outside. Feels like a rainstorm is coming."

"Let me handle him. Load our other stuff in the van, we'll load him after he puts his filthy clothes back on. Need spray everything, cover the piss and shit smell coming from his clothes? Might want to spray some in the tub and van. Make it little more tolerable."

Jake opened the cabinet under the sink and brought out a can of Lysol and a bottle of bathroom cleaner. He laid the can of spray on the sink top, grabbed the toilet scrub brush and the bathroom cleaner bottle, and went to the kitchen and began repacking the items they had brought in earlier.

They loaded everything in the van, including Gonzalez wrapped in an old, tattered blanket and plastic tarp, and hooked up the trailer with the pontoon on it. Jake checked to make sure everything was off, then flipped the main breaker. They pulled out going the opposite way from how they originally came to the cabin, this way eliminated going by the store and restaurant. As far as he knew none of the businesses would be open, but there could be fishermen coming or going.

It started to rain. He hoped the wipers worked.

CHAPTER
29

Driving down the road they didn't say much. Jake tuned the radio to 88.7FM, a PBS station out of Spindale, N. C., played commercial free country, blues and bluegrass. Also gave newsbreaks for the area and nationally. Vince Gill singing the Eagle's *Lyin' Eyes* was playing, helped Jake relax, reminded him of the early times when he and Ariel started realizing their physical attraction for each other. TJ had interrupted, telling him what didn't need to be said, "keep your eyes peeled for any law enforcement, or suspicious vehicles or motorcycles that could belong to the bangers."

The rain had stopped. Jake circled through the lot where they left TJ's truck earlier and dropped him off beside the other truck that had been there before. TJ retrieved his truck and followed him. He turned the radio volume up.

Highway 97 carried them back over the Catawba River. Twenty miles further they came to the outskirts of Chester where he took bypass Highway 9 then Highway 9 toward Lockhart. Nine miles later he turned left onto Roy Wade Road, veering right onto Worthy's Ferry Road. Five miles later he turned onto Leeds Landing Road. He lowered the van's windows, enjoyed the fresh air, Gonzalez stink was getting the best of him. He hoped the chill would bring him out of the drowsy state the nostalgic music had brought on.

The road wound downhill to the Broad River. Jake loved to come here. The trip down the road reminded him of being in the mountains. The terrain dropped off sharply on one side then the other. Olden hardwood trees the only obstacles that could stop your descent if you were to go off the road. Jake and Elena had noticed wooden sleuth-like boxes all along the hillsides, made them think the early settlers had built them, or some like them,from for water channels, maybe for mining gold and minerals. There were many chimneys, old hand-dug wells and graveyards throughout the surrounding woods, remnants when Worthy's Ferry and Wood's Ferry, up the river a ways, had been the only way to ford the river, later replaced by the railroad and bridges for vehicular crossing.

At the bottom of the drive, the road split. A single bar metal gate ended their progress. On the other side of the gate was a wooden kiosk with park information. Four wheelers had made a trail around the gate. He hoped no maverick kids or hunters were around. Beyond this point was the public area with he bath houses, picnic tables, raised metal barbeque grills, a boat landing, and benches along the upper bank of the river.

Jake switched the radio off, got out of the van and checked the lock on the gate, locked, meaning no one else was here. He debated whether to take a chance on driving the van with the trailered pontoon boat around on the muddy trail. TJ stepped down from his truck and joined him.

"Beginning to think you lost."

"This is one of mine and Elena's daytrip places. Occasionally, Elena and I would bring the dogs here on warm days. Those days are probably history for us and our dogs."

"Some friends and I used to take the Turkey Creek canoe trail down to the Broad from below the farm and take out here. I was debating driving the van around the gate. Looks kind of muddy and I don't have four-wheel drive."

"We could hitch it to my truck. Where's that fire tower you talked 'bout? And the bathrooms?"

"The bathrooms are not far. Down by the river. The fire tower is up near the entrance. I thought we could put the boat in and tie it to a tree. Take your truck up to the road that branched off half-way down here as another potential escape vehicle. Then take the van up to the fire tower and get some sleep. I should have already called Ariel. Guess it'll have to wait until morning."

"Later in the morning bro. It's already almost one."

Jake shivered. "Glad I brought my sleeping bag. You okay with my plan?"

"Sounds a little overdone. Hate having my truck where can't see it and get to it. Much of our gear we'll need's in it, on the chance they do find us out here. Ever see any law enforcement or rangers? Our luck another game warden will show."

"Nah man. The ranger station is down the road I suggested you park your truck on. I believe I told you it has been closed for several years. They use it as a maintenance equipment place. Never seen any other law enforcement people. Nearest sheriff's office is back in Chester. Doubt they can afford any patrols out this way. I just hope there are no kids or hunters here on their four-wheelers. However, you're right, our luck has been poor, I'm hoping we've hit bottom and we're on the uphill swing."

"Come on let's get the pontoon in the water. We'll leave the van, put Gonzalez in the back of my truck. Even though he smells like Lysol-scented shit."

Back at the tower, Jake discovered someone had removed the bottom set of steps and put a metal grate with a hasp and lock ten feet up on the fire tower. Jake was almost too tired to climb the framework and walk the guidewires over to the grate, but he did. Another adventurous soul had done the same thing and had cut the hasp on the lock where it entered the base of the lock. From below the lock would have looked untouched. The bottom set of steps had been put on a track that allowed them to slide up and down. They were held in place by a chain that fit into a notch on each side. Jake yelled down to TJ to stand back. He was standing down on the ground shining a flashlight up for Jake to be able to see where to go and what could be done. Jake used the chain as a brake and lowered the steps part way then let go. They sailed down and hit the concrete landing pad with a clang sending pieces of aged concrete outward like shrapnel. One or two hit TJ's truck and he squawked an obscenity.

Jake went down, apologized to TJ, grabbed his weapon bag and backpack then climbed to the top to check for any varmints that may have made the tower their home. He was worn out. The physical and mental weight of the last few days had taken their toll. Reminded him of his days overseas in the combat zones. He had been a little younger then and the adrenaline punch of weapon fire had taken the edge off. How did TJ do it? SWAT team and undercover duty must be like this every day.

He forced himself to go back down. Halfway he met TJ who handed him his gear telling Jake he would go down to get Gonzalez. Jake told him to wait while he took his gear up and he would come back down to help him. TJ went back down without another word. Once more Jake was partway down, and TJ told him to move. Jake leaned way out and away. TJ, Gonzalez wrapped in a blanket and thrown over his shoulder, nudged past, climbed on up.

They laid out their sleeping bags and laid Gonzalez out on the blanket far away from their bags as possible, covering his shivering form with another blanket. Before carrying him up, TJ had put some looser zip ties on him, allowed him to piss. TJ regagged him despite Gonzalez' pleas and curses.

Jake tossed and turned all night. He could not get comfortable. His neck had stiffened. At the sign of first light, he crawled out of his warm sleeping bag, donned his jacket he had used as a pillow and went to the first platform, took a much-needed piss. He came back up and stood looking in the direction of the river. The same night sounds, whippoorwills, and other night creatures he listened to at the farm gave their final odes to the darkness. Way off in the distance he could hear a boat upriver and a vehicle moving away not far in the direction they had come no more than five hours before. Gonzalez was making a muffled snore. He looked over at TJ a few feet away. He was staring back at Jake.

"Hope I didn't wake you," Jake said quietly.

"Been awake. Forgot how uncomfortable not sleeping on a mattress was." He sat up and twisted his body back and forth, side to side. "Hate the thought of having to get up to relieve myself, but this my usual morning piss time." TJ unzipped his bag and stood, walked down to where Jake had gone and let it flow accompanied by a loud fart. "Damn that felt good," he remarked when he came back up. He pulled a thermos out of his bag, poured some in the cap cup and took a swallow making a face. "Care for some less than warm coffee?"

Jake declined. He pulled out a reuseable water bottle that he had filled with green tea and some granola bars, offering one to TJ. TJ had some nutrition bars of his own and a wedge of cheese with apple slices. Jake heard Gonzalez stirring and looked over to see him watching them. Jake knew Gonzalez had not eaten anything since they grabbed him the day before and the only drink had been a little water and the tequila. He put his water bottle on the platform rail where he had been leaning while he snacked, reached into his pack pulled out another water bottle and two packs of cheese crackers sandwiched with peanut butter, walked over removed the gag, pulled out his Ka-Bar and cut his hands loose.

"Here," he said handing him the crackers and water. "Pretty high up, unless you have a death wish would advise you not try anything. He reached down and cut the zip tie on his feet also. "Have to wait to piss until we're ready to go down."

Gonzalez took the crackers in trembling hands, ripped the pack open with his teeth, pulled the top blanket around his shoulders, and began guzzling the water and stuffing the crackers into his mouth.

Jake watched and said, "Better go easy on the water. Once that's gone, you'll be back drinking tequila." Jake and TJ laughed. Gonzalez stared.

When they had finished, TJ escorted Gonzalez down to the platform and waited while he pissed. He was having a difficult time and asked TJ to let him go to the ground.

TJ asked, "Need to squat to piss, that it? Go ahead, you can piss through the grate, ain't nobody here goina give a damn."

After what seemed way longer than most people, Gonzalez finished and buttoned up his pants. "Why you hate on me?" He asked TJ when they reached the tower deck once more.

"Damn. Let's see. You come into my country and break every law that any decent person respects. You run with a gang of other outlaws who thumb their nose at our system and get away with way too many crimes. The worst happens you git caught, you git deported, rejoin your cartel and do it all over again."

"Yesterday, you made it personal with your threats to kill us and our families. You are a foreign terrorist and deserve the same thing from good ole USA as any other terrorist. Fortunately for you, you're still alive. Depending on what happens, you may live to join others like you in a max somewhere, maybe even Gitmo."

"Oh, by the way, care to say how it is you and your brother track each other?"

"He find me. You pay."

"Bring it on. Been threatened by badder fucks than you. What do you think bro, do these fucks deserve a ranking?" TJ looked over at Jake who had come down to join them.

"Not even close," Jake replied.

"My brother have your woman. Hope she dead."

Jake walked over and looked down at Gonzalez. "I wouldn't push my luck if I were you. Maybe we need to regag you. I think maybe cut your tongue out."

Gonzalez grinned and didn't reply.

Jake looked at the time displayed on the cell phone, seven o'clock. "I'm going to try my friend. Probably shouldn't have shit for brains listening in," he said to TJ.

"Stand up you piece of shit." TJ reached down and yanked him to his feet, zip tied his hands while Jake tied his feet. TJ plopped the blanket-wrapped Gonzalez in the bed of his truck and told him to either shut up or he would put the gag back in.

Jake walked over to the truck tailgate and handed TJ his sleeping bag and placed his own on the tailgate next to Gonzalez and began rolling it up. TJ followed suit. The sun was peeking through the trees taking the edge off the morning chill.

"Thought you going to make a call?"

"Before I call, I need to know if there is anything more you thought of that we need her to bring?"

"Clothes for It. Hey you," TJ said nudging Gonzalez, "what about some more clothes, what size you wear?" Gonzalez did not reply. "Maybe we should get some baggy dresses?" He said with a grin glancing over at Jake. "What color dress you like?" He asked poking Gonzalez harder. Turning back to Jake when Gonzalez didn't answer. "Guess you going to have to tell her to get something to fit someone about five feet six, one hundred forty pounds, maybe a lined jacket and a cheap sleeping bag."

"What about food or groceries? I could go for a baked chicken, potato salad and green beans. Grocery wise, I figured apples, bananas, dried fruit, tomatoes, avocadoes, cheeses, nuts, precooked bacon, saltine and other cheese flavored crackers and a large container of Gatorade, salt, and hot sauce," Jake said as he wrote. "Anything else you can think of?"

"Think she's going to be okay with this bro? Most people have a problem being asked to do this kind of favor."

"Why? We're about to give her an exclusive. Unless she has changed, the Ariel I knew would be willing to do this."

"For you? You two must've been more than kissing cousins?" TJ looked at Jake arching his eyebrows.

"Come on man. Okay? We have no way to get this stuff otherwise. Maybe we call Amazon and have their service drop it off." Jake replied with a smirk. "Like I said, if she wants the scoop, she'll do it. I guarantee you any other news person would jump right on this. At least with Ariel, she'll keep it to herself."

"She better. One slip-up, we fucked."

"I need to call. You got any requests?"

TJ looked toward his pack. "Got nutrition bars, MRIs. Got those two five-gallon bottles of water you brought. Food wise, prefer a burger and fries, but to avoid asking her to make a separate stop, we can share a whole chicken with our guest. Ask her bring a double helpin' mash potatoes, no, make it triple, lots of green beans. A jug or two green tea with ginseng and honey, drinking cup or two. Coffee, brought my small percolator, along with my mess kits." TJ rubbed his unshaven, bristly chin trying to think of anything else. "Soap, four, five towels, wash cloths, disinfectant wipes and a bag of toilet paper."

"Tell her use cash only. Eventually someone is going to check on her. Especially after she airs the interview. Tell her rent a vehicle, and again," he emphasized, "pay cash, gotta be rental place like Rent-a-Wreck since the major rentals won't accept cash. Need to come alone, no cameras, voice recorder only. Tell her leave her cell behind, get throw-away, burner phones so they can't track or trace her movements."

Jake looked at TJ, "soap, towels, wash cloths, toilet paper and disinfectant wipes? Would have never thought you were the type. Old rugged, Mr. Independent, off in the bush, macho dude like you."

"Been civilized. You should try it. Might give you a whole new perspective."

CHAPTER
3o

Elena was not able to control the panic attacks. She was being held in a luxury prison, but that did not make the feeling any more palliative. Could this be a hotel? Was it possible there were other guests? Where was she? Could they have taken her across the border? The same questions drummed in her head over and over. She paced back and forth from one corner to the next, Maisy following or watching probably wondering why she couldn't go out as she usually did-- meaning she was having to do her business in the room and Elena was having to clean up afterwards. The room smelled more disinfected than a hospital. Who was responsible, why, and what would be the outcome? The why seemed to be because of something Jake had done. Was he right about Thurmond Tindal? She couldn't put together the man she met, all his wealth, doing something like this. The Latino bitch? There had been Mexicans working on Tindal's property. And this luxurious prison, no Latino person in this area, that she knew, some in California and Texas but not here, had anything like this. Her father was friends with Tindal. Thinking about her father, his cancer, knowing he would not go for treatment once he heard she was missing upset her. Did he know?

And Jake, she had seen the broadcast. Someone had turned on the television, startled her. Who and how did they do that? On the tv was the DA, sheriff, and other law enforcement people. She recognized Bob Hardy, he had been at their wedding. She didn't know he was with Homeland Security. It was in English, not Spanish. America? Had to be.

She learned Jake and TJ were being blamed for her disappearance. A reporter said authorities found blood on the driver's side of her car. Elena had found no cuts. She had checked herself when she took her clothes off before taking her first shower. Nothing. She wanted to scream at the television, "I'm alive. Somebody find me. Please!" The sheriff said Deane was missing and had called in sick. No one had heard from her since. Nor had the authorities been able to get in touch with her husband, Thomas J. Alvarez. The authorities did not know if SWAT Team Officer Alvarez and his wife were victims, or if Officer Alvarez and Mr. Harper were involved in a domestic terror plot. He posited the theory that Jake Harper had gone on a rampage triggered by his dog being shot in a tragic accident. He went on to say that his wife had told family members she feared Jake suffered from PTSD because of his being severely injured. "He suffered this injury as the result of an IED attack while he was in the Army on a training mission in the Philippines." The reporter gave a quick bio for Jake and TJ. An All-Out Bulletin was issued declaring Jake, perhaps Mr. Alvarez, to be armed and dangerous. Anyone who knew of their whereabouts should call 911 immediately.

If she had listened to Jake and TJ, maybe none of this would be happening.

Jake *was* at fault. He shouldn't have provoked that game warden.

She had to get away from the madness. Jake and the farm. Why wouldn't he sell it? Thurmond Tindal would pay more than it was worth. They could move to Louisiana or Texas, be near their children, her family, and friends. Was it because of his children? They had little to do with him. Holding onto the farm made no sense. His kids weren't interested in the farm. They hated coming to visit. Since their marriage, his kids had not been back.

Who was he going to leave the place to? He never gave a definitive answer when asked. He said maybe he would put it into a trust or leave it to a charitable foundation as a camp for disadvantaged children or for therapy for disabled vets.

None of that to benefit her. He knew she wouldn't stay there if anything happened to him. Why not sell? They could do what they talked about doing, get a small house near their children and travel. No. Not yet he kept saying. Then he said travelling was no longer an option because of the pandemic. Consistently, he was adamant, "never would he sell to Thurmond Tindal."

He didn't care how she felt. Their marriage was a mistake. Thinking about Jennifer's dad Tim, made her juices flow. The love making, her orgasm the other morning which Jake wondered about, the whole time she had been thinking about Tim. It was that memory that had stayed with her while she was out for her morning run. Then Dusty. Oh God. She didn't see any way to get beyond this. If Dusty died? That would be the end of any possible reconciliation. She wasn't sure she wanted one.

None of that mattered, she was imprisoned. Where, by whom? Pacing back and forth, she looked up at the camera and yelled, "please somebody talk to me. Tell me what you want."

CHAPTER
31

Bud Jenkins sat in his office putting together the speech Colonel Tindal would be giving at the upcoming York County Fall Festival. He was none too enthusiastic about the endeavor. Knowing Tindal, he would rewrite the speech, most of what was being scripted by him, not included. He had more important matters to attend to. He watched the DA and Sheriff on the network television broadcast state the Harper man and his friend Thomas Jefferson Alvarez were fugitives. No surprise since Tindal insisted on their due diligence.

The news person's interview with the FBI spokesperson who announced the capture of several gang members, locked in a moving van in Charlotte caught his attention. The Hispanic security employees said Arturo would be calling him.

He hoped Arturo had good news. He waited, watched the Harper woman. Had she discovered the monitors? She didn't change clothes in the bedroom. The miniature video hidden in the bathroom vanity light was enough. He had recorded videos. Watched them over and over, when he had time, which had been less than he wished. The video snapshots showed her beautiful body, posed as if for a magazine.

He was looking forward to what the camera in the shower captured--watch her scrubbing herself--imagining his hands and tongue doing to her what her hands would be doing while she bathed.

Back and forth, she went, followed by the mutt, paced. She shouted a plea, looking up to the spy cam. Apparently, she did know it was there. He wanted to go to her, offer his help. In exchange for what? Would she really give herself to him? Would she consider escaping with him, join him to enjoy his soon to be wealth? Had letting her see her husband and his friend on the news helped or hurt his cause?

A decision would have to be made about her fate. He was certain Arturo would be discussing this with him. Arturo may insist on a trade for his brother.

Bud hoped Arturo's brother David had been killed or would be killed along with the now notorious Harper and Alvarez men. That would eliminate any possibility of their capture by the authorities. David coerced, talking, jeopardizing his plans was not an option as far as he was concerned. He was too close. The bids were coming in. He needed to ensure David never talked.

Mark Poponovich, as he called himself, had made a generous offer regarding the Gonzalez brothers' assets. David Gonzalez said he ran a background check on Mark for the cartel and his story had passed their smell test. On this, he decided to trust David's assessment. David had been the go between. Dealing with Paponovich without David had its risks. With David out of touch, he felt he should keep the cartel option open, so he reached out and Mark contacted him directly. To his surprise, Poponovich suggested cutting the Mexicans out completely, He was suspicious, but played along without commitment, thinking this was a card in the hole he could use in his game with the cartel, or, the government, if things went to hell.

Using other sources, even before David vouched for him, he ran his own check. Mark Paponovich was a ghost, tracing his history had proven impossible. The threads did not make whole cloth. Either the guy was very good at covering his tracks, or his story was a fabrication. Claiming to be from the Baltics was an unprovable fact, a strategic move by Mark. Even the Russian Okneyev could not verify his bonafides. At least he claimed not to have, even though he had had Poponovich where he could question him. Had Okneyev learned something? Was that why he left him to die on his freighter that exploded and sank? The authorities were after Okneyev. He had gone dark. Not knowing who Poponovich was concerned Bud, made him extremely wary. Was Mark a mole? If so for whom? The best way to do this was to wait until his plans were finalized and burn Mark Poponovich or whoever he was.

Thurmond Tindal buzzed. He sounded unusually ebullient, summoned Bud to his office. Could be something good Tindal wanted to share, or it could be he found something on Bud, was waiting to show how clever his discovery.

When he entered the office, Tindal sprang up out of his chair, told Bud to take a seat.

"I guess you saw the DA and Sheriff on the news yesterday?" Tindal didn't wait for him to answer. "Looks like Harper will have no choice regarding his land. Surprising that the Alvarez man would disappear. Looks like Harper may have done something terrible to his wife, perhaps to his friend. That is tragic. I talked to the Harper woman's father. Told Sam to let us know if there was anything he wanted us to do. He indicated he would be heading this way and I invited him to stay here."

"The reason I asked you to come up here was to tell you the news in person. Colonel Baker sent word. DoD has approved our contract for The Hive with the contingency that we be able to provide them ten units within a year. The contract calls for five hundred units within five years. It will take three years to build that manufacturing facility across the river, which means we won't have to rely on outside manufacturers after we are up and running."

"I also heard from Southeast Petroleum. They have placed an order for an additional ten units. If I obtain the Harper land, which seems very likely, they have agreed to run the western branch of their pipeline across my land."

"You helped make all of this possible, probably would not have happened without you. For that reason, I have decided to make you a Senior Vice President, as well as COO, with a starting salary of two hundred thousand, plus stock options and incentive bonuses. How does that sound?"

Tindal was rattling on like he was hyped up on something. Bud had often thought Tindal was manic depressive. He always seemed to be up or down. Bud had learned to play along with his moods. He acted like this was great news, thanking him effusively and promising to show him he would do everything in his power to keep the good times rolling. Bud was thinking, 'you pompous asshole, you're right, none of this would have happened without my coercion, some would call blackmail, provided by the videos. *I* made them think they were in your possession. *I* helped make you richer, where is the gratitude, a pittance compared to what you stand to make and there would always be the threat of having it taken away. No thank you. I'll get mine, my own way.'

Bud stood to leave telling Tindal he needed to get back to the speech. He told him he would need to revise it because of the good news. Tindal said he was looking forward to seeing the speech. Then it was back to the old Tindal he knew and had come to hate. Tindal told him to make sure everything was ready for the Festival and to go over every detail with the techs as many times as necessary to make sure there would be no problems. As the new Senior Vice

President, COO of Tindal Industries this was his duty, how he could earn the bonuses. Always the carrot and the stick. Not much longer.

CHAPTER
32

Shortly after he returned to his office, Arturo Gonzalez called.

"My men tell me you wish me call you. Why you not call me?"

"Not the way it happened. Those men said you would call me. Been waiting."

"We bring Harper woman to you then David he disappear. He have GPS chip. This will help you find him. I need you to help find brother."

"Everyone is trying to find the Harper and Alvarez men. I have been looking. They are the ones who have your brother. Did you see the news last night? They are on the run. The police and the government haven't been able to find them. They will not harm David--not as long as we have the Harper woman. And I just received news from Tindal, everything is set for the Festival. The Hive will be here ready for you and your men to take it and be gone, long before anyone knows what happened."

"We talking 'bout my brother. Nothing happen without him. Understand? Find Harper and Alvarez men and my brother. Once have them, we do business. Then no one have need for Harper woman. Not good for police to find her with you. Not good if they find these men and my brother first. You must find them?"

Bud didn't like to be threatened. This damn spic's threat was a problem, especially with Arturo's men wandering the grounds as armed security personnel. A gun battle here would be a major catastrophe. Even if he survived, his plans would be fucked. The authorities would be all over this place. Elena would be found--an investigation would take place. He had hired Arturo's men, so the blame would be on him and a whole pile of shit would fall on him. Of course, Tindal would deny everything. Damn. On the other hand, he could let Arturo go after David--either he and his brother would not survive, or the Harper and Alvarez men might not survive, which would mean the authorities and the Gonzalez boys would be tied up--hopefully long enough for him to make his getaway.

Bud punched in the chip data Arturo had provided him once more and waited on the program scan. Nothing. He told Arturo he was tracking David, so far the satellite was unable to locate him. He promised Arturo as soon as David moved to where he could locate him, he would immediately notify him.

Arturo was not interested in excuses. "You find brother, or you have problem. Others find brother first. You have big problem."

"Arturo we are close to accomplishing our goal. I cannot locate a GPS chip if there is no satellite coverage. You say the Harper man has David. I believe you are right. I have tried to locate the Harper and Alvarez men's vehicles. They do not register either. There is nothing more I can do until they move and as soon as they do, I will pick up their signature and I will let you know."

"Tell me, where you find brother before?"

"Last signature was outside Chester, South Carolina on Highway 9 headed toward Lockhart. They dropped off screen in that area. Listen Arturo, the authorities are out looking. If they see your men, they will arrest them. Some of your men have already been arrested. If any of them talk, you and I will have big problems. We have to be careful. Let's not fuck this up. You do your part and I'll do mine, Okay? We are too close to our goal. Soon as I know something, I will let you know."

Arturo disconnected.

Shit. This was beginning to get complicated. He should have seen this coming. How could he keep Arturo from making a mistake and fucking everything up? Perhaps Paponovich would have an answer. He would have to approach him carefully.

Mark Poponovich was sitting in his tenth-floor office looking across Tryon Street. He watched a high-rise crane swing load after load of wall panels up to construction workers who set them in place. They were constructing a new bank. He admired the dexterity and courage those workers must possess to allow them to work up this high, seeming not to have a care in the world.

Not so for him. He had heard the news from his superior about Jake Harper and the Harper man's friend, an undercover agent working for Charlotte Metro SWAT and Homeland Security, Thomas J Alvarez. He heard the same story from The Gonzalez cousin in Juarez who had informed him of David Gonzalez disappearance, which was not news to him. The cartel big cheeses were not happy about this. Mark had figured this would get their attention. He told them he was monitoring the situation and anticipated finding him shortly. He reminded their spokesperson about having the Harper woman for use in an exchange. The uncle's, the cartel's reply was the same as Arturo's, "first David then drone." Those fucks didn't get it, the schedule was not flexible. Mark wondered what course of action to take to keep this operation from jumping off track. This was his balancing act.

Mark Poponovich had been born to Hannah and Jon Steponovich as Marcel Steponovich. His father had been a very successful industrialist in Poland after the fall of the Soviet Empire. Marcel had been sent to several prestigious schools and ended his education at the Sorbonne University in Paris. As a child he was taught to write and speak Hebrew, Russian, French, and English. During his second year at the Sorbonne where he majored in Science and Economics, he was approached by a young woman at an outdoor café. She said her name was Catherine, she spoke French, but her native language was English. His father, who had wanted him to major in Industrial Management had not been happy with his choice of study and was even more upset with a Gentile girlfriend. The final blow came when Marcel announced he was dropping out of the Sorbonne and moving to America. His family disowned him. The relationship never recovered. Marcel changed his name to Mark Poponovich, didn't contact his family for another five years. His father died shortly thereafter, his mother sold the business and moved to Jerusalem.

Meeting Catherine had been no accident. Unknowingly her actions were the opening act, the art of seduction into the espionage services of America.

Shortly after moving to Washington, she introduced him to Bernard Obberman, who offered him a sorely needed job as a translator at his International Finance Group Corporation. Within two months Catherine told him who she really was and that IFG Inc. was a front company of the government. Mark, a romantic who had read many western thriller and mystery writer's books, was an easy recruit.

Mark spent the next two years in training. He was given classroom lessons and field lessons teaching him the mental and physical aspects of espionage. The classroom part was far easier than the outdoor physical regimen.

Mark had never been one for exercise outside of walking, biking, and dancing. He had been given classical dance lessons as a child. His best moves were learned by watching American television talent shows. He considered himself a hell of a break dancer. But dancing was not what was taught at the Farm, though it did help with learning some moves in self-defense lessons. Mark's father had taken him to weapons courses and hunting, which he was not fond of, sport killing had seemed senseless. This had proven to be one of Mark's strengths, had earned him respect from the instructors. Mark hoped he would never have to use a weapon to kill anyone. He kept that thought to himself.

In the classroom, his aptitude for languages made learning Spanish a breeze. He learned this talent was what had attracted attention to him when he had been at the Sorbonne. One of his father's friends was an agent for the DGSI, wanted to recruit him for their service, but the CIA through Catherine beat them and Mossad, who also approached him, to the punch.

His field training took place in Europe. His cover was with an Investment Bank as a trainee. The drug trade in Europe was on par with the United States, the seized funds and property a large part of funding for intelligence agencies. Mark spent three years learning the ins and outs of money laundering while getting to know some of the key players in the drug cartels, mainly the Russian and Medellin Cartels. He also got to know Teresa Mendoza and several key operatives from Mexico. His later undercover field work had taken him all over Europe, South America, Central America, Mexico, the Bahamas, and Cuba. Three more years of work to build a reputation and background necessary to know the players, earn the Juarez Cartel's trust.

When the competition and conflicts between the cartels made the border of the United States a war zone, they began acquiring more sophisticated weapons, the CIA stepped up their presence. Mark, who had an in with the Juarez Cartel was sent to Miami by his superiors to find out what the rumor of a big move by the Juarez Cartel meant.

Thurmond Tindal's man Bud Jenkins had dumped a golden goose in the Juarez Cartel's lap. They had been in the market for drones to use to transport their product across the border. Other cartels were already doing this, El Chapo and his Juarez Cartel, could not let themselves be left out. Mark had been given a heads up from General McDab his superior about Jenkins' seeking bidders for a new type of drone that Tindal Industries had received DoD DARPA's tentative approval for. Mark had fed this information to members of the Juarez Cartel. This excited them. McDab had given him the green light to proceed. The Gonzalez boys had been sent here from Chicago to take possession of the drone. Mark had been sent from Miami as an Investment Manager for EUAmerica Investment Group to work out the payment details.

David Gonzalez' computer skills had been an asset for the operation. Arturo had worked with Jenkins to put his men in place. Playing Jenkins and Arturo against each other was working as planned. Problems began when the FBI, Homeland, ICE, and the SWAT team entered the picture. The Alvarez man's undercover work was about to throw a monkey wrench into the whole operation. Just as all his work was about to pay off. Not only that, two other characters in the unfolding drama could be a problem.

The Harper man knew of him from Cuba back when he had been working to regain the trust of the cartel. Undersecretary Hardy had been there also. Although, he had not come in contact with Hardy, he didn't know what the Harper man may have told him after he was rescued following the sinking of that damn Russian oligarch Okneyev's freighter in Cuba. Fortunately, none of his people were questioned specifically about him when they were taken to Gitmo after they were picked up following the freighter explosion.

The Harper man could identify him to the cartel if they got their hands on him. That would be most unfortunate for both of them. He liked the Harper man. One of his assignments from McDab was to watch over him. He often wondered why. Seemed the man was quite capable of taking care of himself. It was damn sure in his own best interest to make sure nothing calamitous befell him or his friend, and especially, his damn fine-looking wife. Harper and his women--amazing the man's ability to get more than his fair share of primo ass.

Jake Harper's situation was severe, but there was nothing he could do to help him until he located him. Maybe he could help by keeping an eye on his wife. That was hardly a chore.

In Cuba, Jake had seemed like a player coming off a tragic marriage and fresh out of the military, ready to sew wild oats, not settle down as quickly as he had. Then again, most men might feel and do the same for a woman looked like her.

Mark never did quite know why Jake chose to be in Cuba. Almost blew his own operational cover, all his work Now here he was again. The guy seemed to show at the wrong time and in the wrong place--with the exception of the freighter incident—There was that. Jake had saved his life. But, almost got him arrested along with his crew.

He had informed his supervisor about Harper and Hardy. His cutout said General McDab said not to worry, he would handle any problem. Complications never ceased to exist when working without a net, always the case, a balancing act, your life, and other people's lives always hung in the balance.

Mark emphatically told Jenkins to find David Gonzalez, a priority for the operation and for the cartel. Bud Jenkins seemed less than enthusiastic about being told what he should do and sounded less than enthused about locating David, Harper, or the Alvarez men. Jenkins thought his being with the Harper and Alvarez men kept the authorities' attention focused on them which would make the handoff less problematic. The cartel and Arturo most assuredly wouldn't see it that way. David Gonzalez was a vital part of their operation inside the states. Jenkins' plan had its merits, but should he trust him? Mark had been monitoring Jenkins. Knew he was seeking other bids. He decided to let Jenkins believe he was willing to cut the cartel out. This was a dangerous game to play--for both of them. Nothing new for Mark. Another card, same game. When and how to play his hand was always evolving.

Was this the end of his work inside the cartel? McDab nor his cutout had given him an indication that was to be the case. Where would he go, what would he do? Being a desk jockey without the constant danger didn't appeal to him. He could retire with a nice pension. But what did that mean? He had no family, no wife, or kids.

He would be a wanted man by the cartels. Changing his appearance and getting new papers would not be an issue. He had been living a lie his whole life and he didn't know how not to do that. Working with the cartels had allowed him to live a lifestyle he would never be able to afford on his pension. The adrenaline rush, how could he live without it? Would being wanted by the cartels be enough? Finding closure with this operation was not likely. There would be more Gonzalez boys and people like Jenkins willing to betray their country for money. The cartels weren't going away. As long as there were people looking for ways to escape reality or get their kicks from what these cartels were willing to provide, or people looking to get rich off *sin*, people like him would be necessary. He wanted it to never end for himself.

He continued watching the construction and watching and listening to what was happening at Tindal's place. After Arturo's call to Bud Jenkins, he checked to see where each of the Gonzalez boys were. Unlike Jenkins, as far as he knew, he had many more sophisticated resources at his disposal which he hoped kept him better informed. Anticipating a call from Jenkins, he thought he would put a little fear of his own into him. He would tell him where David Gonzalez was. Show another of the cards he held, see how Jenkins reacted, perhaps Jenkins would expose his trump card.

CHAPTER
33

TJ took his weapons out to check, clean and oil them. His Charlotte Metro SWAT Team sniper rifle lay across the tailgate on a blanket. Gonzalez watched him, made no comment.

Jake asked if he would do the same to his and TJ said he would. Jake climbed the tower expecting reception to call Ariel. It was half past seven. Jake figured she would be up and wondering why he hadn't called. She was.

"Good morning." he said quickly when he heard the connection. Don't use my name."

"Good morning," she said sounding more awake than he expected. "I wondered when you would call. Thought you might have changed your mind."

"We moved. By the time we got here and took care of things I decided to wait. I don't want to talk too long to you on this phone so the first thing I need you to do is go to several places that sell unregistered phones, buy five or so, one from each place and pay cash."

"They call those burner phones, um… She almost said his name. "I know all about them. Why so many?"

"I'll explain later. Once you get the phones, call me at the number I'm going to give you." He told her the number, she recited it back.

He went back down. TJ was cleaning his Remington 700, the civilian version of the Colt M4 Carbine, TJ had already cleaned.

"That was quick."

Jake told him the conversation.

"Good thinking. Where'd you learn that, some video game? You know we never played those things at home as kids. Couldn't afford them. My mother hated idle time being spent on anything, even television. My brother would go to friends' homes to play games or watch tv, then he got mixed up in gang shit. That's how it goes down, huh Gonzales," he said nudging David's foot. "Not me. I read, studied, and spent as much time as I could with Deane. She was and still is my closest friend. How about you bro?"

"The first time I played anything like a video game was in the Army, those simulators used in training. I had too many chores. Our television time was limited just like yours. A local store had pin ball machines. I played those. Still like to play them. My ole man gave my brother and me a billiard table when I was ten or so. Played that as often as time allowed. Started slipping off to pool halls when I got my first motorcycle at fifteen. That's when my ole man and I started having problems. He didn't like the direction I was headed. His ole man had been a rabble rouser, left him with bad memories. I ended up in a gang, started having run-ins with the law and my ole man said I needed military discipline. I offered to join if he would sign for me. He jumped right on it, but my mother talked him out of signing. Two years later I joined. That was after a bigger run-in with the law left me little choice and after I learned Ariel's father had sent her to England to live with her aunt. He wanted to get her away from me. Speaking of Ariel, I better get back up where I can talk."

Jake leaned against one of the roof support beams and watched birds fly to the rails. When they saw him they flew away. There was a time when he had been up here at night, the sounds would come from far away: night birds, bobcats, coyotes, the sound of a train, clanking and chugging somewhere off in the distance, its whistle shrieking a lonesome cry as it approached a crossing. The only sound today, the whisper of the wind in the trees, a few chirps, the pings of the tower's metal heated by the sun, nothing more.

Memories came to him about Ariel. He knew he should not think of her like he did. Especially with Elena in the predicament she was in. But thoughts of Elena texting her old lover and father of her daughter and planning to meet the slimy limey without telling him, well, he couldn't bring himself to feel too guilty about Ariel. All he was doing was asking Ariel for help. He wasn't going behind Elena's back. Would he have contacted Ariel if none of this crap happened? He didn't know. Time enough to sort that out once this was all over. Depending on the outcome. For all he knew he could end up in jail or dead.

It was while his mind strayed back to Ariel's and his past that his burner rang. He hit reception. He waited for her to speak first.

"Jake? You there?"

"Did you do as I asked?"

"Of course. I picked up six phones. You sure this is necessary? I have an iPhone with a burner app--supposed to be secure."

"I don't know. What I do know is what I've heard. But with everything that has happened, and with the authorities convinced we are terrorists, I figured the safest bet is to believe what the conspiracy buffs say."

"Tell me where I can find you?"

"Are you alone?"

"Yes. No one knows where I am. I told the station manager I had a big story to run down. She got someone else for tonight's broadcast."

"Just like that. No questions about the story?"

"She knows me. If I say big that is all I need to say. I am well respected by my colleagues. So. Where do I need to come to?"

"TJ, my partner in crime and I have put together a list of things we need you to do and some supplies we need. You okay with that? I promise what we have to say is worth the trouble. You'll need to have pen and paper."

"As long as I won't be breaking any laws. Meaning if its guns, ammo or something like that, then don't ask."

"Nothing illegal I promise. Meeting with us is not legal. I guess you know that."

"The press doesn't have to reveal their source."

"We are considered terrorists. We have no protection under the law. The Patriot Act says they can hold you, no protection, no legal rights. You sure you want to do this?"

Ariel didn't hesitate. "Jake I would probably do this, even if you weren't someone I knew. I would say "know", but it has been a long time and we haven't seen or talked to each other in over twenty years. Yes. I'm sure I can find a way to protect myself. Give me your list. I hope it's not a long one."

"Ariel, to help protect you and us, you need to go to the bank or an ATM, withdraw cash. You don't want them tracing your moves from credit cards. Leave your iPhone at home. Hopefully, there is a Rent-a-Wreck car rental place somewhere in your area and the people there won't know you. Better still is to get someone you trust that can keep their mouth shut to loan you one or rent one for you. You need to pay cash, that is why Rent-a-Wreck. Is this a problem?"

"Jeez Jake. I'll see what I can do."

"No, not I'll see, you have to do this. It is not just the authorities, there is a gang with sophisticated hackers that are looking for us also."

"That truck they found in Charlotte. That was you and your friend? I wasn't certain. I thought it was the authorities running up charges. Okay this may take me a while. What supplies were you going to ask me to pick up?"

Jake read out the list to her."

"Good gosh. This sounds like more than a day or two of stuff. Who are the clothes for?"

Jake had to think quick.

"I'll explain when you get here."

"Is your wife with you? Is she hurt?"

"No. I need to get off this phone. This is asking a lot from you Ariel. You don't owe me a thing and if you say you'd rather not, then don't get involved."

"No journalist worth a hill of beans would turn this opportunity down. This is what earns writers and news people their awards. Like I said this will take me a while. Tell me where to come and I'll be there as soon as I can."

Jake gave her directions. "Thanks Ariel. I'm glad you are willing to do this," Jake said. And one other word of caution. Act as if someone is watching you with every move you make. They very well may be, or, for damn sure will be, once this airs. Gotta go."

"Right. Okay. I'll be there soon, I hope. I'll call when I am out of town."

Jake looked out, couldn't see far. The pines and the few remaining hardwoods blocked his view. Guess that's why they stopped using the tower. He watched the smaller pines gently swaying in the breeze. As a kid, he and his cousins would climb trees such as these. The sway made the climb more adventurous. Once at the top, they would launch their feet out into space. The momentum bending the tree, their weight carrying them on a ride toward the ground. You were lucky if the top didn't break. Some family members saw this as destroying a crop, refused to see the thrill. Seemed they were always getting punished for this, damming the creek, playing gladiator with corn stalks, their motorbikes the horses--country-life mischief. Ariel thought everything was funny back then.

The day was heating up. The sun had risen to the tops of the trees. Jake felt its warmth on the metal handrail as he descended the steps. Moving around had lessened the ever-present pain and stiffness in his neck. The Gonzalez guy was sitting up leaning back against the bed of the truck. TJ had finished cleaning and oiling their weapons, had put everything back into the truck when Jake reached the bottom. He pulled Jake off to the side to find out how the conversation went. Jake rehashed what had been said giving TJ as accurate an account of what had been said as he could remember. TJ was a stickler for details. Jake had to repeat several questions and answers that caught his attention.

"Should've thought about that. Asking her to bring clothes. Damn. If she paid attention to the authorities' reporting of a missing gang member, we could have a problem. If she thinks we have Elena…Damn bro. Slipups are what get people caught."

"She doesn't know you or what your clothing sizes are. Remember Deane is missing also. I'm sure she'll think of many reasons I asked for the clothes. Hey, I know. I'll tell her it was in case someone was listening in and I wanted to give them something to think about. Don't make it sound so fatal. Alright? Once she gets here, I doubt the subject will come up. Why don't you call Deane? Maybe that'll help take your mind off the what ifs."

TJ started to come back at Jake about his cavalier attitude. Jake and his women. Going to be his downfall. Mine too if he's not careful. Maybe talking to Deane would help.

"Better check on the van and the pontoon. Didn't you say there were toilets and showers inside those bathrooms down at the landing? Need to drop a load, take a shower, who knows when have another chance? You best get cleaned up 'fore your girl crush shows up." He broke into a big grin and left Jake standing there shaking his head while he walked over to the metal tower and began his ascent.

CHAPTER
34

David Gonzalez sat back looking and listening to his captors. He heard about the reporter coming. Perhaps he play on her sympathy. He thought the Alvarez man soft, playing him. Arturo say give pieces of information, keep him close. This torture shit scared him. He knew torture. He knew what torture is, all his life. Never no tire, no fishes, and no snake. He shuddered. Alvarez man again say he do this unless he say where Harper man's wife is? He can no say what he not know.

Arturo no tell him what plan once he capture her. Jenkins man say get Harper woman, then authorities blame Harper man, make easy for them do business, get UAV. Where Arturo? What happen to Harper woman? What must he say.

Jake stood looking at the Gonzalez man. He was staring back at him. Reminded Jake of the Afghanis' tribal leaders' looks when they were contemplating what to tell him and his men when asked about the Taliban. Usually it was a lie, but often lies told more than half truths. His wife's life was at stake. As well as his and TJ's freedom and lives.

"Bet you would like to get cleaned up, perhaps take a piss or a shit?" Jake asked. "Your use to us is getting less and less. Our only use for you is in a trade for my wife. But we can't do that unless we have a way to get in touch with whoever is holding her. For you and your gang's sake, she better still be alive. I need to hear her voice before any exchange can be talked about. I'm sure a smart man such as yourself can understand the situation. All you must do is tell me your brother's telephone number. I will call him and perhaps we can work out a way to make everyone happy. How about that?"

"My brother, he no speak to you. He speak only to me. You no like when he get here. You think he has wife. I not know this. You let me speak, I tell him kill you quick."

Jake walked around the truck to stand on the side next to David. "I will hand you my phone you can call your brother. Otherwise, when my friend comes back down here, I'm going to tell him you need convincing. How does that sound?"

"My brother no talk to you. He may no have your wife. You kill me everyone die."

Jake leaned in over the bed of the truck. "Not everyone will die the same way. If your brother comes to kill us, we may die, but it will be in the way that we choose. You, on the other hand will die many times and beg for death before you will be allowed the relief of death. Understand? Comprende?"

Gonzalez refused to look at Jake. He understand this not doing as asked mean. He afraid they cause him more pain if he not say right thing. Why not let Arturo say what he think? They not find Arturo. Arturo, he find them. Soon, he hope.

TJ came back down the stairs and Jake went over to tell him what he had offered David and to ask if Deane had anything new to tell about what was being reported.

"She said the DA and sheriff have labelled us domestic terrorists. Told her this was political bullshit, trying to make themselves look more important for their reelection campaigns because for us to be terrorists meant we had anti-American ideals or a political agenda. That would make the DA's and Sheriff's actions terrorism if you wanted to get down to the nitty gritty of the definition, she's real worried and wants to tell her story. Deane thinks it's good we goina get our story out to the media. She wanted to know 'bout your friend the reporter, said she wants to tell her her side of the story."

Jake said, "Having Deane talk to Ariel is a good idea. I'm sure Ariel will be all for it. She'll probably ask to interview Deane in person." TJ started to object, and Jake said, "I know that can't happen. You'll have to convince Ariel of that. Anyway. Our friend is thinking about whether to agree to or refuse to call his brother. I need to know Elena's alive and if his brother has her. We can offer an exchange then work out a plan if we feel there is a way to get Elena free. What do you think? I was thinking maybe you can help him make up his mind."

TJ looked at Gonzalez. He was looking at them. Probably trying to hear them or read their lips.

"We know how to convince him. Need to make some calls first, talk to my supervisor, see where he stands. Most likely he'll insist we turn ourselves in. Maybe, talk to my SWAT buddy, have him get a message out about Elena, put pressure on whoever is holding her. That has its risks. The bangers could panic. Counting on the Gonzalez brothers' affection for each other to get Arturo to agree to an exchange for Elena. There's an off chance he doesn't know where she is. If Arturo does, he may agree to an exchange and refuse to let you talk to Elena until then. You thought about that?"

"No exchange without proof of life. We need Arturo's number."

TJ and Jake walked over to the truck.

"My friend Jake asked you to call your brother so he can hear his wife's voice." David opened his mouth to speak, then shook his head no. "Oh yeah. You will. Bet on it. You'll tell Arturo he has to do this. Try to say anything else and my friend doesn't talk to his wife, all Arturo will hear is your screams." TJ turned to Jake standing beside him. "Jake hand him the phone." Jake reached over and David held up his bound hands, then lowered them without taking the phone. TJ looked at Jake. "Hand me the phone, grab a Taser from my bag, other side of truck." He looked back down at Gonzalez. "Going to cut your hands free, don't do as asked, goina shock the shit out of you. We will do this as long as it takes or until you're so fucked, you'll wish you were dead."

TJ reached over and cut David's hands loose and dropped the phone into his lap. "Call your brother or suffer the consequences."

David wanted to hear Arturo's voice. Arturo would know what to do. He punched in the number, heard the ring tone.

TJ ripped the phone out of his hand, disconnected the call. He checked to see if the number was one he had seen. He nodded to Jake. Gonzalez was cursing him in Spanish. TJ reached in from his side and Jake from the other to grab Gonzalez. They drug him to the tailgate of TJ's truck, zip tied his hands and gagged him once more.

"Shall we go up and make this call?" asked TJ.

Jake called out the number to TJ who entered it into a phone they had taken from the garage workshop which he had put the batteries back into. Arturo answered on the second ring. TJ recognized the voice, like David's, a deeper tone.

"My brother, I wait your call," said Arturo in Spanish. Where gringos?"

TJ spoke to Arturo in Spanish.

Arturo began cursing and threatening TJ. TJ waited.

"You can speak to your brother when we hear Elena Harper say she is alive and well."

Arturo denied he knew anything about Elena. TJ cut him short and told him he would give him time to think about it, make it happen. "We'll call back in five hours." TJ looked at his watch it was just before noon. "That will be at 5 o'clock. Either we speak to Senora Harper or you will not like what you hear from your brother." TJ disconnected, told Jake what was said.

"You think he'll answer when you call back?" Jake asked.

"He has her, he will, Better believe it."

"I'll check on the van and pontoon. I need to get cleaned up for our interview."

"You mean you want to get cleaned up for your lovely reunion, don't you?"

"That too," Jake replied. "I want lie. It has been almost twenty-five years."

"Remember you're married."

"Come on man, she knows that. She probably has a boyfriend. Could be married. Her last name is now Gaspard, not Harper."

The van was in the same condition as they left it. When they got to the river picnic shelter bath houses, Jake told TJ he would check on the boat while TJ took his morning nature call and got cleaned up. TJ carried David in the bath house and checked the water. It was on but there was no hot water. This was going to be fun he thought. TJ checked the toilet. The water supply had been turned off. He looked around outside and found the shutoff and turned it back on. After he finished taking his constitutional, he took Gonzalez over, cut his hands loose, waited as he undid his pants buttons and sat on the toilet. David wrinkled his nose and protested the odor TJ left behind. TJ zip tied David's right hand to the handicap bar attached to the wall, told him to do his business and shut the fuck up.

David struggled to pull his pants back up and rebutton them using his left hand. TJ didn't offer to help.

Undressing TJ hesitated then stepped in under the cold spray of the shower, got wet, turned the water off and soaped himself, then turned the water back on and rinsed. The water was damn cold. He was covered in goose bumps. He used a roll of paper towels that he kept in his truck to dry off, then he put on another set of clothes, wrinkled but warm and didn't stink.

Jake came in while he was shaving, looked over at David and took a whiff and told TJ he was going to the ladies' bathhouse.

They went back up the winding road to the fire tower awaiting Ariel's call. Jake kept pacing back and forth across the upper tower lookout with his rifle, like he was on guard duty waiting for his relief. He dared not admit he was anxiously anticipating seeing her again. TJ told him his pacing was getting on his nerves. "I hope she didn't run into any trouble," Jake commented.

"Jesus Jake, she had a helluva lot to do. You're acting like a guy getting ready to go on his first date."

"This may be the most important date I have had since my first date. I hope it goes better than that one, for both our sakes. Make that for all of us."

CHAPTER
35

Ariel wondered why she agreed to go to all this trouble. It seemed overly cautious. I guess if my life were at stake, I would see this as not so extreme she thought. At every stop she checked her mirrors and looked around to see if anyone was paying undue attention to her. A few people were looking at her, probably people who recognized her from the broadcast. That happened often. It took some getting used to.

What made her noticeable when off the air? She often dressed as she was now—off the rack jeans-- she didn't like designer jeans, why pay expensive prices for something with holes in them or, the latest worn, dirty look. She grew up with off-the-rack jeans, worked then, worked now. Today she wore a flannel shirt and her riding boots—was that a throwback look of when she and Jake dressed that way as teens, often to the dismay of their in-town peers? She wore a sequined natural colored leather jacket which she shed. The meteorologist had said today's high temperature would rise from the low forties to the lower eighties. Ariel had brought a pair of shorts and a pair of sandals. Away from the station and doing interview work, she dressed for comfort, not style. She wore no makeup—Jake had always told her he hated makeup.

This was a business assignment, why did she keep thinking about Jake and what he did or didn't like? Admit the truth, your heart raced when you heard his voice. Twenty-five years. She blamed him, tried to forget him. He had abandoned her, leaving her only one choice, listen to her parents, go live with her mother's sister's family in England, away from small community gossip.

She had experienced a failed marriage to a Spanish exchange student, Enrico de Vincenzo y Gaspard, whose family was upper class. School break, his parent's palatial estate, he reminded her of an aristocratic Jake, had she been getting back at Jake? Jake had no way of knowing. So much he hadn't known. Would she tell Jake? Did he deserve to be told?

When her marriage failed, she decided enough time had passed. She had her degree. Her first choice had been in New York with a travel magazine--living there was too expensive. Next, she suffered through five years as a news reporter in Minneapolis--the place was too cold. Finally landing at an NBC affiliate in Columbia starting out as a field reporter, then moving up to her current position as a network anchor. Now here she was doing something most local anchors weren't allowed to do, going after a story. That was one of the privileges she negotiated in her contract. The problem-- this story involved Jake--personal stories were frowned upon.

There was so much Jake didn't know about her and so much she didn't know about him. Who was Jake now?

She had gone online, amazed at his military postings, so much different from her experiences. Two tours served in Afghanistan and Iraq, then the Philippines where he had been severely wounded by an IED. An early marriage to a Natchez, Mississippi debutante and three children who lived in Louisiana with their maternal grandparents. Divorced same dates as his recovery from the IED wound. Further research revealed his ex died of an overdose.

Currently Jake was married to another woman whose family was in Texas. She had disappeared. Getting the answers, a prime-time news story the reason why she was on her way to meet him. She had to admit that was not the only reason. Would she have done all this for any other story? One of this magnitude? Yes. With the mixed bag of emotions? Doubtful.

There was a lot she didn't know about Jake's and his friend's situation. Ariel had laid awake long after going to bed trying to come up with an approach for the interview. After leaving the station with a copy of the DA's pronouncement in hand, surreptitiously copied while the technician was on break, she watched it over and over through almost a bottle of wine. Why were all the feds there? She could understand the FBI's presence, a kidnapping and possible flight across state lines, why ICE and Homeland Security?

She wanted to call the station affiliate in Charlotte, was afraid it would raise a red flag. Jake's friend the Alvarez man had been a Metro Charlotte SWAT team member. How and why was he involved? The Sheriff had hinted Mr. Alvarez and his wife were missing. They had Jake listed as a person of interest in that situation also. There had been a report about a moving van with some gang members inside. Ariel pulled out her laptop, searched that story. Was Jake and his friend involved in that incident? Was that why the clothes? She had more questions than answers.

After tossing and turning and staring at the clock until long after midnight, Ariel got out of bed, pulled out her stash and her one hitter. This should get her creative juices flowing and hopefully put her to sleep. Often this helped. Good thing the station didn't drug test. After a few hits, she thought back about the first time she had smoked. It had been with Jake. A lot of firsts had been with Jake.

Her alarm woke her. She hurriedly took a shower while the coffee was brewing. Grabbed her no spill cooler drink holder filled with hot coffee, a sweet roll, and her laptop, turned her iPhone off, left it in her nightstand and jumped in her Jeep Grand Cherokee. She dropped her jeep off at the airport, took a taxi two blocks to the Rent-a-Wreck car rental place and got the best four-wheel drive vehicle they had on the lot. Paid cash and headed out to complete Jake's list.

She finished shopping at a Walmart near Fort Jackson on Forest Drive. Having purchased the abbreviated list of items Jake had agreed to, she got on Highway 1 and headed toward Camden. At the next exit, she went back on Highway 1 the way she had come before exiting. She took the exit onto Interstate 77, continuously checking her mirrors. She didn't see any vehicles switching lanes with her as she sped up and slowed down, dropping in and out of traffic.

She read Jake's directions she had written down on a scrap piece of paper. She exited onto Highway 97. South of Chester, she turned onto Highway 9. The route seemed simple and straightforward until she turned off Highway 9.

She had gone what she thought was ten miles and did not see the sign for the landing. No cell phone reception. She felt she missed the sign somehow. She checked the rental's odometer; she had gone five miles further than Jake's directions indicated. Ariel decided to turn around. Driving slower than the speed limit and checking every sign on both sides, she finally spotted the large sign. The entrance was around a curve and on top of a hill making it hard to see especially from the other direction.

When she turned into the short road that led to the fire tower, she saw a man approaching carrying what looked like an assault rifle. Ariel stopped the car, wondering what she had gotten herself into. The man slung his rifle onto his shoulder by its strap and waved her forward. She crept forward watching him for any threatening movement. When she got about twenty feet away, she saw the grin. The armed man was Jake. He was taller than she remembered and at least fifty pounds heavier. His slim cute face had become fuller and he was far better looking than cute. Ariel pulled up beside him and lowered the driver's window.

"You scared the crap out of me. God Jake. This seems surreal." Ariel looked him up and down. The camouflage cargo pants ended in combat boots and he was wearing a slightly wrinkled cotton long sleeve camo shirt. He looked like he was a game hunter ready to go into the woods. A well-built game hunter.

"Hello Ariel. I guess it is okay to call you Ariel?" Jake asked with that same lopsided grin--that Paul Newman *Cool Hand Luke* grin. His blue green hazel eyes staring at her—she was amazed how little he had aged.

"Don't be funny. I brought everything you asked for, where do you want me to park?"

He noticed her low country accent was gone. She sounded sophisticated, yet still very much like a born and bred southerner. God she was beautiful even without all the makeup. Her freckles gave her a youthful look.

She creeped forward as he walked alongside. Ariel got out and she and Jake silently stood at arm's length looking at each other not sure what to do. Jake stepped forward and they hugged. She pushed back after a couple seconds. "You smell clean. How is that?"

"There are bath houses down at the river." Jake pointed down the hill.

"And where is Mr. Thomas Alvarez?"

"Up there," Jake said pointing up.

Ariel looked up and saw a man holding a scoped rifle looking down at them. He resembled the actor called The Rock, Dwayne Johnson. The scene seemed even more surreal.

"Hey TJ, you want to come down so I can introduce you to Ariel?" Jake yelled up to him. "Maybe help with unloading the car."

"Figured you needed some time to get reacquainted," he yelled back. "I'll hang up here, make sure we don't get any unwanted visitors. The supplies can wait. Hello Ariel. Jake has been keeping me in the dark 'bout you. Why don't you and Jake decide how to handle the interview. Let me know when you are ready for me."

Ariel stared hard at Jake trying to get a read on him. He seemed more at ease than she expected. She was amazed she felt the same. She wondered how much he knew about her. "How did you know I worked at the station in Columbia?"

"Ran into Bitch. He told me. I thought I mentioned that?"

"You may have. When I heard your voice, it threw me for a loop." She watched his eyes. That same piercing look brought back memories.

The first time she came home from school in his Toyota street racer: no one home, his reluctance to come in, her decision, her bedroom, her bed, her move, his hesitation, his questioning, taking off her clothes, those eyes.

Ariel shook her head and looked around. "Is there some place we can go more private?"

"Just you and me?"

She laughed. "No. Some place out of the sun, where there won't be the glare."

"Glare? Remember I told you this was to be verbal only." Jake glanced up. TJ was pretending not to be watching. TJ and I decided having any kind of background could possibly give a clue as to where we might possibly be. The people after us are good. They have every tech tool and tech person at their disposal."

"Hold on Jake. I thought about what you said. The reason for doing this interview is to get your account of what happened. You are trying to convince the public you are innocent. To garner sympathy, people need to see you, not just hear you. They will judge your validity by looking at your expressions as you speak. You know that. Having a voice only, I'm not sure my station manager would air that." Ariel watched Jake as he glanced up, she did the same, TJ's attempts at not looking were amusing. "What did you tell TJ about us? He's acting like a chaperone or something."

Jake chuckled. "I didn't tell him much. Enough I guess to make him curious." Jake took a step past Ariel and walked over to TJ's truck. She didn't move. He unslung his rifle and leaned it against the truck, the pull on his neck had caused more discomfort. What she said made sense. But where could they go out here that would be inconspicuous? The only place indoors out of the sun were the bath houses, but there was always the possibility some viewer might recognize them. Then it hit him. Often when the Taliban or Isis had a hostage interview, they would put a blanket up. They could do that. But was there enough light in the bath house? The camera probably had its own light source. Would a fisherman or hunter show up while they were doing the interview? And what about David Gonzalez? He had not told Ariel about him. Thankfully, she hadn't asked. Yet Jake decided he needed to talk this over with TJ. "I need to talk to TJ. I'll be right back."

CHAPTER
36

Ariel watched as Jake climbed the tower. She had to convince them to do a video interview. With their rugged good looks, viewers would be more apt to be sympathetic, especially female viewers. Amazing how the opposite sex made judgements about people based upon looks more than anything else. Perhaps gays did the same, she often wondered about that. She wasn't sure why, or why now. Jake and TJ. No way. While she was waiting, she looked around. There wasn't much to see. Mostly pine trees and some hardwoods, a newer model truck and the fire lookout tower. Not many options for a good background. She wanted to take some footage of what she saw, didn't dare piss them off. Maybe Jake was right. There weren't too many fire towers. If the people looking for them were determined, and by all accounts, Jake and TJ were the men of the hour for the authorities and a cartel gang, checking out fire towers would be a priority. Ariel knew she was letting her personal feelings determine what she was doing.

TJ came down instead of Jake. "Mrs. Gaspard, Jake and I talked 'bout your request. Down the hill are bath houses. The electricity is not on. The sunlight should suffice if we leave the door open. We can put a blanket up for a backdrop, do you think that would work?"

Ariel stuck out her hand, "Call me Ariel please. May I call you TJ?" TJ said he would prefer that, lightly gave her hand a squeeze. "TJ, I don't need light.

My equipment has a light source for filming in the dark." God, this guy was a large man, and the women viewers will love him. Those dark moony eyes. And he seems so polite.

TJ yelled up to Jake, "You should probably go first. I'll unload her car and you can set things up with her."

"Haven't been up in a tower since high school," exclaimed Ariel. "Would you mind if I went up to have a look?"

"Sorry ma'am. I'm afraid I can't allow that. We have things up there that I would rather you didn't see."

That made Ariel curious. What could they possibly have up there that they didn't want her to see? Could it be Jake's wife or the missing gang member? The thought Jake's wife was up there possibly injured or worse made her shiver. The Jake she had known would never do anyone harm. His friend didn't seem to be the type either.

"I'm sorry I don't mean to be intrusive. Well, I guess that is not entirely true, I am a reporter after all and that is what we do."

"If I felt I could tell you I would. When this is all over, you'll know. There is nothing more I can say at this time."

TJ walked over to Jake who had come back down. He told him about his refusing to let her go up the tower. "I don't think it a good idea to let her know what we have up there or about our other weapons. Ask her not to mention the refusal or about us being armed."

"Damn TJ. I'm sure she saw the broadcast. She's going to ask questions about what was reported. Probably about the clothes also. How are we supposed to answer? No comment won't look so good. If we are going to do this, we need to be upfront and openly honest about what we believe. I agree we tell her not to disclose we are armed and maybe we shouldn't talk about Gonzalez, but everything else should be fair game. We got to take it to Tindal, the fucking cartel and anyone else involved in taking Elena and causing us to be fugitives."

"We have to be careful about what we say Jake. What we believe and what we can prove, they not entirely the same. We need to stick to telling the story, excluding kidnapping Gonzalez and about our other weapons. If we mention Tindal, and if he is involved in Elena's kidnapping, of which I am not sure, he will deny it. The DA and the feds aren't going to go to his place based upon our word. He owns the DA, and the feds' requirements for searching his property require a judge to sign off and the judge will require reasonable evidence of a crime. If Elena is being held at Tindal's place, my guess is, as it has been, he knows nothing about it. Our friend up there said he didn't know where Elena is. We believe Elena's there. We have no proof."

"After this interview, our next step is to find a way to either get Arturo to make an exchange or find Elena some other way. What we should do with this interview is create reasonable doubt about our involvement. Try to force the investigation to go in a different direction. Maybe your friend Ariel can help with that. But she must be careful, about what she says, for her own safety. She starts digging around in the wrong places--could put her in jail or worse. The cartel and Arturo's bangers don't play nice. And, from what happened to you in the Bahamas, others could be out there, more determined than ever to take you, and those close to you, off the board. Think about it, this could be their doing, with Tindal or not. Could be more than one operation going on here." They both looked over toward Ariel. She was watching them, a frown on her face. Then she smiled, turned her palms out and shrugged. "I wonder if she reads lips?"

"Hopefully, she doesn't have super hearing." Jake held up a finger and said in a slightly louder tone than their conversation, "One second Ariel." She smiled and shrugged again. "I know you have no reason to trust her, but I am willing to bet my life she will not screw us over."

"Okay. But this is not just your life. This is about Elena. You willing to bet her life and mine and Deane's bro?"

That made Jake uncomfortable. What was the best thing for everyone? His only experience with hostages had been in Army training and in combat situations where the hostage lives at stake were not personal. "TJ I'm out of my element here. I have not a fucking clue what is the best way to handle this. Overseas experience with those tribal fucks is a whole different kind of thing. You're more experienced with this kind of situation than I am, tell me what are we supposed to do? If anything, I do causes Elena harm, I don't know if I could live with myself." Jake felt guilty. There were too many what ifs about what had happened in the last five days. He felt a lot of that had been his actions and reactions, and that Elena had nothing to do with where what he did had put her.

TJ saw the downcast look on Jake's face. If the situation had been about Deane instead of Elena, he didn't know if he would be rational. He felt for his friend and Elena, even though his feelings for Elena were more concern for his friend Jake and how Jake felt and would feel if what they did or didn't do resulted in her being harmed or killed.

"There are no guarantees in hostage situations, especially when dealing with these cartel and Mexican fucks. Their hostage negotiations are based on macho threats and retaliation, except when it is family. They value their immediate families as much as we do. Arturo will not harm Elena as long as we have his brother. Remember David is his number two. He had the information, which we now have, to their whole operation. Elena will be safe unless they find us and get David and those flash drives back."

Jake only felt marginally better. He was not certain rationality applied to the situation. Elena's fate was in the hands of irrational criminals and the actions of him and TJ. And to a great extent what they said in this interview. He felt a great weight on his shoulders which caused tension in his neck to return. He twisted it from side to side with his eyes closed. Damn what to say and do. Took a lot of the joy of his reunion with Ariel away. Ariel. He looked over at her. She had gone to her rental and was leaning against the hood looking perplexed. A lot of what happened depended upon her reporting, why not include her in the discussion?

"TJ" TJ had been looking at Ariel also. Upon hearing Jake say his name he looked back to Jake. "Since Ariel is going to report this, a lot of what she reports when she is on the air is going to be up to her and we will have no way of stopping that. Maybe we should include her in this discussion and tell her what we want her to say or not say, don't you think?"

"I was thinking the same thing bro. You're right. Why don't you go over and ask her to join us? I need something to drink. It's starting to get a little warm out here. How about asking her about our meals. I think we should discuss this while we dig into some chow. How about it?"

"Sounds good to me."

Ariel had bought two large coolers—not on their list—one held their lunch request along with some bags containing other food stuff they had requested. The other cooler was packed with ice, a twelve pack of Miller High Life, Jake's old favorite, a bottle of white wine and two 32-ounce cans of green tea with ginseng and honey.

They sat on TJ's tailgate and ate while Ariel sat on one of the coolers sipping on a plastic glass half full of wine. They talked while they ate. Ariel asked them to tell their versions of what had happened. She took notes and made check marks beside the parts she needed clarified and parts that would need to be brought out more strongly in the interview. She also had brought a tape recorder and taped their story. She would be able to embellish the broadcast with anything she failed to question them about in their sit down.

When they finished, TJ and Jake looked at her notes and marked the parts they wanted left out. At one point, after she asked about Homeland and ICE and the incident with the moving van, Jake and TJ went out of her hearing range and discussed how they wanted to handle this. Jake was for telling about David Gonzalez having tracked Elena with Arturo kidnapping her. TJ said that would cause big problems involving his undercover status and would most likely blow the whole operation sky high. "This will piss a lot of people off, could be major repercussions, most of them aimed at me and by association at you," TJ stated emphatically. "Plus, we could be charged with kidnapping."

Jake argued, "If we are going to clear ourselves, how in the hell is that going to be possible unless we name someone else and give credible reasons to implicate them? We tell her she can't report this and explain why. I trust her. I believe she would never do anything to screw us over."

TJ didn't have a quick answer. Jake knew her better than he did. Had known her. He was afraid of opening that door to anyone, especially a reporter. Jake was operating on emotions. If she reported about Gonzalez, his SWAT commander would be pissed, so would all the other fed agencies, including Homeland. Hardy would come under fire and TJ knew his ass would be persona non grata with law enforcement everywhere, if it wasn't already. They would burn him. How to save Elena and his career and keep Jake and him from prison, where in all likelihood, the cartel would make sure they didn't survive? They should have gotten their stories squared away before Jake's friend got here.

"Okay. Suppose we say we had received threatening telephone calls, with texts and pictures of family members from some Hispanic sounding person. We discovered cameras inside your home and didn't know what else to do but warn all our family members and go someplace safe. We can say the York County Sheriff's Department and FBI have been given this evidence along with evidence regarding your dog having been shot, and we don't know why they haven't followed up on it. You can tell the truth about Elena. That you knew nothing about her disappearance until you saw the news report. That you had called her family to ask if they had heard from her prior to the news cast. We'll say we were told if we went to the authorities we would be arrested on the Assault and Battery charge, so we went into hiding in hopes the evidence we gave would clear our name."

"That might work," Jake said rubbing his chin trying to think of a problem with the story. "At least it would throw some heat on the Sheriff's Department and the FBI. We can test the story on Ariel, maybe she can embellish it and throw some extra heat on the Sheriff and the FBI by questioning them."

Jake looked over at Ariel. The sun's rays sparkled off her auburn hair highlighting the deep luxurious red tones. She looked over at them with her blue green eyes—Jake thought, just like mine, must be from our ancestral gene pool. He and TJ went back to where Ariel sat on the cooler twirling her empty wine glass, her notepad on her lap with notes scribbled in the margins.

Jake had TJ tell her their abbreviated, annotated version. Jake asked if this sounded more than plausible.

"You're asking if I believe the listeners will buy it? Depends on who those viewers are." TJ asked her to explain. "If the listener is Mr. or Mrs. Casual News Watcher that doesn't pick a story apart or if they have become sympathetic or empathetic to the person, namely you and Jake, and how I've presented your story to them, could be. But if the viewer has been fixated on the news reports, wants you to be guilty, or is a law enforcement or legal expert, there are holes in the story that make it seemed contrived."

Ariel saw the disappointment on their faces. Look I've been thinking. The best way to handle this may be to give reasonable doubt by making the viewers see how much you care about your wife. That there was no way you would wish her harm or have harmed her. Where is the motive? TJ can back up your testimony, like a character witness. Your character is on trial here. We need to make as many of the viewers as we can, sympathetic. Motive needs to be addressed. Your stepdaughters claim that your wife told her you suffer from PTSD." Ariel stopped talking and she looked up at Jake.

Jake felt uncomfortable. Elena threw that in his face every time they had an argument, or he raised his voice. Sometimes he would throw things in anger or frustration, rarely when they argued, never at her, mostly when working outdoors, when he grew frustrated with a faulty effort. Like his father, he tended to be a perfectionist when it came to his work. He had never laid a hand on Elena or anyone who didn't deserve it, never a woman or child. Elena judged him by the reports of PTSD, especially reports of those who had suffered a traumatic injury like he had. And she judged him by the difference between him and her father, which was more fantasy on her part than reality, since she had not lived around her father since high school whose deployment overseas kept him away for most of that time.

Jake told this to Ariel, glancing over to TJ, for acknowledgement. "Not only that but many vets are said to suffer from PTSD. That seems to be a catchall to explain every incident involving veterans. Am I different since serving overseas and having had the injury? Hell yes." Ariel had laid her head over, looking up at him sideways with a curious look on her face. "Come on Ariel you knew me back before I was in the military, you know I've always had a temper and I have thrown things when frustrated, did you ever personally feel threatened?

"Not personally. Most men where we grew up were that way. That Irish temper was how I think of it. You did tend to have a wild streak. As I recall, you ran with a rough crowd. Got in lots of fights. Always one step ahead of the law was the local gossip."

"Didn't seem to bother you. You never mentioned this back then."

She shrugged, then winked.

"Part of the attraction."

TJ spoke up, "you two can discuss this some other time. How about it?"

"You're right. What about you TJ?" she asked. "You agree with Jake or do you think Elena was correct?"

"Not my department. Jake always seemed level-headed whenever I was around him and Elena. She never asked me about him or said anything about PTSD to me or my wife Deane. Deane would have said something if she had. I'm with Jake about the vet thing and PTSD."

"Since being out of the military, I have been with SWAT units in Miami and Charlotte. There is a lot of stress associated with our duties, but you rarely hear PTSD used by cops to explain cop misbehavior. I could be wrong. With the way things are today, not hard to imagine most people could be diagnosed as having PTSD."

"Elena was frustrated with Jake's refusal to sell the farm. She wanted to move closer to her family and her family was upset with Jake because he wouldn't comply. She often complained about this to Deane and told her about her discussions with her daughter. If the truth was known, her daughter probably put this PTSD idea about Jake in Elena's head."

"Did you not have a good relationship with your stepdaughter Jake?"

"I rarely saw her or talked to her. Elena talked to her every day. They were close. I thought Elena and I had a good relationship. Living on the farm away from her family had just recently become an issue. Part of that was the coronavirus and she found out her father supposedly had cancer and she wanted to be there for him and her mother. I understand that. Then this incident happened with our dog Dusty and everything went to hell from there."

"You said her father supposedly had cancer. What do you mean supposedly?"

TJ cleared his throat and Ariel looked at him. Jake looked away, then back. Jake knew this question was going into the Tindal realm and would lead to another whole set of questions that he and TJ agreed not to bring up.

"I found out her father had been up recently for a visit and Elena had not told me anything about it. Her father and I didn't exactly see eye to eye. I thought it strange that he would make the trip if he was going in for cancer treatment and I was upset that Elena had not told me. Made me suspicious, that's all." TJ seemed to relax. "Before we could discuss this, all this other stuff happened."

TJ heard David Gonzalez move around. Ariel moved her head in the direction.

"Going to be dark soon and we need to get this taping done. Not a good idea to have Ariel here if someone shows up," TJ said quickly.

Jake had heard the sound also. "You're right. Why don't we finish unloading the car? TJ, I'll do that while you go up and grab a blanket."

Ariel looked from one to the other. "What was that noise?"

"What noise?" Jake said. David started banging away. 'Shit.'

"There's someone up there. That's why ya'll didn't want me going up there. "What's going on Jake? That wouldn't be Elena? Tell me that is not Elena. Oh Jesus." She jumped up and stepped back a frightened look on her face. Jake stepped toward her and she put up her hands, dumping her pen and pad, her plastic wine cup rolled away. Ariel stepped back further. She looked around at the car and tried to judge whether she could make it to it before they caught her. No way. O' God why had she come here? "Stay back Jake."

Jake held up his hands. TJ started toward the tower. His rifle leaning against the bottom framework. Ariel saw the rifle and looked at TJ then back to Jake, her eyes bulging. "Hold on Ariel! Jake said loudly. That is not Elena. We didn't want you to see who it was because we didn't want you to be involved."

"Involved in what? This is scaring me. Why don't you let me leave? I promise I won't say a word." She started running toward the car. Jake caught her before she could open the door. He held onto her arm and spun her around.

"Look at me Ariel." She was looking down, suddenly she kneed him in the groin. The shock waves ricocheted up through his body. Jake let go of her and grabbed his cotch, pain etched all over his face. She tried again and he deflected the attempt with his thigh. It was all he could do to reach out to stop her attack. "Stop it Ariel. I'll let you go, but you've got to quit trying to hurt me any further than you already have. I am Jake. I would never hurt you. If you'll give me a minute, I can explain. Please. Just one minute." She continued to struggle.

"Ariel, I love you. I could never do anything to hurt you." Jake didn't know why he said that. Was it true? Somewhere deep inside him, he knew that it was. Thinking of her, then seeing her, had opened him deeper than he wanted to admit. He had expressed the emotion out loud—no way to recall the words. She stopped struggling. He let go of her.

"What did you say? No. You didn't say that. I need to get away from here. This is madness." Ariel turned to open the door expecting him to stop her. She heard the gravel as he turned and was walking away.

You're a fool, she thought. But wasn't that what you wanted to hear? All these years you held onto those words while you hurt and wanted to hate him for abandoning you, not being there for the hell you endured, hating yourself, hating him. Why *did* you come here? You've been trying to rationalize your decision. It bothered you when he talked about his wife. Did he love her? Did he tell her that he loved her? Was it in him to harm his wife or her? Why had he said those words to you? She looked over as he was walking away rubbing his crotch. If he meant you any harm, would he let you go?

TJ had stopped at the bottom of the tower. His rifle was where she had seen it before. He had a frown and a big grin on his face. He looked up and met her eyes and shook his head. No guile or threat shown.

She pushed her door closed loudly. Jake glanced back. She was coming toward him. "No more bullshit," she said. "I want the whole story. I'm going up that tower or I'm leaving. That is up to you two." She came alongside Jake and said softly, "I hope I didn't hurt you too much. Don't ever grab me again or I'll start believing you may suffer from PTSD. Oh, by the way, don't ever tell someone what you said to me unless you mean it." Ariel hurried on toward the tower not waiting to give Jake a chance to reply. She looked up at TJ as she reached the tower. "I'll follow you."

"Glad I'm not Jake," said TJ with a chuckle and started up the tower. "When we get up there, please save your questions until after I take care of our guest. I guess our interview won't be on tonight's evening news?"

TJ climbed on, glancing back to see if Ariel was having any problems. Nope. She was a trooper. He was beginning to like her. Good thing he loved his wife. Jake damn sure had a problem. They both had a problem. Make that all three of them. They would have to tell more of the story than he and Jake wanted to. She would have to decide which was more important, her story or her word. He stopped on a turn landing half-way up and waited on her to join him. The space was tight. TJ felt uncomfortable. He moved up a few steps and sat. He was eye to eye with her.

"Why are we stopping?"

"Before we go any further, this your last chance to make a decision. Up there," he motioned his head back in the direction of up, "another whole story, leaves you a choice: you cannot report it or go to the authorities once you see what's up there. Get you charged as an accessory to a felony if you did, could even be held incognito because of the Patriot Act and forced under extreme duress to tell what you know. No First Amendment Rights will protect you. Or, you can turn around, go back down and we can proceed as we talked about, you can rightly deny knowing anything. Your choice."

"I didn't come here to get part of a story. What I report, how I report the whole story may be another decision, my decision."

"No. *We* will make the decision. The whole purpose of this interview to give our side of certain events in hopes of getting the heat off us, put pressure on the authorities to find Jake's wife Elena. The person up there is involved. To report about him will put Elena's life in more danger, will put your life in danger as well. Before we go any further, you must agree to work with Jake and me on what gets told, and what doesn't. Otherwise, no deal. You can go down report what you will. We will find another way to tell our story."

Ariel stared back at him concentrating on not blinking or looking away. Who was up there? Thinking about what she knew from the broadcasts and what he had said. He said him, so it was a guy. The clothes. The moving van with illegals, the feds, the missing illegal? Had to be. She had never walked away from a story. She had been threatened, hard-hitting reporters often were. She had covered a story in the Middle East involving war refugees and had seen and heard fighting. She had interviewed Theresa Montoya, a notorious cartel drug queen. This was her story, a big one. And it was Jake. He said he loved her. No way was she walking away.

"Let's go."

CHAPTER
37

The ping had been steady for several hours. He had located David Gonzalez. Bud Jenkins pulled up the location. The Sumter National Forest, Leeds, South Carolina Fire Tower. He scanned the surroundings—a wooded road that ended at a park area and boat landing on the Broad River—interesting. Zooming out he saw how remote the area was, then he zoomed in—a pontoon boat tied up near the landing, no other boats in the area, no people in a picnic area.

He traced the road with some effort due to the trees, half-way back toward the fire tower was what looked like an older model van parked near the intersection of another road. Bud moved around the area of the van. Didn't appear to be anyone. There could be a hunter doing some scouting or maybe it broke down.

He moved the pointer further toward the fire tower, nothing until he reached the tower. Zooming in he saw a green late model Subaru SUV with a rental company tag and nearer the fire tower was a newer model black Toyota Tundra king cab, fully loaded including spotlights on the sides and on the roof. He couldn't get a shot of the tag--the tailgate was down, and a man sat on it. He zoomed in tighter. Bingo, the Harper man, holding a Remington assault rifle. Where was David Gonzalez? Where was his buddy and who did the rental belong to? Is that what they used to transport David in?

What now? Notify the authorities? Couldn't do that. That would put Gonzalez in their hands. He hesitated calling Arturo. Arturo would immediately go after his brother. How well armed was the Harper man and his pal? Only naïve idiots would do what they did and not be armed to the teeth. They were neither. For the reward and to free his brother, Arturo's men would be delighted--certainly would mean a battle to the end. Whose end, both sides were seasoned killers?

Did it matter to him and his plan? With the Harper man and his pal out of the way, Elena Harper might consider him as an option. Thurmond Tindal could get what he wanted. The authorities would be tied up investigating the incident. Only problem, the continued search for Elena Harper. Nothing new as far as he was concerned. If the Gonzalez men were eliminated the cartel would be forced to act. Would they come after him? Not if they wanted The Hive badly enough. The best option would be for all of them to be killed. That was a good thought. Eliminate the Harper man and his pal, along with the Gonzalez brothers. How could that be accomplished? Perhaps Mark would like the idea.

He had his reservations about Mark. Was he who he said he was? The more Jenkins had thought about it, the more he doubted it. Not enough intel there. The NSA had too little, said it was because he was from the former Soviet Bloc. Why didn't that red flag him? Did he have ties to the Russian Oligarch, Pietr Okneyev? When asked, Okneyev denied knowing him. Could he be working for another Russian group, or the CIA? Were the NSA geeks watching him? Jenkins still couldn't find any reason to trust him. He had no other choice. For now. Soon it would not matter. The bids on the dark web had started pouring in.

Mark answered almost immediately. He had been sitting back in his swivel, reclining office chair throwing extra sharp pencils into the ceiling tiles. There were ten of them still hanging on, others were scattered across his desk and on the carpeted floor.

"Bud Jenkins, you were on my list to call. Arturo called. He is upset. He called you also. Did he tell you he received a call from the Alvarez man? No. The Alvarez man wants to make a trade for the Harper woman. That's right. I told him not to trust them. They said they would call back at five. They want proof of life, otherwise Arturo will be listening to David's tortured screams. I know. I told Arturo not to even think about going--too risky. I finally got him calmed down. Oh no, he agreed. Said his cousin, she will help with the Harper woman. Have you seen her? Not bad looking if you like them butchy."

Bud was worried. Arturo was about to fuck everything up. Did he actually believe he could waltz right in here take the Harper woman? Probably thinks he can take The Hive also. He didn't have the faintest idea how to fly the damn thing. Fucking, fucked-in-the-head spic. And the dumbass Harper man and his lame-brain sidekick, did they really believe Arturo would trade? The whole plan was going sideways.

"Mark, we are too close to everything happening. Three more days. Fucking Arturo and the Harper man and his pal are going to fuck everything up. Good. I'm glad you agree. I need to know, when you talked about cutting the Gonzalez brothers and the cartel out, were you serious? Sure, you can trust me, can I trust you? I thought so. Look I figured you had to be serious since you were willing to cut these fuckheads out of the deal. I think I may have a way we can do this. I found where the Harper man and his pal have David. You bet. I'm looking at the Harper man as we speak. Hold on. I see the Alvarez man. He has David over his shoulder. Who in the fuck is that woman? Okay. You got it. See what I'm seeing? Damn that's some sweet looking broad. Could that be the Alvarez man's wife? You sure? Right, I missed seeing her picture somehow. Then who is this dish? What is she doing there? That throws a wrinkle into my idea."

"When I first got the ping from David's GPS chip, I checked the area out. As you can see it is remote as hell. Got me to thinking, when we talked earlier, we both agreed it would be better if the Harper woman was not found until after the handoff was made. Putting the authorities onto the Harper man was a great idea. Got him and his pal out of the way, concentrate the authorities' attention elsewhere."

"Then they did the unexpected, took David hostage. That was good and bad. We both agreed. The worst part was with David missing, Arturo started going commando. He threatened me. Had me worried that the whole operation was going to shit. Then bingo. I find David. Fuck Arturo. I thought about what you mentioned earlier, cut out the Gonzalez boys and the cartel, wondered whether you were serious? I know, I know, talking about this is risky, my line is secure, I figured yours was. Good. That's what we are doing, talking about it. Time is running out. Arturo wants to wait. The time is right, waiting fucks everything up. What do I propose? I say everything would be easier if they eliminated each other. You know what I mean? How? That's why I called you. We turn Arturo loose. Tell him where David is. Let them have at it."

Mark rocked forward listening to greedy Jenkins and watching the scene on his monitor. Who *was* that woman? Damn sure a lovely sight, even dressed as a country girl. She could be a model with those looks. Why was she there? Jenkins prattled on. Good God, the man was insane. Let's see how do I put that into my report? Wasn't my idea sir. Like that would work. Why not just tell this idiot Jenkins to send Tindal's drone down the river? Then use it on Arturo and his goons. McDab would have my ass— might as well kiss what's left of my career goodbye.

"I got to think on this. I'll call you back if I think of something. I know, I know Arturo isn't going to be patient. Hold off telling him you found David. Let the Harper woman talk to her husband, see if they can come up with an exchange. That could be present an opportunity when they are all together. Stir the Hornet's nest. I mean The Hive. Tell Tindal it went beserk. A joke Jenkins. It was a joke. I'll get back to you."

Mark sat back and watched the scene unfolding on the other end. Who was that woman? He checked the plate on the car—Rent-a-Wreck West Columbia. He googled the name; the yellow pages directory came up. He clicked on the most likely location's number. He asked the person on the other end for recent rentals on an older model Subaru. The young-sounding female agent read off the privacy bullshit. He told her the car had been driving erratically, ran him off the road. If he had to, he would call the police and that would not be good for their business. All she had to do was tell him who the car was rented to and he would tell his attorney to send a letter. He wanted to let her company know a vehicle of theirs caused damage to his vehicle and he wanted to handle it out of court. Otherwise, he would make a police report for a hit and run and Rent-a-Wreck would be named in the lawsuit. Mark heard the clicking sounds as she was entering her request into their system. She asked him his name and he said Jack Offmeir, which he had to spell. He heard more clicking. After a few minutes, she told him the Subaru Outback was rented to Jane Doe and she gave an address. The clueless agent said Miss Doe paid cash.

"Listen lady I'm not fooling around here. Get serious, Jane Doe? If you're going to lie, at least be a little more creative. Jane Doe? Come on, give me a break."

"Mr. Offmeir that's what is entered into the system. I'm not lying mister. Our agent Thomas Jeffrey did the contract and he's left for the day. You can call him tomorrow. He should be in around nine in the morning." Mark asked her about any video. Yes sir, we tape every transaction, but our policy requires a court order to release that information. I've already given you more information than I should have. This could cost me my job." She disconnected.

Mark needed to know who the woman with the Harper and Alvarez men was. He would contact his supervisor and make a request for one of their tech geeks to hack into the system, pull up the info on her from the photo. The upper pencil pushers in the agency will not be happy to hear the latest developments. Jenkins was right, this thing with the Gonzalez boys was getting close to blowing the whole operation. Perhaps he should contact EL Jefe L, that was how he referred to him, the little fat man, his contact in the cartel, the Gonzalez big cheese, their uncle. Maybe I can convince him to reign in Arturo until a trade for the Harper woman is made. Tell him the boys are about to fuck the op up.

A trade would be the best way to handle the situation. He would need to move fast. Jenkins sounded like he was ready to turn this thing into a blood bath. Was that his plan? Had he already made a deal and the telephone call was to throw Mark off? He would have to up the ante, play to Jenkins' greed. Jenkins could already be putting his contingency backup into motion. If he took other offers, fucked him over. That would be a major problem.

Mark continued looking at the monitor. Was that camera equipment in the rental car trunk? He had seen the woman and the Harper man unloading the car. All those supplies. They were planning on an extended venture. That *was* camera equipment. Who was this woman? What was the equipment to be used for? An idea came to Mark, fuck Jenkins and Arturo's revenge, he would request the agency send a UAV from McEntire JNGB to this location. Put the fear of God into the Harper and Alvarez men. Put them back on the run, out of Arturo's way until the hoped-for trade could be arranged. Mark started making calls.

Good. All he could do was sit back and wait.

He buzzed his assistant, a Mexican girl. She was the Gonzalez big cheese's spy. Mark wasn't worried. Plus, she fulfilled her duties without question.

She came in. He walked around the desk, kissed her, turned her around, and hiked up her short skirt. No panties. She submissively bent over the desk. Time for working out his frustrations.

CHAPTER
38

Elena was tired and frustrated. No one to talk to. The Hispanic woman came and went without a word. Elena had begged in English and Spanish for her to talk to her. Tell her what they wanted. She would do whatever they asked. She pleaded and screamed, pleaded and spoke calmly, nothing worked. Although the woman did look at her and smile occasionally. She also noticed the woman wearing more revealing clothing lately. Apparently, no talking was allowed by whoever was in charge.

The woman brought her meals, brought her the books she requested. Nothing much to watch on the television but at least she heard other voices. They reported daily news stories about her plight, the search for her, Jake, TJ, and Deane.

Time for the woman to bring her dinner. No complaints about the food. Obviously, whoever was in charge employed the services of a chef or an incredibly good catering service. Elena glanced up at the camera. Who was watching her? Where was she being held? What had happened to Jake? Was he in custody, dead? She hoped someone found her somehow. What about her family? Her dad would be looking, Jennifer frantic, of that she could be certain.

She looked down at Maisy lying on the rug. Her belly swollen with fatty growths she and Jake feared were cancerous. Turned out they weren't. Watching her brought to mind Dusty, Elena hoped he was alive. If only someone would tell her what she should say, or do, to end her imprisonment.

Let her go outside, see the sun, moon, sky, anything but these walls. She had already decided she would tell them whatever she knew about whatever it was they wanted to know. She would do almost anything to be set free.

The door lock clicked. The woman came in with a service cart. This was different. Maisy jumped up, yapped a couple times, then laid back down. She was getting accustomed to the woman. Elena noticed she had let her hair down. She normally kept it up in a bun. Made her look younger. She was wearing a colorful flowing skirt and a lacy blouse instead of her usual pants with t-shirts or plain cotton flannel long sleeves, like field hands wore. Elena thought this woman was no more than a girl, ten years younger. She looked pretty without the plain clothes she always wore.

The woman pushed the cart over to the desk, but she didn't unload the food tray. Instead, she turned and walked into the bathroom. Elena heard her turn on the water, the sound of the drain stop being engaged. What did this mean? The woman walked back out, nodded to Elena, pointed with her chin to the bathroom. Elena wasn't sure what the woman intended and hesitated. A frown came on the woman's face. She walked deliberately toward Elena. Elena thought the woman intended to force her into the bathroom, so she walked slowly in that direction, passing by the woman, and stopping inside the door. She reached to close it and the woman put her foot in the way and joined Elena in the bathroom, closed and locked the door. Elena felt trapped.

Turning to Elena she said, "take your clothes off" in perfectly understandable English with a South Texas accent Elena was familiar with. Hearing her command shocked Elena. The sound of a live person's voice was almost overwhelming. The command caught Elena off guard. One was as shocking as the other.

"You talk. Hallelujah. Say something else."

"Take your clothes off now or I will take them off." She moved toward Elena. Elena turned to the side and the woman reached in felt the water and turned the two-thirds-full tub faucet off, turned back around and reached for Elena's arm. Elena felt her strength, remembered her first encounter, and didn't resist. She was scared.

"Okay. I'll take my clothes off myself. Would you mind looking the other way?" The woman released her hand and stepped on the other side of Elena. She did not look away. Elena started undressing slowly, which drew a frown from the woman. "What's your name, will you tell me that much? And why am I taking a bath? I showered last night." The woman didn't answer. Elena finished undressing and stepped into the tub, easing down and back, left hand covering her mons, her right arm and hand covering her nipples.

She kept her eyes on the woman. The other woman reached up and peeled off the lacy blouse, she wasn't wearing a bra, her breasts were firm, capped by larger than normal areolas. Elena wanted to look away but was transfixed by the thoughts racing through her mind. What was going on? Was this woman going to join her in the tub? For what purpose? Bathe her? Drown her? Oh God, please don't let her drown me. The way the woman was looking at her as she stood there made Elena think this woman had something else in mind. Oh Lordy!

Elena was no stranger to what she thought was on this woman's mind. Had lots of time to think about it. In college she had joined a sorority. In the sorority house she shared a room with a pretty blond from Connecticut named Cindi McCulley.

Halfway through the first semester together, she and her roommate had been out with some of their sorority sisters at a local watering hole partying down. They all got intoxicated and caught a cab back to their house. When they got back to their room, Elena had fallen on top of her bed laughing, too inebriated to pull back the covers or take off her clothes. She fell asleep, passed out, whatever.

The next thing she remembered was her roommate removing her bra. The cool air from the air conditioner hit her bare skin and she realized the rest of her clothes had been removed. She quickly opened her eyes and through the light of the streetlamp outside their window, Elena saw that Cindi her roommate had taken off her own clothes and was caressing her breasts as she lowered her face down to kiss Elena.

Too drunk and shocked to resist, so Elena reminded herself, she had lain there while Cindi began French kissing her and running her fingers over her nipples then gently inserted a finger where no woman had ever been before. Despite herself, Elena later blamed it on the alcohol, Elena found herself responding. Cindi used one then two fingers to bring Elena off, inserted the fingers into her mouth and sucked on them, then reinserted the fingers and brought them up to Elena's mouth and Elena allowed her to insert them into her own mouth. Elena was no stranger to her own taste; she had had several sexual encounters with other men including oral sex followed by kissing.

Cindi then began playing with herself and when she neared her own climax, she reached out and took Elena's hand and placed it over her mons, then she pushed two of Elena's fingers inside her. Elena, in a haze did not resist. Soon,

Cindi was moaning and holding Elena's hand in place as she shook. Cindi collapsed beside Elena and brought her fingers up and rubbed them across Elena's lips. This was the first time she tasted another woman.

The next day she requested to be reassigned to another room after telling Cindi never to say anything to anyone about what happened, or she would bring her up on assault charges. Cindi laughed. Later, Elena found out she was not the only sorority sister Cindi had seduced or assaulted. Was this what this Hispanic woman had in mind?

What should Elena do? The other woman reached back and undid her skirt, letting it drop to the floor. She wore no underclothes. Her pubic hair was trimmed, a hint above her vulva. Elena watched as the other woman ran a hand over her pubic area, smiling, she locked eyes with Elena, a haughty, naughty look on her dark-skinned face. She pulled her long hair back and twirled it into a bun and inserted a hair pin to hold it in place. This done she walked over knelt beside the tub, picked up Elena's loofa, squirted Elena's body soap on it and began slowly, methodically to scrub Elena's back. Next, she washed Elena's feet and legs and to Elena's surprise she skipped her private areas, as she moved up to her stomach and breasts. Elena's breath nearly caught in her throat. She dared not resist. She felt certain of what was coming after the bath. The woman leaned over, and Elena thought, here we go, as she felt the woman's breath on her neck, then her ear. Unexpectedly, causing Elena to take in a sharp breath of soap-scented air, the woman whispered to her,

"Don't worry Chiquita, I have no wish to have you do anything you not want. They listen, perhaps watch. No! You must not look, only look at me! I put my hand down toward your pussy in case they watch. If you like I give you relief."

Purely professional, unfortunately this did not make Elena feel more secure. Who were they? Where was the surveillance equipment? She thought the bedroom was the only place with a camera. Oh God, what should she do? If she said no, what would this woman do? In a daze she heard the woman whisper, "Would you like? Move your head say yes or no."

Elena didn't know how to respond. Elena felt certain what the woman would rather she indicate. What should she do? If she indicated no, would the woman leave, or what? Clearly the woman wouldn't be here doing this unless she had been told to. Elena felt she was in a no-win situation. She knew how to fight. Her father had taught her. She was at a disadvantage. The woman had already proven that. Tears began flowing out of her eyes. She nodded.

"Don't cry sweet senorita. I be gentle. I make you feel better. Close your eyes. Relax. Be good senorita, I tell you good news. Relax. Enjoy."

The woman gently began rubbing a soapy finger over Elena's clitoris. Somehow, probably Elena's breathing coming in spurts told the woman her ministrations were having the desired effect, Elena shuddered as the woman inserted her thumb inside her vagina and, for a first, she allowed what she stopped Jake from doing, the woman slowly inserted her middle finger into her rectum. Shortly Elena, despite a part of her wanting not to, she began to move with the woman's strokes, followed by a body shaking orgasm. She whimpered like a baby with the release. The woman leaned in and whispered, "Feel better? Maybe next time you return favor. You learn I can make you feel better than any man can Chiquita."

Elena glanced at the woman. The woman stood and Elena watched. The woman ran her hands over her own body, a lascivious look on her face. Her body had betrayed her; the orgasm had surprised her. Elena felt she should feel ashamed. She had no choice. She had been afraid. She started to speak. The woman put a hand to her lips, made a shushing sound.

The woman pulled her to her feet in the tub, then gently dried her off with an oversize towel. The woman picked a note up off the sink, put her own clothes on, and watched as Elena dressed, then handed her the note.

"Soon you talk to husband. Must say only what is on note. Would you like some tea? Perhaps some crackers, cheese and fruit."

She pulled out a cell phone, looked at the time. "Twenty minutes before husband call. You must not say anything but what on note. Nothing more. Understand?"

Elena said she understood.

"Good," she replied, unlocked the bathroom door, and walked into the bedroom, leaving the door standing open. Maisy was outside the door and the woman pushed her aside with her foot. Maisy snapped at her.

CHAPTER
39

Ariel followed TJ on up. A chilly, stiff breeze blew off and on, swaying the pines, brushing limbs against the tower, swish and screech on the metal. Leaves twisted and turned, falling from hardwood oaks and hickories, gravity pulling them downward. Fall was in the air.

She entered through the opening onto the viewing platform of the tower. A crumpled pudgy Hispanic guy lay on his back in the middle of the platform. He was gagged, his hands and feet were zip tied together. He stared at her wild-eyed.

TJ said, "This the person I warned you about. He's a member of a gang called El Diablos with ties to the Latin Kings and the Juarez Cartel. His brother's the local leader. This one's the second in command and a leading IT expert for the cartel responsible for the kidnapping of Jake's wife Elena."

"They previously sent mine and Jake's family exclusive photos with threatening captions. Moving van, abandoned in Charlotte, reported as loaded, contained a few of his men and some of what was probably stolen computer parts and files. Now that you have seen him, you no longer safe, may not ever be safe. May not look like much but the gangbanger organization he is part of will stop at nothing to get even with us. The cartel, as I'm sure you know, is an international terrorist organization. This is what Jake and I didn't want you to see. We felt it best not to involve you."

TJ walked over, once more rolled Gonzalez up in the blanket and hoisted the Mexican over his shoulder like he was a sack of dogfood. "No reason keep him up here now, probably needs to go to the restroom, let him eat." TJ adjusted the weight. The Mexican protested, the sound muffled by the gag.

"In a coupla hours, we will show his brother he's alive. After his brother let's Jake see and hear Elena, we hope to set up an exchange. It was our intention to have your interview air to provide plausible doubt, get the authorities to do what they should be doing, investigating other leads. There's no certainty regarding Elena's condition or whether she will be allowed to talk to Jake. You need to do your interviews and get out of here. His brother will be trying to find us rather than do an exchange. That may not happen if he doesn't have Elena. If he or the authorities show up, you will be in major jeopardy." TJ took his hostage, started down the tower steps.

Ariel went over to the rail, looked down at Jake sitting on the tailgate of the truck holding his rifle. This was not what she expected. 'You didn't know what to expect,' she thought. TJ was right, she had gotten herself in over her head. But that is what hard hitting journalists do. Get the story, regardless of personal danger. Their news organization had legal experts to advise them what their rights were, any potential liability. Ariel was certain her conservative station manager would insist she go to the authorities. If she withheld part of the story, could they prove prior knowledge? That would be the safe bet, but it diminished the impact. Reporting this kidnapping was a major breaking story. But it made Jake and TJ look like vigilantes and if the exchange didn't happen, they would be in greater jeopardy. How could she do the interview and not use this part of the story? She looked around, watching, and listening. The soft whistling of the wind through the gridwork, now an ominous sound.

When she exited the tower, she saw the Mexican sitting on one of the coolers devouring the remains of the meal Jake and TJ had eaten earlier. Jake walked over to greet her.

"TJ and I were wondering if you brought the clothes we requested? They were for our guest. We need to get him cleaned up and in fresh clothes. While TJ does that, you and I can do our interview. Then TJ can do his. You ready?"

Ariel walked past Jake, TJ and the Mexican without saying anything. She went to the opened trunk, rummaged through a bag, and pulled out a smaller one containing the clothing. She and Jake finished unloading the rest of her purchases and she pulled out the camera and tripod, checked to make sure the battery was charged and laid it back in, and closed the trunk. Jake went to the truck and grabbed a blanket out of the back.

TJ started to object about the camera, decided to let it go. Jake asked him if by chance he had a hammer and nails somewhere in his truck?

"You gotta be kidding?"

Jake went under the tower, searched around on the ground until he found some old screws and a double-hand-sized rock. Ariel asked what that was for? Jake said to attach the blanket to a couple trees.

"Why don't we just do it in the car?"

"With TJ and the Mex out here?"

Ariel didn't catch on until she heard TJ chuckling and saw the big grin on Jake's face.

"Maybe you haven't changed much after all."

This brought more chuckles from TJ.

Ariel got in the car. Jake stood holding her door open, blanket in hand.

"We'll wait for Gonzalez to finish eating. TJ plans to take him down to the bath houses, get him cleaned up, have him put on fresh clothes."

Ariel asked Jake to take a seat in the car so they could talk.

Jake came around to the passenger side and sat down. The car had a musky smell, the seats were worn, a couple star-shaped dings in the windshield. He looked at Ariel. She was a woman now, the only hint of the farmgirl was her clothes. They fit her well. Despite himself his mind undressed her, memories of their youthful discoveries, tasting the forbidden treasures. He shifted in his seat. His balls still ached.

She cleared her throat. His eyes met hers. She seemed to read him. He smiled. She smiled back. She became all business.

"You see we can do the interview in here. You could put the blanket over the door. Or we could dispense with the blanket and I could blur the background. Would save time. TJ said you would be making a call in a couple hours. That doesn't give us much time."

"A good hacker could maybe undo your changes. Isn't that right?"

"Not my expertise. Ready?"

Jake draped the blanket over the door and pulled it closed.

"Any questions, comments before we start?"

"Do not mention our guest, our weapons, definitely, nothing about the hoped-for exchange. Those could and would create a whole new set of problems for everyone."

"As I recall you and TJ said the main reason for the interview was to give your side of the story, have the authorities start an all-out investigation. And you said your intent was to find Elena. If you have any information where she could be, don't you think giving them someone and somewhere to look would be a good idea?"

"These people are dangerous. If they think the authorities are after them, they will get rid of her. How is that helping? It damn sure isn't in Elena's best interests. Nor yours. If you mention their name or implicate the cartel, you won't ever be safe. You said it earlier, this interview should be about my character and Elena's and my relationship. Show I had no motive, nothing to gain from harming Elena. TJ's presence and interview should dispel the rumors about him and his wife. He can testify to the fact I had nothing to do with any disappearances. If you think it will help, we can explain the PTSD accusation. Taking away motive and opportunity, give reasonable doubt. Isn't that what these interviews should be about?"

Ariel's piercing blue green eyes bore into Jake's. "Jake, you and TJ need to explain your Assault and Battery on an Officer of the Law Charge to make you seem less dangerous. How and why did that happen? Isn't that the real start to this mess you are in?"

Uh oh, hadn't seen that one coming. How to answer that without Thurmond Tindal's involvement being mentioned and TJ's undercover operation being disclosed? Jake could use Ariel's help. She could talk to Doc Hunter. Jake wanted to know Dusty's condition. Doc could verify the injury's suspicious nature. He could tell her about the unusual nature of the ammo and wound. An interview with Deputy Coulter couldn't hurt. He could tell what he knew, send her to the FBI lab. Would he? Could cause him problems. For damn sure the sheriff wouldn't agree.

Then there were the thumb drive, zip files, their ace in the hole. No way could they agree to let her have those, see the info. Mark Paponovich. ask him questions, see his face, hear what he might say. Could cause his superiors to shut her down. Get her into major hot water. Jake couldn't allow that to happen.

Deputy Coulter and the Feebs, that should make some people uncomfortable. Ariel could ask the DA and the sheriff about campaign donations from Thurmond Tindal? About the warden's cozy relationship with Tindal. He could talk about this, not mention TJ's undercover operation. They didn't have much time. The gangbangers and the authorities could be on the way.

Jake decided the hell with it, tell her the whole story, leave out TJ's investigation and knowledge of the gang's potential involvement with Tindal.

He started telling Ariel the story. TJ came over, knocked on the car's passenger window, startling Ariel, and him.

Jake exited the car. TJ said their guest was finished pigging out and he was taking him down to get him cleaned up. Jake told him to go ahead he and Ariel decided to do the interview in her rental. TJ reminded Jake he was a married man, not to do anything he shouldn't. Jake simply shook his head, kept a straight face. He hoped Ariel didn't hear him.TJ laughed, grabbed the bag with the clothes, dumped Gonzalez in the bed of the truck, drove around them with a short wave and a grin as he went by.

Ariel asked what that grin was about. Jake told her just TJ being TJ. She squinted, looked straight ahead through the windshield, then looked back at Jake.

"Did you ever think about me?"

"Always. When you disappeared and your parents refused to let me talk to you or tell me where you were and none of your friends could or would tell me anything, I thought about breaking into your house. It was close to two weeks before I found out you had gone to England to live with your Aunt and her family. I couldn't believe you would leave without telling me. There were all kinds of rumors and gossip. Everyone in the community treated me like I had been at fault."

"Weren't you? One of your friends told me you had enlisted in the Army. You never told me. I wanted to talk to you. Seemed you made the decision, didn't feel you needed to tell me. When daddy found out we had been sleeping together, he flipped out. He wanted to have you arrested. I had to promise to not talk to you or see you again. The next thing I knew, daddy and mama had made arrangements with my aunt for me to go live with her. No way to talk on a plane on my way to London. My aunt had strict instructions to not allow me access to a phone, especially, to call you. By the time I found a way, you were gone."

"You had two more years of school. You were smart and I knew you wanted to go to college. What you said earlier about me was right, I couldn't tell you that I was in trouble with the police. The last time I was arrested, to avoid going to jail, my grandmother used her connection with Senator Boykin to get the charges dropped on one condition, my folks had to agree to allow me to enter the military. Sheriff Hinson told my ole man the best thing for me was the military, my ole man agreed. I wasn't ready for college and your ole man would never have allowed you to marry me. I was going to tell you about my decision, was going to ask you to wait for me, but your ole man told my ole man to keep me away from you. Next thing I knew you were gone."

"Why did you say you love me?"

"I don't know. It just came out. You were acting like I intended you harm. I guess in the back of my mind, I was afraid if you left, I might never see you again."

"You're a married man. Your wife is in trouble. Don't you think that is kind of shallow? Wouldn't play well if Jane and John Q Public knew about that. They'd want you to hang, that's for damn certain."

Jake turned his head, looked out through the windshield. The sun was sinking lower; the breeze was turning chillier.

Ariel was right. No need in thinking about what ifs. Hopefully, he would be talking to Elena soon, an exchange would be made. He needed to concentrate on how to make that happen. He needed Ariel gone for her own sake, so there would be no distractions. They needed to hurry with the interviews.

"You're right," said Jake. "We need to get these interviews over with and get you and us out of here. The longer you're here, the greater the risks. I find it difficult to think with you here. Maybe when this is all over, you and I can sit down and catch up. Right now, we need you out there doing your job; perhaps you can help sway Jane and John Q Public. You ready to get started."

"I'll get my video camera." Jake started struggling with the blanket trying to create a cocoon. "Don't worry about it. I can zoom in and block everything out or I can edit out the blanket. Which way do you want me to do it?"

"On the blanket, like we used to." Jake watched Ariel's face struggle between a frown and a smile. "Just kidding. I'm kind of nervous and I try to cover by being a smartass. I'm sorry. If you can edit out the background, then I guess it doesn't matter."

"Jake I could make it look like you were on the courthouse steps, if I wanted to." Ariel set the camera up. "All I need the blanket for is to provide a darker background. I can put in another background later. Why don't we do it outside, place the blanket over the tower framework?"

"Fine by me. Better for us if we put space between us."

Ariel left his comment unanswered. He draped the blanket and got her approval. She turned the camera on and zoomed in on him.

"You look rugged. Should create sympathy among some female viewers. Don't look so smug. Here we go."

"My name is Ariel Gaspard, NBC Columbia, reporting live from a remote location I cannot disclose."

"I am here at the request of Jake Harper and Thomas Alvarez for an exclusive interview. Mr. Harper and Mr. Alvarez are wanted by the authorities for Assault and Battery on an Officer of the Law in York County, South Carolina."

According to witness statements, Mr. Harper's family dog was shot while accompanying Mrs. Harper on her morning jog. The critical wound to their pet was created by an unknown assailant with an unknown weapon using what has been described as for military use only--restricted ammunition. The incident was investigated by two York County Sheriff Deputies and Game Warden Walter Crandall. A verbal exchange between Mr. Harper and Mr. Alvarez with the game warden led to assault charge levied against Mr. Harper and Officer Alvarez."

"Mr. Harper. Officer Alvarez and you say that Warden Crandall appeared on the scene when you, Officer Alvarez and your wife Elena had stopped at the site of the shooting after taking your dog Dusty to Doctor Hunter's Veterinary Hospital in McConnells, is that correct?"

"Correct. We stopped there to await the deputies' arrival and to protect the scene for the investigation."

"Mr. Alvarez is an officer of the law, a former retired military veteran and a member of the Metro-Charlotte SWAT Team. You are a former veteran who was given a medical discharge after nearly twenty years of service. Both of you served overseas with several tours of duty in the Middle East, is that correct?"

"Yes."

"You stated that the wound to your dog Dusty was suspicious, appeared to be from a weapon firing a bullet, you described for military use only. You and Officer Alvarez determined this, due to your experience in the military, is that correct?

"Yes. That is correct. The ammunition fragments were sent to the FBI. t am certain they can confirm this."

"You also stated that while waiting for the deputies, Warden Crandall appeared. You said he didn't seem interested in investigating the shooting, rather he seemed more interested in provoking an incident with you and Officer Alvarez. Why would he do that?"

"Warden Crandall and I have a history that started when he became a game warden. The place I live was my maternal grandparents' home and land. After my grandfather died, the hunters from an adjacent hunt club, came and went as they pleased, hunting my families' land. This included Warden Crandall, who used his position to allow only members of this hunt club to hunt there without any family member's permission."

"When I moved onto the land, a man, well-known in the area, who owned the hunt club was not happy. He is, as he has been, determined to buy my land. I have declined. I want the land to be preserved for future generations. This man has used Warden Crandall to continuously harass me. I believe Warden Crandall's appearance at the scene where our dog Dusty was shot was not to investigate, but rather to deflect the investigation of my dog Dusty's shooting. Rather than wait for the deputies as we requested, he deliberately provoked the incident with Mr. Alvarez and me."

"The warden's friend owns the land that surrounds your property. His name is Thurmond Tindal, isn't that who you are referring to? And isn't it true that Mr. Tindal is the man who has been trying to buy your land and has used the warden to press you to sell?"

"That is correct."

"Why would Mr. Tindal want your land so badly and why would Warden Crandall do his bidding?"

"You would need to ask Thurmond Tindal that question."

"Besides the assault charge, the York County District Attorney Gerald Sumners and the Sheriff Dale Yates are saying your wife has disappeared, as has Mr. Alvarez and his wife. Shortly I will interview Officer Alvarez, whom I have seen and talked to. He will attest his wife is alive and well. According to both you and him, your wife Elena was kidnapped and is being held by party unknown. You asked me here for this interview. Why?"

"To assure the public I had nothing to do with my wife Elena's disappearance."

"Why should the viewing public believe you? Who do you think took her and why?"

"First off. Let me say I love my wife. And, if she's listening, I want her to know that. And I want her captors to know I will do everything I can to get her back, and when I do, she better be safe and unharmed."

"My friend and fellow vet TJ Alvarez' family and my family received threatening photos and messages. The sheriff department knows this. When a sweep was made of our property numerous miniature game cameras were found inside and outside our residence. Not knowing who was making these threats, we wanted our wives to go some place secure. Mr. Alvarez sent his wife to an undisclosed location. Our plan was for my wife Elena to give her deposition to the authorities concerning the altercation with the game warden then join Officer Alvarez's wife. She never showed. Officer Alvarez was with me when she left our house. I thought she might have decided to go to her daughter's house. I talked to her daughter. She had not heard from her. My wife never answered or returned any calls. Mr. Alvarez and I tried to find out where she was, without any luck. I later learned, from news broadcasts, her car was found abandoned with blood on the driver's seat."

"Makes me think somebody didn't want her telling what really happened."

"Would her deposition have helped in yours and Officer Alvarez's defense?"

"She was the only witness. Her testimony is critical to our defense."

"Perhaps the motive is the half-million dollar reward offered for the safe return of your wife and for your arrest."

"Whoa. Stop the camera."

Ariel did.

"A half million-dollar reward? Who is offering that?"

"The amount was all that was reported. You didn't know?"

"Hell no. Everybody and their brother will be looking to collect. Damn."

"Another reason why this interview is important."

"Another reason why all of us, including you, better be careful."

"You want to continue I hope?"

Jake thought about the reward. Who? He wondered how he could find out. Ariel had moved from behind the camera. She was staring at him.

"Sorry. That reward amount threw me for a loop."

"Jake there's no need to apologize."

"Be nice to know who's behind that reward offer. My bet it's Tindal."

"I'll see what I can find out. Ready?"

"Yeah. Go ahead."

Ariel looked down at her notes, then cut the camera back on and resumed.

"You and Officer Alvarez have been on the run trying to find your wife and clear your names. Why not turn yourselves in and let the authorities do this? The police and FBI are better equipped and trained to handle these situations, why not let them handle it?"

Jake paused. He had been looking down. He shook his head and looked back up. She would edit that out. Made him look uncertain.

"Because they have been more interested in arresting Mr. Alvarez and me rather than investigating other possible suspects. The DA and sheriff have been accusing me of being a criminal with all kinds of false charges. Even going so far as to label us domestic terrorists. They claim I did all these things because I suffer from PTSD. They have said we are armed and dangerous. There is no evidence for these accusations."

Ariel cut the camera off and stepped back.

"Jake I need to get this reward thing out there. The reward has already been made public so there's no reason not to."

"Some people might have missed it. This will just incentivize more crazies. Ah hell. Fuck it. Go ahead ask away."

"There has been a reward offered to anyone who has information leading to your arrest. Aren't you afraid some people might use that as a reason to do you and Officer Alvarez harm? They could claim self-defense. Why not turn yourselves in?"

"I hope no one gets the chance. We will turn ourselves in as soon as my wife is released. Then we will provide proof these ridiculous charges are false. The authorities could do the same if they did their jobs."

"Why do you think the sheriff and DA are more interested in arresting you than they are in finding your wife?"

"You need to ask them? In my opinion, they are using this for political reasons--a major contributor to their campaigns I bet is behind this—perhaps the same person offering the reward. The same one who wants me out of the way. I have something he wants. He will do anything to satisfy his ambitions. I believe this is all connected somehow. Our dog Dusty getting shot, the threatening photos, the cameras in and around our home, and my wife Elena's disappearance. Our dachshund Maisy was with my wife. She is also missing. The authorities have evidence. The public should demand they do their jobs. Demand justice."

"Anything more you want to say?"

"Whoever has my wife, whoever is behind this, you will be found. Turn my wife loose. Otherwise, you better hope the authorities do their job and find you first. One more thing, I want the viewers to please report anything you see or hear to the FBI, not the local authorities. Elena, I hope you hear this. I love you. I will do whatever I have to, to get you home safe."

Ariel switched the camera back off.

"I hope this works."

"Some editing, add other interviews from people you mentioned and…"

They heard TJ's truck coming up the hill. Sounded like he was in a hurry.

CHAPTER
40

TJ was forced to drive slower than he wished down the winding road. He slowed to look at the van. Did not look like anyone had messed with it. Once he reached the bottom, he saw the sun was not far above the ragged tree line. Soon it would drop behind the treeline on the distant hill across the Broad River. He drove on past the bath house area to check on the pontoon. It was still there. A solitary vessel rocking in the breeze-stirred murky water. He circled around the parking area pulling as close to the bath houses as possible. Climbing down from the truck, he reached back in the rear passenger area and grabbed the bag of clothes Ariel had bought. He forgot the soap and towels Ariel brought with her. He dug out his almost empty liquid hand soap bottle and the roll of paper towels, along with one of the Tasers.

He unsheathed his Ka-Bar and cut David Gonzalez hands and feet free. Brandishing the knife and taser, he told David, "You try to run, and I'll give your head a perm with this thing. A word of caution, even if you were to get away, which we both know isn't going to happen, these woods are full of snakes, many of them poisonous."

David looked at him bug-eyed. David reached up to take the gag off. TJ waved the knife, "Huh uh. I didn't tell you to remove that. You will do as I say, when I say, if not, you will suffer the consequences. Something for you to think about while you are in the shower. You can bet this taser with you wet will do more than curl your hair."

"The water is cold. So, if I were you, I would wet myself, soap myself with the water off then turn it back on and rinse. The nice lady brought you some clean clothes." TJ laid the bag on the tailgate. Here take these paper towels and liquid soap. You can remove the gag before you get in the shower. I will be outside the door waiting. I can see inside the bath house so don't think about anything but getting clean. Let's go."

TJ stood outside the door. He kept his ears open and glanced inside ever so often. Most of his attention was taken up watching an eagle circling around and around, gliding up and down in the wind currents ou over the river. It tucked its wings in and made a kamikaze dive toward the water, pulling up at the last moment as its talons snagged a fish. With the meal in grasp, it swooped back to the distant hillside and landed in a towering pine tree. This was the first time TJ had seen an eagle this close. It was like a silent nature film being seen with background sounds of running water, deep inhaling breaths, and Spanish curses. The water stopped as the Eagle landed. TJ took a quick look and watched Gonzalez quickly turn his back on him as he used the towels to dry off.

He glanced at his Luminox Special Ops time piece. A little after the 1600 hour--less than an hour until they called back. Would Arturo hold up his end or had something bad happened to Elena? He and Jake needed to discuss their options. He was to do an interview. It would have to be brief. Ariel needed to be gone before the call. TJ wondered if Jake had thought anymore about Elena and the exchange. Would Jake need Ariel if the call didn't happen? No matter. Ariel needed to be gone. They needed to be on the move.

David was shuffling his feet putting his shoes back on. TJ looked back, turned around, something shiny caught his eye. He saw an object come down and hover just above the treetops near the boat launch area. TJ's first reaction was to duck back into the bath house. He looked past the door jamb with one eye, keeping his body out of sight against the wall. He heard David moving toward him shouting. He saw it also.

"I tell you my brother he find me. You fucked now."

TJ reached out an arm and swept him back, knocking him down in a heap several feet from the bench where his soiled clothes lay on the concrete floor.

"Shut the fuck up and stay put or I'll use the taser on you."

David pushed himself up into a sitting position. "My brother he kill you. I be glad."

TJ whirled around, fired the taser, shocked David enough that he jerked backwards onto his back. TJ hurried over, stuffed David's dirty shirt in his mouth, flipped him over, zip tied the shirt into his mouth, zip tied his hands and feet together and propped him up against the wooden slat dressing bench. David's eyes had rolled back into his head. TJ laid a finger across the carotid area of his neck—his heart was racing. TJ's was also. He walked back over to the doorway and peered out. The UAV had moved. He crouched down and leaned his head out past the door frame. Nothing. He hurried over and crammed the rest of David's dirty clothes into the bag. There were more new clothes in the bottom. He threw the soap bottle and the paper towel roll in along with the ones David had used to dry himself. Took the bag, picked up David lifting him up, tucked him under one arm and hurried to the truck—all while looking frantically for the UAV.

He threw David in the back over the side rail. He fell on his back with a loud thump. TJ tossed the bag in the backseat and moved as fast as possible to get into the driver's seat. He spun the truck around kicking up dirt, grass and gravel and tore out of the parking area. Going as fast as he dared, he slid past the locked pole gate and floored it. He straightened as many curves as possible, almost sliding off into one of the deep wooded ravines which were descending into shadows on each side of the narrow road. He glanced into the mirrors; wanted to look back to see if the thing was tracing him but didn't.

How did they find them? Was it Arturo? David had said they knew how to locate each other. No way Arturo gained access to a UAV. How was this possible? How did they know where to look? Ariel? The car, her camera, anything's hackable. Had she let something about them slip out? He hoped not. Fuck. Go. Go. Go. Get the fuck out of here! That looked like a military UAV. That would mean military authorization. Who could do that? It was illegal.

The who and how kept running through his mind as he fought to stay on the narrow winding road. Memories of the Middle East, desiccated, faceless vaporized bodies--images he rarely reflected on--the thumbdrive of Tindal's UAV and the shredded dummy. He zipped past the van. What should they do with the van and pontoon? Leave them. Jake may not like that idea. He checked the time. His truck display said 4:15. Forty-five minutes before they made the call. They needed to make that call. They needed to get out of here. He nearly missed the tower. He braked hard and slid to a stop short of Ariel's rental.

Jake was standing by the passenger side, Ariel beside him, camera in hand. Hope that thing is off, TJ thought coming to a stop. Not that it matters now. He jumped out, looking around for the drone.

CHAPTER
41

"They found us. There was a UAV down by the river. They know we are here." He shouted to Jake. Jake immediately began scanning the sky. "Is that damn camera on?" He asked Ariel as he started toward her. She had the camera pointed up. She had been looking up then she and the camera swung toward him. "If it's on, turn it off."

Ariel's startled face caused him to pause.

"Ah what the fuck does it matter. They know we're here. Tell me Ariel, you didn't tell anyone where you were going or who you were meeting?"

The question caught Ariel by surprise. TJ's sudden approach and startling comment had created all kinds of thoughts. "No. I did as Jake instructed. Why would I?"

Jake continued to scan the sky. TJ rarely got this excited. "Maybe the drone belonged to some amateur. Lots of people have those damn things."

"Damn thing was a military one. No doubt and no doubt it saw me. We can't take any chances bro. We got to get the hell out of here. If they know where we are, they will be here soon. For all we know the authorities could have a chopper on its way."

"A little more than thirty minutes until we make the call. I've got to know Elena's alive. Set up an exchange. If we leave, I may not get cell coverage in time. If the authorities have a chopper on the way, we're fucked. Maybe we should split up."

"Whoa bro. Splitting up? We need to stay together. Ariel needs to get out of here." He looked over to Ariel.

"He's right Ariel. You need to get out of here. How soon can you put my interview on the air?"

"I could climb the tower and upload to the station from here. They could have it on the six o'clock news. I'm sure they'll have a breaking news alert as soon as the station manager reviews the footage. The national network would run with it immediately, guaranteed. But I haven't interviewed TJ."

"Can't take the time," TJ threw in walking past her to gather up the coolers and other stuff they had pulled out before he took Gonzalez for a shower. "You caught me on camera. I bet you did so earlier and again a few minutes ago. That will have to do."

Ariel turned around watching Jake and TJ picking up the coolers and walking back to his truck.

"I'm sorry you think I would be so underhanded. I assure you I have not taped you and never would without your permission. Think what you will. If you won't give me an interview, then let me stay until the call is made. Once the viewers hear Elena is alive and not being held by you, the authorities will be forced to look for her elsewhere."

"No. The call's to arrange an exchange. If they hear we have Gonzalez," TJ said sliding the cooler in, "they charge us with kidnapping. Now how do you think that helps us?"

Jake had placed his cooler on the tailgate and had walked around to look closer at Gonzalez, who was not moving. "Ariel, TJ is right. Go upload your footage, then get out of here. You can help us by questioning the DA, the sheriff, Deputy Coulter, Doc Hunter, and anyone else you discover that is involved and has evidence. If you can, see Tindal, his man Jenkins and any of his employees. I wouldn't bother with the warden. Put pressure on them through the media. Be careful with Tindal, he has a lot of influential friends. I will call you to let you know about the call, hopefully, the exchange. I would appreciate it if you could check on Dusty's condition when you talk to Doc Hunter. I would like to know how he's doing. You need help with your camera?"

"No. I can manage."

"You need to hurry."

She stared at Jake. Nodded. Went to the tower.

Jake walked around to TJ at the other side of the truck and spoke so Ariel couldn't hear. "Is he okay? He doesn't look so hot. What did you do to him?"

"Had to taser him. He'll be alright. The ride up here probably rattled him. As soon as she leaves, we need to check him and his clothes for a GPS chip. Get her out of here," TJ spoke softly and emphatically, his back to the tower and Ariel. We need to make plans fast." He glanced over his shoulder following Jake's eye movement.

Ariel had turned around, was walking their way. She had followed Jake's eyes and expression and partially read his lips as he spoke to TJ. Jake headed her off. She saw his worried face.

"Has something happened to the Mexican man?"

"No. If you're going to upload the interview, go do it now and get going. I wouldn't want you to be here if our adversaries do make an appearance. You wouldn't want that either, believe me."

Ariel made a move to step around him and Jake put out his hand catching her across her chest. He felt her firm but forgiving breasts push against his forearm and hand. Her breath caught and he felt her heart vibrating beneath his touch. She stopped and looked at him. He didn't know how to read her expression. He dropped his arm and grasped her wrist lightly.

"Ariel please do as I asked. It's for your own good. I promise I'll get in touch, tell you what I find out. I hope you will do the same. I wish we could talk more but that is not possible at this time. Either go up there or leave. You've got to be out of here in ten minutes. We need to get Gonzalez ready, make sure he knows what to say and not say." He squeezed her wrist, brushed his hand over hers and walked on past to finish loading the remainder of the items left where the coolers and TJ's truck had been.

Ariel followed him, stopping by her open driver side door to retrieve one of the burner phones.

Jake's touch was still there, emotions welled up inside her. A part of her wanted there to be something. Another part of her was torn because he was still a married man with a wife whom, if she was alive, would have a lot to say about what the future would be. Was there a future with him and his wife?

She shook her head, brushed a few loose strands of hair back across her left ear, took the phone and her camera, walked past Jake without looking or saying anything more and climbed the tower. She needed to switch back into professional mode.

CHAPTER

42

Undersecretary Robert Hardy had received the call from the NSC. There had been a request for UAV surveillance from one of their sister agencies. The target was none other than Jake Harper and Thomas Alvarez, two fugitives declared armed and dangerous. They had been surveilled via satellite up-feed in a remote area of the Sumter National Forest named Leeds, South Carolina on the Broad River. Undersecretary Hardy had called for a videoconference with the individual initiating the request and had been connected to the Director of the CIA's Clandestine Unit, General McDab. The general would not reveal the name of the agent but assured him this was part of an ongoing operation to determine the location of a person of interests to his agency. Hardy said he would talk to Homeland's Secretary. He requested that no action be taken until he had cleared this with her.

Hardy was flummoxed. Apparently, TJ and Jake had stumbled into a CIA operation. TJ must have learned something from his CI that spooked him. That thought had come to him earlier when the moving van with the gang members had been discovered. Seemed his hunch was correct. What had he learned?

TJ was supposed to gather evidence, not act without permission. Had he jeopardized the task force's operation? He and Jake may have put the skids on Homeland's Tindal investigation.

He knew Colonel Thurmond Tindal from their prior service as intelligence officers. That was not in his file and he saw no reason to include it. He wanted his report to not seem prejudiced.

Tindal had been vetted by Homeland as a matter of course when he applied to DoD for developing a UAV weapon system—a system that utilized military and civilian satellites' classified information vital to national security. He had passed the preliminary investigation and was given the permit to proceed. Final approval by Homeland for DoD would have been issued once the system had passed the development and testing approval process. This had not happened. Someone had gotten the former POTUS to sign off on the project, cutting the timeline and bypassing many phases of the process.

Hardy's boss, HS Secretary was in the dark, so she claimed.

Hardy was not satisfied. TJ came to him with questions regarding Tindal's potential involvement with the shooting of Jake's dog. Hardy tried to warn TJ and Jake off, apparently his admonitions had fallen on deaf ears.

His investigation into Tindal Industries turned up numerous times when Tindal had received contracts when other longtime contractor's bids had been less expensive. Hardy knew this happened all the time. That was how Washington politics worked.

One problem was not whether Tindal had used influence peddling to obtain the contract for his UAV, rather did the system have a potentially fatal flaw which would have been discovered, if the process had not been shortcut? Another problem Hardy discovered was no agency had run a thorough background check on Tindal's employees at his home-based operation.

Tindal had reportedly used hostile takeover tactics to acquire a smaller company, Marberry Industries which was a research and development company that developed military hardware for the Department of Defense.

Tindal subsequently moved the operation to his private property after he built his home and the adjacent building where he housed the research and development business. There had been no government oversight prior to, during or after construction. This shouldn't have happened.

Had Jake and TJ stumbled onto a connection to Tindal's proposed UAV project and the cartel members TJ was investigating? Was TJ's CI the missing link? Did this pose a threat to national security? Homeland and the DoD would be held responsible if they missed this as a matter of course. And DARPA would not give approval to Tindal's project.

Was Tindal behind Jake's past problems while working in the Bahamas for Homeland's op? Was TJ correct, is there a connection to Jake's and TJ's current problems? What was CIA Clandestine Operations' McDab's interest?

Hardy knew firsthand that Tindal had been involved with CIA operations during his military career. He also worked for the NSA, before quitting and starting his own weapon sales and manufacturing business. Why the CIA request for UAV surveillance of Jake and TJ? What kind of operation was the CIA running on continental soil? Why had he, as Homeland Security Undersecretary for the region, not been told? The bigger question was, did the CIA Operation pose a problem for the task force investigation and Homeland's Tindal Investigation?

Homeland Security's Secretary listened to Hardy's objections to the CIA request, said she didn't see any threat to Homeland's investigation. She said she would talk to the CIA Director and voice her concern. Hardy asked the secretary if she knew about any domestic CIA operation. She knew the CIA was working with the DEA, FBI, and ICE on their ongoing border operation at the request of their directors and congress. Hardy asked her to request the CIA not give the local authorities information regarding the UAV and satellite surveillance and to please share with him what the UAV surveillance showed, and any actions they intended to take using the info they obtained. She agreed to pass along his request. Hardy doubted the request would be made, and if made, would not happen. Something told him, he was deliberately being kept in the dark. Why?

CHAPTER
43

Five o'clock was fast approaching. Jenkins had watched the recording of the Mexican woman's and Elena's encounter over and over. He would never have guessed anything like this would happen. The Mexican woman had a nice, well-shaped body, not as desirable as the Harper woman's, but he wouldn't crawl over her to get to the whores he had shared a bed with. He wondered if a threesome would be possible. What a treat that would be. If things didn't work out with the Harper woman, he could always sell the recordings to some smut peddler. It would be a shame if the final recording was a snuff film--the last thing the Harper woman ever did. He would keep these recordings in his personal folder.

For now, he had to make certain nothing happened to force a change in the schedule. Bud debated trusting Mark, whoever he was, and decided the best bet was to let Arturo know his brother had been located before he found out from Mark or a cartel hacker. He hoped this didn't turn into a problem.

Arturo had heard from the Alvarez man and was expecting a mutual proof of life call. That was why he sent the spic whore-dyke to get Elena prepared. Bud wished he could have been part of the preparations. Maybe tomorrow. If an exchange could be arranged, and if Arturo listened to Bud's request.

One extra day, the York County Fall Festival, Thurmond Tindal, the local politicians, and Colonel Baker would be at the event for Tindal's big announcement. The show and tell would be a big fiasco. He wished he could witness Tindal's and his pals' reactions when the demonstration failed to occur. If everything went as he planned, he would be on his way with his prizes to a place where he could live the good life. No more Tindal, no more cartel, no more ex-wife, and the alimony. He would have what should have been his father and mother's life that Uncle Sam had screwed them out of. Fuck you all so very much.

A day and a half. That was if Arturo and Harper and pal didn't fuck things up. Arturo had so far refused to accept his request, his plea to wait, make the exchange in accordance with their long-time plan. Bud had implored his patience. One extra day, he told him, and the cartel could have the Hive with the Bumblebees without any problems. Arturo would be reunited with his brother David. Then could exact his bloodlust by doing whatever he wished to the Harper and Alvarez men. Whether that included the Harper woman was yet to be determined.

His plan was taking shape. Lisa had inserted the NM0099 chip into his head. He suffered headaches for a couple days, but when they ran the test it worked as designed. He could control The Hive remotely once he got used to the uncanny sensation of the neurotap. It was as though the implant and he were one. And it gave him access to the worldwide web. Dr. Guthridge had been reluctant, had to be coerced. Jenkins told her Tindal gave the go-ahead. There was a lot of opposition to the concept in Washington. Tindal had told Colonel Baker a demonstration would quash their fears. Baker thought the timing wasn't right. Jenkins didn't care about the demo. The implant was another bargaining chip and, like The Hive, a much-sought-after asset once listed on the dark web.

Dr. Perkins AI, IA brain interface did not have DARPA approval, no FDA or other regulatory body approval. Dr. Gallagher had improved the implant. Made it more valuable and without DARPA approval and registration, like The Hive, not technically illegal to possess or sell.

Dr. Perkins was fired by Jenkins when Perkins claimed he should have the patent rights to the implant and Hive. Tindal insisted Dr. Guthridge and her team continue hers and Dr. Perkins' work. The Hive and the implant were his, so Tindal claimed. Jenkins would soon prove that claim wrong.

"Get the Hive and Bumblebees' DARPA approval, then work on getting the implant approved," Tindal told Dr. Guthridge.

Jenkins demanded she insert the implant, despite her reservations. He said Tindal was convinced this would wow the big boys with a demonstration--sell them on the idea of having the ultimate UAV field weapon.

She and Dr. Perkins developed the Hive and implant for peace-keeping use. Implanting Jenkins alarmed her. She was given no choice. She placed the implant. Her report to Poponovich and McDab would contain this information along with her objections to doing the implanting. If she hadn't she would have been terminated. They needed her here. Besides, these were her babies.

Jenkins had everything he needed. What Tindal, no one knew, there would be no Bud, no demonstration, no wow moment for all parties concerned. Another blow for Tindal. This morning news sources had reported The Atlantic Coast Pipeline contract was being cancelled. Bud found the news greatly amusing. He had been looking forward to Tindal getting fucked over for a long time. Being the key part of future fucking made it extra special. A pity he won't be there to see it first-hand. Just have to use the implant to pull it up off the cameras.

Bud watched the satellite feed connected inside his head and projected on the monitor. The feeling was still uncomfortable, but at least he no longer felt nauseous.

His thoughts created a split screen. One showed the Harper party preparing David Gonzalez. He looked like he had been asleep and just woke up. Had they drugged him? Had he missed something while his thoughts and senses were enjoying the Harper woman's performance with the whore-dyke? The woman in the rental car had left. Bud followed her movements until the GPS lost contact. No matter. He could pick up her camera rig's smart chip later after the call.

The Harper woman was seated on the big bed holding the rugrat mutt reading the instructions the whore-dyke had given her telling her what to say and how to act. Both parties had warned their captives not to stray from the script or the call would be terminated.

Remarkable how each hostage holder seemed to be thinking the same way. The effect for Bud was like watching a hologram, he felt he could reach out and touch the actors. If only he could touch the Harper woman. The sensation he felt was almost the same. No fulfillment.

Arturo was set for the three-way call. Bud Jenkins would be able to hear. Arturo had been told, and both parties wrongly believed, no one would be able to locate them. He needed to know if Arturo intended to do as had been agreed upon, or whether the murderous spic's bangers had been sent on their way after his brother's captors. Bud hated to think he would have to use his backup plan. Backups seldom worked out as well as hoped. Bud watched.

CHAPTER
44

TJ and Jake had to pour water onto David Gonzalez face. They pulled him into a seated position against the cab of the truck. His back rested on a blanket, a dazed far-off look on his face. "How much juice did you hit him with?"

"I'm not sure. When that UAV appeared, he tried to go running out of the bath house, I reacted. All I could think of was to shut him up, stop him, so I could see what that thing was going to do. I zapped him; more than I should have I guess."

"I hope he can convince his brother to let me see Elena."

"He's alive. Arturo will see we're not fucking around, make him willing to make the exchange."

"I hope so. I hope Elena is okay. What about the zip drives? You know he's going to know we have those."

"Let's hope that doesn't come up during this call. We need to insist, no further talk until a transfer is made. You didn't mention those to Ariel, did you?"

"No. Why would I?"

"Just checking bro. I wanted to touch base with Deane before we make the call." TJ looked at his watch. Fifteen more minutes. He had planned on texting Hardy and talking to Deane. A teaser for Ariel's breaking story had probably aired by now. "Guess it'll have to wait. I'll get Gonzalez." TJ put the sim card for his personal cell in his pocket. He retrieved it, replaced the throwaway's sim with his other one so they could have video capability when they made the call. He then walked around the side of the truck, grabbed David's arm, and slid him over. Gonzalez didn't resist. TJ threw the blanket over his right shoulder, pulled David back to the tailgate and hoisted him onto the blanket across his shoulder. David's lack of resistance concerned him.

Jake followed TJ up the tower steps. Sunlight was leaving the treetops. At the bottom, dusk was settling in.

Once on top, TJ tried to leave Gonzalez standing, but his legs failed to support him. TJ lowered him down and slung the blanket over the railing and leaned him back.

"Hey motherfucker," TJ slapped his face peering into David's vacant stare. He blinked. TJ slapped him a little harder. "You going to talk to your brother or sit there like a knot on a stump?" No reply. TJ looked back at Jake who shrugged. "Guess it doesn't matter. All we have to do is show he's alive." TJ checked his phone, two to three bars.

"Hope he isn't faking," Jake replied. "Be a shame if he starts saying shit that we don't want his brother to hear. I need to see and hear Elena."

TJ once more looked at his watch. "It's showtime." TJ looked at Jake. "You ready?"

Jake nodded. His palms were sweating despite the dampening chill that had descended with the dwindling light.

TJ hit the redial for Arturo. Arturo answered immediately. TJ switched the phone over to video with the speaker volume turned up. His face became visible to Arturo.

"Where is brother?" He barked in Spanish.

TJ turned his phone, so David was visible, then quickly turned it back so his own face once more filled the screen. Arturo started making demands to talk to his brother. TJ ignored this.

"My friend wishes to see his wife before we go any further." Arturo started protesting and threatening. TJ said, "Now or I end this call."

Jake had moved over next to TJ. He saw Elena and Maisy sitting on a four-poster bed. Where was she? Looked like a luxury hotel room. She looked like what he imagined a hostage felt like. Her lovely blue eyes seemed to have a faraway stare, her mouth was set, no smile, no frown. Maisy lay motionless on her lap watching whoever was operating the phone or camera. The image was there, then gone.

"Elena hold on. We'll see you soon." Jake shouted, not sure if she heard.

TJ cut the video feed on his phone. Arturo continued protesting and cursing TJ. TJ said, "Here's what has to happen, we agree on a time and place for the exchange."

Arturo said, "We do today. I bring woman to you. We make exchange."

"I don't think so. The day's gone. Needs to be in daytime. We need a place where both of us feel safe. Somewhere the authorities can't find us. I'm sure you understand. No posse. You come with Jake's wife and Jake and I come with your brother."

"Better in dark. We do tonight."

"No. Tomorrow. Name a place. We see if we agree."

Arturo did not immediately reply. They could hear him having an animated conversation that was muted so that what was being said was not clear.

"We meet tomorrow other side river from Senor Tindal's place."

TJ looked at Jake. Jake shrugged and silently mouthed, "Could work. Make it early. No. Make it about this time."

"Tomorrow at this time."

Jake wanted to recce the area and be set up in case Arturo had other plans.

"You and one other man with Jake's wife. No posse. No tricks. We'll be watching you." TJ disconnected the call.

"You think we can trust him?" Jake asked.

"Hell no. But we now know several things. Elena is alive. And did you notice the background, too nice for Arturo and his crew, Tindal's property, not much doubt. Arturo was talking to someone in the background. Probably someone trying to trace the call. I didn't talk long enough I don't think." He looked at his time piece. "Less than five minutes. What concerns me is that UAV. TJ walked over to David. Jake watched as TJ crouched down and checked his carotid again. David made no move. TJ looked up at Jake who squatted next to him.

"Man must be in a state of shock, no pun intended. Heart rate is a little high, don't know if something else is wrong that could explain his condition. We need to check his dirty clothing for a chip. Despite your misgivings about the drone, this fucker has said more than once, he and Arturo know where each other is at all times. They don't have a drone. They're trying to buy Tindal's. I need to call Deane. While I do that why don't you take our friend down and get him in the truck and check his dirty clothing. Think you can carry him by yourself?"

"What kind of question is that?" Jake twisted his neck back and forth. The pain was there as always, but he knew carrying David would not make it any worse, as long as he kept the weight equally distributed.

"Don't talk too long, we need to get the boat, finish loading and out of here. Like you said, if that UAV was looking for us, won't be long before we have company. I've been thinking, perhaps, if it was a military UAV, it was some desk jockey on a training exercise."

"Best to be safe than sorry."

Jake knelt.

"How about helping me get this fucker across my shoulders." Jake took David's arms while TJ took his legs and they placed him across Jake's shoulders. TJ helped Jake to his feet. Jake bounced him once to settle the weight and headed down the steps. A half-moon had appeared, its light reflecting off the dull weathered metal steps.

TJ texted Undersecretary Hardy. *Have Cartel's Gonzalez. Thumb drives. Find Mark Poponovich--Cartel moneyman--CIA? Cartel after UAV from Tindal. Elena at Tindal's.* TJ removed the old sim card, placed the newer one back in a throwaway and punched in Deane's throwaway number already registered from an earlier call.

Deane saw the *Breaking Story*. She told him it had been repeated several times on the local stations. One network affiliate reporter interviewed York County DA Sumners and Sheriff Yates. Each one called it fake news. The FBI spokesperson said they had no comment due to their ongoing investigation. TJ told Deane about the hoped-for exchange.

"This should be over soon. Once we have Elena, Jake agreed for us to turn ourselves in."

"Be careful. There are a lot of people out there that will do anything to collect that reward. I don't trust the local law enforcement people either."

"Neither do we. I hope the feds beat us to Elena. I plan to turn Jake and myself over to them. Gotta go. Love you. Hope to see you soon."

Jake was in the truck. TJ got in the driver's seat. He looked over at Jake. "Did you check his clothes?"

"Yep. Nada."

"I wonder why Gonzalez seemed so certain Arturo knew where he was." This puzzled TJ. He felt they were missing something.

"Nothing in his stinky-ass clothing."

"You're welcome to check when we get to where we're going. We need to get the van and boat. I know a place we can drop them which should be okay until this is over. We should be safe there for tonight. Puts us closer for tomorrow's meetup. If it happens."

They were on the road. TJ in his truck with David now secured in the back seat, pontoon on trailer hitched to the truck and Jake in the van. They retraced their route back to Highway 9 which took them to Lockhart, where they turned onto Highway 105. Ariel called. He told her Elena was alive and they were arranging an exchange. She said that was great news. She wanted to know more but he told her that he would have to get back with her.

She told him that she had not spoken to Dr. Hunter, but the night attendant said Dusty appeared to be doing better. Doc Hunter was keeping him lightly sedated. She told Jake about the excitement his interview had generated.

"The national networks are reporting the story, some have teams already in the area. Others are sending teams. This is like an Eric Rudolph coverage. They all want to interview me. I may have to go into hiding. Any ideas?" she asked with a laugh. "Sorry. The good thing: the authorities are getting roasted. Being pressed for answers and investigative reporters all over them. Jake, we didn't get to have the goodbye I hoped we would have. I loved seeing you again and I hope this won't be the last time we see each other. I didn't know how I would feel or how we would react to each other. You still mean more to me than I ever wanted to admit. I think, I hope you feel the same way. I'm sorry I know this is not something you want to hear right now."

Jake had mixed emotions. He felt guilty like he had betrayed Elena. In the back of this thought was Elena's own betrayal. Would their marriage survive this ordeal? He didn't know.

"Ariel, I have no idea what is going to happen in the next hour, much less tomorrow or the next day. I feel guilty when I think of you. I cannot deny how much you mean to me. I have to get through this first, then see where this leaves Elena and me. For now, I need to be there for her. Damn I hate this. If only we could take back time. Hold on a minute, I'm going to put you on speaker, I need both hands. You need to talk to York County Sheriff Deputy Dan Coulter. Do it securely. Did you get that?" No response. "Damn it!"

Jake turned onto a narrow gravel country lane near where the Pacolet River merged with the Broad River. A few minutes further brought them to a drive. At the end was a house surrounded by woods. It belonged to a family friend, a fellow vet currently in Syria. Jake doubted anyone would come here in the next several days. This was down river, about seven miles by road and less than two miles by water on the opposite side from Tindal's place. They could crash here tonight. Make plans for tomorrow. He laid the phone down to maneuver the van and keep an eye on TJ with the boat as they drove slowly through the woods.

When they came into the clearing where the cabin was, he pulled over to let TJ by. After TJ pulled past, he picked the phone up from the console.

"Ariel you still there?" The cell reception had grown weak, which was good and bad. Good because tracing would be difficult. Bad if they needed to talk to someone.

"I'm here. Can you hear me? You're breaking up."

"Barely. Probably going to lose you. Did you hear me? Talk to York Deputy Sheriff Dan Coulter. Be discreet."

"Okay. I don't know if you heard me. I said I understand about yours and Elena's situation. I hope she is okay, and you can get her away from whoever has her." She briefly lost connection. "Damn. You there?"

"I'm losing you."

"Don't move I heard you. Anyway, I'm sorry, but I have to ask-- Jake, please don't think ill of me, but I would like to be there when you make the exchange. If not, then whenever you and Elena are ready to talk. Forgive me. This is my job. This whole situation sucks. I feel lousy asking."

"That's okay. Let me see how it goes. I can't speak for Elena. I will do my best to let you have the interview, but…we'll have to see. I need to get off the phone. You need to keep yourself safe, like we said these cartel bangers are dangerous and they are everywhere."

"You're the one who needs to be careful."

"Remember my track running chant? You can beat me…"

"But you'll never defeat me. Make sure that remains true Jake."

CHAPTER
45

TJ got out of the truck and came back to Jake. "Where am I supposed to turn around?"

"We'll have to take the trailer loose and move it by hand, then you can turn around."

"We're not far from Tindal's place. Figured this was secluded enough and close enough by road and water if need be. Tomorrow we can recce his place to set up for the exchange."

"Problem is we have no way out by road if they track us."

"There is. It's down near the river. It was an old mule path for pulling barges up-river back in Colonial times. All the way up until the Twentieth Century. My friend's family, along with the other property owners, have kept it clear. They use it as an ATV trail. It's kind of narrow."

"Shit. Hope it's not narrower than their drive."

"You can look at it when we put the pontoon in. There is a small dock to tie it off. We need to unhook the trailer and push it over there." Jake pointed to the other side of the cabin. "Turn your truck around, we'll reattach the trailer and back down to the launch pad."

They launched the pontoon and Jake tethered it to the dock while TJ walked up the ATV trail. He saw lights up around a bend, looked about a half mile distant.

"Guess I could make it in four-wheel drive, Don't want to scratch my truck," he said to Jake as they walked back up to the cabin. TJ pulled his truck up, backed it parallel to the cabin on the river side just off the ATV trail. If need be, he could go either on the trail or back out the way they came in. They unloaded David, propped him up against the wall of the small front porch.

Jake reached underneath a rock at the base of a shrub near the steps of the front porch to retrieve the front door key.

The cabin was an open floor plan with two bedrooms and a bath upstairs. A balcony overlooked a modest living area and a small kitchen. There was another bath and a laundry area underneath the balcony area toward the roadside. The river side had two sets of French doors that opened out onto a deck that ran the entire length of the cabin. One end of the deck was covered and had a covered set of steps that led down to the storage area underneath. TJ walked out, stood on the deck. The glow of the moon revealed landscaped steps which extended down to where his truck was parked and the dock beyond.

Jake joined him saying "I guess we better keep all lights off. I'm going to eat a little something and turn in. I'll stay downstairs on the sofa, keep guard for a few hours. You can take one of the beds upstairs. I'll wake you around 3. You okay with that?"

"Think I'll get my sleeping bag and gear, stay out here under the covered area. That way we have the front and back covered. No need to wake me. I'm still a light sleeper. Old habit from 'Stan." He headed toward the doors. "Believe I could use a snack also."

Inside they sat at the small eating bar and ate crackers, cheese, nuts and drank water by the light of a lamp they set in the laundry area with the door slightly cracked. David lay on the floor where they had placed him. "You think he may have had a stroke or something?" TJ asked.

"That's possible," Jake replied. Good thing for Elena and us, he's still alive. Oh, by the way, I thought about the chip thing. A lot of pet owners have chips put under their pets' skin; some people have done it also. You think maybe the Gonzalez fuckers did something like that?"

TJ sat silent for a second considering the possibility. "Wouldn't surprise me. The cartel damn sure would be able to track him that way. Where would be the likely place to put it if he has one?" TJ got up and took a pen light from a pocket, walked over to Gonzalez, rolled up his sleeves, checked the backs of his hands, his arms up to the elbows, around his neck, behind his ears, his thick, curly scalp, his feet, legs up to knees. "I don't feel or see anything. Damn sure not taking his clothes off. You're welcome to if you like." TJ covered inert David with a blanket.

"No thanks. Hell, it could be inside him. You believe he has one?"

"We better assume he does. Arturo may have his bangers looking for us. GPS. Wait a minute, my RF scanner will tell us if he has one."

TJ's scanner located the chip on the side of Gonzalez' heel.

"Now what?"

"I could cut it out. Might be messy and could get infected."

"Fuck that."

"Fuck it," TJ said. Maybe in the morning?"

"Guess we'll both have to sleep lightly." Jake looked at his phone. One o'clock. "Only five hours until daylight. Won't be getting much sleep anyway." He tried twisting his aching neck, the damn thing was stiffening up in the chilled, humid night air.

"Damn it," TJ said getting up, leaning back to stretching back. "No way I'll be able to sleep knowing we can be traced. He probably wouldn't feel a thing. Too bad if he does."

Jake checked the cabinets. Found a first aid kit and a tube of superglue. Grabbed an old towel and a roll of papertowels. He held Gonzalez. TJ took his knife, made an incision. The chip was not deep, not much tissue to be embedded in. The cut didn't bleed as bad as was expected. Gonzalez didn't move. They cleaned the cut, put iodine on it, superglued the cut shut.

"Good job," Jake said.

"Thanks, Dr. Harper."

TJ mashed the chip using a pair of pliers, went down to the river and threw it as far out as possible.

"Hope they haven't already tracked us here," Jake said.

"We'll know soon enough."

CHAPTER
46

Just before dawn, TJ's half-conscious mind heard a window-vibrating noise echoing through the woods. He sat up. Could it be trucks or machinery? No. The sound was the deep-throated rumbles of motorcycles, and it was coming from the direction they had travelled the night before. TJ jumped up, grabbed his assault rifle, and hurried to the closest set of doors. Jake was already up and grabbing his weapons. "You heard it too," TJ said as he entered the room. He handed his rifle to Jake and reached down to grab Gonzalez. "Fuck," he said when Gonzalez hit his shoulder, "the motherfucker pissed all over himself and the blanket." They rushed down the back steps. The bikes were coming down the gravel road.

Jake started toward the dock. TJ was putting David in the back of the truck, "forget the boat bro. We need to get going."

Jake ran out the dock, jumped in the pontoon and went to the back and yanked the gas tank out, disconnected the quick coupling, then twisted the battery cable loose, and ran back up the dock to the truck, put the gas tank in next to the swaddled Gonzalez and jumped into the cab.

"Wanted to make it difficult for someone to take the boat. Never know, we might need it."

TJ accelerated and they eased out of sight before he gave it more gas. They bounced down the rough trail. Jake twisted around and watched the lights come across overhead through the trees in the direction of the cabin. They came around the bend and saw the neighbor's lighted dock. The house appeared dark.

"Need to turn up the neighbor's launch ramp area when you see it, head back out to the gravel road. Question is do we make a run for it by going right or head back to the cabin's drive and do something about them? If they found us here, they'll soon be on our trail again."

"What you mean do something 'bout them?" TJ asked. "They armed and it's goina be a gunfight if we stop. The neighbor is sure to call 911," TJ turned uphill on the other side of the neighbor's cabin. He swerved around two vehicles and plowed through their yard.

Jake watched as the gas container slid, and Gonzalez rolled, from one side of the truck bed to the other. "Did you check to see if Gonzalez was still alive?'

"No time. He is or he isn't, nothing to be done either way. I say if we're going to do it here, we do it where the pavement starts. Shit. I hate what this goina to do to my truck. Insurance people goina love it."

"If we survive, you mean, don't you?"

TJ pulled his truck across the gravel road around the bend before the intersection of the paved road. They jumped out, opened the back doors, and TJ started pulled Kevlar protection gear out of one of his bags.

"May not be an exact fit, but that's the breaks," he said tossing one over to Jake. They each checked their weapons: Jake his Remington 700, TJ his Colt M4. They each had extra magazines along with their sidearms.

"Ready?" TJ said.

"Ready."

Jake tossed the vest back. "I've got one of those." He picked up the shoulder and arm guard and slipped it over his head. Next came a leg protector, then his com helmet TJ was already decked out. They did a quick com-check. TJ pulled Gonzalez onto the tailgate of his truck.

"Damn he stinks." TJ felt his carotid again, the pulse was barely detectable. "He's alive. Just."

"If he dies, there'll no exchange with Arturo," Jake stated, an edge to his tone.

TJ looked across the bed of the truck at Jake. "Arturo has other plans bro. Doesn't intend for us to be there for no exchange. Probably never did. We'll get Elena. First, we have to deal with these motherfuckers. Help me get this stinking fucker over to the wheel."

They pulled him out and TJ used bungee cords to hold him in a sitting position at the driver side front wheel. The banger bikers would see him when they came in sight of the truck.

TJ turned to Jake who was once more checking his rifle and pistol. "These bangers ain't no army, don't know shit 'bout assault tactics, won't be attacking in no organized manner. Most likely come charging, straight at you. I'm going over there," TJ pointed to a copse of small trees about fifty yards away. "Hopefully, they'll see their friend here and stop. They'll wish they hadn't."

"And if they don't stop, then we take them out. That will make the law dogs happy. Then…" Jake didn't finish. There was automatic weapon fire coming from the cabin area. Next an explosion vibrated the ground and flames shot up over the trees. "Shit! They set Donnie's house on fire. Fuck! I'm going to kill these bastards." Jake came around the truck and TJ grabbed him.

"Too late bro. Soon they know we ain't inside, be headed this way. We do according to our plan. Looks like your chance getting' ready to happen,"

TJ and Jake heard the rumble of the motorcycles cranking up. "Here they come. Get behind the truck." TJ donned his helmet, the visor up, he turned and trotted in the direction of the trees.

The Harleys and other bikes could be heard through the trees. By the sound, Jake knew they were turning off the drive onto the gravel road. In a matter of minutes, Jake saw them two by two, six of them total. They came around a bend in the road, picking up speed until they saw the truck. One of the front men motioned with his hand, the riders split up. They slowed, came to a stop long enough to retrieve their weapons. They were almost parallel to TJ's position. Jake glanced over. He didn't see any sign of TJ.

The front man, must be their leader, was talking to them, deciding what to do. So much for not being organized. They were too far away for Jake to hear them through his headgear. They were backlit by the light from the cabin fire. How long before the neighbors' calls to 911 brought the police and volunteer firemen to the scene?

The leader rolled forward. The others stayed put. Once he was close, he shouted to Jake in Spanish, "give us our friend, we let you go."

Jake wasn't sure how to reply. "Arturo made deal," he yelled back, "my wife for his brother."

"Arturo?' The leader shrugged. "We take friend, you live you die, no care. Where other man?" They were looking around.

"You'll soon find out."

The leader started motioning to the other bangers indicating that they circle truck. Before he could lower his arm, a shot rang out and the tank on his motorcycle twanged and fuel began spurting out. The leader's bike pitched sideways. He was thrown over. The bike exploded. Jake heard the shots and watched as two more of the other bangers' tanks ruptured and exploded. The other three bikers throttled forward to check on the leader who was scrambling to his feet, beating at the flames on his legs. The leader yelled at them. They began shooting into the woods and at Jake. Shots pinged, bounced off the hood of TJ's truck where moments before his head had been. When their shooting stopped, Jake raised up over the hood of TJ's truck, and shot the one coming at him in the shoulder, pitching him backwards off his bike. TJ's next shots took out the wheels on the other two bikes before their riders, guns blazing, could reach the place he had been. Their AR-15s continued to spray bullets wildly into the trees as they laid their bikes over.

TJ stepped out from his new position down the road from where they thought he was. He ordered them to throw down their weapons or die. He fired twice more; the rounds kicked up gravel where they stood, tearing holes in their two bikes. They looked down at their ruined motorcycles, then at each other, and slowly looked back at TJ as if they weren't sure what to do.

Jake heard the siren in the distance, the bangers apparently did also. The leader yelled at his men in Spanish. They all began running toward the trees in the opposite direction from TJ.

TJ fired some shots over their heads and trotted back toward Jake and his truck. He stopped, deposited his weapons in the back seat. He checked the damage to his truck. "Fuck me," he yelled.

Jake came around the truck, checked, made sure none of the bangers were in sight. He bent down to help TJ lift Gonzalez.

TJ asked Jake, "You okay?"

Jake replied, "I'm fine. How about you?"

"Pissed. Look at my truck. Just think what my insurance company's goin' to say."

They had to hurry and load Gonzalez into the bed of the truck. The sound of sirens drew closer.

They jumped in the truck. Jake decided to hold onto his weapons in case the bangers reappeared before TJ got them out of range. He told TJ to go the opposite direction on Highway 105.

CHAPTER
47

'That fucking hothead idiot would fuck up at a one car parade.' Bud Jenkins could not believe what he was seeing. Arturo's men went after the Alvarez and Harper men and got their asses handed to them. This was about what he expected. How did Arturo think anyone would trust him now? Bud felt he had no choice, he couldn't wait. Arturo was not going to stick to any plan. His words and actions didn't mean shit. No need to contact Mark. Bud felt certain he had seen the same fucking nightmare. Why hadn't Mark called? Bud had to assume the worst. Mark had not called because, like him, he could see their whole anticipated plan had gone to shit. How come the cartel big cheese, Mark said was their uncle, didn't reign Arturo in? Bud felt he had to know. Certainly, he was in no position to bargain except through Arturo, perhaps neither was Mark.

He had been leery all along about bargaining with these fuckers. Good thing he had posted the sale on the dark web. Time to forget about the cartel. He would take the best bid or bids—the most secure and most likely to pay bids. Why not?

It was time to expedite his getaway. The news broadcasts will undoubtedly bring the feds. And the Harper and Alvarez men will have interrogated David Gonzalez; and he had to assume they had seen the missing files loaded with incriminating evidence of collusion with Tindal Industries; and now, because of that stupid spic's actions, the Harper and Alvarez men could very well be on their way here also. He had to hurry.

Bud packed the thumb drives with the files into a nonscanable, secure wallet. He used his implant and looked in on the Harper woman. She was watching the video feed of her husband and the other woman, now identified as Ariel Gaspard, an anchorwoman for some Columbia, South Carolina News Station. Bud had edited the video feed to make it look like the Harper man and this Gaspard woman were being intimate. The Harper woman was watching the screen, tears flowing down her cheek. Tears of anger or of pain, he did not know.

Bud had made the decision to take the Harper woman with him. If she didn't want to share herself with him, he felt certain he had a way to change her mind and at least get her to go with him, then see how it went from there. If not, she would make a tasty treat until he could unload her to any number of sleazebag foreigners. No one need be the wiser. The authorities already had their suspect.

Bud texted the Executive Air Transport and placed his order for a helicopter pickup to take him to Charlotte Douglas International. This would be a handy diversion for when the authorities start their search. He scheduled it for ten o'clock. Pickup on the landing pad down by the river. Thurmond had an early meeting with the York Festival Coordinator and would be gone. He had less than four hours to prepare for his exit.

He thought his plans through again for the umpteenth time. First thing was to erase all evidence that would implicate him—all connections to Arturo, Mark, and the cartel. He checked his new identity and the ones he had prepared for the Harper woman, just in case. He booked separate and several airline tickets for her in her name to various destinations. He booked several flights in his real name and others using their fake identities to places far from where he was headed first.

Time to put his plan into motion, implement the arrangements made with one set of people--he and the Harper woman would simply disappear. These people didn't know the Harper woman would be coming with him--he hadn't known at the time. He would send the prearranged signal notifying them he was on his way as soon as he was airborne. The billing for the unused tickets paid for with Tindal Industries' credit cards. Wait until Tindal's accounting agency receives those bills.

The authorities would continue to blame the Harper man for her disappearance. Bud would post the footage of the Harper and Alvarez men's shootout with Arturo's men on an *You Tube* anonymous site, along with the edited video of the newswoman and the Harper man. The ones the Harper woman was so moved by—that should provide the authorities with the motive, keep that nosey news bitch busy answering questions, casting doubt on her scathing stories—interviews with the Harper man—easily dismissed, that was Tindal's problem, he hadn't been implicated, no skin off his back. After he was gone, Tindal will have his hands full trying to explain what happened, be interesting viewing—from afar. The probing interviews out there, shown on news' feeds nationwide, will continue to grow, the news vultures, like her, will go on a feeding frenzy and he will get the last laugh.

He could see her and her crew, parked outside the front entrance, waiting. The guards' attempts to make her go away had been futile.

Jenkins called the guards, instructed them not to let her or anyone else onto the property without his or the colonel's authorization. He needed to get to moving, not that it mattered, by the time anyone discovered his absence, he intended to be in the air, on his way to a place where no one could touch him. The Hive, the implant data, his to sell to whichever party bids the most. He had files showing all US satellite locations, including the top-secret military ones. He didn't intend to sell them. They were for his own security, in case Uncle Sam threatened him.

He would soon have the wealth to live the life he always dreamed of.

He sent the signal. His plan was now in motion. By tonight, he will be long gone, out of the country—with or without the Harper woman.

CHAPTER
48

Jake looked back at the glow in the sky created by the fire as he and TJ sped down Highway 105. Adrenalin from the events made his heart race, what now? Donnie Franklin's family would be upset. How soon would Donnie know? Jake felt responsible. The van, trailer and pontoon would implicate him. He would find a way to make good on his intentions to rebuild the house for them.

For now, he and TJ had to concentrate on saving theirs and Elena's lives. He looked down at Gonzalez rocking with the movement of the truck. Was he dying, perhaps already dead? What would his death mean? TJ said his pulse was low, made him fear Gonzalez had suffered a stroke. What should they do with him—drop him at a clinic, on the side of the road? And how were they going to rescue Elena?

"Where to?' TJ asked.

"I want to take a close look at Tindal's property. We can do that from across the river. I hope we've seen the last of the bangers Arturo sent after us. Think he has a way to track us?"

"From what just happened and what our friend back there said--could be Arturo has another way to track us. Have to assume he does, and if not, the cartel certainly does. But I'm more worried about that UAV and what that means. If the authorities are the ones possibly tracking us, we're fucked."

Had Homeland sent it? TJ worried. Were they still being watched? If so, wouldn't matter about Arturo and the bangers. TJ knew Hardy was already shitting bricks. He dared not mention Hardy's name to Jake—nor his warning, ordering them to stay away from Tindal. Hardy said Homeland had had their eyes on Tindal's place, did they still? He and Jake were contemplating a major security breach—he needed to warn Jake, but he doubted it would deter Jake. Jake was fired up, no need in adding fuel to the fire or try to put the fire out. And who could blame him? If it was Deane, nothing would stop him wanting to know, and he knew Jake would be right there with him. Jake interrupted his thoughts.

"We need to get rid of Gonzalez, he needs medical care."

"And if they revive him? He could testify against us, you thought about that? Then there is Elena? Arturo has shown his hand. If Elena is on Tindal's property in Arturo's guard, and his brother is found held by the authorities, comatose or worse, dead, Elena may never be found."

"I see no alternative for me. I'm going to recce Tindal's property, then I'm going to find out if she's there. If anything has happened to her, it's going to be Tindal's ass and as many of the bangers that I can take with me. You can come or you can drop me off."

"Too late for that now bro. I said we were going to take it to them. We just have to be smart about it." TJ felt Jake's frustration. "You said it yourself. His place is heavily guarded, towers with monitors, and a UAV. You need to get real bro; you'd need an army."

"Stop. Go back. We missed the turn."

"And our friend back there?"

"There are a couple building basements we can put him in. Hopefully, their surveillance signals can't penetrate the dense foliage and earth. We have to chance it. We're running out of options and time."

When they arrived at Pinckneyville, TJ asked where this supposed town was? A small stone remnant was all that was left of what had been a cul-de-sac on what had been the town's main street. The road continued to the Broad River, where, from Colonial times until the early twentieth century, a ferry service had provided portage across the Broad River. A bridge for the railroad system made the ferry obsolete. The ferry had been part of the Colonial Road System that stretched from New York and Philadelphia to Charleston. The road dividing Jake's land from Tindal's had once been part of that same system. A granite marker, CHRLS on one side and ASHEV on the other, with kilometer distance numbers, once stood on the road dividing Tindal's and his property. It disappeared soon after Tindal acquired the Hill family property.

On the Broad River side of the cul de sac was a two-story brick wall with holes made by repeated bullet impacts. There were vulgar slogans and satanic symbols and messages spray painted, targets on the wall around the blasted holes. To the right were what remained of wood sided, tin metal-rooved structures. Bars remained on one window with a sagging door on the same building, perhaps the jail during or after the Revolutionary War period when Pinckneyville was the County Seat. The sagging buildings stretched for fifty yards or so, each unit having a common wall with the adjacent one.

Jake directed TJ to the left where another crumbling brick two story building stood on the highest point. This was thought to have been the Colonial District Courthouse, later became a Four County South Carolina State District Court House until each county built their own Court House. This was the building, whose basement where Jake intended to place the inert Gonzalez. Jake searched the building basement for snakes, found none. He and TJ laid him on the dry smooth red clay floor. They hurried because TJ's truck was exposed, due to the lack of any tree coverage near the structure.

"Head past that lone brick wall with the graffiti painted on it. You may have to use four-wheel drive--the ruts can be deep. This will take us down to the river across from Tindal's place. I'll tell you when to stop. Hopefully, no one will hear us. Go slow."

"No shit. You sure you know what you're doing."

"If you'd rather, you can drop me off here. You don't have to do this you know. You've done more than your share."

"Gone way past turning back now. Lest you forgot, wasn't just you and your family threatened. Look at my truck, it's fucked. Somebody's going to pay."

"I guess I'm trying to say thank you. I'm glad you're with me."

TJ turned his truck around where Jake told him to. They grabbed their rifles and scopes. TJ also had a pair of binoculars with night vision, infrared and heat sensing capability which was not necessary at this time--the sun was rising over Tindal's property.

Lying prone next to some trees a hundred feet from the water's edge, Jake and TJ studied the movement across the river. Two Hispanic men were on the dock where two boats were moored walking back toward what appeared to be a bottom-brick, top-metal hangar. Jake was amazed at the landscaping—trees and shrubs lined terraced steps of granite climbing from a large patio up, level by level, past a huge swimming pool to a palatial home on the hill.

Two more men and Butch and Billy emerged from the hangar and spoke to the first two and what could be a woman in fatigues. The bangers had guns strapped to their sides and AR-15's with bump stocks slung over their shoulders.

Jake raised his rifle and put the sights on Butch. It was tempting. He hoped he had a chance up close and personal later.

"See that?" TJ asked. "That UAV we saw on the computer was hovering over the hangar. Gone now. Damn."

"I missed it. I was looking at Butch and Billy. They were talking to those armed Hispanic guards and that feminista-looking Hispanic. You think those are some of Arturo's bangers?"

"Most likely." TJ scanned the house and saw no one on the upper terrace. "Say they have Elena, we need to figure out where? We can eliminate the house. Has to be the hangar or that other building up there on the hill near the house."

Jake rolled over onto his back to relieve the pressure building on his neck. Through the partially de-leafed poplar tree, he saw what's called a Carolina blue sky. Such a beautiful day, maybe his last.

TJ's phobia concerning water was now in play. He hoped Jake didn't dis his fear. "How we goina get across this damn river? I'm not a swimmer. Never learned how, wasn't a helluva lot of water in the Hood. We'll be sittin' ducks. And then there is our unconscious friend. We can't just leave him here." TJ said.

"We tear the place apart and find Elena. Hopefully, she's there along with Maisy. We get them and ourselves safely away from there and we fuck up anybody who gets in our way. Especially Butch, Billy and Tindal. God, I would love to get my hands on Tindal."

"Be easier, we had a boat."

Jake eased up into a seated position, his eyes on the distant shore. He looked over at TJ. He was staring hard at the water. Jake understood his fear. When he was a preschooler, he had been taught to swim the hard way.

"I remember what it was like to want to learn how to swim. When I was around five or so, me and my family had been on a river, offshore from Springs Park, headed into the landing. My brother Charlie had wanted to swim in. Our dad cut the motor off, Charlie dove in and started for shore, and for some fucked-up reason, I started making a racket, didn't know why, brotherly competition most likely, can't remember what my idiotic thinking was about. My mother told me I needed to learn to swim first. I don't know what possessed me to push the point. My father stood up, picked me up and threw me in the water and said swim. He started the boat and headed to shore, my mother screaming her head off. That's how I learned how to swim."

TJ remained quiet for a minute or two. "Ain't no way you gonna throw me in bro. And, I learning to swim today. Alright? So, we need plan B."

"Damn. Okay. There is a possibility we can take care of that. What say we go back down river and get the pontoon? We could come up the river in it, Take them by surprise. Make it a whole lot easier in and out."

"By now that place goina be crawling with firemen, emergency personnel and police, not to mention, the SBI and feds, once the cops trace the van back to you."

"I took the temporary dealer tag off. They'll think the van belongs to my buddy's family. They should have the fire out by now. That wooden cabin won't be anything but charred smoldering rubble. There might be a couple volunteer firemen, a neighbor maybe hanging around. If there are any police, they'll be busy investigating the motorcycles and the reports of shooting. We go back from the other direction, take the boat, get the hell out of there. Anyone tries to stop us, we scare them off—after all we're armed and dangerous criminals."

"That's crazy bro. Never work. We can't threaten a bunch of innocents. Damn good chance there'll be police there. We're already in over our heads. I say we wait until after dark. There is no way in broad daylight. First we have to figure some way to get over there. Maybe we need to go back and come in from the road."

"Can't wait until dark. The road has a fence and guards. Take us too long to get there. Got to figure Arturo knows by now we escaped the bikers. There's boats tied up at Tindal's dock. I could swim over and take one of them."

"Say you manage to get over there without being seen or getting your ass shot, how you going to pull that heavy ass boat against the current bro? No way."

"The river is shallow except for a few areas. You can wade across in most places. I've done it numerous times. Come on we're wasting time. Either I can do it, or I can't. I won't know unless I try." Jake stood up and leaned against the tree keeping an eye across the river.

"If we can wade across, why bother with the boat?"

A funny idea hit Jake. "Twain's Huck Finn and Tom Sawyer. A raft. We build us a raft."

"You got to be kidding?"

"Got plenty of wood up on the hill. You got rope I'm betting. Doesn't have to be big. Just large enough and strong enough for the three of us and our kits."

TJ shook his head. "That's the old country cracker Jake I been wondering where it went. Been noticing a new giddyup--I believe that's what you hillbillys call it—anyway, you seem more enthused since we had that little skirmish. Miss it don't you?"

"Yeah, I miss the action. TJ, there's something else you should know. I can't help but think Elena helped bring this upon herself. Makes me feel guilty to think this. But there it is. Part of me wants to do this; find her make sure she's safe. Another part of me can't help but feel our marriage is over no matter what."

TJ stared hard at Jake. "Think you better concentrate on one woman at a time partner."

"What do you mean?"

"You know what I mean," TJ turned back up the hill and said, "come on Huck, let's git that raft built. Guess you figured we would use the wood from those derelict structures."

CHAPTER
49

Tomorrow. Thurmond Tindal was happy, overwhelmingly ecstatic. Jenkins and Dr. Guthridge said everything was ready. He wished his mother could be here to see him announce the proposed manufacturing facility in Pinckneyville, the old town named for the man for whom she had given him his middle name. Now it would be attached to Tindal Industries' largest enterprise. He would become an industrial king and the people in the area would see him as their hero. Once he acquired the Harper land and the pipeline went through, his economic success would be assured. His chauffeur interrupted his thoughts.

"Mr. Tindal there are reporters blocking the entrance, what you propose I do?"

"Tell the guards to clear a path." That Gaspard woman had been hounding him since yesterday. He wasn't about to dignify her allegations with a statement. After tomorrow, no one would care. He wished they'd hurry up, catch Harper and his nigger Cuban friend. Someone banged on his window as they drove through. Good. Now he could prepare himself for the morning meeting with the Festival Committee.

"Sir, that news van is following us."

Tindal looked back. "Let them. They're wasting their time. If they try to talk to you, ignore them, or say no comment."

Tindal's car pulled into the municipal lot in front of the Greater York Chamber of Commerce Building, housed in an old Rail Depot Building. The lot serviced the York County Library as well. Tindal was surprised by the number of cars and people in the lot. He saw the local police, FBI and ICE vehicles and personnel in the lot. His driver parked, got out and opened his door. When he stepped out a tall middle-aged FBI agent stepped forward, introduced himself as Agent Gerald Lacey. He asked Tindal to come with him.

Once they reached the walk to the Chamber Building, Agent Lacey, to his surprise Mirandized him. Another agent stepped forward and handcuffed him.

"This is outrageous. What's the meaning of this?"

Agent Lacey said, "Thurmond Pinckney Tindal you are being charged with Interfering in a Federal Investigation, Employing Illegal Immigrants, Misuse of Federal Funds, Employing Prostitutes to Commit Extortion and Bribery. Do you understand your rights as I read them to you?"

"I want to speak to my attorney. This is preposterous! Agent Lacey, I will sue you and the FBI!"

"You can try. I have warrants signed by a federal judge that allows the FBI and ICE in conjunction with Homeland Security and the NSA to search your property and seize all records and detain all personnel pertinent to our investigation." Agent Lacey leaned in and said in a volume only those nearest could hear, "you better hope that we do not find Mrs. Elena Harper on your premises." Then Agent Lacey turned to another agent and said more loudly, "Take him away."

Ariel and her film crew were standing close enough to record the arrest and show Tindal's face. "Yes." She said pumping her fist by her side. "Come on we need to get back to Tindal's property." She and the crew hurried back to the van.

CHAPTER
50

Building a raft that would float was no easy task without the necessary tools. Jake and TJ pulled the weathered boards off by hand, some splintered, others were too rotten for their purpose. When they had a stack laid out, large enough for their weapon kits, they carried the comatose David Gonzalez, then the materials, upstream. They used rope, which TJ had in a rucksack, too lace them together by going over and under the boards and around two light dried-out logs. They managed to lash them into a raggedy semblance of a raft that would have made Twain's Jim laugh.

TJ checked his weapons, made sure he had the extra magazines ready for quick reload. Jake did the same. TJ was smiling as if he had remembered a private joke. Perhaps it was because of their situation which to an outsider would have been hilarious. It wasn't for Jake, especially the struggle to move their catastrophe waiting to happen into the river while trying to remain invisible from the assholes possibly watching from the other side. They had camouflaged themselves, Gonzalez and the raft with twigs and leaf liter.

No shots rang out. Which was a good thing.

"Wish I had brought my wetsuit", Jake said just before entering the water. The river's current did not look or feel strong at the edge. Soon he found out, the adage, 'looks can be deceiving.'

"Maybe once my nuts finish shriveling, I will be okay," Jake muttered after stepping out into the chilled stream.

The weight of Gonzalez made the raft sink down, miraculously the raft stayed afloat. Gonzalez had not moved. "If this doesn't revive him, I guess nothing will," TJ hoped their weapon kits stayed dry, that their raft didn't come apart, and everything didn't end up in the murky water.

He and Jake waded out, pushing the raft out into the current, trying to work their way across before they were swept too far downstream. They quickly discovered the current was stronger further out. They struggled to keep their balance. Several times the raft almost got away from them. The ropes cut into their hands and wrists. Each one of them slipped several times, causing the other to wrestle the raft as it seesawed with the imbalance. TJ looked like a fish out of water, kept cursing Jake under his sputtering breath.

Jake kept his eyes on the far bank, hoping to get across before they were discovered or TJ began yelling. Intermittently, he scanned the horizon watching for signs of the drone they saw earlier. Jake gave special notice to the poles with video monitors and sirens, spaced at regular intervals rising above the River Birch and other wet feet trees and shrubs along the bank. He was certain, feared, soon as they hit shore, armed men would be there.

They discussed what they could do if the UAV saw them and attacked. TJ believed, if they could disable the mother hive as he called it, maybe this would disable the bumblebee-looking drones. Jake hoped he was right. Images from the demonstration witnessed on one of Gonzalez laptop's thumb drives of the mannequins exploding, shredded bits of fiber all that remained and thoughts of Dusty's innards blown open, made his already adrenaline pumped, nervous cold body shiver with anticipation and dread. Memories of war zone battles that seldom worked as drawn up by personnel back at the safety of headquarters, gave him pause. He hoped their hastily thought up assault plan worked.

Fortunately for TJ, they didn't have to tread water very far, just in the middle. They struggled their load up the bank onto a muddy shelf near the edge of Tindal's orchard. Jake made a low hiss to get TJ's attention, pointed two fingers at his eyes, up to one of the monitoring poles. TJ nodded. They pulled the raft into some low shrubs, the only shelter available, and tied it off. They quickly unloaded their weapon kits, then struggled, slipping, and sliding, to get David Gonzalez body up the muddy bank.

They moved into the orchard, as they had initially planned, using the trees as cover. They struggled staying low with Gonzalez while wending their way through the trees to the massive structure set off from the house. When they finally made it, they propped Gonzalez against the wall. Jake went right toward the house end of the building, and as planned, TJ moved off toward the hangar.

Jake noticed a couple of window wells. He knelt to try to see in. They had bars on the outside and shutters on the inside, nothing to see. He moved on toward the front in a low crouch, staying behind shrubbery, a couple feet off the stone wall.

TJ slipped through the orchard, moving slowly, trying not to draw attention to himself. There was a slight breeze and enough leaves on the fruit trees he hoped gave him enough cover. The cover soon came to an end, ending at a paved runway. He knelt and checked his twenty. He only saw two of the banger guards. They were at the corners of the hangar, their backs to him. Looked like he needed to back track to the higher part of the runway. If he stayed low, he should be able to get across without them seeing him. He checked out the security surveillance towers. Looked like they were set to scan sideways and toward the river. Not back toward his position. But once he reached the other side of the tarmac, he might get into their range.

He would just as soon shoot their asses, take them out one by one and be done with them and join Jake but then there would be no hope for his career in law enforcement. He wasn't certain there was even if he didn't fire a shot. He had to restrain himself. Unless he had no choice.

Where was that damn UAV? He didn't see it. He tried a mic check. No reply from Jake. He had no way of knowing if that was good or bad.

He had to make his move. He checked himself over: Kbar on left hip, Springfield pistol on right, M4 locked and loaded, taser velcroed to his vest, and his kit with a tranq gun and the gas and stun grenades inside went across his shoulder. He scooted across the tarmac and darted to his left to the river side of the hangar. He eased around the corner, moved to the other end, slid around grabbed the banger stationed there, put him in a chokehold and pulled him back around the corner, and held him until he quit struggling.

He pulled out his tranq gun. He needed to get in closer to the other guard. In his head, he knew the clock was ticking. He hoped Jake hadn't run into a bad situation and needed backup.

He hurried around to the riverside of the hangar and ran to the far corner facing the dock with the boats. Around the corner was where the overhead doors were. They were open and he could hear voices. Sounded like Butch and Billy were having an argument. Good. He eased out into view of the other banger guard and before he could react, TJ tranqed him. Then he slipped around and entered the hangar.

"Hello boys. Jake sends his regards."

Butch and Billy jerked around when they heard him. Billy was holding the remains of a joint. He dropped it. TJ quickly stunned Butch with the taser. Billy tried to run. TJ caught him before he could get around a small passenger jet and reach the man-door at the other end. TJ spun him around and coldcocked him.

Retracing his steps, he stooped over Butch and punched him, rendering him down for the count.

He needed to check on Jake. Tried his voice mic again. Still no reply.

He darted out the side door, caught a glimpse of something overhead. Before he could react, he felt a sting on his neck, above his vest. He dropped to his knees, reached back, nothing, he caught a glimpse of one of the bumblebee-looking things, thought he saw the mothership, the hive-looking UAV's shadow.

He reached up, jerky, slow motion, pulled his M4 scoped rifle off his shoulder. His vision became blurry. He wiped his eyes on his sleeve twice, rubbed his eyeballs in between wipes. His sight wavered, right eye sliding on and off the scope as he tried to acquire a target. Where was that damn hive-looking UAV? He caught a glimpse of movement from his blurred left eye. He looked up, attempting to focus, saw the fuzzy conical shape hovering in the near distance. TJ, as quick as his off-balanced body would allow, slid down onto his back. He thought he had his left arm cradling the barrel of his sniper rifle. He struggled to feel the trigger. Thought he felt the rifle fire. Another sting, the world faded to black.

Jake reached the front of what he discovered was a garage, found the people entry door unlocked. He pulled the door open, slid in against the wall, his pistol up and ready. The garage was full of vintage, collector automobiles. He crouched down, headed toward the back, found a short hallway with elevators. He saw a door with a light shining from inside, a set of steps. The elevators had a security keypad, so he took the steps. On the next level, he stopped, cracked a door, on the other side was a wide, well apportioned, hallway with marble looking chair rail and tile. No movement, no sound. So much for security. This puzzled Jake. How was it the video monitors on the shore, around and inside the garage had not seen him? Or had they? Could be a trap?

What did it matter now? Jake wondered if TJ had found another way in, was he already in their clutch? His mic didn't get a response from TJ. In for a penny, he stepped into the hall and moved off toward the short end to his left.

At the other end was a thick ornate mahogany door. It was unlocked. Jake opened it, glanced back down the hall, slipped inside. It was a well-furnished suite like you found in luxury resort hotels, like the one he had seen behind Elena. It was empty. Jake went back out and down the hall. Halfway down, he discovered another suite, empty as well. At the end of the hall was a door made to look like part of the wall. He didn't see any way to open it. He ran his hands around the door and the wall it was mounted in, pushed, and couldn't get any movement. To the right was another inlaid mahogany door that had another staircase and elevators behind other ornate mahogany doors. The doors were locked. Jake took out the electronic lock pick devise TJ had given him as a birthday present. He unlocked the door to the stairs using the picks just the way TJ showed him.

He took the stairs two at a time down to another level. He figured he had to be below grade. This time there was a heavy metal door with a keypad. He wasn't about to go back. Maybe they had been following his progress. In South Carolina, the law allows you to shoot a trespasser if you feel your life is threatened. Jake knew he looked threatening, was considered a dangerous felon, therefore he was fair game no matter the law. He hoped Elena was here, if not he might die in vain.

Pulling out his K-Bar, he pried the cover off the keypad, pulled the wires loose and crossed what he knew were the hot to the lead and the lock clicked. On the other side of the door was another hallway. He heard sound coming from behind a door to the right. Sounded like someone was hurrying his way. He ducked back inside the door, held the knob with his left hand with his pistol in his right. He heard the sound of steps rushing by through the crack in the door and saw the back of a tall woman. She was dressed in lab clothes, her hair in a bun. From the rear, tall and slim, shapely looking. She knocked on a door several times, the door cracked open. A male voice. Jake struggled to hear what was being said. He heard what sounded like the woman saying something about Tindal, guards, federal agents. He could not make out what the man said. Soon the woman turned, Jake closed the door and listened. The sound of her feet came back by his door. He heard another door close.

Tindal? FBI? Jake immediately took this to mean Tindal had notified the FBI. They were on their way. Could they already be here? He needed to hurry. Where was TJ? He needed to find out if Elena was here and do it quickly.

Fuck it. He went through the door after looking both ways. No one, not even a sound other than the air movement from the overhead AC vents.

His only hope was to find her before whoever had her hid her anticipating the FBI and police arrival. Jake decided the man would be his best bet. He went down the hall to the door, put his ear to the cold metal and listened. He could hear clicks like fingers on a keyboard, some shuffling and light tapping, sounds of someone putting things in a case, then steps and the sound of a door opening and closing.

Jake pulled out his K-Bar, pried the face off, then disabled the keypad lock on the door. Inside the room were rows of monitors. On several of them figures and numbers scrolled down the screens. Jake didn't care. On another monitor, he saw the man, he now knew from the thumb drives was Jenkins, enter a room. There was Elena and Maisy. Jake felt elation and anger welling up in him. He felt the hot sting of tears as he watched Elena go off one monitor, then appear on another inside a bathroom. That perverted son of a bitch had been watching Elena, his wife. Jake hurried over to the other door. He was so upset he dropped his K-Bar twice, finally he disabled the keypad releasing the lock.

One the other side of the thick metal door was a semi-dark hallway that curved to the left. Jake could not see far. He started to call out to Elena, had to restrain himself. Jenkins could be armed, possibly use Elena as a shield. In the distance came the echoing sound of a door closing, echoing sounds of hurrying feet, moving away. Jake moved fast as he dared, wanted to run, scared the sound might reach them. He had not gone but a few paces past the doors set into the concrete walls when he heard noise, like the hum of a motor. He felt a sudden change in the atmosphere. Jake moved on cautiously. The tunnel curved to the left. He saw light, the sounds appeared to be a hydraulic motor. A door was opening.

Jake waited, watched, and listened. He heard a light clicking sound coming toward him. He leaned back against the wall his sidearm pointed in the sound's direction. Two things occurred simultaneously— the hum of the motor stopping and Maisy beginning to yap. She was just a few feet away. Jake knelt. She ran to him, whining, jumped onto his legs, and began licking his face. He picked her up in his left hand, moved back against the cold concrete wall. Elena called Maisy's name. Jake ran toward the light. He saw Elena, then Jenkins his weapon coming up, pointed his direction. Jake hit the floor, Maisy yelped, a couple rounds ricocheted off the walls. Jake checked Maisy, she was okay, when no more shots were fired. He stood, moved slowly, cautiously toward the opening.

The door was closing. He feared Jenkins was waiting for him to stick his head out.

There came the sound of a plane, he saw it move past the end of the tunnel. He ran, darted through the half-open door at the end of the tunnel and saw the plane's tail section as it went over a slight rise of the runway. The plane lifted off into the air banked left, disappeared over the woods of Pinckneyville. Jake felt deflated.

Jake ran out onto the tarmac and watched the plane as it banked and sailed over the trees across the river above the remains of Pinckneyville and disappear. He tried to reach TJ by mic. Again, no answer. Then he saw the bodies at the hangar, one looked like it could be TJ. He heard the sound of footfalls coming from Tindal's residence, and shouts from on top of the hill in the direction of the garage. Jake turned and ran toward the river. When he and Maisy, reached the far corner, he felt a sting, two more strides around the corner, his legs gave way, he felt himself falling, then nothing.

CHAPTER
51

Before Jake, TJ and the feds arrived, Bud Jenkins had been purging the files, when an alert sounded from the security system. Checking the camera monitors, he saw Jake and TJ make their landing on the bank upstream at the end of the runway, down from the start of the orchard. He zoomed in, saw the Alvarez man handing up weapons to the Harper man who stood on the upper bank. He rejoined him at their makeshift raft. They struggled to bring David Gonzalez up the bank. They were dressed in combat gear including helmets with cam coms. They were well-armed prepared for an assault.

Shit. He saw them enter the orchard carrying David Gonzalez. Damnit, they would have to appear just as he was about to finish his tasks. Another forty-five minutes and he would have been out of here with the Harper woman. Let The Hive take care of them. A bonus for the authorities when they investigate his disappearance—live demonstration of The Hive's capabilities.

Time to get moving. He started the trojan horse programs, checked everything to make sure he wasn't leaving anything he wanted behind, grabbed the case of thumb drives, went to the rear door which led to the tunnel where the private suites were. As he was entering the code, he heard loud rapping on the corridor door. He cracked it open, Lisa's grim face stared back at him. Damn, what now. He didn't have time for this.

"Mr. Jenkins did you hear from the guards? They tried to reach you. They called me when you didn't answer. The guard at the gate said federal agents are here with a search warrant. They said Mr. Tindal had been arrested. It's on the news. What is going on? Do you know?"

Bud acted surprised. "I had not heard. Don't panic. Tell everyone I'll check with Mr. Tindal's attorney. And Dr. Guthridge say nothing to the authorities. Let the attorney handle this and hold off telling the others until then." He closed the door. This changed everything. He opened a drawer, retrieved his Colt .45, loaded a magazine, chambered a round, slid the weapon into his belt on his hip, and covered it with his jacket. He hurried back over to the tunnel door, entered the code, opened the door, and ran down the hallway to the Harper woman's room.

She was sitting on the bed reading a book. The little mutt started yapping soon as he entered the room.

Elena was shocked by Bud's sudden appearance.

"Mr. Jenkins, What are you doing here?" All kinds of thoughts ran through her head. His appearance made no sense. Was he here to rescue her? Why was it just him?

"I don't have time to explain. Get dressed fast. We've got to get you out of here before those Hispanics find us here. Hurry it up now, I must get you out of here and on the way to your father; he waits to hear you are safe."

"My father? Why didn't he come with you?"

"He sent me. We don't have much time. Get dressed. We have to go."

They hurried down the tunnel. He opened the hydraulic-operated door to the runway. He checked the satellite feeds. He calculated the Harper and Alvarez men would be at the entrance in less than ten minutes. Ten minutes to the entrance--five there and five more to the house and garage lab. The Hive awaits them. He had hoped it put a stop to their ill-formed assault. Where was it? He watched them lay David Gonzalez against the wall of the garage then split up; the Alvarez man vanished back into the orchard and the Harper man very shortly was seen in the upper hallways wandering in and out of the guest rooms. Jenkins last saw him in the hall outside his office.

Earlier, while he was getting prepared, before Lisa appeared, he sent info to The Hive to arm the Bumblebees with the knockout formula. Not that he had any compunction about killing, but, if by any chance he failed and was captured, he would rather not face a murder rap. He had watched The Hive come around the hangar, the Mexicans, and the redneck idiots Butch and Billy near it were caught off guard. Butch and Billy ducked back into the hangar. Some of the

Mexicans ran, others dove to the pavement. The Cessna, he had been moved earlier, now awaited him on the runway.

The Harper woman seemed perplexed. They had come to the end of the tunnel and waited for the hydraulic motor to open the exit door. The mutt started its piercing bark and ran back up the tunnel. The Harper woman called out to it but it disregarded her echoing demands. He heard, then saw, the Harper man in the tunnel. He fired off a couple rounds. They ricocheted down the tunnel and he saw the Harper man had dove to the floor. Before the Harper woman could look back, he took her hand. He rushed Elena to the passenger side of the plane then ran around to his side while she climbed in. He caught sight of the two guards laid out at the corners of the hangar and the Harper man's buddy sprawled out on his back outside the side door. His weapons were scattered beside him. He didn't move. Jenkins chuckled, then climbed onboard. He started the plane, accelerated up the runway and soon they were airborne.

"Maisy," the Harper woman exclaimed. We left her."

"What?"

"My dog Maisy. We left her. She ran off down the tunnel. I hope they don't do anything to harm her."

"I'm sure they won't. You need to buckle up. It will be a short flight to Greenville Spartanburg Airport. From there my dear will catch a private commuter jet and have you safe in Texas by nightfall.

CHAPTER
52

When Jake opened his eyes, a nurse was standing over him shining a light into his right eye. He tried to sit up; he was strapped to a table. He looked right then left, he saw the nurse step back.

"Where am I? Why am I strapped down?"

She didn't answer just turned and left the room. Shortly the door reopened. Jake glanced down, saw Bob Hardy enter shaking his head. He was dressed in jeans, a button-down dress shirt and a blazer. The typical preppy bureaucratic Washington I'm going to bullshit or fuck-you-over look.

"Hello Jake. Glad you could rejoin us."

"Did you catch him?"

"Who?"

"The man who shot at me, Tindal's man Jenkins. He had Elena. Did ya'll catch him? Is Elena okay?"

"No. But we will. I doubt he'll harm Elena. She is his hostage. He needs her. Seems he had her all along, fixated with her apparently. I'll tell you all you want to know later, if you agree to what I am about to offer." There it was that here it comes expression on his face.

"Offer? What do you mean offer? Fuck you and fuck your offers."

"You don't have much choice. You see I'm prepared to get all charges against you and TJ dismissed if you accept my offer. TJ has already agreed."

"Where is TJ? I would like to talk to him. And would you please take these damn restraints off me. I want to talk to TJ first."

Hardy's expression became a frown. He walked out without another word. A few minutes later he reemerged accompanied by TJ.

"I'll leave you two alone for a few minutes. TJ don't go into any details about the offer. He needs to tell me whether he accepts or not. Then I will explain." Hardy once more left the room.

TJ was dressed like he was getting ready to step outside to grill out or play with his dogs. He had on a long sleeve tee, his typical cargo pants, and flip flops. Jake noticed a bruise on his forehead. He walked over to the bed and released the restraints. "Not supposed to do this, but what the fuck."

Jake sat up twisted his neck, rubbed his wrists and ankles where the restraints had dug in. TJ's ever-present grin looked strained.

"What happened to you? Fall out of bed?"

"Something like that."

"Okay. Out with it."

"Jenkins took Elena and got away. The bastard sicced that damn drone on us. Didn't know shit 'till woke up here. Hardy said I needed to talk to you."

"Where'd you disappear to? How'd you end up here? Last I recall, I went one way, you were headed back into the orchard to go to the hangar."

TJ recounted what happened to him.

"Damn UAV, think I shot at it. Next thing I'm here strapped down, woke to see Hardy, same as you."

"You decked Butch and Billy. Hope you fucked them up."

"Probably need some repairs."

"Wish I'd been there."

Jake felt woozy. "Go on. Out with it."

"Don't have many options. Won't let you leave until you agree or say you're not interested. Might want to hear Hardy out. May surprise you, otherwise, I'll just leave it at that. What they offering's incredibly strange--so I thought. More down your alley than anything I can relate to. 'Bout all I can tell you. You accept, all charges will be dropped. Oh, by the way, feds arrested Tindal. He's out on bail, much doubt he will stand trial. Betcha he won't ever mess with us again. Might like to know, Ariel was a prime reason behind his arrest. She's here. Been asking about you. They told me to tell you Dusty's out of the woods, on the mend. Maisy's still with Doc Hunter also."

"What about Butch and Billy and David Gonzalez, his brother and the other bangers?"

"Butch and Billy were arrested by Deputy Coulter, prints were on the cameras. The motorcyclists and other bangers they caught are in ICE custody. David Gonzalez's in a hospital. Wasn't the taser that fucked him up. He's a diabetic, suffered from low blood sugar, something like that. The Diablos are in federal custody. Most likely, all that'll happen they'll be deported. I've been put on administrative leave, pending an investigation. SWAT Commander's not happy about the outcome. Said I went off the reservation, jeopardized years of work. Hardy says he'll handle it, since I'm agreeing to his offer. Gotta go bro. Hardy's at the door. He'll explain the deal. Know you'll do what you think best. One more thing, I've decided it's time I conquered my fear, I'm going to learn how to swim."

"Good for you."

TJ left and Hardy reentered.

Hardy came in, stood next to the bed. Jake thought, 'here comes the sales pitch.'

"Can you make it quick. I'd like to get out of here."

"Jake you and I have known each other since you were discharged from the Army. I talked you into working with Homeland once before. Sorry you feel I fucked you over. You pulled my ass out of a jam, and for that I am grateful. However, in case you forgot, I did help pull your ass out of the drink in Cuba. Now I am here to help you out of the jam you and TJ are in. Homeland Security needs people like you and TJ…"

"Stop right there," Jake said. "I did my time with Uncle Sam. I don't owe you or them anything. If you want to repay me, then do it, no strings attached."

"Okay. If that's how you want to play it. I don't think you will like how that turns out. Knowing you, even as little as I do, and, that is more than most people, I know you want answers and revenge. And, your farm Jake, the legal system will eat you up, you'll lose everything. Even if your attorney gets you off, you'll end up destitute. If you lose, which is a distinct possibility, you could end up in prison. The cartel's members will be waiting for you." Hardy paused; his expression grew more severe. He saw he wasn't getting anywhere.

"Just listen. I have a way for you to avoid all your legal problems, save your farm, stop Tindal." That caught Jake's attention.

"You want someone like Tindal taking your farm? I don't think so. Could, probably will happen, if you don't accept my offer. By the way, I guess you know Tindal was arrested, has his own legal troubles. We know he wants your land and why. You can prevent this from happening, get the answers to most, if not all your questions, put an end to your troubles—that is if you join TJ as a special agent. The assignment would be to find Jenkins and Elena, recover the property Jenkins stole. Be an opportunity to pay off your debts, for real this time. You and TJ are more familiar with what has happened and have a personal vested interest in seeing this through. The government, Homeland Security, has made locating Jenkins and recovering their property a top priority. That means Elena also. You will be working with me. Few people inside the government, none outside of a select few, will ever know anything about you, your involvement. Come on Jake. Here's your chance at getting even." Hardy stopped talking and stood there staring down at Jake.

Jake hated to think Hardy and TJ were right, what choice, did he have? Going to prison and dying at the hands of the cartel's insiders was not what he saw as a desirable option. Losing his ancestral farm, damn sure could happen. What would become of the animals—where would Dusty and Maisy go? Elena. He wanted to know if she left of her own volition--had she played him for a fool? And Tindal could afford a legal battle. The thought of Tindal getting his land…

"So that we understand each other, if you people fuck me over again..." He left the threat unfinished. "You said government property, correct me if I'm wrong, Jenkins was Tindal's man. Aren't you really talking about something that belonged to Tindal?"

"Sign and find out."

Hardy opened a folder and laid it on Jake's lap. He read over the enclosed papers, hesitated, what the fuck was this? Sounded like something from a sci fi book.

"Is this for real?"

"Sign and find out."

He signed all the documents, in triplicate, including nondisclosure and top-secret security clearance documents.

Hardy said, "It will be good working with you again. We'll say I owe you one for that fiasco in Cuba; let's make certain that that ongoing op, and this related one, ends successfully. We will find Elena; you need closure. You cannot disclose your involvement to anyone, family, friends, anyone, especially your lady news friend Ariel Gaspard. As far as anyone knows, you and TJ are being quarantined for possible exposure to a coronavirus variant."

Hardy told him he would be staying at the clinic for a simple medical procedure. He had signed a waiver, holding the clinic and the government harmless, bunch of legal mumbo jumbo. He had breezed through it, probably should have read all the fine print. Hard not to have second thoughts.

Hardy described the neuro implant Jenkins had received, told Jake, like Hardy himself and TJ, he would have one placed in his brain. In addition, a medical procedure, CRISPR or something similar was planned to fix Jake's injured spine.

Jake thought he had awoken in the Twilight Zone. He had read such things were being developed, he had no idea if what Hardy said was possible. This chip, had he given away his privacy? Could he or should he trust the government? What choice did he have? This meant no more worrying about the farm and Tindal. Tindal? Wait a minute. Hardy had taken the papers and left. What could be done could be undone if it was not to his liking. Or could it? This would be a whole new chapter—No. A completely new book of his life.

CHAPTER
53

Elena and Jenkins flew on a chartered flight to south Texas near El Paso. They arrived there at night. Jenkins had been pleasant to her, seemed to be riding a high, she didn't think it was drugs. Other than a mixed drink for him and a glass of wine for her, she had not seen any reason for his ebullience. She was glad to be out of her confinement but couldn't help but feel something wasn't right. When they took off, she saw where she had been held. It was Tindal's estate. This didn't make sense. Jenkins had been nice. She couldn't bring herself to believe he or Tindal would have done this to her. Was he taking her to her father?

She asked to borrow a phone to call her daughter. He handed her a phone without hesitation. Jennifer asked where she was. Elena told her somewhere in the air headed to Texas to meet her father. Before they could continue their conversation, the phone went dead.

When they arrived in Texas, she once became concerned because no one she knew was there to meet her. Jenkins took them to a private residence. The people were nice, but knew nothing about her father, or so they said.

Jenkins disappeared after the introductions. Later he returned and came to her room. He said he had business to take care of and had arranged for her to be taken to meet her father the next day. Then he said something strange. He said if she wanted to, she could remain with him and share in his newfound good fortune. He told her she could have everything she had ever dreamed of and more if she chose to be with him. Elena was caught off guard. That this man would propose this to her was shocking. It made her wonder about his motives, past, present, and future. All kinds of scenarios ran through her head. The way he was staring at her, eyes cold and beseeching at the same time. He sat there on the edge of her bed, made her uneasy. Was he crazy? Did her father know she was here?

Oh fuck, what to say?

"Mr. Jenkins, I never expected this. After what I've been through. I don't know what to say. I need to think about this, perhaps after I have had time to get beyond my ordeal. And, you know, I am a married woman. Plus, my father, you know him--this is sudden. Can we talk about this tomorrow?"

Jenkins reached over and took her hand.

"Call me Bud, my given name was Buddy Walter Jenkins, but I've always been Major Jenkins or Bud to everyone who knows me. I know this is sudden. What I'm trying to say is I was taken by you from the first time I laid eyes on you. Your husband doesn't appreciate you. He's a fool. After what you've been through, I'm sure you know that. Your father, Sam is my friend. We served together overseas. I've always admired him. He told me he doesn't think much of your husband. He thinks you deserve better. I know you do. I can make that happen. Once you get to know me, you can forget about not having the things you want. I will make it my goal to keep you happy."

Elena gently pulled her hand away.

"Mr. Jenkins, Bud, you seem like a nice man. Let me think about this. I'm sorry, if you don't mind, I need to get some rest. I'm not sure what to think at this time." Elena let out a sigh. "I need to lie down. Maybe, after I have had some sleep, I will know better what I should do."

Bud rose from the bed. "I'll see you in the morning. It will have to be early. I must meet someone mid-morning. I would like for you to accompany me if you decide to accept my invitation." He handed her a small, locked gold-inlaid case. "This is valuable. Hold onto it. Tomorrow I'll open it for you." He leaned down, kissed her on the cheek.

She wanted to cringe but smiled instead and said, "thank you."

After he left, Elena went to the door and listened. She heard his steps receding, then the sound of a door opening and closing. She rushed over to the window. It had bars on it.

She ran to the door. As she reached for the handle, she heard some noise outside her door. Putting her ear to the upper wooden panel, she heard Jenkin's loud protest, "we were to meet in the morning." Followed by the sound of another door slamming. Then quiet. Elena slowly opened the door. Jenkins was going down the stairs in the company of four people. It looked like three men and a woman, but she couldn't be sure. She waited until she heard the front entrance door close then she ventured through the house. It appeared she was alone. An old-fashioned telephone sat on a desk in the corner of the small living room off the foyer. It had a dial tone. She dialed 011880 and her parents' home number to call them collect.

Her father Sam told her to get out of the house, go to the nearest hotel and call him on his cell to let him know where she was.

Four hours later at three in the morning, Jennifer and Sam arrived to pick her up. It was a tearful reunion between the two women. Sam was his usual stoic self. The only reaction came when she thanked him for having Bud Jenkins rescue her. Her father looked around to where she sat across the aisle from him on the chartered plane, an odd look crossed his face. After a short pause he said he was glad it worked out. He began lambasting Jake, blaming him for causing everything. Elena tried to argue, but he wouldn't listen.

They arrived at her parent's place outside Houston as the sun was coming up. Another tearful exchange took place with her mother. Then she excused herself, pulled her daughter aside to borrow her cell phone, went to her old bedroom, called Jake.

CHAPTER
54

Jake was hesitant to answer his phone when he saw it was Jennifer. He considered not answering, thinking she was calling to curse him some more. He told the masked Ariel who the caller was and that he was going to answer. She stepped out of the room.

Jake was shocked to hear Elena's voice calling his name in a weary sounding tone.

"Elena, oh Jesus, where are you? Can you talk?"

Elena said, "I'm at my parents' house. We just got here. I wanted to see if you were okay. Jennifer told me you and TJ were in a clinic, possibly under arrest, in the custody of federal authorities."

Jake told her the charges would be dropped. He and TJ were not under arrest, they were in a clinic as a matter of precaution, having tested positive for a coronavirus variant. He asked if the authorities knew she was safe. She said she had not talked to anyone and didn't know. She didn't think so. Jennifer and her parents had not said anything to anyone as far as she knew. She then told him about her rescue by Bud Jenkins.

Jake told her the feds were looking for Jenkins. He asked if she knew where he was. She told him about what she witnessed, wanted to know why the feds were looking for him.

Jake told her.

"All I know is he was the one who helped my father rescue me, Jake."

"He was the one holding you hostage Elena. The feds have evidence to prove that. If you hear anything more from him, you need to find out where he is and call the FBI or call me and I will call them. Do you understand?"

He heard her breathing.

"Jake I'm not coming back to the farm. I need to take time to find out what is best for me, and you need to do the same."

"I agree. Take as long as you like. The feds are going to want to talk to you. They may want you to come back here."

"They will have to come here. I don't intend to ever come back to the Carolinas."

"You know I can't and won't be leaving the farm. I guess you are saying we're through, is that what you mean? Does that slimeball Teddy have anything to do with your decision?"

"Jake. Don't even go there. I saw the news footage of you and your ole girlfriend, that news woman. And no, this is something we both knew had to happen. To leave the Carolinas or not is up to you. But I will never come there again. As for us, I have said this numerous times, I want to be near my family—my daughter in Louisiana, my parents in Texas--either one. You have children in Louisiana, yet you refuse. I said I wanted to live with you down here--I'm not sure if that is any longer true--too much happened this last week. I don't see how you or I," there was a pause, "how we could ever put this behind us. I'm sorry Jake, I need to go. I hope we can find a way to talk. I need time."

Jake stared at the phone. Elena had hung up. She hadn't even asked about Dusty and Maisy. He didn't get to tell her the good news, Dusty was hanging in there and was showing improvement. Ariel said she learned this from Doc Hunter when she was doing her investigative interviews. Ariel gave him some more good news--the sheriff and DA were under investigation by the feds involving their connections to Tindal.

Ariel had been waiting outside in the corridor and was peaking in through the glass viewing section of the door, watching while he talked to Elena. She pushed the door open slightly and asked if it was okay to come back in.

"Yeah. Hey, I'm glad you came by to give me all the good news. I hope we can talk more when I get out of here."

"I'll need to do a follow-up. You and TJ are big news." She hesitated, waited for him to say something.

"How did the conversation with Elena go?" He remained silent. She saw a far-off look cross his face. "I guess it's none of my business."

"Nah. Doesn't look like you'll get to interview her unless you go to Texas." Then he told her what was said.

Ariel said she was sorry. That wasn't what she wanted to say. She walked over to his bedside. They locked eyes and she didn't have to say what she was going to say. She could see he already knew. She leaned down…

Warrior veteran, roguish, Ron Marshall is a graduate of UNC Charlotte, where he lettered in wrestling and LSU, where he played rugby. He and his dog Streak spend their time on his farm in the Carolinas and visiting friends and family in Louisiana, or wherever he finds interesting people and places to inspire his writing.

**SPY OP
A TASTE OF PARADISE**

THE WAR AFTER THE WAR SERIES

A Jake Harper & TJ Alvarez Novel

Book I

Now Available

THE OFF SWITCH

RONALD K MARSHALL

A JAKE HARPER AND TJ ALVAREZ NOVEL

THE WAR AFTER THE WAR SERIES
BOOK III

Ron Marshall

PRELUDE

"**H**ow do I turn this damn thing off?

"Off? Why on earth would you want to turn this thing, as you call it, off?"

"Privacy. Some people, me being one of them, enjoy privacy. I have to have it."

Doctor Perkins, his nametag said, shook his head, a confused look on his face. "Privacy?" He pronounced the word with a soft I, not the hard I Jake was accustomed to. Had to be a transplant, British maybe, perhaps a New Englander.

"Look Doc, when I'm alone, all by myself, or, with certain people, doing things most decent people don't talk about, making whoopie, or whatever-- things I don't wish to share with other people if I choose not to, that's called privacy. So, now I ask you one more time, how do I turn this thing off?"

"Oh. I see," he said with a chuckle. By the look on his face, Jake doubted it.

"Mr. Harper, the NM0099 is programmed so you can censor such thoughts and actions. You helped program it. It is a part of you. It knows when you want privacy. You could consider this your on and off switch, if that is what you wish. The NM0099 is learning this as we speak. Concentrate. Give it a name if you like. Give it key words for these commands. You and your devise are teaching each other. I say again, the NM099 is part of you. Give yourself time. Give the NM0099 time. Before long you will take it for granted and would no more want to be without it than you would an arm or leg."

CHAPTER
1

Almost heaven. Jake stared up at the beadboard ceiling of hundred-year-old deep yellowed brown knotty-heart-pine wood. The ceiling fan, as old as he was, spun the morning light as it creeped across the ceiling, the air refreshing, invigorating, titillating, his skin moist with sweat and their love juices, the inhaled scent a pleasant reminder of the love/lust desire fulfillment, feelings far beyond mere memories from youth and the substitutes since. His hope, that it would never end. Almost. If only…

Jake's sleep had been interrupted many times during the night, memories of his military brothers, torn, disfigured, dead. His once stiff, nearly immobile neck had been a reminder of his personal brush with death. Failed marriages, alienated children, his dog lying sedated, trying to recover from near-mortal wounds—battle scars foreign and domestic. His estranged wife, a practical nurse, termed it PTSD. Now this implant--an alien inside his head.

He had earlier done his best to keep from disturbing Ariel, his childhood sweetheart. He now lay next to her. Their lovemaking a welcome reprieve, an intense burn slowly dying down from its feverish pitch. The thought of the implant sought to rob him of the postcoital bliss they both deserved. He refused to let it. Not this time. But there was the impending mission.

"You seem distracted?"

Jake looked down at her. Her luxurious auburn hair, mussed from their love making, framed her lightly freckled face, contrasting with the deep pools of her hazel, emerald-green eyes staring up at him from her head on his chest.